SEEDS OF FATE

Lewis Cox

SAPERE
BOOKS

SEEDS OF FATE

Published by Sapere Books.

20 Windermere Drive, Leeds, England, LS17 7UZ,
United Kingdom

saperebooks.com

ISBN: 978-1-80055-125-1

For my brother, Trevor Gordon Lewis, whose great joy it was to visit Luniette.

CHAPTER 1

"You're late! Just ten minutes too late! There she goes. Pity you lost count of your time, miss. Wherever did you get to? There aren't many places for a girl to hide on Luniette. Them chaps up to t'lighthouse spots every stranger in no time. I wonder they didn't warn you. But didn't you hear t'hooting, calling all passengers aboard?"

There followed a spate of words in a croaky old voice — something about folks who were so deaf they couldn't or wouldn't hear what everyone on the island heard, the ship's call.

As the old salt was toothless, and spoke with a clay pipe in his mouth, Anabel could only understand a quarter of what he said. But she could guess very well.

Any girl might have felt a fool under these circumstances — but not a girl like Anabel, who was able to face her misadventure with a smile. She was still breathless from scrambling over the rocks to reach the beach in time to catch the pleasure steamer *Lady Elizabeth*, only to arrive too late to go aboard, for the ship was now well out to sea on her homeward journey from the island to the mainland port.

Thinking that all passengers were aboard, the loiterers, their fun for the day over, had gone home to their cottages on the plateau above the cliff; and the children who had watched the "piggy-back" landing of the passengers with much merriment and frank comment, had raced home to tea. The beach was empty save for Anabel, the girl who had missed the boat by minutes, the old salt in corduroys and navy jersey, and a few cheeky gulls perched watchfully on the gunwale of a boat drawn clear of the tide high on the shingle.

She stood staring at the stern of the *Lady Elizabeth*, which looked like the end of a fat duck swimming importantly out to sea, and she told herself she had never felt so annoyed.

Yet, as Anabel looked seawards, she remembered something, and her irritation melted, and a queer smile twisted her lips, for there was irony in this new situation, one which might be turned to advantage. With every passing second the distance between the steamer and Luniette widened, and the mainland, which had appeared so solid when she was upon it, seemed now to have grown suddenly dim and unreal, as ghostly as the uneven blue smudge above the horizon. While she listened absently to the old man who took a chuckling delight in her misfortune, the more practical part of her brain was wondering what she should do next, arranging the immediate future, planning where the night would be spent; and how she would manage for necessaries, and what money was in her purse, and whether her compact was full of face powder, and numberless other small things which made for comfort.

But the something Anabel had remembered helped her to overcome any one of these difficulties.

She had left London abruptly, to escape meeting Paul Brycon. His loverlike persistence for a year had been the talk of mutual friends, and the subject of a gossip-writer's query in a daily press column. Paul's attentions had been flattering and amusing, for he was good company, and Anabel had thought herself in love with him, and only waited for him to declare *his* love. It had been a shock to read in the morning newspaper that he was married to a girl outside their circle of acquaintances. For a while, the world rocked under her feet. Anabel's first reaction was anger at this cavalier treatment, then humiliation and hurt pride drove all other feelings from her heart. She faced friends with almost brazen coolness, said she had known all about Paul's engagement and that she wished him the best of everything. But even as she spoke, perhaps too glibly to sound true, she guessed that no one believed her. To them she was as a woman scorned. It was easy to imagine they were laughing at her misfortune.

Then, after meeting Paul and his bride, a happening which called on all the courage she possessed, Anabel turned tail and ran away. She came down to Bankshire, running away from humanity, wanting only to be alone, holding herself aloof from everybody in the hotel where she stayed, freezing any tentative advances — and the result was boredom. For Anabel was used to having people around who made a fuss of her, not because they were attracted by any personal charm or beauty, but because she was the only daughter of Samuel Robinson, the great international financier. Not that Paul could ever be accused of wanting her fortune. To be fair, he had made it plain since the first day of their friendship that her money — or that which she would one day inherit — was a barrier to any closer relationship. She had fancied, stupidly it seemed, that the difficulty was overcome. The conclusion was wrong, and shook her sense of judgment in people. Great wealth meant power, but that did not spell happiness.

Now that the first edge of grief and wounded pride was blunted, Anabel realized that she missed her friends, and was lonely. *Ennui* drove her to join the crowd crossing from Bettycombe for a day trip to Luniette.

Here, after lunching at the comfortable hotel on the island, she had wandered away for a walk, sitting on the rocks, just around the corner from and out of sight of the landing-beach, in a sheltered spot, facing the Western ocean. And with the wind in her dark-brown hair, and fine spray from the waves, which splashed ceaselessly against the rocks, on her face, she had thought of — Paul. Unseen, forgotten, Anabel had daydreamed of the might-have-been. Only dimly, through colourful, wishful dreams, had she heard the insistent note of the ship's hooter, and it had meant nothing to her. Everyone had been warned by the ship's purser aboard the *Lady Elizabeth* that the steamer must leave on time to catch the tide at Bettycombe. There was no excuse for anyone not hearing or disobeying, for the hooting was loud and prolonged, the island small and the atmosphere calm and still.

When Anabel awoke at length from her foolish, clinging daydreams, and realized how time was passing, she had rushed back to the beach — but too late.

Now, turning to look at the old man, she wondered if it mattered much whether she stayed in an hotel on the island or the hotel with all its up-to-date amenities at Bettycombe.

She smiled in a friendly way at him.

The old salt had finished talking. It had been obvious for some time that the girl was not listening to him. His eyes considered her, noting that she was pretty enough in a direct kind of way, with nice blue eyes, good teeth and a clear skin; and with wavy brown hair that was lifted softly from her broad forehead by the wind and glinted with golden lights in the afternoon sun. He was struck by the weary air which hung about this girl, clouding her looks, and thought she must be tired, and perhaps a little disappointed at the position she found herself in. But it was strange to be young and tired. The two did not go well together in his mind. Perhaps she had been seasick on the way over?

"Well?" Anabel asked at the end of his lengthy scrutiny, when he withdrew his eyes and stared pensively at the gulls.

"I was wondering if you could handle a boat," he answered at once.

"I am a competent sailor," was the confident reply.

He nodded approvingly. "And if you've got much brass," he added audaciously.

Anabel's smile faded. She replied coldly, "That's not your business."

"You'd be surprised," the salt told her. "I've lived too long to be told that money's worthless. I know that if a feller has money in his pocket, he counts. If he's rich, with several hundreds to his fingers, he can buy a boat — and a boat, like this old 'un of mine, means a packet of money. See?"

Anabel nodded. "I shan't tell you that money is valueless, but I do know that a lot of money can be a curse, certainly a bar to happiness," she replied bitterly, thinking of her own blighted life.

"Don't you believe that — not if you're sensible, and I think you are. Money can buy everything — even happiness."

Anabel would not argue. It would be impossible to change this man's set ideas. She asked, "What's your name?"

"Dai."

"You're Welsh?" She glanced towards the north coastline of the Channel. "From over there?"

"Aha!"

"Is there a shop on this island?" But she knew the answer before the words were out of her mouth. She corrected herself, "I mean — I suppose people are sometimes left behind like this, and have to spend the night here? But if I can't buy things, is it possible to borrow?"

Dai laughed — a raucous sound which frightened the gulls perched on the boat, waiting hopefully for titbits cast up by the tide. They took to the air and flew about in circles, screaming defiance at him.

"How like a woman!" Dai took his pipe from his mouth, and spat with a rich sound among the pebbles a yard from his feet. He was in a good mood, having made over a pound carrying people across the shallow strip of water from the *Lady Elizabeth*'s small boats to the beach.

"How should I know what ladies want? I'm a bachelor, I am. Better go up to the hotel. They'll set you up. We're not savages here, look you — except the children, and they're proper savages, a regular plague messing about with my boat."

"Are there many visitors on the island?" Anabel glanced over her shoulder at that part of the square-built white hotel which was visible over the top of the low Cliffside.

"What, here? We're underhoused as it is, with no room for strangers. The hotel is empty. There's nothing to attract visitors here. They can walk over the island in a couple of hours. There's the ruins, and the remains of the battleship as ran on the rocks some years back, but we've no cinema or shops or anything that folks seem to want nowadays to live. There's nothing for idlers to do all day but listen to the wind and the sea and these plaguy gulls; and there's only the lamp in the lighthouse to break the monotony of the night — if you can't sleep. There are two lights. The lower one is fixed, but the upper intermittent light brightens every twenty-two seconds. Folks say that counting the seconds sends them to sleep. Of course, for them as likes the sea there's ships passing up and down-channel, into port and out of port; and the pilot cutters which run out to put on or take off the pilots. But that wouldn't interest you. 'Ee come from Lunnon, don't 'ee?"

Anabel nodded and spoke slowly. "I'm not so sure. It sounds — exciting."

Here was something fresh, not the traffic of the road whose rumbling sound she had heard since she was born, but the silent traffic which plied along sea-lanes.

Dai looked at her unblinkingly. He, too, spoke slowly, because here, on Luniette, there was time to live. "I don't know about exciting. I've lived here man and boy for over seventy years. I remember when we was no more'n fifty people on this island with five houses amongst the lot of us. This life suits me and I like it, but then, I don't know no other. But the young 'uns aren't so content."

By this time the steamer was a black dot in the sea, with the thin thread of black smoke stretching behind her funnel and dissolving into space.

Anabel moved. "I'll go up to the hotel and see what they can do for me," she said.

"Aye, better find a roof, for there'll be no boat for two days, and perhaps not then if the weather's bad. The wind has shifted a couple of points since the morning."

"What would the worst weather mean for me?"

"Waiting for the weekly mailboat which comes over from Combeford every Thursday."

"I see. Well, thanks. I'll be seeing you again soon."

"Oh, sure. I'm here most mornings."

"Thanks for your help."

He made a gesture of repudiation. "You're welcome, miss." He replaced his pipe between his lips and returned to his contemplation of the sea.

Anabel picked her way over the pebbles and climbed the steep pathway leading up to the hotel, which was set back from the cliff among pastures, in a chosen spot on sloping ground so that one had a magnificent sea view from the front windows. The building looked like a simple whitewashed farmhouse with barns and stables about it, with no pretensions of being an hotel.

Here was the solitude she had so often craved lately, a quietness broken only by the crackle and rush of waves breaking on a pebbly shore, the swish of seawater washing rocks, and the quarrelsome cries of gulls fighting over food on the beach. Here, amongst a few strangers, she could recover confidence in herself.

Presently she reached the hotel, pausing in the porch to read the licensee's name, which was written in small black lettering over the hotel door. "Sarah Ann Groom," she read.

Anabel crossed the threshold, her footsteps echoing in the empty, flag-paved passage, and lingered in the pleasant coolness, expecting someone to come forward to inquire her business.

But there was no sign of life in the place, which had apparently regained its habitual state of drowsiness after the departure of the midday visitors. Anabel walked along the passage towards an open door leading to a yard at the back. Here, in a cow-byre on the far side of a cobbled square, she heard voices, and someone was playing a tinny mouth-organ.

The talking and music covered the sound of her approach, and she was standing in the open door of the stable, looking into the soft darkness, before those within realized that a stranger was in their midst.

Then the voices and mouth-organ stopped abruptly. A woman and two young men stared open-mouthed at her. The men wore corduroys strapped below the knees, and Welsh flannel grey shirts which were open at the neck, revealing skin tanned to a mahogany colour. They looked swarthy, with red lips and strong white teeth.

The woman's eyes, hard, round and brown, appraised Anabel's clothes swiftly. The men noticed that her shoulders were broad but feminine, her hips were narrow as a boy's, and there was grace and lissomness in her figure. Their eyes glistened.

The three moved forward slowly, looking as though they saw a ghost. For apart from Anabel's unexpected presence, as she stood there with the sun and light behind her, bathed as it were in a golden beam of dust-filled sunshine, she did not seem real. Her features were small and elfin, and she was dressed in smart clothes.

And then Anabel spoke, remarking obviously, while suppressing a desire to giggle at their astonishment, "I've missed the boat."

Indeed, the more she thought of her predicament, the keener was her pleasure. For once in Anabel's life, her day could not be planned. It was impossible to see even one hour ahead into her future.

Apparently her light-heartedness mystified the three people, because they exclaimed in unison, "She's missed t'boat."

It was so like a stage chorus taking up a cue that Anabel smiled, and though the woman's face stiffened immediately because she felt herself being laughed at, the young men's faces brightened, and their red lips widened into dazzling smiles.

"Whatever'll you do?" inquired the woman in a sing-song voice, so that Anabel guessed that once she, too, hailed from the north coast of the Channel.

Anabel shrugged. "Make the best of it, I suppose. It isn't a tragedy, providing you can fix me up. Have you a telephone?"

She was used to looking after herself and ordering her own life without considering or consulting others. There was a sturdy independence about her which was not lost on the onlookers, who judged her to be a person of some importance.

The woman went close up to her. She was plump and elderly, and dressed in shabby black with a black-and-white checked Welsh flannel apron tied around her waist to protect her skirt. "Come this way, miss," she invited respectfully, as though she had reached a conclusion about Anabel's status in life which demanded a show of respect.

"You are Mrs. Sarah Ann Groom?"

"Why, yes. How did you know?"

"I saw your name over the door as I came in. Besides, I caught a glimpse of you through the hatchway in the kitchen while I had lunch."

"I remember you, too, miss," was the reply.

Sarah Ann Groom had cooked the lunch enjoyed by visitors from the boat who had patronized the hotel for a meal. She had also collected the tips given to Mabel, the waitress, who was a halfwit and had no idea of the value of money. Sarah Ann had been too busy serving to notice the visitors. But after lunch, when she saw the size of the tip Mabel had received, Sarah Ann had taken great interest in Anabel's back.

So that now her manner was deferential, though behind the respectful expression on her face was a calculating mind. She reminded herself that there were several spare bedrooms upstairs, and here was a rich young lady, who knew how to spend, needing a bed!

Sarah Ann led the way indoors, pausing on the doorstep for Anabel to precede her into the hotel. But the girl stood back. "You know the way," she said smilingly. "I suppose you are used to this sort of thing?"

The little act of courtesy was not without its effect on the landlady.

"It does happen sometimes in the summer months, when the pleasure boats bring trippers, but mostly they're ready to leave when the time comes to go. There isn't much to see, and when they've had a meal and a look round they wander down to the beach and wait for the boats. It's the fresh air they like, the trip here and back, and to say they've been on Luniette. Though I've never had a young lady alone before, only men — and once a couple. But there's nothing for you to be afraid of —"

"Good gracious, I'm not afraid!"

Sarah Ann nodded. "I thought not," she replied approvingly.

By that time, they had walked along the cool passage and had turned into a small bar, a cosy intimate little room full of every kind of good cheer. There was a high counter with three tall polished brass beer-handles in the middle; an old-fashioned telephone on the wall at the end; sawdust on the flagged floor; and two low square windows, one facing east and the other south, with shutters and broad window-seats which gave an air of ease and comfort with a silent invitation to relax.

Anabel exclaimed at the glass-backed shelves behind the counter, which were well stocked with full shining bottles and ruby, green and crystal glasses. "What lots you have to drink for such an isolated spot," she said, noting the shapes of the bottles and the labels on them. There were rare liqueurs and old brandies.

Sarah Ann was surprised at the remark. "That's nothing," she replied offhandedly. "You should see my cellars where I keep the good stuff. There's not overmuch on those shelves. And men get thirsty even on Luniette with water all around them. They can't drink salt water."

Anabel laughed. "But who *is* here?"

"There are the islanders, mostly farmers and fishermen; and there's a naval unit camped out at Shutter Point. There's been talk that the Navy may take over a part of Luniette, and that'll mean more business for me, for though they may have their own stores, the boys like company and cosiness when they drink. Material for huts is already here, with the workmen living in tents in a meadow. And I heard —" She broke off suddenly and compressed her lips, but soon opened them again, for she had the garrulous tongue of the lonely woman. "There, I've been warned not to talk to anyone. It's supposed to be a secret, though everyone around these parts knows full well what is happening. One day soon, so these naval chaps say, there's going to be a war, and — You are English, miss?"

Anabel nodded carelessly. The question sounded superfluous. She went over to the telephone and opened the dog-eared telephone book hanging from a nail in the wall. "I'll ring up my hotel at Bettycombe and tell them where I am, or they'll wonder what has happened to me if I don't turn up this evening. And perhaps you can lend me what I need for a night?"

The landlady smiled faintly. "I'm sorry I can't oblige, miss; but you can have a pair of my son's pyjamas — new ones," she offered.

"They'll do. Will he mind?"

"He won't know. Alf used to work at the lighthouse, but he's gone over to the mainland this three weeks. He was a naval reservist and has been recalled."

"Oh! And I am your only guest?" The question was perfunctory, for Dai had already told Anabel that the hotel was empty.

"The only *visitor*," emphasized Sarah Ann. "There's the officer in charge of the naval unit who's here on business. He's a nice gentleman, though, and I'm sure won't worry you."

Anabel sighed inwardly. She did not answer. She knew that it was not a question of the man worrying *her*, though he might well do so if he knew who her father was. The only man she had ever met who was not impressed by her father's wealth was Paul. Just thinking of him brought a bitter, wry expression to her mouth. Aware that the landlady was looking at her curiously, she lit a cigarette and glanced out of the south window, at the light and shadow on the rolling down-land and the cottages lying dreaming in the mellow afternoon sun.

The peace was broken by the shrill shouts of children and the barking of dogs, and presently some cattle were passing the window. They came herded closely together, with a dull clatter of hooves on loose stones and sad protesting moos, passing in a cloud of dust and flies.

And then they were gone in diminishing sound. The dust settled again, and peace, like a drowsy cloak, was resumed.

Anabel turned to Sarah Ann, who was standing behind her with hands folded across her apron. "I think I'm going to like it here very much," she said.

The latter beamed with pleasure. If only this nice young lady would stay for a while! She replied, "You'd like it better if I could give you my best room."

"Why can't you?"

"It's where the Lieutenant-Commander sleeps, miss."

"Turn him out," advised the arrogant Anabel, accustomed always to having the best of everything, even if she had to pay an extravagant price for it and it was at the expense of someone's convenience.

"I don't feel I could do that," replied Mrs. Groom dubiously.

"Why ever not?"

"He wouldn't like it."

"Refer him to me. I'll settle him. You admit he's not a real visitor, but someone you felt you had to accommodate."

Mrs. Groom smiled. "It isn't so easy as that, miss. He's a nice gentleman and I've done my best to make him comfortable, but I've never thought to cross his will. I'll take you upstairs, miss, and you can see all my rooms. Maybe you'll prefer to have a land view instead of looking at water."

Anabel nodded. "I'll phone Bettycombe first," she decided.

Mrs. Groom did not leave the bar while Anabel telephoned her hotel, though she retired discreetly behind the bar counter and polished some of the glasses on a shelf as an excuse to wait. Meanwhile, it was easy to listen to the telephone talk. It delighted Sarah Ann to hear that Anabel was staying at the best hotel at Bettycombe.

'She's paying at least three guineas a day over there,' she told herself. 'If I charge even a third as much, we shall both be more than satisfied. I wish I could give her *his* bedroom, but if I do what will the Lieutenant-Commander say?'

Then Anabel was taken upstairs.

As the landlady had said, the naval officer was occupying by far the best bedroom — a huge double room with many windows, and a fine panoramic view of the sea, which was a dancing blue waste sparkling in the afternoon sun, with the faint lavender-blue coastline to the north and south.

Anyone on Luniette, which lay like an obstruction athwart the fairway of the Channel, would have a clear view of any traffic going into or leaving one of the many ports on the shores. A collier, with a thread of black smoke streaming from the funnel, deeply laden, was coming down-channel with the tide.

On entering the room, Anabel had crossed over at once to the window. The view was like a magnet to her, used as she

20

was to stuffy town streets. But soon she turned her back on the glorious seascape and looked about the room, which was spacious and clean. It was, of course, inhabited, and Anabel frowned heavily as she noted a man's hairbrushes on the dressing-table, a bottle of hair-oil, a telescope in a brown leather case, and a discarded starched white collar.

"What does he pay for this room?" she asked abruptly, adding without waiting for an answer, "Whatever it is, I'll double it."

There was a pause. The landlady's eyes glistened avariciously. Then she spoke, and there was genuine regret in her voice. "It's no use, miss, I daren't let over his head."

"Are you afraid of him?"

"Perhaps I am a little."

"Well, I'm not. I'm sure, though, he won't mind moving out for a night. I'll explain to him if you won't," said Anabel impatiently.

"That's just it. No one likes being upset for a night. It might be easier if it was for a week or a month." And Mrs. Groom waited expectantly.

After a little while, Anabel heard herself say, "Well, it could be for a week or a month. Who knows? Supposing I like it here so much that even if the weather keeps fine and I can return to Bettycombe I won't go? I'm only supposing, of course, but now what about it?" Yet Anabel had already made up her mind definitely. The more opposition Mrs. Groom showed, the greater was Anabel's wish to occupy this room.

"Will you see the other rooms before you decide upon anything, miss?" Sarah Ann queried respectfully.

But Anabel waved aside the idea. "You've shown me the best and I like it. None other will do."

"Then if it's like that," said Sarah Ann slowly, "if you might be here, say a month, of course that would be different. But you couldn't stay without clothes."

Anabel smiled triumphantly. She had won her way. "Are you afraid that I shall upset the Lieutenant-Commander, then go to fetch my clothes, and change my mind about returning to you? I can send Dai across to Bettycombe for my baggage."

Mrs. Groom shook her head. "Don't you suggest such a thing to Dai, miss. He'll jump at the suggestion — or he would if he could get his feet off the ground — but he's too old to make the journey safely now. And even if he managed to sail over, he'd forget what he went for. His memory's fading with age. But one of the naval chaps might be crossing. They're always pleasuring around in the pinnace."

"It doesn't matter who goes so long as they fetch my luggage."

Mrs. Groom felt enthusiastic, an emotion only slightly dampened as her eyes fell on the hairbrushes placed neatly on the white cover of the dressing-table. "You don't think you'll be bored here, miss?" she said hesitatingly.

"Why should I be?" Then sharply, because Mrs. Groom had not welcomed her with open arms, and she was accustomed to being warmly welcomed — where she paid her way — Anabel said, "Don't you want visitors here? Don't you wish me to stay? Is there anything wrong with the place?"

"There's nothing wrong with Luniette. It's only that you may want a more exciting life than we can offer you here."

Anabel frowned. "But that's exactly why I shall like it. Anyhow, Mrs. Groom, what's the betting I shall be sorry when my time here comes to an end — whether I leave tomorrow or next week — or even next month?"

"I never bet, miss," was the prim reply. But the older woman looked flushed and excited at the prospect of new young life in her house. She could not have put a name to it, but there was a quality about Anabel, a something in looks or manner — or perhaps both — which promised fun and adventure to people with whom she came into contact — and Mrs. Groom was no exception.

The latter said, "Don't you want to know my charges, miss?" and waited expectantly for Anabel's face to fall and her voice to sharpen, as people's usually did when the cost of a pleasure was questioned.

But Anabel, without pause, answered recklessly, "No, ask me whatever you think fair." She turned almost dramatically to the open window, listening to the boom and thunder of sea dashing against the rocks below, and smelt the ozone in the air. She waved her hand. "This view alone is worth a queen's ransom."

CHAPTER 2

Anabel had tea, with bread and butter, jam and clotted cream. Afterwards, replete, she sat on a seat in front of the hotel and smoked, her thoughts hazy, and senses dulled by the ceaseless sound of the sea, the stillness of the atmosphere and the drowsy heat of the afternoon sun.

Being on Luniette was like living in another world. She felt far from her world, existing in a lotus-like land which soothed instead of fretting her nerves. The vision of Paul that had been before her tormented mind for weeks seemed a little fainter, and for the first time since the tragedy Anabel was able to summon up the energy to think, 'I must not dream about him anymore. I must forget him.' Then she went inland to explore the island, passing some cottages where children were playing, and skirting the church, which was perched on a rocky hill and made her think that this was the church the forsaken merman had visited when he came up from the sea to find his mermaid-wife.

Beyond the churchyard was a hill leading to an eminence from the top of which Anabel was sure a bird's-eye view of the whole island could be obtained.

She had not gone far when she found the track led downwards to the sea on the western side of the island. This, in turn, led past some ricks of last year's harvest, the hay greying in the sun, to a farmhouse built in a dip of the downland.

Anabel stood still, undecided whether to continue the path to the house or retreat, and saw the tall dark figure of a man cross the cobbled yard and enter one of the outbuildings.

He paused at sight of a stranger, stared, then moved on.

Anabel sensed a certain hostility in his attitude, and retreat faded in her mind.

Instead she turned her face westwards, where the sea foamed and dashed against numerous small islets, some of which were no more than big rocks in the sea. She walked swiftly through long grass towards the cliffs, where gales and bad weather had created great rifts in the ground among the brambles and dog-roses.

Anabel was so busy looking at the sea breaking with almost frolicsome delight over the small islands that she did not look where she was going, and suddenly found herself without footing or hold, falling headlong down into a broad fissure in the earth.

She screamed loudly, and, as though triumphant of her downfall, the gulls rose in flight and seemed to echo the thin sound.

Happily Anabel fell on earth which had collected with time on rocks above high-water level, and which recent rain had rendered soft, and so no harm was done.

After a lengthy pause, during which she felt her body gingerly with careful hands to see if any bones were broken, satisfied, she scrambled to her feet. Angry with herself, she bent to brush her dress vigorously.

"Of all the fools!" Anabel cried aloud, shaken by her fall, and wondering how on earth she was going to climb the steep rock face without help, or indeed if this ledge of rock under her feet would not be covered with water at high tide. But even as she wondered, shaking her skirt and throwing back with an impatient hand the hair that had fallen over her face, Anabel heard a man's voice calling anxiously from above her head.

"I say, are you hurt?"

She looked up, and saw that it was the man from the farm. A wave of thankfulness went through her. "No," she replied, "but I deserved to be. I didn't look where I was going."

He seemed relieved to find that she was unhurt. He told her, "I was afraid this might happen. That's why I followed and tried to stop you, but apparently you didn't hear me."

"The sea makes so much noise. It's bedlam."

The man smiled, and the smile transformed the sombre expression on his face. "This is gentle to what it can be," and he continued looking down at her upturned face.

"Well, what are you going to do about it? I don't want to remain here all night," said Anabel impatiently.

He laughed. "You won't be able to get up without help. The earth is soft and there's no hold."

"Get a rope," directed Anabel, feeling cooler now that help was at hand.

"No need. I know this coast and what liberties can be taken with it, and how this cliff face reacts to kindness." Here he laughed as though he had made a joke, but Anabel, shaken and dishevelled, did not see any cause for merriment. Her face became wooden. "Wait a bit, and I'll be down."

She stood leaning against the rock face, looking out to sea and listening to the surf dashing and splashing so tirelessly far below her. And now she had forgotten to daydream. She did not think of Paul, only of this queer predicament, and of the fierce repellent face of her rescuer. Presently he was standing beside her on the ledge of rock, a look of unwilling admiration in his eyes.

"You weren't afraid?" he asked.

"No, and you'll say that's because I didn't realize the danger."

"And did you?"

"No, because instinctively I knew I wasn't in danger."
Anabel spoke lightly, and he looked at her keenly,
unaccustomed to the sound of a quick tongue, evidence of a
swift brain.

"You were within an ace of death," the man remarked
quietly.

"How interesting!" Anabel's light mocking voice replied. "I
wish I'd realized it."

"Why?"

"I might have been amused at my reactions."

"That sounds *blasé*."

"Does it?" Anabel replied indifferently.

"You're a visitor. You must have come by the steamer
today."

"I was *left* by the steamer," Anabel said grimly. "When I got
up this morning in my hotel at Bettycombe, I quite thought I
was going to sleep there tonight."

She talked lightly. It was her habit now to make light of pain
and discomfort. She had learned to dissemble before people
who must never guess the weight of the pain in her heart.

The man looked at her for several minutes, taking in the
finely drawn features, the high cheekbones and the width
between her blue eyes. He observed the sun glinting in her
dark-brown hair, and heard the light careless laugh that was
both crystal clear and musical. His eyes searched for detail,
noting the lovely skin and the few freckles on the bridge of her
nose.

He said, "You don't seem to mind very much."

Anabel shrugged. "Why should I? What's the use? They've
fixed me up at the hotel. I'm going to be comfortable."

In turn, she saw that his face was strong and brown. Even
the mouth was strong, though too tight. It was only afterwards,

remembering his features, that Anabel realized he was repressed. Now, as she saw his obvious strength, she thought of him as virile.

He said, "I'm glad you missed the steamer."

"Are you? Now what is that to do with you?" Anabel was amused, and did not know how provocative she sounded.

He eyed her keenly, from head to toe, then he sighed deeply. "I suppose you'll laugh when I tell you this means a glimpse of civilization for me?"

Anabel did laugh, but not mockingly as he had feared, but gently, because she felt sorry for anyone who longed for the civilization she represented. "Are you so much in the backwoods here?"

He nodded glumly, brought out a packet of cigarettes, offered her one and took one himself, and they lit up.

"Can't you do something about it? Why don't you go into Combeford every week by the mailboat?"

"Because there's no one to work the farm if I leave it for a week."

"There are the pleasure steamers in summer." Anabel tried to help him.

It was the farmer's turn to laugh, an odd sound, like a man who does not often laugh. Indeed, he stopped in the middle as though afraid and ashamed of the sound of his own voice. "We call them 'flappers' because they seem so irresponsible. They are at the mercy of weather and tides — useless to me when it's a case of *must* get back."

"What about the fishing-boats from Bettycombe? I know *they* call here."

The farmer shook his head. "Undependable."

"It seems I can't help you, then."

"Not if you can't think up some new way."

"You should know those better than me."

"Oh, I've stopped thinking of ways of escape years ago."

Anabel was just about to say, "Is that why you're so sour? Why you look so sombre and funereal?" But she bit back the words. While they stood alone together on this narrow ledge of rock, twenty feet below the top of the cliff, and double that many feet from the base of the cliff, it might be unwise to be personal. Besides, she was comfortable. There was no hurry to return to her hotel. And talking to this man took her mind off tragic things, stopped any foolish daydreaming.

She asked presently, "Then what made you settle here?"

"My father lived here. He bought the farm from a Frenchman, and came here for his health. I was born here, at the Bella Luce farm. I went away to the mainland to school, and when my father died I came back. Once I had a motorboat of my own, and for a while I used to get away. Perhaps my mother thought I was absent too much." He glanced at Anabel and compressed his lips. Then he continued tonelessly, "Now the farm takes all my time. I've sold the boat."

"Quite a life story," Anabel commented lightly. "But you shouldn't make yourself a martyr to duty."

"I don't feel a martyr, but my duty is here."

"With — your mother?" And Anabel thought she understood the position clearly — the determined mother with her son tied well and truly to strong apron-strings.

"She lives with me."

Anabel threw the end of her cigarette far out to sea, and leant over to watch its flight as the wind curved it back against the rocks below.

She glanced ruefully at her hands, at the dirt-edged nails which she had dug wildly into anything solid which might stay

29

her headlong fall. She had not realized the strength of her instinctive desire to live until she saw her grubby hands.

"Well, if I were you —" began the self-willed, opinionated Miss Anabel Robinson, with a carefree toss of her head, when the farmer interrupted harshly:

"If you were me, you'd do exactly as I have done. You'd realize, as I have, that there's no escape."

"I wouldn't admit that," Anabel replied sturdily.

"Because you're silly. Thank goodness I'm a practical man."

"You're the silly one," Anabel said, beginning to laugh.

At first, the farmer seemed fascinated at the way her eyes crinkled up with merriment; then he remembered that a secret joke caused this mirth, and he was not sharing it.

"If you're laughing at me —" he began haughtily.

"I'm not," Anabel replied, sobering a little, "though your outlook is priceless and I ought to laugh at you for a sobersides. I'm laughing at myself, and the queer fixes I seem to fall into. You must forgive me. It's been such an unexpected kind of day for me. First of all I miss my boat through daydreaming, then for the same reason I fall down a cliff, and meet you in this outlandish spot. It is certainly time for me to wake up, or goodness knows what'll happen to me next."

"I don't believe in dreams," the man told her firmly. "They're misleading, a part of wishful thinking, and unpractical, while, of course, there's always the awakening, which must come inevitably."

Anabel sobered then, and an odd frightened look crept into her eyes as she remembered her own special awakening with Paul, and the agony of those endless nights and never-to-be-forgotten days when she heard he was married.

The farmer was watching her warily, not sure of her mood or whether she were laughing at him or not, but certain that he had surmised a look of fear and misery in her eyes.

Seeing this, Anabel threw back her head and laughed again, so that he told her half-resentfully, "You don't appear to mind these things much."

"What d'you expect me to do? And anyhow, why should I care? I like adventures, and there is no one to worry about me!"

"Have you no family?"

"Well, there's my father. But he's in Australia, and I don't expect him back in England for some time. Besides, he's just got married again, and is on his honeymoon."

"That hurts you?"

"No." But she said it too quickly, almost violently, and the man knew that she was bitter. "Why should I care? I like him to be happy." Anabel gazed at him earnestly, and saw how unsmiling this man's face was, how intense were his brown eyes. "Don't you ever laugh?" she demanded.

"Not often. I've laughed more since I've been talking to you than I've done in a year. There's nothing to laugh at."

Anabel shook her head dolefully. "D'you really mean that?"

"I seldom say what I don't mean."

"Then you're the eighth wonder of the world, and should be in a circus, or museum — or Madame Tussaud's. It's a mistake."

"What is? Not to pretend a bit?"

"No, to let yourself be too serious: not to laugh. Well, if you know me long enough, and you can spare the time off from your Bella Luce farm, I promise to teach you how."

It was a rash promise, and Anabel regretted it as soon as it was made. She waited for him to beg her to show him, perhaps to inquire into her methods.

Instead, the farmer said calmly, "That's what I mean you to do."

"Oh!"

"It has been my intention for the last five minutes."

"I say, how long do you think I'm staying on Luniette?"

The farmer paused before he replied slowly, "I don't know, but I have a hunch that you will be here for some time."

"We shall see," Anabel said darkly and with some dignity. But it was difficult to maintain a cool dignity while standing close to a man on a narrow ledge of rock above the sea, when she might unthinkingly overbalance, or he might push her into the sea.

She looked upwards, and saw how her fall had broken off clumps of earth with long grass attached, and felt the insecurity of the cliff, though the part she was leaning against seemed solid enough.

The sun was beginning to sink, turning pink as it slid down behind the lavender veils of colour in the west. And the wind was rising, as though to prove the truth of Dai's prophecy that the weather was changing. It swayed the long grass that grew at the cliff's edge, giving it an ethereal silvery sheen.

Anabel's eyes came to rest on the farmer's saturnine face. She said, "And now I must go back to the hotel."

He nodded. "It's about time."

"It must be, if I want my supper, and I'm hungry. Will you help me?" She looked inquiringly and trustfully into his eyes.

"Of course." He turned inwards, taking her hand as he did so, and squeezed his way into the fissure and the darkness beyond.

It was rather a weird experience for Anabel to turn from the light and face the unknown blackness with this stranger. She was not frightened, only her heart beat fast with anticipation.

"It's rather like being dragged into Bluebeard's chamber," she said to his back, and was surprised to hear a tremor in her voice.

"I promise you I won't kill you. I want to keep you for another day," was the answer. The words were simple enough, but the echo of his deep tones made them sound terrifying. And then he said, "It is kind of you to trust yourself to me like this."

"I have no choice," was Anabel's reply. Her voice sounded like a stranger's amongst the echoes, for the wind whistled eerily into the fissure, and the incessant thundering of the sea against the rocks below the cliff resounded with a dull reverberation as of heavy gunfire.

And as the couple proceeded slowly, squeezing forward in the narrow curving passage, so the various sounds — their own voices, the gulls' cries, the wind and the noise of the sea seemed to combine into an unnameable satanic howling — Anabel felt the hold on her hand tighten, and took comfort in it. Her shoulders felt bruised, and she wondered dully how much longer this horrible slow progress would last.

Then suddenly they were in a kind of pocket, a space which was merely a widening of the granite fissure, and looking upwards, Anabel saw the blessed blue of the sky. She was astonished to find herself trembling violently; though she was sure that she felt no fear, of course there had been terrific tension on her nerves and muscles. Her hands, too, were clammy, while her arms felt weighty and strangely tired.

She smiled at the farmer in the wan light that filtered down, and his clasp tightened on her sticky fingers, though his face still looked grim.

He did not pause long, but began to ascend the steep side of the 'pocket', and letting go Anabel's hand, he told her, in what sounded like a hoarse whisper, to hold on to his ankles and steady herself as much as possible. Without his encouraging voice to swell the strange music, the queer cacophony of sound changed to a mournful tone, but, oddly enough, Anabel did not hear it.

Within five minutes, which seemed like an eternity of time, the adventure lay behind Anabel, its horrors fading quickly. After a little while she realized how quiet it was, and turned to thank her deliverer.

But he brushed aside her gratitude. "It was nothing. I am only too glad to have been of some help."

"You saved my life," she panted.

"Rubbish! This isn't an uninhabited island. Lots of people must have seen what happened to you, and knew that I was helping you." He waited while she recovered her breath and the curious trembling of her limbs, which he pretended not to see, ceased.

It was Anabel who started to move, speaking easily, as though there had been no recent terrifying experience to ratch her nerves. "I really must be going," she remarked, just as though he were trying to keep her with him.

The farmer turned at once, and they walked side by side, in silence, swiftly across the field. "What's your name?" he asked abruptly.

"Anabel Robinson."

"Anabel!" he repeated below his breath, as though memorizing the name, or savouring the music of each syllable. "Mine's Smith — Robert Smith."

"But my friends call me Bob," Anabel felt sufficiently recovered to tease. "No, I don't think they'd dare. You've never been anything but Robert."

"That's so," he agreed sombrely.

When they reached the footpath which led to the farm, a tall gaunt woman dressed in black was waiting for them. So still she stood, with her arms crossed, her elbows cupped in her hands, and with hair parted in the middle and drawn down in two curtains on either side of her face; and wearing a small black shawl folded over her flat breast which was fastened with a large cameo brooch. She might have been a figure stepped out of a bygone age, a puritanical figure with dark eyes like her son's. Only instead of looking sombre, her eyes were cold and disapproving.

"Who is she?" asked Anabel softly, and the smile that was in her eyes and playing around her mobile mouth died away, frozen by the icy stare.

Robert had no time to answer, for they were close to the statue-like figure. Then he said awkwardly, speaking directly to the older woman, "This is Miss Robinson, Mother. She fell down the cliff. I knew this kind of thing might happen one day. That was why I told you the dangerous ground should be fenced off. Now I *must* see about it."

He sounded unnerved and excited, and spoke in quick jerky sentences. It did not occur to Anabel that these might be the natural reactions to his adventure with her. She imagined him to be afraid of his mother.

The latter shook hands stiffly with Anabel, who thought, 'She doesn't like me, but she's the sort of person to freeze out anyone who might be friendly with her son.'

Mrs. Smith spoke in a metallic voice. "Well, it has happened, and Miss Robinson appears to be none the worse for her experience. If she should ever come this way again, she will no doubt be more careful where she walks. And no one else is likely to walk on the cliff for years — if ever, so the fencing can wait. There's more than enough work to do on the farm without rushing to do extra jobs."

Anabel felt irritated when Robert nodded in agreement. She did not know that he had long since ceased to argue with his mother, who had a habit of grinding at a fellow until he gave in to her wishes for the sake of peace. Turning her head to stare at him, Anabel saw that his expression was more saturnine than ever.

'What a repellent couple,' crossed her mind. She caught her breath quickly when Mrs. Smith said:

"You were down the cliff together for such a long while I thought something really serious had happened, and was wondering whether I should send for help." But she was looking at her son as she spoke, and waited for him to answer.

He said at length, "Miss Robinson fell down, and she needed time to recover. It's no joke tumbling unexpectedly down a hole."

"It wasn't particularly funny," admitted Anabel, glad that her adventure had ended so well, refusing to allow her mind to dwell on it, though as yet she could not get rid of the feeling that everything about her had the shape and quality of a dream, and that any moment awakening would come.

"I suppose not," Mrs. Smith agreed, fixing her mournful eyes curiously on Anabel's face, and noting with some inward perturbation the appealing beauty in her expression.

But the girl did not see the look. She had turned her head and was looking at the farm, a grey building whose latticed windows shone like diamonds in the mellow light of the sun, nestling among trees, appearing like a small oblong jewel in an emerald setting.

"What a lovely homestead!" Anabel exclaimed in admiration to Robert. "Surely it is a Queen Anne house? There is something so old-world and reposeful about it."

Robert looked pleased and told her, "The house was built by Frenchmen who took the island by a trick in William and Mary's reign. It should be solid, for it has stood up to over two and a half centuries of storms — and storms can be something to remember on Luniette."

"How interesting! I had no idea such a place existed here." Anabel wished the Smiths would ask her to their home.

"And why not?" interrupted Mrs. Smith almost inimically, as though Anabel had somehow disparaged the island.

"I don't know," hesitated Anabel, at a loss how to treat this cold, reserved woman, "except that Luniette struck me as a rather barren island — sombre, wild and un-get-at-able, with only the one landing-place."

"But you don't know our island." Now there was no mistaking the hostility in the older woman's tone.

"I was speaking from impressions. Of course, I saw it for the first time this morning," Anabel said quietly, looking straight into Mrs. Smith's eyes, adding hastily, "but the sea is marvellous, a restless waste of every shade of blue and green; white froth and sparkling spray. But —"

It was Robert who intervened with what seemed to his mother, listening and watching the two young people, a disquieting excitement in his voice, "What you need, Miss Robinson, is a guide to take you round and show you places of interest, someone who knows little Luniette well, who lives here —"

Robert stopped abruptly and his face darkened, for Anabel's eyes had crinkled with amusement at his suggestion; then he continued almost resentfully, "Not me. I wasn't thinking of myself. I'm too busy on the farm to play guide to chance visitors. But you seem interested, so before leaving try to see the view from the Policeman, the pyramidal rock over there. It's the highest point on the island. Then there are the ruins of Morisco Castle, where pirates once lived who plundered the island and pillaged the neighbouring shores; and the ancient chapel is worth seeing. And beyond the lighthouse there is a remarkable chasm, called the Devil's Cauldron — but after today you'll probably wish to give that kind of sight a wide berth."

His voice had changed. It was as though Robert had forgotten that his mother stood close to them like a disapproving sentinel. The cliff adventure with this lovely strange girl had formed an intimacy between them which he, at any rate, would not easily forget. In retrospect, Robert knew he would remember the feel of her slim body against his, the clinging touch of her hand.

"I don't think I've lost my nerve," Anabel said slowly, repressing a shudder at the memory of her way of escape from between those merciless slate and granite rocks. "And you make Luniette sound so intriguing that I wish I could stay to hear more."

No doubt in his desire to keep Anabel there a little longer, Robert would have been ready to tell her all he knew about the island, but his mother felt they had dallied long enough. She put a warning hand, roughened with toil and gnarled like an old tree with rheumatism, on her son's arm, saying, "If Miss Robinson wants to get back to the hotel for supper she will have to hurry, or she'll lose her way in the dark."

Anabel felt dismissed. She looked at Robert, whose face a few moments ago seemed young and animated. Now it was dark and inscrutable, as though the old woman's words had contrived to shutter his thoughts, leaving his expression a blank. If he were surprised at his mother's ungracious and aloof attitude, or her scarcely veiled dislike of this girl who had been thrust willy-nilly into their lives, nothing showed on his face.

"It's a clear path downwards to the churchyard, and you can see the hotel from there," he said to Anabel in a flat voice, and did not offer to go with her.

The girl nodded, saying slangily, "I shall be okay. Thanks again for saving my life. You don't know how valuable some people think it is."

She left mother and son with a gay wave of her hand, though with keen disappointment in her heart.

Anabel Robinson was not used to being slighted. Usually people jumped to gratify her slightest wish. Despite the fact that Mrs. Smith had a lovely homestead, she had ignored Anabel's hint to be invited inside, and had pretended not to see the girl's dirty hands, or that a short rest after such an experience might be acceptable. Mrs. Smith had shown no curiosity about Anabel's movements, or how the girl came to be staying alone in the hotel.

"What's wrong with the old hag?" Anabel asked herself angrily, when she turned at a bend in the path.

Mrs. Smith's black-gowned figure, like a slim pole, was greying into distance; but Robert was standing still just as Anabel had left him, looking at her, and a queer elation came over the girl. For these few moments he seemed to have forsaken his mother to watch a stranger.

Anabel thought wrathfully, 'One would think I was trying to steal her precious son, but for what use? As if I would, though the old witch deserves to lose him.'

On impulse Anabel laughed mockingly, though she was then too far away from Robert for the ribald sound to reach him, and blew a kiss on her fingers — an audacity that both surprised and amused herself because she did not want to kiss Robert Smith — or indeed any man ever again.

But quick as Anabel's movements were, before she could turn her face homewards, she saw Robert raise his arm in salute, and though it was impossible to see the expression on his face at this distance she guessed that he was smiling.

Anabel ran down the hillside towards the churchyard, a place of dark yew trees and old grey stones, memorials to islanders and shipwrecked mariners, obviously a lonely spot to be avoided after dark by those afraid of spooks. Here she scattered a flock of sheep pasturing below the stone wall, which ran madly down the slope towards the sea.

There was a glimpse of the slated roof of the hotel, almost hidden in shadow in the lee of western winds and the setting sun. A curl of blue wood smoke rose spirally from a chimney; and presently other threads of blue smoke could be seen against the clear evening sky, rising from unseen chimneys among the trees.

CHAPTER 3

At the hotel there was bustle and noise, the sound of men's voices and deep laughter, the smell of good ale and the pungent scent of tobacco. The conviviality came wholly from the little bar, which seemed to be bursting with friendliness and cheer.

As Anabel entered the hotel and passed the open door of the bar, a man hailed her, detaching himself from the crowd as he spoke.

"Hallo, there. I've been waiting for you for ages. Come in and have a drink. I'm sure you need one." A tall, dark naval officer, with intensely blue eyes, advanced smilingly, glass in hand, to meet Anabel.

And instantly, at the sound of his voice, raised to carry a friendly welcome, there was sudden silence in the bar, and Anabel, glancing behind his broad shoulders, saw dozens of faces turned in her direction, some smiling broadly, but all wearing an air of pleased expectancy that was intensely gratifying after the cold reception she had experienced at the hands of Mrs. Smith.

Then Anabel found her hand grasped and held in a generous grip which made her forget the screen of faces in the immediate background, and forced her to focus all her attention on the compelling personality of this man with his heartening welcome and warm clasp of her fingers.

He was saying, "When I woke up this morning, something seemed to tell me my luck was in. How do? I'm so glad you lost your ship today — at least, speaking for myself. I guess you are pretty sick about it, though." And still holding her hand in strong fingers, he drew her within the heated bar, which was dim and lamp-lit. "We're all friends here, and jolly glad if you'll join us. Come in: don't be afraid."

Anabel hesitated. "But I need a wash. I'm filthy."

"Don't bother, you can wash later. You'll feel better after a drink. We're all straight from work and dirty."

A narrow lane was made for the couple to advance which led direct to the bar itself. Anabel smiled impartially at everyone, and all the men, young and old, returned her smile with interest. It was in the nature of a triumphant progress, for each man tried in his own way to make her feel welcome.

Sarah Ann Groom was smiling behind the counter, nodding approvingly at the effect Anabel was creating upon her customers. Simple Mabel was beside her mistress, sporting a scarlet ribbon in her fair frizzy hair; and one of the young men Anabel had seen in the backyard earlier in the day, the one who had played the mouth-organ, whom Mabel called Olly. His shirt was still open at the neck and his sleeves rolled up, but now he wore a large sacking apron.

By that time the customers, a little excited now that there was a pretty girl in their midst, had returned to their drinks, and the talk and laughter were several degrees louder.

Having reached a point when he could go no further unless he vaulted the bar counter and pierced the mirrored wall at the back of it, the naval officer turned to face Anabel, his blue eyes smiling in frank, friendly fashion into hers, and reluctantly released her hand.

"Now what can I get you? What do you like to drink?"

"You seem to know the ropes here; what do you advise?" Anabel replied, and though her tones were crystal clear, such was the din in the bar that the naval officer had to bend his head close to hers to hear what was said.

"Righto — well, what about a gin and lime? That's a clean drink."

"Please, I shall like that."

The naval officer gave the order to Mabel. "And remember, only a dash of lime, Mabel," he added darkly, as though warning Mabel against watering the drink. Then he begged Mrs. Groom to refill his own glass. "The same as before, Mrs. G."

When they were both served, he picked up his glass. "And now for a toast: or rather a wish. To a long stay on Luniette for you."

Anabel smiled. It was difficult not to feel happy in the presence of such gay spirits even though she felt tired, bruised and dirty, with a longing for a bath and rest.

She raised her glass and touched his. "To my stay here, but not too long or perhaps I shall wear out my welcome," she qualified.

"That's not fair of you. But here goes." They both drank to the toast. The naval officer put his glass down. "We'd be a couple of sillies to make up our minds as to how long you'll be here, because the weather rules our doings on this island. We're at its mercy. And in case no one has already warned you, there's a terrific storm brewing, and you wouldn't dare venture to cross to the mainland for days — perhaps weeks."

While speaking, he took out his cigarette-case, and opening it offered it to Anabel. "Smoke?"

"Oh, you are a pessimist! Thanks." She took a cigarette, then bent her head towards the lighter he flicked to life.

"It's the truth. Of course, I'm a selfish brute, speaking, as usual, for myself. It's deadly dull here, and I'm so fond of life with a capital L. I couldn't wish to keep a girl like you here." He lit his cigarette and took a deep puff at it.

"Like me!" Anabel echoed.

"It wouldn't be a fair deal." But there was no regret in his tone, only a gaiety which Anabel found infectious.

"You don't know. As a matter of fact, this kind of loneliness has a special appeal for me because I live in London — you know, hot streets, smells and flies. I've had life with all the letters capitals, and I'm sick of the sight of a restaurant with a dance band and all that goes with that sort of thing. It's the simple life for me."

The officer looked at her with interest. "I can't hope to get away from Luniette for ages — perhaps ever, until I'm old and bent and gracefully retired to chicken-farming, or however I end my days. And you're a godsend, so I hope you'll stay here — a present from heaven — a girl who talks my language. I say, let's make the most of your visit here, whatever its length."

Anabel laughed. "Of course. That's what I intended on doing." She blew an expert wavy smoke ring into the thick atmosphere of the bar, and watched it dissolve and merge into the haze which filled the room.

Her companion looked on approvingly, his eyes on the long line of her throat. "O-o! But you don't know how to set about it."

"Well, how did you spend your afternoon?"

"How?"

"You went up to Bella Luce farm, tumbled down a fissure, were extricated by Smith, the farmer, wasted a precious hour talking to him on the rocks, and —"

"You seem to know all about my movements since I landed here," Anabel said tartly, undecided whether to be annoyed or not.

"Rather! Considering I — and I daresay most of the males marooned on this island — have been watching you through my glasses all day with great interest, I think I should know."

"What nerve!"

"Oh no, we've been having a glimpse of heaven, and I know you won't begrudge us that." But he laughed gracelessly, and Anabel's annoyance fled.

"Silly!" was all she could think of to say.

"Smith is a handsome chap, I grant you, but as sombre, heavy and sour as lead."

"He's all right, or would be if you knew him."

The officer smiled wryly. "Perhaps he got on with you. He'd be a difficult chap who couldn't — you're so sweet. But I confess to not being able to get under Smith's skin." As though talking of Robert Smith bored him, the officer picked up his glass again. "And now for another toast," he cried happily. "To the gods who sent you here — I'd like to make them my deepest salaams."

But it was hard to talk progressively in the general hubbub around them. Anabel had to shout to make herself heard. She fanned her hot face with her handkerchief, and only succeeded in producing a heat wave.

"This is truly awful," the officer said, and put his hands to his ears. "I shall melt, and you may indulge in a faint if we stop here much longer."

"It's terribly hot," shouted Anabel, and put a moist hand to her throat, which ached through producing so much sound.

"Let's go over to the window," the officer said, and wondered why he had not thought of it before. But he had been too much engrossed with Anabel to trouble much about his surroundings. He ordered fresh drinks and carried them with difficulty over men's heads across the room, to the seat beneath the open window — Anabel following in his wake.

Here it seemed a little quieter, or the peace reigning outside made it seem so. Anabel sank down on the seat, put her glass down on the sill, sighed with relief and looked out to sea. There were more shadows over the heaving watery waste now, and often the wind blew the top from the waves and sent the spindrift flying.

The officer, his arm resting carelessly on the window-ledge, fixed his eyes on Anabel's face, noting the beauty of the gentian eyes placed so widely apart, and that the whites of Anabel's eyes were very white, making the eyes seem larger and bluer; and he measured the length of her lashes in his mind's eye, brownish spears curling back on themselves, and gold-tipped as though the sun lingered on them.

He began to speak. "Now listen, Anabel —"

There was that in his voice, a caress Anabel had often heard in Paul's voice, which jarred her complacency so that the sea view lost its interest and her calmness fled.

The use of her Christian name, said in that drawling, sweet tone, meant that this stranger liked her, that he wished to be friendly. It might mean he was paving the way to make love to her, and that she would not tolerate.

She looked sharply at the officer and snapped, "Who said that was my name?"

"Don't be angry, please. It's in the hotel register which is on the table in Mrs. Groom's sitting-room, and written in a round childish handwriting for king or beggar or poor naval chap like me to read. It is such a sweet name and suits you down to the ground. And mine is Tim."

Anabel considered his face in silence for a while. He was unsmiling now, and his face in repose, though strong, was kindly, with nice eyes and sensitive lips. "Tim what?" she inquired.

And after a little while, still smiling gently, he said, "Just Tim."

Anabel told herself she knew what that meant. They were to skip acquaintanceship and leap into friendship, which would be Anabel and Tim.

She was conscious of a slight confusion of mind, and to cover it she asked, "What do you do with yourself all day here?"

"Work, mostly." He leant forward, ostensibly to see something the better from Anabel's side of the window, but in reality to bring himself closer to her. "See that lighthouse?"

Anabel turned her face to look in the direction he indicated. "Yes?"

"Well, just below there, near to Shutter Point, where the *Oakham* went on the rocks some years ago, we are preparing a camp."

"A camp! But who will want to camp here towards the end of summer?"

"I can't tell you. It's terribly hush-hush."

Their eyes met, mysterious and questioning.

"But you've aroused my curiosity," Anabel complained.

"I only told you what I was doing in this forsaken spot," was the quick reply, and as though realizing that he was talking too much, Tim changed the subject abruptly. "But don't let's talk about me. There's nothing new anyone can tell me about myself, and I want so much to know more about you."

Anabel shook her head, not wanting to meet Tim's friendly advances. "I'm only a bird of passage — hardly interesting news," she said almost coldly, aware that Tim's interest in her was increasing with each passing moment.

"Maybe, but something tells me you won't be that to me. And you can't help being interesting; you're the most wonderful creature that has happened on this island since I've been here." And again there was that queer low intimate note in this man's voice which seemed to promise that the friendship between them which was so strangely begun was destined to continue until — oh, well, who knew where friendship between man and woman ended and love began?

The idea frightened Anabel, who had made up her mind after the tragic Paul episode that never again could she go through any more heartache for a man. But that did not prevent her laughing with Tim, and refusing to take seriously the friendship he was offering so generously and blatantly, with the eagerness of a lonely man with gregarious instincts.

It was obvious to Anabel that both amusement and forgetfulness lay in Tim's society; and she laughed softly, answering, "You say very pretty things, and being an ordinary girl, I love hearing them. But I can't help thinking that in spite of the loneliness of your existence on Luniette, you've managed to keep your hand in very well. You sound so — practised. There are girls on this island?"

Tim laughed too — a bluff, hearty sound. "Of course, there are a few, but none to touch you." And as an afterthought, as though remembering one girl who stood out from the rest, "Did you happen to meet young Naomi up at Bella Luce?"

"No, the farm seemed particularly devoid of youth, I thought. Who is she?"

"Smith's sister."

"His sister! You surprise me. Mr. Smith didn't strike me as the kind of man who had a sister."

"Because there seems such a lack of feminine influence in his outlook on life and manners? Well, he has a sister, and that stoic woman, Mrs. Smith, is her mother — and an ill-assorted mother and daughter they are."

"Is Naomi pretty?"

"Very, in a wild way. I always think there is foreign blood in her." Tim's careless answer was meant to hide the measure of his attraction to Naomi Smith, but did not deceive Anabel.

"She sounds uncivilized."

Tim laughed. "Could one expect anything else from a girl born and bred here?"

"There is a school, I suppose?"

"Of course. It's attached to the church and is run by Parson and his wife. But Naomi has probably forgotten all she ever learnt at school. She's dairymaid up at Bella Luce now."

"What fun!"

Tim grinned. "Tell that to Naomi. She'll say you don't know what you're talking about. Being dairymaid up at the farm, under Mrs. Smith's eye, isn't the playtime it was to Marie Antoinette and her court ladies over a hundred and fifty years ago."

Then Tim moved restlessly, obviously finding it boring to talk about the Smith family. He was sick of the inhabitants of Luniette. Perhaps he had been cooped up too long in this island, whose entire length was only two and a half miles, and considerably less in width.

He coaxed, "What is London looking like just now?"

But Anabel had no time to tell Tim what he longed to hear, for Mabel interrupted them with a message from Sarah Ann Groom. Speaking to Tim, the maid simpered, "Missus says to tell you if you've quite finished your drinks, sir, that supper'll be ready in a quarter of an hour."

"Righto. I won't be two ticks having a wash," Tim replied, finishing what was left of his drink and rising to his feet. And to Anabel, as though to hurry her too: "There'll just be time for you to have a quick bath."

Once more the throng parted to make way for Anabel to leave the bar-room, and several men said 'goodnight' to her as she went, a civility she returned with a gay smile.

Mabel followed them into the hall, where it was cooler and quieter, the noise from the bar-room sounding like the humming of busy bees. Twice the maid opened her mouth as though to say something to Tim, then thought better of it and closed her lips again. She went behind them upstairs, gasping so audibly that Tim stopped on the landing and, facing her with some exasperation, said, "Now, Mabelle, I can see that something's hurting you — get it off your chest and quickly. What is it? Well —" impatiently — "say it. Don't stand gasping there like a fish out of water on the point of suffocation."

Anabel had paused too. She looked inquiringly and with some amusement at Mabel, who was patently fond of Tim, gazing at him adoringly as a pet dog might look at its master.

Mabel took a deep breath and blurted out, "Don't go into your room, sir. It's not yours any longer. It's hers," and without waiting for him to speak, Mabel turned tail and clattered down the stairs, shouting, "Yours is opposite."

"Don't break your neck," Tim called out after her; then he turned soberly and wonderingly to Anabel. "Now what exactly did that girl mean? Perhaps you can tell me?"

It was twilight on the landing. The sun had set long ago, daylight was fading, and objects inside the hotel were losing their familiar daytime appearance, and becoming shadowy and strange. Someone had lit a small oil-lamp and fixed it on a bracket on the wall at the far end of the landing, but as yet the light was pale, and only served to deepen the shadows.

Anabel met Tim's eyes squarely. Mystery evidently irritated him, for his was a simple straightforward personality.

It had already occurred to Anabel that there must have been sharp conflict between Mrs. Groom's conscience and avarice, that the landlady's moral cowardice had prevented her from facing Tim, and she had deputed to Mabel the task of telling him, guessing rightly that her guest would feel annoyed.

Anabel walked straight to the door of the large best bedroom, and with her hand on the knob said lightly, "Mabel was trying to tell you that I have taken your room. You've been superseded, dispossessed, or dislodged by me — turned out, in fact. Too bad, of course, but these things do happen sometimes, but you'll get over it I've no doubt — and it may be for only a night. Who knows?" Anabel had purposely spoken in a gay tone, avoiding looking at Tim. She thought, 'But if this had happened to me, I'd kick up no end of fuss.'

Yet she jumped as Tim's voice sounded close to her shoulder. There was a hard note in it which held the warning that Tim was a stranger to her, that the Tim who had been so friendly towards her in the bar downstairs — the gay, light-hearted, convivial spirit, the easy companion, the would-be trifler — was only the surface of the real man. Then he had seemed soft and pliable to womanly influence. It had been very misleading. Underneath there was granite, which was in the stern timbre of his voice. This was a man impatient towards change, intolerant of petty deceit, a master and leader first and a friend afterwards. And as Anabel realized this, something within her exulted. It was as though the swift crack of Tim's voice, the curt words, acted like a goad to her jaded spirit, and brought to life the dead thing that was her heart — or that which she had supposed was killed by Paul's cruelty. Her pulses began to flutter, for here indeed was metal to her liking.

But there was no answering laughter in his tone as Tim snapped, "Why have they happened?"

Anabel paused and shrugged. Still keeping her fingers on the doorknob, she turned to face Tim, quickly averting her eyes, however, when she saw his stern face with all the former friendliness gone out of it.

"Because, I suppose, I wanted the room so badly I simply had to have it," Anabel said lamely, feeling confused and hurt by that cold, composed quality in Tim's voice which gave no hint that he could ever again speak softly.

"And so you bought Mrs. Groom over? Go on, tell me — I want the truth. I'm so sick of lies." But what Tim meant was that he was sick of women's lies.

"I haven't told you any — yet," Anabel said plaintively. Then seeing that he waited for a reply: "Well, yes, I told Mrs. Broom she could charge me what she liked because no other room would suit me." Anabel was aware that she must sound like a spoilt creature to Tim, but she blamed him for asking awkward questions.

Tim said, "Thinking that everyone must have his price?"

"And so he has," Anabel flared, trying to remember an old tag of her father's.

"You know queer people, perhaps. Obviously you are rich enough to pay for a whim. Yet had you troubled to ask me to let you have my room, the one you coveted for its view, I suppose, I would gladly have moved out to please you."

There was a pregnant pause. Dimly, Anabel remembered Paul saying similar words to her: "You take too much upon yourself, thinking money is everything that counts. There are other things worthwhile in life which may mean happiness. But you have so much to learn before you can hope even to notice those things, I despair for your happiness."

Was wanting this special room one of the 'other things' to which Paul was referring? Anabel's heart ached, as it always did when she thought of Paul, but she said quietly, "I'm sorry you are so put out. If I'd dreamt you begrudged me this room, I wouldn't have asked for it."

"I begrudge you nothing. It's the method of obtaining your ends that annoys me. I can't stand people working against me behind my back," replied Tim swiftly.

"Those are hard words, and they don't fit the occasion," Anabel complained. "It's usually held up against me that I'm too frank — too blunt. There's no need for me to be sly. Remember, I hadn't met you when Mrs. Groom showed me this room. If I had —"

"What on earth has that to do with it?" Tim blazed. "Don't you understand it's the principle of your behaviour that counts?" Tim was finding fault with her, treating her like a perfect stranger — no, worse, like an enemy, and Anabel felt her temper rising. Tim was putting her in the wrong. It was unfair of him and impertinent.

She said stiffly, her tone measuring the distance between them, "I said I was sorry. Of course, I'll change my room at once."

To Anabel's annoyance and amazement, because she had expected him to treat her apology graciously, Tim cried, "You jolly well shall!"

Anabel's face whitened with quick anger, but she managed to remark steadily — if coldly, "It is easily done, because I have no luggage, as you know."

She moved away from the door with what she hoped was dignity, and stood forlornly in the middle of the wide airy landing, wondering what she should do next.

And as Anabel remained there, her bruises and her dirty appearance making her seem limp and beaten, she happened to glance at Tim, whose anger had matched her own; and that sense of humour which had helped her throughout life, even when things were blackest, came again to her aid.

She smiled. "You win," she admitted, "but how inglorious you have made me feel."

Involuntarily Tim took a step towards her. He held out his hand, meeting her more than halfway, for he, too, could be generous.

Having shaken hands solemnly, Tim opened the best bedroom door and flung it wide. "Of course you can have it," he told her in a more friendly tone. "But it's awfully bad for your character when men give in to your whims. I wonder if they've moved out all my gear."

Anabel went into the bedroom. "Come and see," she invited cordially. "There's nothing of mine here." But she noticed that the room had an unoccupied look, though the bed was turned down and a pair of striped flannel pyjamas was laid out on the sheet. A toothbrush in a transparent holder with a new face-flannel and a tablet of soap were on a marble-topped washstand.

Anabel seized on these toilet requisites. "Now show me where the bathroom is. I'm so grubby, I'm sure you won't know me when you see me again."

"Well, don't be too long; it's already late," said Tim, and led the way to the bathroom.

But though they had shaken hands and were friendly again, there was a new reserve in Anabel's manner that was not lost on Tim.

'She's not used to the mental spanking I gave her,' he thought grimly, as he went into the room opposite to his former bedroom. 'But now Miss Anabel knows I won't stand for any nonsense. I wonder who she is.'

CHAPTER 4

It was half an hour before Anabel, bathed and with her clothes brushed, went down to the dining-room, where she found Tim waiting for her at the only table laid for supper. It stood before the open window, and there was a globular oil-lamp, set in the middle of the white damask cloth, which shed a mellow glow on Tim's face.

He had been reading an old newspaper which he laid aside at Anabel's approach, and rose as she looked tentatively around the room.

"At last! Do you always keep people waiting?" Tim grinned.

"I had to be clean," Anabel told him.

"Of course, but, dirty or clean, you look good to me."

"And I didn't wash for your sake."

"Why should you?" Then Tim gazed quizzically at Anabel. "You've never had to consider others, have you?"

"What makes you say that?"

"It's an impression I gained of you."

"You mustn't believe too much in impressions," Anabel said impersonally.

"I'm open to change," Tim grinned. "But you haven't been over-long. It's only that I missed you, and I'm hungry, which I'm sure you must be, too. And Mrs. G. has sent Mabelle in twice to see if you are down."

By that time Anabel had joined Tim at the table, and she said calmly, "That was Mrs. Groom's fault. If she had done her duty and told you that your room was changed, we shouldn't have wasted time quarrelling on the landing and making ourselves unhappy."

Tim was full of contrition. "Did I make you unhappy, Anabel?"

"Of course."

"I'm sorry. Let's stop that particular war — forget it, shall we? After all, you won, so you can afford to be magnanimous." He pulled out Anabel's chair, which faced the window, from which there was a fine view of the greying sea, and was close beside his own, a position Tim had chosen carefully before Anabel entered the room.

As she sat down, he pushed her chair forward under her knees.

"That do?" Tim asked, looking down on the crown of her head.

"Perfectly, and what a gorgeous view! It looks windy out there."

"I told you there was a change coming in the weather. We don't feel anything here because this hotel is in a hollow of the hillside, and the wind is behind us." Tim sat down in his place. "Mrs. G. apparently thought we'd like to sit together for our meal," he offered as an excuse for supping with Anabel.

"Or she wanted to save lamp-oil," said Anabel spitefully.

"That's catty! D'you mind eating with me? It's more matey."

Anabel smiled. "You haven't asked me, but you may have supper with me."

Tim looked nonplussed for a moment, then he laughed. "Oh, it's to be like this, is it? Well, I don't suppose either of us will suffer for being polite to the other."

Anabel surveyed the table. "But you shouldn't have waited if you were hungry," she said, noting that their plates were already served with slabs of cold meat and mayonnaise sauce, while there were dishes of attractively arranged salad on the table.

"I'm not that hungry. Besides, I like your company. Half the fun of eating is talking to your opposite number at table."

Mabel burst open the door, which Tim had carefully closed when Anabel came into the room, looked vaguely about her and disappeared, leaving the door wide open.

Both Anabel and Tim looked round in surprise; then their eyes met and they smiled at each other with understanding.

"Mabelle's gone to tell Mrs. G. you're down." There was a bottle of light French wine on the table, and Tim drew Anabel's attention to it. "I don't know what your taste in wine is," he told her, "but I ordered this thinking you might like it. I haven't drawn the cork, so if you have a preference for any other kind, there's no harm done, and I'll tell Mabelle to take it back and bring something else."

Anabel bent to read the label on the bottle, and saw that it was a brand of wine often served from her father's cellar at home. "That will do nicely," she said, and Tim was pleased.

"Righto, then I will draw the cork."

Mabel returned with a dish of chipped potatoes which she banged down on the table, and having smiled in a lingering kind of way at Tim, she withdrew, leaving the door wide open.

Tim rose and shut the door. "It would seem meaningless jargon to Mabelle to tell her that an open door creates draught. And to say it gives me a pain in the neck would give her the ell of liberty she is for ever seeking to take with me," he said laughingly.

"You have obviously made a great impression on her. While you are in the room, Mabel takes no notice of me," remarked Anabel.

"And you don't like that," grinned Tim.

At first Tim and Anabel chatted lightly of this and that, but presently, when the keen edge of their appetites had worn off, and the wine had mellowed their thoughts, the talk turned to London and people — and soon they discovered some mutual friends which formed a solid link in this agreeable friendship so strangely begun. It seemed natural, soon afterwards, for Tim to talk of his people; and Anabel learned that Tim's father was a parson of the austere, aesthetic type — a recluse — who shows little human understanding of its children, and rears them almost in secret.

Anabel looked at Tim closely, with more attentiveness than she had hitherto shown him. A kind of pity wakened in her heart for him, though she drove it resolutely out, recalling in time that they say pity is akin to love, and such an idea was far from her mind. But Anabel marvelled secretly that a boy obviously born with a hunger for society, as Tim was, yet deprived of it by a short-sighted parent, should have, in manhood, such a normal outlook on life.

Anabel thought it might be fun to give Tim a little of the pleasure he had missed in life. "You don't appear to take after him," Anabel pointed out, helping herself to a second portion of apple pie and clotted cream.

"People say I am like my mother — and she, poor soul, is dead."

"So is mine," Anabel told him calmly. "She died when I was born."

"But your father is alive?" asked Tim, thinking that if Anabel were an orphan it would explain her independent spirit, that wayward recklessness with which she was able to face the trying experiences of the day.

"Oh yes, but Father's seldom at home in London. He's busy, and I seldom see him."

"What does he do for your bread and butter — and jam?"

Anabel paused. There was such a mistake as talking too much and too fast, not realizing that the conversation was growing intimate, with a free-and-easy give and take of all sorts of ideas. Too late, Anabel saw that her old habit of being a good mixer was letting her down. She was reluctant to tell Tim her father's business, knowing that it would at once label her 'rich girl', an opprobrious tag even for a short time. It might cramp Tim's style, as it had Paul's, and so spoil a pleasant friendship.

Unfortunately it was impossible to lie, for Tim had already shown that he was not a man to be trifled with — deceit was anathema to him. So Anabel said in a shamefaced way, as though she were confessing her father to be a failure or felon, "Father is an international banker. He backs governments — you know," and waited breathlessly for Tim to speak.

It is true that Tim looked at her sharply, being more struck by Anabel's manner than the actual words she used, though Anabel was not to know that. The full impact of her father's business did not occur to Tim until afterwards — in the middle of the night, when he could not sleep for thinking of the girl.

But now Tim remarked with mock sadness, "Your father may be a busy man, but he spoils you by giving you too much freedom, too much money and a colossal independence. Perhaps I'm old-fashioned, but I believe these things, in super form, are bad for a girl, especially if she's pretty, like you."

Anabel breathed a sigh of relief that a difficult moment was passed. "Why?"

"Partly because they make you a prey of unscrupulous men."

Anabel laughed loudly. "That really is funny. Do I look the unhappy victim?"

It surprised her when Tim nodded, saying, "You don't seem to me to be particularly happy in spite of the fact that laughter comes easily to you."

"But I can assure you I am — terrifically happy," Anabel hastened to say.

Tim shook his head wisely. "That's what *you* think. But I wish I could do something to make you really happy."

"I've told you —" began Anabel pettishly.

"All right. We'll let it go at that."

After supper, while waiting for coffee, Tim suggested a stroll outside, and presently the two went, side by side, down the path to the beach, and stepped across the line of seaweed thrown far up the shingle by the rough tides. And so to the edge of the sea where the waves broke rhythmically and sullenly with a rustle and drag on the shingle in their ceaseless ebb and flow.

A moon was shining, turning the restless sea to silver, and the rocks at the side of the small bay to velvet. The tide was out, revealing serried rows of rocks draped in seaweed. "We call these the 'Praying Nuns', but they're treacherous, too," Tim told Anabel. "Dai gathers his mussels for bait from that weed." Anabel stooped and picking up a flat stone, sent it spinning and hopping across the sea; and Tim watched the play of her figure, admiring its grace.

Anabel turned to Tim suddenly. "Aren't I clever? I've never played ducks and drakes since I've been grown up."

"You poor little rich girl," Tim commiserated, but his tone was serious, and the eyes that were looking at Anabel were soft and eager, like those of a young boy.

Anabel stood still, staring at Tim wonderingly. "Why," she exclaimed, at length, "you're much younger than I thought; you're only a boy."

Tim smiled. "How old did you think I was? I'm not exactly a Methuselah."

"No, but you seemed old — about thirtyish; but in this half-light, you don't look a day more than twenty."

Tim burst out laughing, and the sentimental moment passed. "As you say, it's this kindly light; and I'm more than thirty, though I don't feel nearly so decrepit as I may appear to you in full daylight."

It was Tim who suggested they should return to the hotel for coffee.

Anabel turned with him at once. "It seems such a pity to leave this gorgeous night," she exclaimed, looking towards the dark hillside of the island.

"Lovely!" said Tim, but Luniette had long ago lost its attraction for him, and he found more to study and admire in Anabel's clear-cut profile.

Anabel saw a light shining in the darkness, a solitary orange spot in the deepening night. "Surely that light isn't at the Smiths' farm?" she questioned, pointing up the hill as they climbed, single file, up the cliff path.

"You can't see Bella Luce from here. It's in a dip of the downs, practically invisible from the east. It lies open to the west, if you remember. That light comes from a cowman's cottage on their land. He's the one old labourer left to them, a chap named Reuben, quite a character, with a bent back and a fringe of hair circling his face," Tim told her.

Anabel added, "But there's a light moving on the footpath beyond the churchyard."

"Ah, that would be Naomi riding her bicycle downhill."

"You sound very sure," Anabel commented curiously.

"Naomi does the same thing every night at this time — or she has since I've been here. That's what I hate about this island life: you can bank on what everyone is going to do each minute of the day. Naomi's a native, and runs true to island form. Not that she likes it on Luniette any more than I do, but her home is here and she's stuck. I feel sorry for the kid. It must be pretty awful to want to clear out and be unable to."

"Why can't Naomi leave Luniette?" asked Anabel, thinking that Tim and Naomi must be close friends.

"She has to help on Bella Luce."

"But that's fun."

"Fun!" echoed Tim. "Well, most things are fun for a short while. It's when fun becomes routine that it grows dull."

"I wouldn't mind working on a farm."

Tim shook his head. "It's no future here for a kid who likes life."

Something in Tim's deep voice caused Anabel to pause and turn to look at him. She was standing on rising ground, and so Tim's face was on a level with hers. It was grey and shadowy in the moonlight, and Anabel could not see his eyes, which were deep set.

"Why are you stopping?" Tim questioned. "Go on."

Anabel smiled. "No reason at all," she replied lightly. "But I'm longing to meet Naomi."

"You will, and soon. She'll probably have coffee with us presently," was the calm reply.

There was a short silence, during which Anabel frowned, not liking this unusual cavalier treatment. Then she said meaningly, "Oh! Is that an island habit, too?" Something seemed to drive Anabel onwards, a quick urge that might have arisen from anger, and she hastened her steps, and so gained the top of the cliff, from which vantage point could be seen the whitewashed facade of the hotel.

Said Tim to Anabel's uncompromising back, "I gave Naomi a standing invitation, ages ago, to come down whenever she liked. In fact, I begged her to take pity on my loneliness."

Anabel did not know what to think about Tim and Naomi, so she told herself crossly, 'The man's a born flirt — the most odious kind of man.' But in her heart Anabel knew this was not true. Tim was the lucky possessor of a blithe spirit. He could not stop himself being friendly to either man or woman.

Tim was able to draw level with Anabel now, for the path was considerably wider. The two unconsciously hurried their pace, and each looked ahead towards the door of the hotel.

At long last Anabel spoke, replying to Tim's previous remark, which he had already forgotten. "Which, of course, Naomi did."

Tim glanced sharply at his companion. "Eh! What do you mean?"

"Nothing: just what I said." Anabel's tone was cold.

"You sound hateful, Anabel."

"Sorry —" laconically — "I shall leave the hating to Naomi. She won't like meeting me." Anabel spoke with such prim satisfaction in her tone that Tim longed to shake her.

"Why ever not?"

Anabel shrugged. "Women never do like me."

"How conceited you sound!"

"Do I? But it's true."

"What rot! Naomi will be delighted with you. You'll cheer her up, Anabel."

"Shall I?" And Anabel thought rebelliously, 'How cheery for me!'

"You don't sound enthusiastic. But humanly speaking, and I am appealing to your intelligence, what Naomi needs, and is pining for, is young society."

Anabel did not say so, but she thought Tim would have shown more wisdom in appealing to the heart instead of her intelligence. She said, "Then I mean it when I say I'm wild to meet Naomi."

It was annoying to hear Tim championing Naomi's cause. And it was unusual for any man to dream of putting any girl's name before the magic one of Anabel. There was surely something wrong in such procedure?

But Paul had succeeded in doing so. For the first time since that unhappy episode, Anabel wondered if she had been mistaken in what Paul had done to her. Had Paul merely wounded her pride instead of trampling on love?

'Perhaps Luniette is already doing me good; or the island has cast a spell over me so that I do not feel for Paul as I once did,' thought Anabel.

Tim had not bothered to answer her, and the two gained the hotel in silence. Naomi, dressed in a white skirt with large red flowers painted on it and a scarlet jumper, was waiting for them, sitting on a wooden seat placed in front of the dining-room window of the hotel. Her face was turned expectantly towards Tim and Anabel. And her bicycle was propped up against the side wall — with a man's bicycle.

Naomi was not alone.

Almost before she glanced at Naomi, Anabel had seen the loose-limbed dark figure of Robert Smith resting on an arm of the seat, his long gloomy face seeming to stand out against the white wall behind him.

As Tim and Anabel approached, the brother and sister rose; and while Naomi's eyes flickered curiously from Tim to Anabel's face, Robert's were fixed immovably, and with a kind of fierce possessiveness, on Anabel.

Tim waved his hand. "How good of you both to come down," he cried cordially. "Now we'll have a party, just what I've always longed for on Luniette." And to Naomi, and with that special smile he reserved for the girl, for whom he felt warm friendship, "I've been telling Anabel all about you, while, of course, you've heard all about her from your brother." Tim turned to Anabel. "I want you two to be friends," he said.

The two girls nodded unsmilingly to each other.

In one long, swift, practised and appraising glance, Anabel had summed up Naomi — what she looked like — her clothes, which were old-fashioned but definitely suited to her — and something of the working of Naomi's mind, judged from her straight glance and unsmiling face.

Naomi was younger, and without Anabel's 'nous'. She arrived at similar conclusions about Anabel, and took longer over the process. Anabel was like a moonbeam, cool and remote. Anabel's clothes were chic. And Anabel liked Tim.

It was as Anabel had foretold: Naomi hated her.

Meanwhile, Tim had nodded genially to Robert. "Hallo, Smith; we don't often see you down here of an evening."

But Robert neither saw nor heard Tim. He had eyes only for Anabel — hungry, mournful eyes.

"I've been worrying about you, wondering if you felt any the worse for your experience this afternoon. I told Mother afterwards that we should have invited you to Bella Luce to rest awhile. We must have seemed very rude and inhospitable to you."

"Not a bit. Why should you ask a stranger into your home?" Anabel replied easily. "And there was no need to worry about me because, you see, I'm quite all right."

"Not tired?"

Anabel found this sympathetic inquiry of Robert's most healing after Tim's brusque treatment, and in answering she lowered her voice to a sweet intimate softness which was, however, not lost on Tim, who found himself taking quite a lively interest in this encounter.

"Not very."

"You'll feel stiff tomorrow, when your bruises come out. I'm afraid I treated you roughly, but I was so anxious to get you to the top of the cliff. I wasn't so gentle as I should have been."

"Now, you are not to blame yourself for anything. You have no idea how delighted I was when you joined me on that horrid ledge above the rocks. No one could have done better. You deserve so much for your help." Anabel spoke with more earnestness than she would have used had she not seen out of the tail of her eye that Naomi had appropriated Tim as her own special property, a position he appeared to like. Until now, Anabel had thought the afternoon's adventure a trivial affair — rather a nuisance considering she had torn her dress and dirtied her hands, but nothing certainly to dwell upon.

Anabel expected Tim to interrupt, and he did so. "This is Smith's lucky day, too," Tim said loudly. "He happened to be on the spot when you most needed help, Anabel." Then remembering his duties as host, "I'll go and find Mabelle, and tell her to bring coffee out here. We may as well make the most of this evening, for we'll be glad to be shut in tomorrow."

Anabel laughed unbelievingly. "I wish you'd stop joking, Tim."

"Joking, am I? All right, you just wait until the tide turns." Then Tim went indoors.

Naomi and Anabel were sitting on the seat now, and the former said angrily, as though she were willing to use any pretext to start a quarrel with Anabel, "Why should Tim joke about the weather? What he says is always right."

Anabel looked at Naomi with surprise, then smiled indulgently. There was an active dislike of Naomi growing in Anabel's heart; and side by side with it was a feeling of pity for Naomi, who had an exhausted look on her young face, one which surely had no right to be there.

Anabel told herself fiercely, while she continued to smile fatuously, 'She can have Tim. Let him fall for those large, round brown eyes, the dark curls and youthful contours of Naomi's face. None of them knows it, but I'm through with men. I don't want him.'

And aloud Anabel teased, "I thought Tim said it to keep me here on Luniette. He's so bored here — alone."

"He has me," Naomi breathed fiercely.

Anabel agreed smilingly, "Oh yes: Tim has you."

Then Anabel looked out to sea. How right this meeting with brother and sister was. There was an inevitability about it. Everything fitted in so perfectly, even the hate and jealousy that had reared their ugly heads. It was almost as though Anabel could feel the electric cross-currents of emotion that seemed to spin and spread between them with the intricacy of a spider's web. She smiled as though at something funny; but suddenly, at sight of Naomi's tragic expression, Anabel knew it was funny no longer. Naomi was suffering deeply, for a rival in love was something new to the island-bred girl and she had no experience how to deal with her. It was with a feeling akin to relief that Anabel heard Robert speaking.

He was saying, "And another reason why I came down tonight was to ask you to tea at Bella Luce tomorrow afternoon. I am bringing down some butter to the sheds behind here which is to be exported to Combeford, and could take you back with me in the cart. It'll be rough going, but I'll oil the springs, and try to make you as comfortable as possible, and anyway, it will be better than toiling uphill."

This was an unexpected invitation after Mrs. Smith's uncompromising attitude earlier in the evening. Besides, Anabel had now made up her mind not to linger on Luniette. A longing for peace was uppermost in her thoughts, yet it seemed to Anabel that peace was the last thing she was to be allowed. Wherever men and women met together, there was plotting and intrigue. Anabel hoped that by this time tomorrow she would be back in the hotel at Bettycombe, this uncomfortable adventure in the past. She hesitated for so long to answer that Naomi, watching her closely, said bluntly, "She is thinking up an excuse because she doesn't want to come."

"You're quite wrong, Naomi," it gave Anabel some satisfaction to say. And to Robert, who was waiting anxiously for her reply, "I was wondering if I should still be here. You see, if it is possible —"

Robert pointed seawards at the grey waste of water, and then up at the moon ringed with a misty halo, and over to the south where trees on the top of a high cliff were bending before the rising gale. "Don't let the quietness and peace of this sheltered position deceive you, Anabel. It is often like this in the hollow beneath this high cliff, which takes the brunt of the westerly gales. No boat will be calling here tomorrow."

"But if the weather's that bad, and I have to stay here, shall I be able to get to Bella Luce?" Anabel inquired.

"There's only one bad part, and I shall be with you," Robert told her.

After a short pause, Anabel said slowly, "Then if Mrs. Smith wishes it —"

"Of course, my mother told me to ask you."

"Then I shall love to go," Anabel answered briskly. "What time will you fetch me — about four-ish?"

"Oh, before that."

"But can't I find my own way to the farm? You won't be able to spare the time."

"I shall make time; and though you may be able to go alone to Bella Luce, it will be no trouble for me to pick you up with the cart."

Robert spoke so eagerly, and was evidently so glad she was visiting the farm, that Anabel felt a thrill of excitement at the prospect of seeing the inside of Bella Luce, and said happily, "I can't wait until tomorrow."

Naomi rose abruptly and left them, apparently seeking Tim, for she disappeared into the hotel. A little silence fell between Anabel and Robert, and presently the latter said shyly, "That's the first sensible thing Naomi's ever done — to leave me alone with you." And he slid from his perch on the arm of the seat and sat down beside Anabel, who moved aside to make room for him.

Anabel smiled, saying lightly, "I don't believe Naomi gave us a thought. She's gone to find Tim."

"Oh, that chap!" And after a while he said, "Naomi's fallen for him."

"I'm not surprised. From her point of view, he's the nicest man on Luniette."

"What do *you* think of him?"

Anabel shrugged. "I've only known him a couple of hours."

"Quite long enough to have formed an impression."

"Well — he seems nice and friendly enough. But you must know more about Tim than I do."

Robert replied grudgingly, "I believe he's popular."

"I'm sure of it. He strikes me as a man who knows what he wants, and goes after it — nicely."

"Then for Naomi's sake —" began Robert tentatively, so quietly that Anabel could not mistake the meaning he was trying to convey to her, "I am glad."

'It doesn't mean that because Tim is kind to Naomi she can have him for her own for the asking,' Anabel thought. And aloud, she said reflectively, "Naomi has the knack — largely because she is such a child, and one would like to shield the very young from knocks — of making people feel sorry for her."

"I don't understand —"

"No? Then I'm afraid I can't explain."

Robert sighed then, and did not speak again until Tim came out carrying the coffee on a large tray, with Naomi hurrying at his heels like a devoted dog.

"I quite forgot when we wandered down to the beach just now," Tim said to Anabel, "that this is the one night in all the working week, the night of nights to Mabelle, when supper must be gobbled at the risk of acute indigestion, so that Mabelle can wash up and vamoose. It's all my fault, and I will give Mabelle a bigger tip than usual on Saturday, to make amends, and remind myself that such a thing must never happen again. It is Mabelle's night off, and nothing or nobody must stand in the way of her downing dishcloth and apron. While we were gazing soulfully at the moon, Mabelle vanished into thin air. In other words, she's gone home with her boyfriend, Joe."

While Tim was speaking so brightly, Robert had risen and brought forward a garden table with a green wooden top and iron legs, and Tim placed the coffee-tray squarely on it.

"No, don't you help me, Naomi," Tim advised. "I can manage. You sit down and I'll wait on you."

"Where will you sit?" asked Naomi.

"Oh, anywhere. That chair looks comfortable. Bag it before brother Robert seizes it." And Tim began to pour out the coffee.

"I shall sit by Anabel," said Robert loudly.

Naomi added softly, in a voice intended for Tim's ears alone, and with a sweet intimacy not lost upon Anabel, "And I will put my chair beside you, Tim."

"Righto, but you must promise not to jog my arm and upset my coffee as you did last night — or I shall soon be too shabbily clothed to mix in ladies' society."

"Oh, I never mind how you're dressed," giggled Naomi.

"But Anabel does," grinned Tim, and to Anabel, with a direct look from his blue eyes which she found disconcerting, "Don't you?"

Anabel nodded vigorously. "I'm terribly particular."

"How do you like your coffee, Anabel?" inquired Tim. "Black or white — or half-in-half?"

"Black, please, and very sweet."

"Two lumps?"

It was Robert who took Anabel's coffee from Tim's hand and brought it over to her. Then he offered her a cigarette, and struck a match to light it.

"And Naomi likes lots of milk — you see how I remember your tastes?" smiled Tim, looking down at the eager face so close to his arm.

Then Robert placed his case of cigarettes open on the table for anyone to help themselves, and left Tim to attend to Naomi's wants.

Presently they were chatting and smoking, with Robert sitting beside Anabel, and Tim seated opposite, with his legs crossed, and to all appearances at ease, his eyes meeting Anabel's now and again through a veil of smoke.

And was it Anabel's fancy that Tim's eyes were amused and full of a secret understanding. It was as though Tim might be saying with those eloquent eyes of his, "What fun this little party is which you and I are giving, my dear." Or it might be, "Did you ever go to such a queer party as this, and meet two such insanely jealous people? Our only salvation is not to take them seriously."

The amusement in Tim's blue eyes deepened into laughter. For it was not an easy party. The Smiths were not good guests, and if either thought that matters were not progressing as he or she wished, displeasure was shown in glowering expressions or long silences of the brother and sister. Tim had to not talk too much to Anabel, but give nearly all his attention to Naomi, otherwise the girl would sigh heavily and stare sorrowfully at him.

And Anabel had to not joke with Tim, or talk of mutual acquaintances, and show any real friendship for him, for then Robert smoked furiously and fell into a brooding silence.

So the burden of entertaining fell with increasing force upon Anabel and Tim, and neither realized just how hard they worked until it was time for the Smiths to go home.

It is doubtful whether Robert or Naomi would have had the courage to break up the party, because that would mean leaving their rivals together; but suddenly Tim bent forward and peered at his wristwatch and said almost briskly, "Listen! I can hear Mrs. G. saying, 'Time, gentlemen, please!' The bar is closing for the night." He turned to smile at Naomi, who was sitting back in shadow, indulging in one of those wretched silences which she did not seem able to help, and which had marred the evening. "It may not be the witching hour of midnight, when the spooks come out to haunt us, but it is time for us to turn in — if we want any beauty sleep, and I know I need mine." He got to his feet, and slowly Robert copied him.

"I suppose we must go home now, Naomi," said Robert reluctantly, helping his sister to her feet with ungentle pressure on her arm. Then he turned to Anabel, who had risen quickly as though she felt relieved that someone had at last made a move, and held out his hand. "*Au 'voir*, Anabel — until tomorrow. You won't forget?"

Anabel shook her head. "I won't. Goodnight, Robert."

All four moved in a body round the corner of the house, and Tim and Anabel stood together watching the Smiths mount their bicycles and depart.

"I wonder that they troubled to use bicycles," said Anabel, when brother and sister were out of sight. "It is impossible to ride them further than the churchyard, when they'll have to dismount and push."

"That's their funeral," shrugged Tim.

Anabel agreed, then: "And I'll say goodnight now, too. I'm terribly tired."

"I don't wonder. I had no idea those two could make such heavy weather. Naomi wants spanking; I've never known her to behave like that before."

"You've never given her cause; or have you?" laughed Anabel. She turned away from Tim to enter the hotel, then paused to say, "Don't forget to bring in the coffee-tray."

"By Jove no: I was forgetting the thing. I say —" in a wheedling tone — "must you go in just yet?"

Anabel paused. For her, the night was young, and it was a lovely night. She said, "But my beauty sleep?"

"You, of all people, don't need that. I've been watching you all the evening: you're as lively as a cricket still; as sparkling as the ace of diamonds."

"Really! And I thought you had eyes only for Naomi," Anabel told Tim demurely.

He laughed. "Now don't you start any nonsense by taking a leaf out of Naomi's book — that awful 'if I can't have all I'll have none, but you shan't enjoy your bit' rot. It would sit ill upon you." And in a different, coaxing voice, "Come and sit down for five minutes. Do. I promise I won't keep you any longer."

"All right, if you are sure Mrs. Groom won't lock us out."

"For the next half hour, she'll be busy counting her takings. And I doubt whether the doors in this place are ever locked."

So they sat on the seat outside the dining-room window, which someone, fearful of bad weather, had closed for the night. And Tim said lazily, but with an undercurrent in his voice which belied the lazy quality, "Look, Anabel; the moon has gone behind those ominous blooms of cloud. There is the change I promised you in the weather."

Anabel was resting with her hands folded in her lap, and her feet thrust out before her, with ankles crossed. She had refused the cigarette Tim offered her; and he had snapped his case shut and returned it to his pocket, saying, "Then neither shall I smoke. You don't want me to." But Anabel did not contradict. Her brain really was tired, and she hadn't her accustomed alertness of spirit. Now that the watchful Smiths were not there to hold her attention, she could relax. She was aware now that the bar was quiet, and the hum of men's voices had ceased. It was some time since Anabel had heard the thin, reed-like quality of Olly's mouth-organ. But with the decrease of homely sounds about her, Anabel was conscious of the distant soughing of wind over the downlands, and the insistent thudding explosions of heavy seas against immutable rocks. She was aware, too, that there was a dampness in the atmosphere, a smell of dank seaweed, and furtively Anabel passed her tongue over her lips, tasting the salt in the air. She felt weary, but at peace.

But now Tim was speaking, and as though to call attention to what he was saying, or to emphasize his words, he touched Anabel's hands. Stretching out his hand, Tim put it over hers, which were lying clasped loosely in her lap. "It seems you're meant to stay on Luniette," Tim whispered.

Anabel could feel the pulse of his warm fingers on hers, and a queer longing to let Tim do his will with her shook her soul. But only for a brief moment.

As usual, thoughts of Paul had come to Anabel with the accompanying bitterness which Anabel felt would always be connected with memories of Paul. Anabel decided that if she could not profit from her tragic experience with Paul, and was ready to fall easily into the first man's arms which offered themselves, then she fully deserved all the consequences such an act might bring her.

So after one lightning glance at the bright light behind the heavy clouds — which was the moon playing hide-and-seek — Anabel pushed Tim's hand away brusquely. "Don't ever do that again," she breathed in a cold tone. "I am not Naomi Smith, who is ready to drop into your arms like a ripe cherry; nor am I the sort to bring comfort to relieve your *ennui* on Luniette. I am Anabel — a practical if charming person."

It would be as well, Anabel thought, to let this man see that she had no illusions about herself.

Tim sat up. "As you were!" he apologized. "I won't do it again." And now he brought out the inevitable cigarettes and offered one to Anabel. She took one, and Tim helped himself too, and they both lit up.

'We should have done this five minutes ago,' Anabel thought steadily. And Tim asked curiously, "What was Smith telling you not to forget tomorrow?"

Anabel followed his lead readily. "Nothing much, only — hold everything! — I've been invited to tea at Bella Luce tomorrow."

"And you're going?"

"Of course. Why are you so surprised? Why shouldn't I?"

"No reason whatever, only — well, it may be you're going to have a glimpse of Bluebeard's chamber." And Tim's voice was nettled for some unknown reason.

"That sounds rather sinister. What's wrong with the people at the farm? I can't imagine anything evil hidden in that lovely homestead."

"I believe it is a very nice house, though I haven't been inside myself."

"But how odd! I should have thought Naomi would have invited you there long ago."

"She did — and I refused."

"Oh, wise and cautious man!" exclaimed Anabel. Then, "Why?" Realizing that she might sound presuming on their short acquaintanceship, Anabel apologized. "Sorry, I shouldn't have asked you that." She rose slowly from her seat. It was late, and time she went in.

"Oh, I don't mind *your* knowing, but keep it under your hat. There's nothing to take a fellow like me to Bella Luce. I'm not especially interested in the past, and old houses, or the family —" Tim was explaining elaborately, when Anabel broke in laughingly.

"Not in Naomi?" There was disbelief in her tone.

"Naomi's a kid, and not to be taken seriously." Tim spoke shortly, as though annoyed at the coupling of his name and Naomi's. "And I draw the line at making a public exhibition of myself by robbing the cradle. There is a limit to fun."

So that was the measure of Tim's friendship with Naomi? Anabel felt sorry for the girl, though beneath her pity was a kind of relief which would have been puzzling had there been time to think it out.

"Naomi's not over-young for —" Anabel frowned and stopped, aware that she was perhaps speaking too frankly.

"Go on," said Tim sharply.

"Perhaps I oughtn't to say it, and you're bound to get conceited, but you must know you're a smash hit with Naomi."

"Pooh, that's nothing, and just because there's no one else on Luniette for Naomi to dig her sharp young claws into. At her age, a girl must have someone to practise on." Then Tim began to laugh uproariously. "How serious we've grown about me. Yet I haven't made your mistake, my dear, of running into trouble — and still more trouble. Lord, Anabel, but you're an ace for attracting queer adventures to yourself." And Tim looked triumphant, feeling he had scored off Anabel.

"Oh, I can take care of myself," replied Anabel quickly, resenting Tim's remark.

"I'm sure you can — ordinarily; but Smith's not an ordinary fellow — he's dynamite. And if I had a sister —"

"And have you?"

"No, but *if* I had one —"

"But, Tim, how can you suppose what she or you would do if you've never had a sister?"

"Well —" shortly, annoyed at Anabel's laughing manner and precise words, which seemed to ridicule his interference — "if there were some girl I liked — as I do you — I'd say give

78

Smith a wide berth. He's ruthless when he wants anything. I happen to know."

"And you think he may want to keep me at Bella Luce? Oh, that's too funny!" Anabel went off into peals of light laughter.

Tim watched her soberly. "I hope you'll always be able to laugh at this as you are doing now. Only perhaps in retrospect your friendship with Smith won't seem so funny. You aren't so practical and level-headed as you would have people believe. I should have thought it pretty obvious that Smith is greatly attracted to you. He made no secret of his feelings for you tonight; and I think it an act of kindness on my part to warn you to be careful. But if you don't choose to listen, that is your lookout."

"I see. Thanks."

"Don't thank me. The advice is gratis."

"I'll remember." Anabel was still smiling good-naturedly, as she said, "Well, goodnight, Tim."

Tim rose then and held out his hand, but Anabel chose not to see it, sure now that she must never, if she valued her own peace of mind, be too friendly with this man.

Here lay her danger — not with Robert Smith, but with Tim.

Tim's hand dropped to his side. Once again he was conscious that for some reason or other, Anabel was withdrawn from him. "Goodnight, Anabel, and sleep tight in my room; while if you do happen to be awake, remember that I am, too — and thinking of you."

'Thinking of you'! They were words that tore at Anabel's heartstrings, and her eyes were flooded with sudden tears.

Anabel left Tim with a laugh, but on reaching her room she shut the door quickly, when the shaky laugh became a sob.

Paul had said those words to her — once, and now the memory of them, reawakened by Tim, brought an almost insupportable anguish.

CHAPTER 5

During the night the weather worsened, and sometimes fierce gusts of wind swept around Rat Point, on the southern arm of the sheltered landing bay overlooked by the hotel, and sent spray flying like fierce rain across the pebbly beach, where it fell on the stones like the sound of hail.

Giant waves thundered against the rocks, and broke in foaming wildness on the beach, where it lay like froth until the next wave swept it away and spread a mantle of fresh froth.

The moon was hidden by a grey ceiling of dark cloud with swiftly moving tails and jagged wisps of purple blooms scudding towards the north-east.

The noise of the elements woke Anabel, who got stiffly out of bed in the early dawn to lower her window, for rain of cloudburst proportions was coming into the room, wetting the curtains and splashing on the floorboards beneath the window. Everything was damp, even the bedclothes.

Anabel peered through her window, but could not distinguish the sea through the grey perspective that seemed to fill the square of pale light in her window-frame, though she knew the 'grey perspective' to be the sea.

'They were right,' Anabel thought. 'There'll be no boat calling here today.' And she went back to bed and tried to sleep, even resorting to counting numberless phantom sheep which occupied the footpath on the way up to Bella Luce.

But without success, for Anabel's brain was in obstinate mood, thoughts crowding thick and fast through it until she was wide awake with no prospect of sleep. And each thought seemed to revolve around Tim, which made Anabel angry as well as wakeful.

And as morning approached, the storm appeared to increase in intensity. It rained without ceasing all day.

Mrs. Groom said to Anabel after breakfast, "It's set in for the day, miss. And I've a message for you from the captain, who left an oilskin and sou'wester for you to wear if you've not changed your mind about going up t' Bella Luce farm this afternoon for a cup o' tay. And he said as how I'm to lend you my sea-boots. His would be too large for you and would wear holes in your stockings in no time."

Anabel's chin was raised slightly. She knew that people often discussed Anabel, the daughter of Samuel Robinson, in tones of awe, because there was a certain glamour in being *au fait* with the doings of the only child of a wealthy father. But these people did not realize the position she held in the outside world, and had not that excuse to talk.

Anabel was annoyed to find that Tim had discussed her day's plans with Mrs. Groom, and had no idea that the slightest news on Luniette is interesting. Yet it was proof of Tim's thoughtfulness for her, Anabel's, comfort, that he had left word for his clothes to be worn to keep her dry, and Anabel soon relented.

"I intend to keep my promise to go if Mr. Smith comes down for me," Anabel said primly to Sarah Ann, whose brown eyes searched her guest's face closely, wondering what there was already between the farmer and Anabel.

"Oh, he'll come for you all right," Sarah Ann affirmed now. "Though I must say I've never known Smith look twice at a young lady before, and we've had some good-lookers on Luniette from time to time. We always thought he was a woman-hater — leastways until last night. You could have knocked me down with a pin when Mabel came whispering to me in the bar as Smith was come down to see you. If I had'na been so busy with the boys, and me short-handed because of my son Alf re-joining, I'd have taken a peep or two and seen how the land lay myself, that I would, look you."

"You all seem to take quite a lively interest in my doings, Mrs. Groom," Anabel remarked tartly.

"Why, of course. We like a bit of gossip, and we don't get visitors like you every day. And to think young Smith's gone all sweet on you, quick as a stroke of lightning. Well, I never did. But p'raps he thinks that saving your life gives him an interest in it? That might be it — but it's a proper surprise to me and all."

The sing-song voice ceased as Mrs. Groom drew breath, and Anabel took the opportunity to say, "You'll oblige me, Mrs. Groom, by not talking about my friendship with Mr. Smith. It is quite casual; and you are reading all sorts of silly things into a chance meeting. Indeed, it is quite chance that I am on Luniette at all."

Mrs. Groom nodded, as though to confirm her inward thoughts. "They say that all the big things in life depend on chance. If — if — if — I've so often said these words myself. But, look you, it isn't only me as is at fault. Mr. Tim didn't think my expressed ideas silly. He seemed quite put out at breakfast, when we had our usual morning chat — and a bit off his feed, though *that* might be due to his sleeping in a strange bed last night. Now, speaking for myself —"

"Has Mr. Northorn gone out?" Anabel cut in quickly.

"Oh, this long time since, miss; and he won't be back until five o'clock."

That determined Anabel, who knew it was absurd to resent Tim's thought for her, one he could only transmit to her via

Mrs. Groom. Anabel decided that if Robert did not come for her, she would find her own way up to the farm for tea.

When Robert drove up to the hotel door about three in the afternoon, Anabel, dressed in Tim's oilskin and sou'wester, and Mrs. Groom's rubber sea-boots, was waiting for him in the porch.

Robert made no remark about the vile weather, because from experience he knew exactly what it would be like, and the downpour having started, was likely to continue without a break until the following day.

Though dressed in oilskin and sou'wester, Robert, driving under the hood of the van, was comparatively dry.

His sombre face lit up, and he smiled attractively at Anabel, who waited for him to get out of the van and join her.

The bright flash in Robert's eyes was dulled almost immediately as he saw how Anabel was dressed for the weather, in a man's oilskin which, though large, served its purpose well. It was an easy guess that the clothes belonged to Tim.

"I'm so glad you didn't change your mind, Anabel, though there might have been some excuse for it in this weather," Robert said as he joined the waiting girl.

"Weather wouldn't stop me," said Anabel smilingly, holding out a damp hand which Robert took in both of his, and pressed so hard that Anabel was reminded of Tim's warning.

So the two stood for a long moment, with Anabel's hand between the man's strong fingers. Then gently Robert released her hand, and the slowness and gentleness were like a caress.

Robert said, "But you needn't have borrowed an oilskin."

"I didn't; they were wished on me with an order to wear them."

Robert told her, "I guessed you'd have no protection against the storm, and brought down Naomi's raincoat with me. It's weatherproof and warm," and he turned to the van, reaching under the seat where it was dry, and brought out a bundle of clothing which revealed a long coat, storm-cap and rubber boots.

"How kind of you both to think of me," smiled Anabel; and partly because it was to be expected that Mabel, the reporter, was watching the scene from some point of vantage in the background — and also because Robert had gone to so much trouble to come down to take his guest up to the farm in comfort — Anabel unbuttoned Tim's oilskin and took off his sou'wester.

"I shall wear the things you brought me," Anabel said, much to Robert's delight. "Besides, they fit me so much better, and I'm vain enough to want to look nice even in the wind and the rain."

But Anabel was awkward removing the clumsy oilskin, and Robert exclaimed, "Why, you're stiff. It's that tumble over the cliffs yesterday. You should have gone to bed directly you got back, Anabel."

"Should I?"

"And I blame myself you didn't."

"But I should have missed you last night." Anabel did not realize how provocative she both sounded and looked.

Robert seemed unable to tear his eyes from her face. "Yes, that's true."

"You'd have been disappointed: or wouldn't you?"

Robert was helping Anabel to put on Naomi's raincoat, and was not so absorbed in the process that he did not catch the soft, intimate appeal in Anabel's voice. How could Robert know that Anabel was speaking for the unseen, but listening, Mabel's effect?

Robert came round to face Anabel, and began to fasten the coat at her throat. "You know I would," he whispered, adding, "but I must button this coat well up under your chin. You are a precious person and mustn't get wet, or you'll catch cold and perhaps die."

Anabel laughed. "I'm not so fragile as that."

They went out of the porch, Anabel bending her head to the noisy storm which seemed to ride up with renewed energy on purpose to smite the girl; and Robert helped Anabel into the van, where he covered her knees with a waterproof covering, and tucked the mackintosh around her feet. For once Robert's face was lit up with a carefree smile, and it crossed Anabel's mind how good-looking this farmer was.

Then he got in beside Anabel, dragged the covering over his own knees, and chucked the reins with a "Gee up," so that the old roan mare started spiritedly on her way uphill.

The route lay beyond some wretched-looking cottages with slate roofs, tucked in under the hillside, on the other side of the churchyard, away from the sea. It was little more than a stony cart track, deeply rutted with laden hay-wagons that had passed over it recently, in bad weather, and was partly overgrown with grass.

"After being cooped up all day indoors, you don't know how good it is to be out — even if it is raining," Anabel told Robert, speaking loudly because the wind was blowing strongly and it was difficult to be heard.

He replied, releasing a hand to stretch across her knees to make quite sure the covering was snugly in place, "Are you sure you're dry? There's no sense in getting wet."

"I'm lovely and warm: feel." Anabel brought her hand from a pocket under the rug and touched his fingers, which were cold and wet.

For a long minute Robert remained still, and looked down at the hand which lay on his own like thistledown. It appeared useless to Robert because it was white, yet had his glance been more impersonal he might have seen that Anabel's fingers were long and capable, and there was a firmness of touch which belied any idea of feminine delicacy.

"Yes, you are warm," Robert admitted in such a queer throaty voice that Anabel stared, wondering what was the matter — and then calmly removed her hand.

Behind the churchyard, a place of dark dipping trees and long narrow grass-covered humps, Robert halted the horse, and when Anabel turned her head in mute questioning he said, "This is where I give Sue a breather, before she puts everything she's got into her collar to pull us up the steep part of the hill."

Anabel did not believe that Sue was the cause of Robert's stopping at the bottom of the hill. There was a deeper meaning to this sudden caring for his horse. Then quickly Anabel took herself to task for being so suspicious. It was not Robert's nerve that should be questioned, but her own jumpy nerves. All the same, it seemed to Anabel that for no special reason what had promised to be an ordinary outing had taken on a tense, dramatic quality; she would be blind not to see that Robert's manner was excitable, while his hands trembled and he appeared unsure of himself.

And seeing these tell-tale signs, Anabel wondered whether she had been wise in trusting herself to this strange man, and to his mother and sister, both of whom so obviously hated her.

Anabel did not let Robert see how worried she was, but replied lightly, "Sue seems to know what you have in store for her," and helped herself to a cigarette from the packet Robert held out in silent invitation. "Thanks."

"Once we get going, Sue knows we daren't stop, or the wheels, light as they are, will sink into the mud," Robert replied somewhat grimly, so that Anabel felt instantly ashamed of her suspicions, and cried:

"Oh, you shouldn't have called for me. The invitation was understood to be dependent on the weather."

"Not with me," was the prompt answer. "I meant to come for you anyway."

"Well, I hope Sue won't suffer; she doesn't deserve unkind treatment," commented Anabel.

But Robert remarked hardily, "It didn't occur to me to consult Sue. I'd be sorry, of course, but even if I knew she'd drop dead after making the trip to get you to Bella Luce, I'd still start out."

Anabel glanced sideways at the clear-cut profile, aware now that Tim had been right when he called Robert ruthless. It was a word that arose naturally in Anabel's own mind in connection with the farmer.

It was a business to light their cigarettes, for gusts of wind and rain were caught up now and again under the roof of the van with resounding bangs, when Anabel felt a fine tickling rain on her face, and the coldness of a draught. But Robert unbuttoned his coat and made a screen of one side of it, and Anabel buried her face against Robert's chest, near a warmth which would hold out against any kind of weather, in order to light her cigarette.

When she straightened again there was a deep flush under Robert's swarthy skin which stained his face a brick red, and a pulse beat fast under the skin at his temples.

Laughingly, realising the effect her nearness had had on Robert, Anabel took his cigarette from trembling fingers, stuck it in his mouth, and held the glowing tip of her cigarette carefully to his.

"Got it?"

"Thanks." Robert jerked away his head, and Anabel, leaning against the narrow backboard of the seat, began puffing with evident enjoyment at her own cigarette.

While they sat and smoked, and Sue rested preparatory to her uphill task, Anabel's thoughts raced on ahead to Bella Luce, and she wished it had been possible for her to have made a more impressive appearance to the Smiths at the farm. She remarked, "I wish I had on some decent clothes for my visit."

"You look lovely as you are," Robert replied quickly, not understanding the swift workings of his companion's mind, or her wish to impress his mother.

"It's only a jumper suit, and high time it went to the cleaners," Anabel told him disparagingly. "And to make bad worse, Mabel spilt some coffee over it this morning."

"That girl!" Robert commiserated. "But the dress suits you, Anabel. Somehow I can't visualize you in any other clothes."

"Because you've never seen me in others. And don't you know, Robert, that is about the worst thing you could say to a woman? It means I'm dull — a dowd."

Robert smiled. "You know better than that."

"What is so annoying is that I've got stacks of clothes in my hotel at Bettycombe."

"Well, it wouldn't take long to fetch them across."

Anabel shrugged. "This is the only invitation I'm likely to get on Luniette, unless the parson's wife asks me to tea; and it's not worthwhile bringing more clothes here for that. But I do wish I'd had a decent dress to wear this afternoon. Mrs. Smith will see me at my worst — and I can look so nice."

"You're lovely, Anabel, so why worry about gilding the lily? Mother will think your dress marvellous. Even I can see there's a something —"

That was the truth, and Anabel gave Robert full marks for recognizing style and taste, for the dress was an artist's creation.

And oddly, Mrs. Smith had already passed judgment to Naomi on Anabel's expensive dress.

"But the wearer is useless, eh?" laughed Anabel, who had already guessed that Mrs. Smith divided everything in life into two categories — useful or decorative — of use or useless. And Robert laughed at this understanding of the workings of his mother's mind.

Then Robert said more seriously, "But you won't be leaving Luniette just yet, Anabel." A brilliant thought came to him as he saw Anabel's face lengthen. "Tell you what: if you want some clothes, I'll get them for you."

"Will you? When?"

"Tomorrow, if I can persuade someone to let me have a boat."

"A little boat out in those raging seas!" And Anabel looked towards what she could see of the raging seas, and shuddered. "You're crazy to suggest such a thing."

"Not so crazy," Robert said calmly, "when it is considered I know how to handle a cutter as well, perhaps better, than some of these men on Luniette."

"I shouldn't dream of allowing you to risk your life for the sake of a few clothes."

"There's no risk, and it would make you happy to have them."

"Of course it would, but not at any price. I'm not that callous."

"Then I shall go," he decided.

"You mustn't, Robert. There's your work."

"Joe must carry on; and though Naomi's bone lazy, she's no fool."

"Please forget what I said," Anabel coaxed. "I mean it, Robert. What would your mother say if anything should happen to you through me?"

Robert laughed. The sound echoed eerily in the wind. "Mother would probably kill you," he remarked.

Anabel did not take the words seriously. Who would? "There, what did I tell you?" she said angrily.

Then, reluctantly, Robert threw away his half-smoked cigarette, and gathered up the reins which he had looped on a hook somewhere above his head.

"I suppose we'd better move on," he remarked with a deep sigh, much to Anabel's relief, "or Mother will think we're never coming."

Presently they proceeded uphill at a snail's pace with the mare's head well down, and straining at her traces.

"I think we ought to get down and walk," Anabel said more than once, her admiration for the old mare rising.

"Don't be silly, you'd never make it against this wind," was the reply.

It was noticeable that now both had raised their voices, for the sounds of the elements had increased. The country grew barren and wilder, visibility was poor, even nearby objects being hidden in a mist of rain.

"You see what I mean?" shouted Robert.

"I can't see far ahead," Anabel screamed, catching one word and putting her own context to it.

At the top of the hill the ground was green and spongy, and seemed to fall away towards the west, leaving them exposed to the full force of the gale, and, to make matters worse, the cart turned into the wind which was coming straight in from the Atlantic.

Anabel wondered how long it would be before the springs were torn away from the wheels.

Talking was, of course, impossible.

Ahead of them was the field Anabel had crossed yesterday. It seemed a long while ago, and the scene was unrecognizable in the storm — grey, barren and lonely, with death hidden in these treacherous crevasses.

'If I hadn't chanced to tumble on a ledge, I shouldn't be here today. And if Robert had not been on the spot to help me, I might not be having tea at Bella Luce this afternoon. I shouldn't have known Robert. Perhaps Tim would have saved me. And if —'

Just thinking of Tim gave Anabel comfort. She caught herself up on those little, but important, 'ifs' — seeds of fate! There were no other words for them. While Anabel was thinking thus, her hands clapped to the flaps of the storm cap which she had tied down over her ears to shut out the sound of the wind, the roan mare swung round into the blessed shelter of the valley. It was not quiet here, but compared with the fury in the teeth of the gale it was like heaven to Anabel, who was conscious of feeling storm-tossed. And there, like a dark gem, beyond the haystacks grouped like small houses on either side of the glen, was Bella Luce.

Robert turned to look at Anabel, who had exclaimed with joy.

Loosening one hand from the reins, Robert rested it gently on Anabel's knee and smiled down into her eyes, and the mare, knowing there was a warm stable to greet her, broke into a trot.

CHAPTER 6

Robert drove the van round to the back of the low white house, saying, "The front door is kept barred on a day like this. Indeed, it is only open on the warmest days, which are few on Luniette, for there is always a breeze on an island."

Anabel laughed and agreed slangily, "You're telling me. I am feeling quite bruised with fighting the wind." But the tussle, far from getting her down, had exhilarated Anabel, for her cheeks were pink and she was in great spirits.

A fierce-looking sheepdog, chained in the cobblestoned yard, greeted them vociferously, and Robert shouted angrily so that the dog crept, with tail between its legs, into the dark kennel. But to Anabel, in a different voice, Robert said, "I'm sorry to say we're here. I could wish the journey were ten times longer."

He pulled at the reins, stopping the van before the white back door — or what was once a white painted door, for the wood showed through the paint, which had worn thin with time and weather, and was dirty, while the lower panels of the door were scratched by dog's paws.

Anabel was looking about her with ready interest, only giving half of her attention to Robert, and she spoke absent-mindedly. "Sorry! But why?"

"Because I've had you to myself for only half an hour; and now I've got to share you." And Robert leaned over Anabel, and the highlight in his eyes sent a queer thrill through her — exciting and yet repulsive.

Anabel drew back. "That's being selfish, especially when you know —"

"That the drive was just a means to an end? Go on, say it, I don't mind — or rather, I do mind, but I can't do anything about it because you don't care."

"Well, I made no secret that I wanted to see inside your house."

"And you think that is why my mother asked you — just to see an old farm?"

Anabel was startled. "Didn't she?"

Robert did not reply. He pulled himself up, tossed the reins impatiently forward over Sue's broad back, leapt out of the van, and ran round to the other side, where he helped Anabel, who was encumbered with heavy clothing, to alight.

Releasing herself swiftly from Robert's clinging arms, Anabel went forward to the shelter of a narrow porch built over the door, and embowered with a profusion of honeysuckle and fuchsia, hanging dripping and dejected in the rain.

In spite of the sweet-smelling flowers, Anabel, who had pictured a lovely, well-kept, period house, found that seen at close quarters some of the glamour of yesterday had gone. Here was age and decay — careless treatment of old-time things, bordering on vandalism.

"You go ahead, Anabel," said Robert, as she paused undeterminedly, not knowing whether to wait for Robert or to knock at the door. "Walk right in. I must take Sue to her stable. I won't be long."

Robert drove off, and Anabel faced the closed door with a queer mixture of expectancy and reluctance in her heart. The forbidding picture of Mrs. Smith, and a remembrance of Naomi's open dislike, flashed across Anabel's mind. She wondered why the mother, who had only yesterday been at such pains to warn a stranger to keep off the farm lands, should change her mind in a matter of hours, and invite that stranger to her house. Anabel was sure now that the invitation had not been given to please her.

It didn't make sense, for Mrs. Smith was an opinionated woman; and it was difficult to understand what pressure had been brought to bear on the older woman, and by whom. And here, Anabel felt she saw a glimmer of light, for Robert's interest in herself was plain, and she would have been blind not to see it. It was easier to understand Naomi's attitude, for obviously the girl looked upon Tim as her own special property, and would resent the appearance of a rival. Naomi might wish to gauge the power of her rival.

Anabel had no illusions about Naomi, and began to wish she had not accepted the invitation to the farm. But unfortunately it was not easy to retrace steps in the storm which seemed to continue unabated, though in the shelter of the farmhouse the wind and rain were not so fierce.

And then, as though to write '*finis*' to the wishes taking form in Anabel's mind, and stop any idea of retreating, there was a sound of footsteps on flagstones, and the door was opened suddenly by Naomi. The girl seemed in a better temper than yesterday, and to go out of her way to make a pleasant impression, for she smiled youthfully in welcome, as though her past sulkiness were forgotten.

Anabel held out her hand, saying, "Oh, hallo, Naomi," and wished she felt as cheerful as she sounded.

It amused Anabel to realize that while she herself was at a disadvantage in disfiguring top clothes, looking her worst after being buffeted by the storm, Naomi had evidently spent time and care on her toilette. The girl looked exotic in red trousers and an emerald-green blouse, the brilliant colours showing up the mass of thick dark curls and dark eyes — and what great eyes they were, velvet, luminous and unfathomable!

"Hallo!" said Naomi. "So you *did* come!" And her hand met Anabel's across the threshold in a limp clasp — an action which spoke louder than any words.

Then the two girls had drawn apart, and the door was closed. Standing in the narrow, bare stone-paved passage, Anabel began to undo the borrowed coat. "Did you think I wouldn't?" There was a dank smell in the air, of dampness and rot, and Anabel thought what a 'hotbed' for rheumatism the house must be in winter time.

"We weren't sure until we heard Con barking," said Naomi.

"Why ever not?"

"Because you come from a town, and you might be frightened of our weather."

"You surely don't expect anyone to look upon this storm with affection?" Anabel smiled as, with Naomi's help, she freed herself from the coat, then pulled off the cap. "Where shall I put these?"

Naomi took the cap and coat. "It is pretty bad today… I'll dry these things in the kitchen ready for you to wear back."

Anabel would have liked to say, "Must I wear these ugly things?" but it wasn't the ugliness which troubled her so much but that the things belonged to Naomi. But that would seem ungracious, so Anabel patted her hair into order and said, "Thanks. But even if the weather had been worse, I think I should have tried to come here. You see, I *said* I would." Those who knew Samuel Robinson would have said how like Anabel was to her father at that moment.

Anabel turned slightly away and took out her compact, and began to repair the damage to her make-up caused by the wind and the rain. The act of doing this made her feel better able to cope with this situation, which was unlike any position she had ever been in, and which was fashioning itself so strangely. Anabel replaced the compact in her bag.

Mrs. Smith came into the hall. The older woman was dressed in the same ankle-length black dress that she had worn yesterday, but somehow the perspective indoors was different, for Anabel thought with fresh dismay that she had never met anyone taller, gaunter and grimmer than this woman, whose straight up and down figure so closely resembled a pole.

"How do you do, Miss Robinson? I heard what you said to Naomi just now. Do you always keep your word?" And Mrs. Smith extended her hand formally, and the clasp which followed was neither tight nor loose, but just meaningless.

Simple words, yet uttered in that silent passage, with the periodical gusts of wind thudding against the outside of the house, they seemed fraught with a terrifying meaning.

"I try to," replied Anabel, speaking lightly purposely, realizing with some inward dismay that, though Mrs. Smith had invited her to the house, she was unwelcome. 'There is nothing in common between us,' Anabel thought. 'She's not my sort.' And aloud: "And, of course, Robert was kind enough to fetch me in the van."

"I know. But Robert has wasted half a day's work." Mrs. Smith spoke vexedly.

"Oh, I say, I'm sorry. If only I'd realized —" began Anabel, more mystified than ever as to why she had been asked to Bella Luce. 'It's not because Mrs. Smith loves me,' ran her thoughts.

"It would have made no difference. My son is stubborn. He, too, likes to make up his mind about all sorts of things — often against sounder advice. It is a pity, because in this case we are so short of help on the land nowadays."

Anabel thought she knew then that Robert had prevailed upon his mother to ask the stranger to their house, and a warm feeling for the dour Robert grew like a flower in Anabel's heart, so that she told herself, 'Poor thing, he can't help the blight that has grown on him.'

"I could have refused to come," Anabel said reflectively, "but I should have been disappointed, for as I told you yesterday afternoon, I *wanted* to see the inside of this house. That isn't just curiosity, because we once had a Queen Anne home like this, in Sussex, and I wished to compare the houses." Then placatingly, looking appealingly at Mrs. Smith, who continued to stare at her in a withdrawn manner, "I never thought yesterday that I'd ever come up this hill again, much less see your house." And Anabel laughed, trying hard to break through the frozen crust which was like a barrier between them, and which Mrs. Smith appeared to delight in keeping there.

"Neither did I," was the frank reply, "but we decided over supper last night —"

"Oh!" escaped from Anabel's lips as the older woman stopped suddenly as though she had said too much. So the family could talk!

Mrs. Smith's eyes lost their trance-like look, and she looked sharply at the girl, and gave a hoarse chuckle followed by a grunt.

But Anabel sensed the keen scrutiny, and turned her eyes away from the hard, desiccated face, and purposely looked blank, deciding to give nothing away either.

Then Mrs. Smith began to talk loudly, and when she paused to gather breath to continue, Anabel said to Naomi, who had taken the wet clothes to the kitchen to be dried, and had now returned, "It was good of you to lend me your clothes." But that was a polite expression — merely for something to say to break across Mrs. Smith's talk, and to gain relief.

"Thank Robert for that," Naomi replied indifferently. "It was his suggestion."

"And I'm afraid I may have to borrow them again to go back to the hotel."

"Of course, because it'll still be raining, and you mustn't get wet," said Naomi. "That is understood."

Anabel glanced quickly at Naomi, suspecting irony, and was surprised when the latter suddenly said, "And I'll fetch them in the morning."

"Please don't bother, I'll send them up," returned Anabel, fearful of bringing down Mrs. Smith's displeasure on Naomi for neglecting work. Apparently anyone who stopped work on the farm must be viewed with bitterness.

But Mrs. Smith interrupted, "Naomi will go down for the clothes." It was like someone propounding an unalterable law.

"But —" began Anabel in some astonishment, her eyes going from mother to daughter, when Mrs. Smith intervened again.

"What is your reason for not wanting Naomi to go to your hotel, Miss Robinson?"

Anabel's eyes widened. She was conscious of hard tones, and bitter, inimical expressions, and wondered, 'What on earth have I done to them that they should hate me like this?' Anabel said, "There's no special reason, only I thought it would be more courteous if I returned Naomi's clothes."

"But why be courteous to Naomi? I know she's only a child, but —"

Anabel felt confused, not knowing what to think, or how to treat this queer woman. "I don't think you understand, Mrs. Smith. I was merely trying to save Naomi extra trouble. Of course, if Naomi wants to come down..." There was a shade of asperity in Anabel's voice.

Then Robert came in and inquired, "Why are you all standing here?" And to his mother, "We are using the best parlour?"

Apparently it was an unfortunate question, or Mrs. Smith was in a difficult mood, and ready to put a wrong interpretation on anything anyone ventured to say, for now she nodded grimly and replied emphatically, "The best of everything — china, silver and food. We must let Miss Robinson see that we are not entirely uncivilized."

Anabel longed to plead, 'Don't put yourselves out for me. If it is your usual custom to eat in the kitchen, please let me join you there for tea now.' But one glance at Mrs. Smith's compressed mouth and stern expression decided Anabel not to make any such suggestion. It would be bound to fall flat. But Anabel did say, "I'm sure you're not," reserving the right to tell herself passionately that the Smiths' manners badly needed polish.

"Because," went on the horrid old woman, "if we give you that impression, you might spread it abroad that we live like savages, and that might be too bad," and Mrs. Smith glanced at Naomi, who was staring at her mother with a comic blend of expression in which anxiety lest too much should be said, and approval of what had been already said, struggled for mastery.

Anabel saw the odd look, though she could not put a name to it, and aware that she must defend herself against something hostile, half smiled and protested, "But I don't know anyone to tell — even if I wanted to, which I don't. Everybody on Luniette is a stranger to me."

"There are others at your hotel," said Mrs. Smith grimly.

"Only Tim Northorn — and I don't suppose he would be interested," said Anabel, speaking with deliberate carelessness in a soft, disarming voice.

Mrs. Smith rose at the affront. "And why shouldn't he be interested in Bella Luce when he knows my children so well?"

Then it dawned upon Anabel that this invitation to tea was not so much Robert's wish, but Naomi's. Robert was probably a pawn in this, as yet, obscure game which Mrs. Smith and Naomi were playing with preconceived understanding. It was Naomi who wanted her, Anabel, in their house; Naomi who had made an ally of her mother, so that together they might be strong enough to put a stop to any friendship that might develop between the two guests staying at the hotel.

That was Anabel's latest interpretation of this strange invitation that had been worrying her since she stood on the threshold of the back door of the farm waiting to go in. And it happened to be the right one.

Anabel told herself wryly, 'If they only knew how needless are their fears, but they don't know, and I can't tell them about Paul.'

Meanwhile, Mrs. Smith led the way down one passage and along another, into a small panelled room of beautiful proportions, having a delicately carved wooden mantel with narrow alcoves, shell-shaped at the top, and fitted with shelves on either side of it. The original bluey-green paintwork told of past glory, for the room was now shabby and in urgent need of redecoration, though Anabel felt that had this been done, plaster and paper would have been used to cover the lovely panelling. The furniture was poor and of mixed woods; the chair-covers, curtains and carpet were faded and threadbare.

But the silver on the tea-table was old and beautiful, and the flowered china tea-service had the line and colouring of old Rockingham with panels of flowers, and it was all Anabel could do not to exclaim with delight at the tea-table which would have graced any great house.

Mrs. Smith drew a chair up to the tea-table, and the others sat in chairs at a little distance from it. Naomi lounged at ease, a picturesque modern figure somewhat out of place in that old room; but Robert was erect and pale, making rather a formidable and forbidding figure in that feminine-looking room. There was something of the past in that sitting-room which was not visible to the eye — the spirits of those who had gone before and left their mark. For there seemed to linger in the atmosphere, like a fine essence, that which was not understood by the Smiths. It was alien to their hard, dour natures, and unconsciously they passed it by.

Each time Anabel lifted her eyes she seemed to feel Robert's burning gaze fixed on her, and the prolonged stare gave her a feeling of acute discomfort.

Hastily looking past him, Anabel fixed her eyes, through the window, on the western seas — a grey-green vista blurred with runnels of rain on the window-panes. But there was no vision in Anabel's eyes, for she was thinking hard and fast about this queer family.

'What on earth made me come?' Anabel asked herself from time to time. 'Such small fish! Why do I bother with them?' And she dug her teeth almost viciously into a 'split' filled with jam and cream, which was only one of the delectable homemade goodies on the table.

It took Anabel some moments to realize that it was the Smiths who had gone out of their way to bother with her, and she tried to get to the bottom of their intrigue, all the while giving an impression of intelligent interest in Mrs. Smith's talk.

And when, at length, she found Robert's unblinking gaze confusing, Anabel concentrated on talking to Mrs. Smith, who was neither young nor beautiful, and had never been either, though she had a powerful and compelling personality which had a mesmeric effect on Anabel.

Then Anabel observed that Mrs. Smith's eyes were often on Naomi, who was obviously the child of her old age and the apple of her eye. Naomi must have everything she wished for, and was spoilt and inclined to be tyrannical. Yet, seeing Naomi so young, round and pretty, it was in Anabel's heart to feel sorry for the girl. 'Living here is all very well at the moment, but soon, when Naomi grows up, she'll find out that this island has nothing to offer her — if, indeed, she has not discovered that already, which makes her difficult to manage. After all, what has Luniette to give Naomi? There's bound to be trouble.'

For Naomi was talking, with a mounting excitement that was bound to have reaction in depression, of great cities, showing an unflagging interest in London, its amusements, what other girls wore, and how they did their hair. And such talk was plainly annoying to Mrs. Smith, who strove to stop it, so that Naomi undutifully advised more than once, "Oh, do shut up, Mother! Because you are old and past that sort of thing, and there's no one to care two hoots how you do your hair, is no reason why you must wet-blanket every scrap of joy in my life."

Anabel could have slapped Naomi for this petulance, but she saw then the attraction Tim would have for Naomi. They both liked the same things, and it was feasible to think that when Tim left Luniette he might have an appointment at the Admiralty, and enjoy some of that gay London life both he and Naomi longed for so openly.

Presently Naomi said to Anabel, "You've had such fun; no wonder Tim wants you to stay on Luniette for a while."

"Nonsense, as if Tim needs cheering up. He's such a good mixer, Tim can have quite a cheery life anywhere — even at the North Pole."

"Then he did press you to stay?" Mrs. Smith inquired.

"Yes."

And instantly the atmosphere grew electric and quiet.

Everyone had finished eating and drinking tea, and Robert was on his feet, handing round a box of cigarettes.

Mrs. Smith broke the silence to say, "You seem to be great friends with — er — Tim, considering you met him only yesterday."

Anabel pretended to think this over, then she teased gravely, "We should be because we have so much in common. And, remember, I bagged his room. Tim didn't like that at first, and we quarrelled — but we couldn't keep that up, of course."

Anabel spoke easily, and Robert's face darkened. "It must be difficult to know a fellow starting from scratch, when it's only hearsay where his roots are. There's a certain risk in talking to a stranger in the bar of an hotel, and having to accept him at face value."

"Shut up, Robert!" said Naomi angrily.

Anabel gave Robert a straight look. "I'm willing to bet Tim's all right," she said quietly, conscious of resentment that Robert should criticize her friend.

"Possibly, but there's nothing behind the fellow. He's all talk and smiles, but it doesn't mean a thing."

"What do I care? Why should Tim be serious with me?"

Mrs. Smith said darkly, "So long as you know, Miss Robinson."

And Naomi burst out, "Don't you dare to spoil Tim for others!"

"But, Naomi, why should I? That's a queer thing to say to me."

"Because you're so grand you might easily turn Tim's head."

Anabel laughed. "I don't believe that quality would impress Tim; and I've never been accused of spoiling a man before."

Naomi cried angrily, "You're laughing at me, but remember I am warning you."

For a long moment the smile on Anabel's face looked set, then she relaxed and smiled again — only the smile was more polite than friendly. "I don't know why we are discussing Tim, and with such animosity. I'm sure he'd hate to think we talked about him like this. I rather fancy, too, that Tim can take care of himself and be trusted to make and keep his own friends without our interference." And once more Anabel thought angrily to herself, 'The fools! If I weren't so crushed about Paul and was fancy free, this kind of talk would be a fine incentive for me to throw myself into Tim's arms.'

It was Robert who ended the acrimonious talk, by saying abruptly, "That's enough, Mother. Anabel would like to see the kitchen and dairy before she goes."

"Would you, really?" Mrs. Smith asked dubiously.

"I should love to," Anabel replied promptly.

So they went out to the kitchen, where Anabel was shown a disused bread-oven built into the brickwork at the side of the hearth, and a covered-in well from which drinking-water was still drawn up in a bucket on a chain; and into the dairy, dimly lit through slatted windows, with wide stone slabs on which rested large cream-pans, and where two large butter-churns stood.

Here was an old woman, whom Mrs. Smith called Keziah, with her skirt turned back over a dark petticoat, and pinned behind at her waist. She had just finished scrubbing the stone floor, which was still dark, damp and glistening.

Keziah looked humourlessly but slyly at Anabel, but did not return Anabel's polite "Good afternoon."

"She's deaf and dumb," Robert explained from the doorway.

This knowledge depressed Anabel, and now she no longer wondered that Naomi was anxious to come down to the hotel every night. It wasn't escape to Tim and a promise of life, but escape from this.

'One of these days, she'll run away to the mainland,' Anabel thought, 'and I don't blame her.'

Outside the dairy, and while waiting for Mrs. Smith to give Keziah an order in pantomime, Anabel said to Robert, "Is there a fashion for Biblical names on Luniette?"

"Not that I know of."

"There's a corner in them here, at Bella Luce."

Robert smiled as he realized this for the first time. "So there is, for my mother's name is Mary."

"Oh!"

There was a world of meaning in that sharp exclamation, and after a short pause Robert felt constrained to say, "Anabel?" and it was as though the word stuck in his throat.

"Yes?"

"You mustn't take any notice of what Mother says. I mean, don't let anything she says put you off us — and me in particular, for that would be a disaster. You see, Mother is insular, and because she has lived here so long seems to think that Luniette is her kingdom on earth, and the people on it belong to her." He gave Anabel an odd look. "Besides, Naomi put her up to speak about Northorn, but I expect you could see through that business. It was clumsily done, anyway."

Anabel nodded absently. The two were standing on the cobblestones in a covered way between the dairy and the house. Anabel was gazing at the deserted grey courtyard, and listening to the melancholy drip of rain from a stopped gutter pipe. Though it was summer, everything smelt of dampness — a humidity that was depressing.

Behind, in the dairy, were Mrs. Smith and the shrewish Keziah. It was quiet in there, for the women were communicating with each other in a silent pantomimic manner.

Ahead, through the open door leading into the kitchen with its huge scrubbed deal table, chopping-stool and old-fashioned range, was Naomi teasing a kitten.

Anabel thought now that the girl in her red trousers and green blouse looked tawdry and out of place, and there was a look of cruelty on Naomi's face as she teased the kitten.

Anabel said, "I suppose it was a difficult matter for anyone to discuss with a stranger, as I am; and I am afraid that sincerity made your mother blunt."

"To rudeness," Robert finished as Anabel stopped short. "You're hurt, and that's the last thing I want you to be." He spoke with almost savage passion.

"Only a little. It doesn't matter."

"But it does. I blame Naomi for that. The girl is utterly spoilt."

Anabel thought, 'You both are.'

"Naomi fancies she's fallen for Northorn, and while it lasts she takes herself seriously," continued Robert, speaking in a low tone so that only Anabel could hear what he had to say. "If anybody should come between them just now, I think Naomi would cut loose and leave Luniette; and that, of course, would break Mother's heart. It's fear of losing Naomi that makes Mother so rude to you."

"I know. That is why Mrs. Smith asked me up here today: to find out how dangerous I am," was her quiet reply.

"Well, yes, and it was clever of you to tumble to the truth. But now I've explained it all, you won't feel quite so hurt." And Robert's eyes drew hers like a magnet, so that Anabel saw the anxious look in his.

"Your mother and Naomi would like me to leave Luniette as soon as possible."

"But *I* wouldn't," Robert replied, and his chin was obstinate.

Anabel smiled then. "It is difficult to please both sides. Your mother must be torn to pieces between you and Naomi; and no wonder I am disliked as the cause of it all. Just supposing I told Mrs. Smith that Naomi has nothing to fear from me?"

Robert's face brightened, then he said, "I'm not so sure about that."

"But would Mrs. Smith like me any better?" Anabel persisted.

"I don't know —" dubiously — "but would you care?"

Anabel was forced to admit, "Not much. But it isn't pleasant to be driven away from Luniette."

"Don't go," pleaded Robert.

When it was time for Anabel to leave, and Robert had gone round to the stables to bring Sue to the door again, Mrs. Smith followed Anabel and Naomi into the stone-paved passage.

The older woman went to the narrow window by the side of the door and looked up at the unrelenting grey sky which was still heavy and murky with rain. "I really think it is trying to clear a little, Miss Robinson; you'll be able to go back to Bettycombe tomorrow after all." Mrs. Smith's tone said, 'How pleased you will be at that: or won't you?'

Anabel faced her squarely, well aware that this was the crux of their meeting — that it was unpleasant, but must be got through. "But I'm not going," she said clearly. She heard Naomi gasp.

"Not going!" echoed Mrs. Smith.

"No, I've made up my mind to stay and rest awhile. Mrs. Groom has made me very comfortable at her hotel, and I mean to spend the remainder of my holiday on the island."

Anabel spoke calmly, then she turned quiet eyes on Naomi, who was flushed with anger, and snorted, "Holiday! Why, life is one long holiday to girls like you."

"Perhaps I should have said 'rest' instead," Anabel said gently.

"You are making a big mistake," Mrs. Smith told Anabel.

"Perhaps, but I think not. Even if I don't get the peace and quiet that could be obtained here, I shall, at least, have a change of life which I feel I need." Anabel could not be blind to the fact that Mrs. Smith and Naomi had exchanged dismayed glances.

"But what about your clothes —" began Mrs. Smith, knowing that Anabel could not linger long on Luniette with only one suit of clothing.

And now Anabel hesitated. Should she tell Mrs. Smith that Robert had volunteered to go to Bettycombe for her suitcases? Such news would be bound to stir up further animosity. Yet there could be no secret comings and goings on Luniette, where everyone knew all about his neighbour, and took pride in passing on fresh news. Sooner, rather than later, Mrs. Smith must know if Robert went to Bettycombe.

Anabel said boldly, "That's all settled. Robert has offered to fetch them across for me — if he can borrow a boat."

"Robert has said he would go to Bettycombe for you?" Mrs. Smith cried incredulously. "But that's impossible."

"Why?"

"Robert is not a lady's man, and it wouldn't occur to him to suggest getting your clothes."

"Yet Robert told me he would, and I think he meant it."

The two women eyed each other, as though measuring strength, and capacity for truth, and the extent of Anabel's power over Robert.

Then Mrs. Smith cried out bitterly, "Oh, Robert meant it all right." And suddenly, vindictively, she demanded, "What kind of a girl are you, to come out of the blue so unexpectedly, and cast such a spell over my son that he neglects his daily work to fetch and carry for you? This is outrageous. We are a simple people and resent outsiders interfering in our business. Why don't you go and leave us in peace? We were happy enough until *you* came. Do you realize, Anabel Robinson, that had you been born in the Middle Ages, you might have been burnt as a witch at the stake?"

Anabel listened in silence, then she said with disarming gentleness, "I don't feel like a witch, Mrs. Smith. Honestly, I tried to dissuade Robert."

There was a long silence, during which the older woman's thin lips curled disdainfully, while her mournful brown eyes took fresh stock of this girl. "Tosh!" Mrs. Smith spat out the word, then she opened the door, and as one mind, the three women stood hopefully on the threshold, looking out at the wind and rain which to Anabel seemed as bad as ever, and waiting for Robert to come from the stables.

Anabel was saved answering Mrs. Smith's impatient exclamation, for the clatter of Sue's hooves was heard on the wet cobblestones; and presently, with a dashing show of temperament reprehensible in such an aged mare, Sue was drawn up almost on her haunches outside the house.

"Sorry I kept you waiting," Robert apologized to Anabel, with what his mother thought unnecessary humility, "but I had a job getting Sue into the shafts. She may be old in years, but when the fit seizes Sue she can be as skittish as a flapper." And Robert bent forward beneath the hood of the van the better to see Anabel. "Either she went ca' canny, and I thought she was a funeral horse, or she bucked like a bronco at a rodeo."

Anabel shouted back, "Perhaps she belonged to a cowboy in a previous life."

"Shouldn't be surprised. Anyhow, I had to take the whip to her," was the reply.

As Sue was sweating a little and frothing at the mouth, Anabel thought that the punishment might have been severe, but she made no comment.

"Are you ready? Shall we go?" Robert asked Anabel, and drew aside the protecting mackintosh from the seat beside him.

Anabel's spirits rose now that she knew the time for departure had come. She turned smilingly to Mrs. Smith, held out her hand, and murmured thanks for the lovely tea. Then Anabel did the same to Naomi, whose youth made her look defenceless, and the latter said defiantly, "Don't forget, I shall be calling for the mac and cap."

"I won't forget," cried Anabel over her shoulder, splashing into a puddle outside the door in her haste to leave the depressing influences of Bella Luce. She ran so close to Sue's head that the mare tossed her big head angrily out of the way and backed nervously, so that Robert, who was leaning out of the van, with both hands outstretched to help Anabel up, shouted furiously.

In a few moments Anabel's hands were in Robert's and he was ordering gently, "One foot on the hub of the wheel, and don't miss the step or you'll hurt your shin. Carefully now,

Anabel." He drew Anabel in beside him, and proceeded to tuck in the mackintosh securely, with such care that Mrs. Smith, watching, called impatiently from the door:

"Hurry up, Robert. You can't expect Sue to stand still all night."

"Do her good!" Robert waited to call back. "If Sue plays me up, there'll be no bran mash for her when we return."

Anabel nodded and smiled to mother and daughter, looking on from the comparative shelter of the doorstep.

Then the van drove slowly away from the shelter of the house into rain which seemed to fall obliquely, like delicate steel rods driving into the sodden ground.

Again, as when they had come over this ground a couple of hours ago, Anabel and Robert appeared to drive into the worst of the storm — or it worsened at their approach. Now they could hear the rushing wind and the thunder of surf against rocks below the steep cliffs to the west, while gusts swept along the sheltered valley and were imprisoned under the hood of the van, so that Anabel bent her head lest the roof of the van should suddenly be ripped off.

Bad as the storm was in the valley, it was infinitely worse when they came to an open track and had to run the gauntlet of the full Atlantic gale for a short time. Then the van rocked so badly on its loose springs, Anabel involuntarily brought out her hands from underneath the mackintosh apron and clung to Robert's arm for safety, a proceeding that was greatly to his liking. And if Anabel were not so afraid of being capsized, she would certainly have felt squeamish.

But all emotion dried up miraculously when she heard Robert laugh — a queer, triumphant sound which rose discordantly above the shrieking storm. It seemed so much a part of Bella Luce, with its dry rot and smell of decay and melancholy atmosphere, that Anabel loosened her hold sharply, pushing her hands once more under the protecting apron.

The satanic sound stopped suddenly.

By that time Sue had dragged them to shelter, and the rocking ceased. They crossed a muddy patch where Sue slithered — and then came the stony ground of the lane which descended steeply to the hotel.

It was like the end of a nightmare, and Anabel took a deep breath of thankfulness that the worst perils were over.

Robert spoke then. "Why did you do that?"

"What?" Anabel was looking at the deep curve of the bay below the hotel, and at white seagulls against grey skies. A thrill of joy went through her, for here was something she recognized. It was like meeting an old friend. And down there, below the grey-green foliage of the wood, was the hotel — her home.

"Take your hand away from my arm?"

"Oh! Well, there was no necessity to leave it hanging on your arm."

"Were you frightened?"

Anabel admitted reluctantly, "I suppose so."

"I am frightened, too."

But Anabel would not have that. "You are too absurd!" she cried.

"Oh, not of the storm — I've been in far worse storms than this — but of you." And after a pause, "I sometimes wish I could get drunk, Anabel, and this is one of them. A little Dutch courage is a useful thing for a timid man."

Anabel grinned. She knew quite well what Robert meant, but knew he must not be taken seriously. "I don't. It would be hateful, and I'm sure Sue would bolt and tip us out." Anabel sounded frivolous, but Robert chose to ignore this.

"Don't you want to know why?" Robert asked roughly, to hide the deeper, warmer feeling that surged through his heart for this girl, and tried to find some tangible expression which might bring some satisfaction to himself. He was almost ashamed to confess that romance had come into his life for the first time. Anabel, he felt sure, would have no use for amateurs.

Anabel guessed how Robert was feeling, and such a sense of revulsion arose in her that she felt sick. At all costs Robert must be stopped making confession. Soon after leaving the hotel with him to visit Bella Luce, Anabel had known how it was with Robert and wished she had not gone with him. Now it was the one thing she dreaded, to have a heart-to-heart talk with Robert, who seemed so undisciplined, and could certainly be relied upon to behave violently.

'Why does the Smith family behave in this plus way?' she thought angrily. 'Why can't they take things quietly and easily, like other people have to?' She said, "I'm not interested."

There was that in Anabel's tone, a stern coldness, an aloofness as of withdrawing from him, which stopped further revelations from Robert. Though he longed to tell this lovely queenly girl what was blossoming in his heart, he dared not risk alienating her by declaring his emotions so soon, for however long Robert felt he had known her — forever and ever — actually he had met Anabel but twenty-four hours ago. Common sense, that practical streak in Robert's character, inherited from his mother, warned him that a girl like Anabel must neither be rushed nor would be likely to take seriously a declaration after such a short friendship.

Robert sighed.

Sue was picking her way carefully downhill, almost sitting on her haunches, when she came to a particularly steep bit, and Robert held the reins firmly with both hands.

He felt tied in more senses than one; and obviously this was not the moment to talk about love. If he tried to do so, and Sue slipped and broke a shaft, his mother's recriminations for his carelessness would spoil the glamour of his romance. Robert knew from experience that his mother had a habit of dissecting and devastating any gay display of emotion.

So Robert sulked, much as Naomi had done last night, when Anabel had seemed to claim more than a fair share of Tim's attention. Robert's lower lip was thrust out like a teapot spout, and his eyes, staring at some spot between Sue's ears, were dark and brooding.

The van skirted the churchyard wall, past the dripping yews and the lichened gravestones; and a dog sprang across the track, and paused to bark at them, making more noise when Robert lashed at it with the whip.

Then Anabel caught Robert's deadly expression and began to laugh again, though in lighter vein because now they were nearer people. "Why do you spoil life by taking everything so seriously?" she asked.

Robert stared at her morosely. "Aren't you ever serious?"

"Oh lord, yes; but not now. If you want me to be happy —"

"Are you happy, Anabel?"

There was something so wistful in the tone that Anabel composed her face and said more gravely, "Terribly. Why shouldn't I be?"

"And have I something to do with it?"

Anabel longed to shout, "Nothing!" Instead she said lightly, "Oh, that would be telling."

Anabel had not the courage to tell Robert that he had nothing to do with her mood. What affected her was the curve of the beach, the glimpse of an hotel chimney seen through the trees, and the bark of a dog, all of which had reminded her that she was home. She felt like a prodigal who has journeyed in a far country and was now home again.

What would Robert think if she told him, 'This afternoon has been like a long nightmare; I'm glad it is over'?

The gloom of early evening spread like a grey shroud about them, but down here the rain seemed finer, lighter; warmer and mistier, and Anabel's face was wet with the sharp spray blown under the hood from trees by the wind. There was a sense of peace and happiness in her heart which the weather could not affect. Anabel thought of Tim. He would be back at the hotel, and most probably he would be in the bar.

And even as she thought this, Sue came to a standstill before the open door of the hotel. Anabel was home — with a sheet of muddy water between her and the hotel — and Tim running out joyfully to greet her.

CHAPTER 7

"Thank goodness you've come, Anabel!" Tim cried, running out into the rain, leaping across the pool of murky water, and coming round to Anabel's side of the van. "I was beginning to think they had kidnapped you up at Bella Luce, and that I should have to find my way up there in the dark to rescue you from Bluebeard's chamber." And as though he saw Robert sitting glowering beyond her as a real person for the first time, instead of just the driver of the van, Tim said cheerily, "Hallo, Smith, glad you brought Anabel back safely. As I was just saying —"

"I heard you," was the uncompromising reply as Robert prepared to get out of the van.

But seeing this, Tim moved too — and his movements were rapid, because he was standing out in the pouring rain, with wet trickles running down his neck; and he was untrammelled by heavy top coverings.

Quick as thought, Tim tore aside the mackintosh covering Anabel, and slipping his arms about her as though she were a package just arrived by post, he lifted her out of the van, and carried her, a protesting figure, into the hotel.

As Tim did this, he paused long enough to call out to Robert, whose slow movements had given his rival a long lead, "Don't get down. Stay where you are. I'll look after Anabel."

Robert took no notice of the suggestion.

"Oh, Tim!" Anabel protested laughingly, relaxing now that she was back and well away from the heavy, stultifying influence of Bella Luce.

"Don't you like me to carry you?" He grinned.

"I'm too heavy."

"You know you're not. And you can't tell me I'm out of breath. But say the word and I'll dump you in the pool where you'll be sorry."

"If you do —" and Anabel thought Tim quite capable of doing such a thing — "I'll hold on to you so tightly, you'll be dragged down too."

But the short journey was not without slight mishap to Tim, for with the added weight of Anabel he could not judge his balance nicely, and did not quite clear the pool, and stepped into the water.

"Now you're wet," said Anabel, instinctively turning her face towards Tim's shoulder, away from the water which came up like a spout.

But Tim only laughed gaily as he set her down in the porch. "As if I care." Then he looked at Anabel in surprise and began to unfasten the coat she was wearing. "Whose clothes are these?"

"Naomi's; they're quite snug."

"But I left word this morning you were to wear my oilskin and sou'wester. Didn't Mrs. G. pass on my message?"

"Yes, but Robert brought these down for me."

Tim helped to take off the coat, and Anabel pulled off Naomi's storm-cap. "Oh, he did! Then Master Robert can take them back. It'll save you the trouble of returning them." And swiftly Tim rolled up the hat with the coat, and turned to toss the bundle to Robert. "Hey, you! Take these back with you, and many thanks to your sister for the loan."

Robert, scowling furiously, was slow to hold out his hand. Either Tim misfired, or Robert was a shade too late to catch, but his fingers clutched only a sleeve of the coat, which fell apart, and the cap dropped into the pool.

Of course Tim may have thrown it at that moment when Anabel remembered Naomi was to fetch the clothes herself, to make an excuse for visiting the hotel, and put a staying hand on Tim's forearm.

"Robert mustn't take those things," Anabel said.

"He's got them." Tim dusted his hands as though he had rid himself of something unsavoury. Actually the coat was damp and his hands were sticky. As the full import of her words dawned upon him, he glanced keenly at Anabel.

"Get them back."

"D'you mean I'm to go out again in the rain and bring them in? Not on your life. It would be a fool's errand and give Smith the laugh over me."

"What do you care if he does?"

Tim half smiled. "That's the funny part of it. I do care. Odd, am I not? But it might be worth playing the fool to see that fellow's face dissolve in a grin."

"Be serious, Tim. I want those things."

"If you tell me why they are such beautiful and prized keepsakes," said Tim ironically. "Such dull gear, Anabel. It surprises me you want to see them again."

"I promised Naomi I'd look after them until she fetched them."

Tim studied Anabel's face. "Nobody would steal them," he said gravely. "I don't know what it's all about, but it sounds silly. Anyway, you've got me beaten." And Anabel could not be sure whether Tim's solemnity was a mockery or not. "In that case, I'd better rescue the cap, which I see Smith is fishing out of the mud with his whip. What a slack way of doing things!" And Tim strode straight into the pool and picked up Naomi's cap. "Better give me the coat too, Smith," he said, stretching out his hand to Robert, who was stowing away the newly folded coat under his seat. "Anabel wants all this gear just for the pleasure of giving your sister the trouble of fetching it. I must say, the ways of women are unfathomable."

Robert said sourly, and without looking at Tim, "*I'll* give it to Anabel."

"I shouldn't bother to come in. I'll do it for you," replied Tim amiably.

Robert turned his head then, and Tim, catching the look in his eyes, kept back a whistle with difficulty. "I said I was coming in."

"Okay — just as you please." Tim shrugged, wondering what all this ill-humour was about, and whether Robert and Anabel had quarrelled and what about.

"I want a drink — a long, strong one."

"Oh, of course. I should have thought of that. Rotten night, isn't it? Come in and join me in a quick one before you toil up that hill again." And Tim stood back to give Robert room to get down.

But neither man looked pleased at the prospect of the other's company. Tim was conscious of his wet legs, and the drips of rain that ran beneath his collar and made him feel as though he had a lukewarm poultice round his neck.

"I'll join you presently with Anabel," said Robert slowly, in a loud voice, as he pitched up the reins in the roof and got out of the van. As he wore rubber boots, the pool had no fears for him.

Anabel, waiting uncomfortably on the threshold of the hotel, overheard Robert's remark and answered quickly, "Count me out. I'm going upstairs for a bath before supper."

Both men looked crestfallen. With Anabel there the situation was drear enough, but without Anabel it would be hateful.

"You're not wet?" Robert asked anxiously, coming close up to her. "I tried to keep you dry."

"And you succeeded jolly well," Anabel answered warmly. "I don't know what I should have done without your help, because even if I'd managed to reach Bella Luce, the thought of making the return journey alone would have been a nightmare. As it was, the drive downhill was a pleasure — or it would have been if the weather were kinder."

Robert's face glowed and his saturnine expression lifted momentarily, and Tim, watching him, thought, 'It's the devil himself laughing. Anabel had better beware of this man.'

"Very prettily said, Anabel," applauded Tim.

"I think Anabel meant it." Robert spoke quietly.

Anabel gave Robert her hand and looked into his eyes, her expression candid and kindly. "Of course. Thank you for everything this afternoon." Anabel meant, 'Thank you for timely interruptions, for being so frank with me I knew where I stood with your mother and Naomi.' She turned to Tim, who was looking at her with understanding and a mocking light in his eyes. "I had the most marvellous tea up at Bella Luce."

"Did you? I haven't had that pleasure, but you must tell me all about your visit at supper." Tim pretended to be surprised when Anabel's face darkened, for both knew that in coupling her name with his Tim was annoying Robert. "Here," went on Tim, as Anabel withdrew her hand from Robert's clasp and turned to leave the two men, "take this stuff," and he pushed Naomi's coat into her arms. The dripping cap Tim hung on a nail outside the door. "Mabelle can wring that out later."

Robert looked on morosely. "Shall I see you tomorrow, Anabel?" he asked.

Anabel was already mounting the stairs. Now she paused to say smilingly and encouragingly over her shoulder, "Only if it's fine. My clothes won't stand too many damp days. I believe they've shrunk already."

"Don't you worry about your clothes; you shall have them soon," Robert told her so emphatically that Anabel laughed outright.

"What a man you are for defying people and the elements!"

And Tim called out with that lazy indifference in his tone which angered Robert so much that he wanted to knock him down, "Smith may get himself disliked for defying people, but he can be drowned if he defies the elements — and both begin with d."

Robert made no answer, but in the last glimpse Anabel had of his face she saw how dour and dogged he was — and they also began with d.

Later, when Anabel and Tim sat at supper in the lamplit room, the latter had a grievance.

"You let me in for a bad half-hour in the bar with Smith. What on earth made you leave me alone with him? Smith practically emptied the place for Mrs. G. He's not exactly a popular bloke, believe me."

Anabel said, "I was cold and wet, and wanted a bath."

"You weren't wet, though sheer depression might have made you think yourself cold. I suppose you took a bath for comfort, and to buck you up?"

"No, to be clean," Anabel corrected sweetly, but tempered the sugary tone with a placating smile, remembering that Tim had been wet too. It would have been uncomfortable hanging about in the bar with a friend, but must have been horrid drinking with Robert, for the two had so little in common.

"Well, I'm waiting; go ahead." And as Anabel did not answer — chiefly because she had just eaten the Smiths' bread and felt she should not discuss the family — Tim did it for her. He had not Anabel's inhibitions, and considered himself a closer friend to her than the Smiths, and said, "You have the blues. That was exactly what I expected would happen if you persisted in visiting that farm on one of the worst days of the year."

"I couldn't foresee the weather when I accepted their invitation."

"Everybody here warned you. People living on an island learn to read weather portents, and what they say about it is usually right."

"I hate to be beaten by weather, and I don't like breaking my word."

For a second it seemed as though she had said something surprising, and which Tim liked, but his perverse mood was too strong, and he replied almost paternally, "Evidence of a small mind, with no resilience, m'dear; though I've no doubt you'd break your word if it suited your purpose."

"You *are* put out," Anabel replied mildly.

"I've already told you so. And weather or not, you'd still be blue after visiting Bella Luce. One has only to look at the inhabitants of that farm to know that depression is in the atmosphere of the house — and depression is catching, like measles."

Anabel raised her slender brows in disbelief. "Naomi is vivacious enough."

"Naomi's young, but she'll be affected, too, if she doesn't break away soon."

"She may marry and settle down."

Tim stared, his blue eyes brilliant. "There's no one on Luniette for her to marry." And then Tim saw a queer expression flit across Anabel's face, and he went on impetuously and incredulously, "You aren't thinking *I'd* ever look at Naomi in that way, are you? For goodness' sake, get such a wild idea out of your head!"

Tim spoke so wholeheartedly, obviously never dreaming that anybody could take his friendship with Naomi seriously, that Anabel felt sorry for the girl who had openly fixed her hopes on Tim — hopes that were in her heart, alone, and were doomed to be unfulfilled.

Why did men lead women on to make fools of themselves? Why did Tim single Naomi out and allow her to think she was his Number One special?

The thought made Anabel angry, and she said tartly to Tim, "Then is it wise for you to be so friendly with Naomi? As you say, there is nothing in it, and she's only a child, but if I can, surely Naomi might easily mistake your interest?" And once again Anabel knew that she had stepped beyond the bounds of friendship between Tim and herself, and she noted that each time it was when they spoke about love.

Tim put down his knife and fork with a clatter and pushed his plate away, for his appetite had fled suddenly. He looked sternly at Anabel, and though his eyes were brilliantly blue still, there was also a steely quality in their depths.

For a moment Anabel felt that she glimpsed the real Tim which was usually hidden under the easy, attractive exterior.

"Look here, Anabel, you mind your own business, and don't try to tell me what I shall and shall not do." Tim spoke so hardly and coldly that Anabel flushed and then grew pale, and for a moment there was a queer, unaccustomed pricking behind her eyes.

She opened her mouth to defend herself, and to tell him why she had spoken thus — but that would have meant revealing Naomi's secrets. No matter how carefully the subject was approached, it was too delicate a thing to be discussed by acquaintances, and Anabel felt that Tim would never understand.

Closing her lips into a determined line, Anabel held Tim's gaze for a long moment, showing that though she would not speak, she was unafraid of him, then looked away — first through the storm-splashed closed window, and then at her plate — and calmly went on eating her supper.

Annoyed by her stubborn indifference to his mood, Tim rose suddenly, and leaning over to the window, tugged down the blind and shut out the offending night. Then he sat back in his chair and watched Anabel eat. "You seem to be enjoying that salad," Tim remarked after a while, his tone half-resentful.

"It is very good." Anabel's voice was calm. There had been time to school her feelings.

"Do you advise me to try it?"

Anabel raised her heavy eyelids and their eyes met, when she smiled suddenly. "Have some?" Anabel pushed the bowl across to him.

Then, presently, Tim said, "I don't want to squabble. Can't we get on to a safer subject?"

"What?"

"Well, cut out the talk about Naomi and me. Tell me about Bella Luce — the house, I mean. Remember, I have only seen the outside, and then through glasses. It looks old-world and reposeful, and takes my mind back to bits of poetry I used to learn by heart when I was young."

Anabel paused, then she said, "Dare I suggest that you should never go inside Bella Luce — unless you want to be disillusioned?"

"I shall never go to see the Smiths."

"Yet it was interesting; and they have marvellous silver and china — and the tea was…" Anabel hesitated, then grinned, "scrumptious."

"Now that would interest me enormously."

Anabel talked, and gradually their squabble was forgotten — so much so that Tim felt free to ask jealously, "And didn't friend Robert while away the monotony of the journey up and down by making love to you?"

"As you would have done?" Anabel asked lightly.

"As any fellow might want to do — with you."

Anabel smiled and shook her head. "The answer is no," she replied, with mock regret in her tone.

"But I bet he wanted to."

"I am not a thought-reader."

There was a short pause, then Tim said with quiet satisfaction in his tone, "That sounds as if you were indifferent."

It was not so much the words, but the way Tim said them, which gave such significance that Anabel flushed deeply, and was annoyed with herself for doing so.

They seemed to have reached a turning-point in their friendship.

And oddly, because nothing specific had been said to draw them closer, Anabel felt less bitter about life, as if, in this remote spot, she had found a brick wall against which she could lean in comfort.

After supper, when they smoked in silence, seated in comfortable chairs drawn up on either side of the wood fire which Mrs. Groom had lit for their comfort on the brick hearth, Tim roused himself to say to Mabel, who was clearing the table:

"We won't wait coffee for visitors tonight, Mabelle. Bring it in, fresh and hot, as soon as it's ready." And presently, when the coffee-tray stood on a low table between them, Tim asked, "Will you pour out, Anabel?"

"Don't you want to take your own?" Anabel suggested dreamily, wishing Tim would pour out both his and her cups.

"No, I like to watch a woman's fingers with a tea- or coffee-pot. There's something soothing and pleasant in the sight, when a fellow's tired."

Anabel sat up slowly, and drew the coffee-table closer to her chair. "I wasn't watching when you and Naomi poured out the coffee last night, and so I don't know how you like yours?" She glanced questioningly at Tim.

"Do it just as you think I'd like it," Tim said quietly.

"That's an undertaking." Anabel threw the end of her cigarette into the fire and stretched out her hand to pick up the coffee-pot. But she drew back quickly with a gasp of pain, for the pot had come straight from the hob and was hot. "Ouch!" Anabel pressed her hands together.

Tim was full of contrition. He crossed over to Anabel and bent over her hand, taking it and holding it gently between his own. "That's all my fault for telling Mabel to bring it hot, and then forgetting to remind you to be careful. Shall I get some soap for it?"

But Anabel shook her head. "It's not that bad," she said, but her face was red with pain.

Tim did not see this. He had uncovered Anabel's hand, and was looking down at her soft pink palm. "Such a little hand, Anabel, and so useless — and now in pain."

With a slight struggle, Anabel freed her hand. "It can be quite capable when I like," she told him.

Later, Anabel asked, "Is your coffee as you like it?"

"It is exactly right."

"Does that emphasis mean you are telling the truth, or just being polite?"

"It's so true I should like another cup."

There was a little desultory talk, and then a long silence, which was broken by Mabel coming in to remove the tray and replenish the fire.

Shutting the door tightly after her, Mabel reported to the kitchen, "I believe they've quarrelled. I was in there for five minutes, doing up the fire as slow as you please, emptying the ashtrays and all, and they never said so much as a word. But it isn't his fault. He's a dear, and I'll do anythink for him."

Having digested this, Mrs. Groom warned, "Now, Mabel, don't you go prying into other people's business. You attend to your Joe. You'll be losing him one of these fine days, look you, if you're not careful."

Meanwhile, Tim had broken the long silence of sheer contentment. "Anabel?"

For a moment she remained silent — puzzled. That was how Robert had uttered her name earlier in the evening, outside the dairy at Bella Luce — tentatively, as though he had something portentous to say, and was afraid to begin.

Then Anabel asked, "Yes, Tim?"

He was not looking at her, but into the fire which crackled with the new wood Mabel had thrown onto it; and he was drawing hard at his pipe. "I want to tell you something." Tim braced himself to make a confidence.

"What is it? Not your life-story?" Anabel spoke lightly. They had eaten a good supper and drunk sound wine, and the room was warm and cosy. The atmosphere was ripe for confidences.

"Well, yes, in a way," Tim replied. And after a long pause, "It's not very easy to say. You remember just now, when you spoke about my friendship with Naomi, how cross I was?"

"At my interference?"

"That wasn't the real reason I was angry, though it seemed unnecessary for you — or anyone — to warn me against Naomi. Poor girl, she doesn't realize that no girl can ever interest me. But you had reminded me of something — someone — a girl I once knew. As a matter of fact —" here Tim withdrew his eyes from the fire, and removing his pipe from his mouth looked hard at it — "I was engaged to her when I was posted to Luniette. Then, soon afterwards, a mutual acquaintance wrote to me that this girl — my *fiancée* — was going places with another fellow, and of course I didn't believe him.

"And then, one day — I remember it was a lovely morning after a dirty night, with a lot of blue sky, and heavy white cumuli spreading on the horizon, and the sun literally made the choppy seas dance. It was rather like a painting. Well, where was I?"

Tim slipped a couple of fingers inside his collar as though to release some constriction at his throat. "Ah! On a morning like that, my *fiancée* wrote, enclosing the ring I had given her. It took the bottom out of my world. And the worst of it was that I couldn't do anything about it because she told me she was already married to the fellow. And was I bitter? I swore I'd never let another girl make a fool of me, and I won't.

"But the world doesn't like a fellow with a soured outlook, so I cultivated a grin and tried to make a joke of life — and played with any girl who came along. That's me — as I am now."

"Naomi?"

130

"I said any girl, and that goes for Naomi, and you, too." Tim laughed shortly, took a deep breath and began to smoke his pipe again. "Well, that's my grouch."

Anabel did not answer at once, for while Tim was speaking, anguish took possession of her once again — longing for Paul came back afresh.

Anabel had tried to push herself deeper into the chair, and leaning her elbow on the padded arm-rest, had put her hand over her face, shading it from the yellow lamplight, and hiding its expression from Tim.

She remained silent for so long that Tim asked curiously, "And now what do you think about that?"

Slowly Anabel raised her face from the screen of her hand, and Tim saw how white and drawn it was, with a pinched look about the mouth, and the eyes which stared across the softly lit room at him were tragic.

Tim was aware of a sudden tension in the atmosphere, though he could not see how his story should affect Anabel so deeply. She did not strike him as a girl with much thought for others. And dropping his eyes from the torture in Anabel's, they fell on her hands, which were clasped tensely in her lap, and he drew his brows together — puzzled — fascinated.

Presently Tim repeated his question.

Then Anabel made an effort, and summoned all her strength to answer him, for he was waiting and watching, and delay meant that he might probe her secret.

She replied colourlessly, "Thank you for telling me."

"Is that all?" he echoed blankly.

"What do you expect me to say?" she asked quietly.

"Aren't you sorry for me?"

"Oh, if it's pity you want —" she cried out impatiently.

Tim rose, and plunging his hands in his pockets paced restlessly to and fro on the hearthrug. "I don't know what I want. But I'm still lost. The bitterness I feel, the grudge I have against life, remain, and do not seem to lessen with time. Can you explain that?"

"It's cold comfort, but they do," Anabel heard herself say. "Time does heal."

"How do you know? You can't have had such an adventure — you're too young and gay. Anyhow, it's an experience I wouldn't wish my worst enemy to have."

"Yet it must be fairly common."

"What makes you say that?" — curiously — swiftly, struck by her quietness.

"Because, Tim — your story is mine also." Then, speaking with a little rush, as though afraid that if she spoke slowly nothing vital could be said, Anabel told him, "That is why I left London to stay at Bettycombe among strangers, and my reason for wanting to remain on Luniette — any place where I can find sanctuary and forget — any spot on earth where life is different and interesting."

So that was what was the matter with her — the pale, scared face and twitching hands! Tim came to a stop before her chair, looked down on the crown of her head, and in a voice deep with sympathy said, "Oh, you poor little thing!" He drew a chair close to hers and sat down by her. "Tell me about it, Anabel." He held out his hand to her.

But she shook her head decidedly. "I'd rather not. It's something I don't care to speak about." And she locked her hands tightly together.

"I have reminded you of your trouble, and you are upset."

"A bit — but I'll be all right presently. Go away."

Her voice was so urgent that he found himself complying with her wish that he should 'go away'. Tim straightened, and, walking over to the fire, kicked the loose pieces of wood together, so that the embers blazed afresh with new life; and then he added a couple more logs from the wicker basket standing on the side of the hearth.

By that time he judged that Anabel should have control of herself, and turning to face her, Tim laughed shortly. "It's queer that two people who have been ground in the same mill should meet on this lonely island. Obviously we are predestined to cheer each other in adversity. It is something in common between us, Anabel, and we should be very good friends."

Anabel nodded. She had recovered her poise; and shaking herself mentally she said in a stronger voice, "But I must take Naomi's side in all this. She is the innocent victim of your bitter outlook. You are punishing her for something she has not done, and never could do to you. It isn't fair."

Tim was the least conceited of men. He would have been blind not to see how Naomi enjoyed his company and hung on his words. She made no secret of her liking, and used every opportunity to be with him. It was he who treated the friendship in a matter-of-fact way. He said now, "If I told Naomi the whole bag of tricks about myself, and how I'd been chucked, and my life blighted, d'you think it would make the slightest difference to her feelings?"

Anabel shook her head helplessly. She guessed that even if Naomi were told that Tim's heart was sealed against every woman's charms, the girl would still think she held the key to open it. For surely the power of the very young lies in their inability to accept defeat — perhaps not even to recognize it.

"But why must you go out of your way to be so friendly?" she asked presently.

"I wasn't aware I did."

"It is very deceiving."

"That's not your worry." And then Tim turned the tables neatly upon Anabel. "But the same thing surely applies to you and Robert. Since yesterday he's been neglecting work to sit at your feet. Even I have spotted that much."

"He saved my life."

"You mean, he was first to help you when in a predicament. You know, Anabel, this Smith *is* dynamite." And Tim watched Anabel closely, waiting for the explosion. Considering they were strangers, each interfered too much in the other's life.

Anabel for some reason did not rise to the occasion, but made a great show of searching in her bag for a cigarette, and could not find one.

Seeing this, Tim handed her his own case, and retired to his chair on the other side of the hearth, when he knocked the ash out of his pipe against the side of the stove. While doing this, he said in his normal speaking voice, "Our patrol cutter will be going over to Luvelly tomorrow. We've got a unit at the 'Red Lion' there. She could make the round trip, and call at Bettycombe to collect your baggage. If you'll let me have a chit for the people at your pub to hand it over, I'll see you get your gear safely."

"That's awfully kind of you. I was wondering when I could have a change of clothing. I was afraid I might have to wait for the mail-boat from Combeford."

"You'll have it before then. The gale will have blown itself out by early evening, though there'll still be high seas running; but our chaps will make the effort because they want their mail and some fresh stores," was Tim's reply.

One of the logs on the fire had burnt through, and the two unburned ends fell inwards from the andirons onto a heap of white-hot wood ash, and sent up a shower of sparks which were colourful and gay, and the logs burnt with renewed vitality.

Tim settled back in his chair and, crossing his knees, relaxed, finding a certain joy in lighting his pipe; and presently he tasted an unusual but definite flavour in his tobacco, something he had not done for months. Then he looked half-smilingly across at Anabel. "I'm not so busy that I won't have time to show you the sights on Luniette —"

Anabel's eyes widened in surprise. "But you told me it is so dull here."

"So it is, because I've exhausted the sights; and anyway, I've had to play tourist solo, which you must admit isn't much fun."

"What is there to see beside the ruins of Morisco's Castle?"

"Oh, so Robert's already offered to show you round," was Tim's comment. And he thought, 'Smith's a faster worker than I'd have given him credit for.' "The church has some wonderful stained-glass windows in garnet and gold and old forgotten blue colourings, and in fine weather we could visit the Hen and Chicken Reefs on the west coast of the island. At low tide, some unusual birds are found there. And for something to interest you within a stone's throw of this pub, there are fairies."

"Fairies!"

"That's what I call them, but you can name them as you please, leprechauns, ghosts or hobgoblins, but they seem to me to be young fairies —"

Anabel laughed merrily, and after a moment Tim joined in with her, so that Mabel, listening outside the heavy oaken door,

135

on her way from the stairs to the kitchen after preparing the bedrooms for the night, was able to report to Mrs. Groom:

"Them two have made it up again. They're laughing."

"Have you been listening again, Mabel?" Mrs. Groom asked in vexation.

"Oh no," was the virtuous answer, as Mabel's eyes looked sadly at her mistress. "But as I was passing the door my shoelace give out —"

"That's enough. There is a saying as listeners hear no good of themselves, and I hope you heard the worst —"

"They was talking about fairies —"

"Oh! Them! I do so hope 'e won't go filling Miss Robinson's head with them old ghost stories —" Mrs. Groom cried anxiously.

Meanwhile, Anabel told Tim laughingly, "It's no use telling me sailors' yarns —"

"It's not a yarn; and you know I'm not soused — I'm serious."

"I'm too old to believe in fairies —"

"But I've seen them, I tell you."

"Well, I won't dispute it, but I'm sure it must have been after you'd spent the evening in the bar," was the laughing retort.

"You're not fair to me. I saw them when I was perfectly sober — on a Sunday evening. It was in May, during a heatwave which followed a wet spell."

"Where?"

"In the churchyard here."

"On Luniette?"

"Aha! I'll show you if you like." And when Anabel nodded vigorously to show that she 'would like', Tim said, "But when you see them, you must apologize for suggesting I was drunk when I spotted them."

"Okay," she replied gaily. "We'll go to the churchyard together, and you shall show me — fairies."

"At midnight, though," Tim yarned.

"I knew you'd make it difficult. But okay, midnight is a witching hour, though what on earth you were doing out at that hour I can't think."

"I was coming down from going the round of the patrol, to see that the men were at their posts — and I was alone."

"Did the fairies speak to you?" asked Anabel suspiciously.

Tim said, "That's right, laugh. No, they didn't speak to me. I don't suppose they saw me. They — were dancing."

And so were Anabel's eyes — in profound disbelief. "In the moonlight, of course?"

"Oh, of course —"

"How soon shall we go?" Anabel's voice was eager and amused. How absurd this tale of fairies sounded, but she was interested. This, after all, was something different.

Tim was delighted with her reactions. "If it's a warm day tomorrow, and it should be — we'll go along after dark the following evening," he decided.

They parted for the night on a gay note.

Anabel did not believe in fairies, and thought that Tim had made up this tale to help her forget her troubles. And though realizing how kind it was of him to want to help her, she soon forgot about him, for the interest could but be a passing one.

By the time she reached her bedroom and had shut the door, black depression descended upon her once more.

There was an aching, lost feeling in her heart which made it seem like lead in her breast. She did not light the candles in her bedroom, but went over to the window facing the sea, and pulling back the curtains, raised the sash which Mabel had closed so carefully against the weather a short while ago, letting in the wind and the rain, and kneeling down, Anabel rested tired arms on the sill, and looked out into the grey-black distance that was the sea.

And it was as though Anabel removed the brake from her remembrance — something she had striven to keep in place all the evening, but which could now in the solitude of her room be released. She began to cry — deep, heartrending sobs which shook her figure as wind shakes a reed. Anabel cried more violently than ever before in her life, entirely forgetful that on the morrow her eyelids would be swollen and purple, and her head would ache. And having begun to cry, it was difficult to stop.

Its very violence made Anabel's grief short-lived, and presently, feeling lighter and freer for having rid herself of this weight of misery, she threw off any pretence of self-pity, and looked seawards with clear eyes. For all that had happened — or not happened — between Paul and herself, she must take the blame, and anyway, it was silly crying over the past which must not count anymore.

She heard the thunder of waves dashing against immutable rocks, but the roar sounded far away. The nearer and steady rhythmic break, fall and sweep of waves crashing over shingle in the bay below the hotel could be clearly heard.

As Anabel's eyes grew accustomed to the night, she made out the black rocks at Rat Point, edged with white foam, and the serried ranks of the 'Praying Nuns' which kept their eternal vigil on the beach at low tide. So that meant the tide was running out!

Now and then, as though to emphasize the blackness of the night, momentarily revealing things that darkness hid, and showing the wildness of the seas, were intermittent flashes from the lighthouses along the dangerous and rocky southern coastline of the Channel — Merry Point, far away to the east; and E.S.E., the nearer Laver Point, and other lights whose names Anabel did not know; while, of course, every twenty-two seconds came the brightening upper beam — and the glow from the stationary lower lamp — from the white lighthouse standing like a candle on the southern extremity of Luniette. This last turned the black night into a ghostly grey, revealing the tossing sea, with white-crested waves and blowing spindrift, and the rain looking like fine steel needles slanting down from heaven to drive into earth.

There were groups of smaller lights which moved slowly eastwards, and which belonged to some vessel homeward bound to one of the big ports.

The lights going in and out, and the moving lights on the sea, created a friendly atmosphere, for men were behind those lights — human beings like herself — and Anabel did not feel alone in the darkness anymore.

After a long while, her nerves soothed, Anabel moved away from the window, leaving it open to the sounds and smell of the sea, to the fresh wind and the rain.

With the turn of the tide, was it her fancy that the rain was falling more softly? The beam of the lighthouse lamp was no longer barred by 'steel knives', but filled with a moving mist, of the quality of diamond dust; while the dull roar of the sea beating against the sharp rocks had dropped to a kinder note.

Anabel undressed slowly in the darkness and got into bed — too weary now either to think or feel, and forgetting to count sheep which had become a nightly habit — and soon she fell asleep.

CHAPTER 8

In the morning Mabel announced to Anabel, who was eating a lonely breakfast, which was served for convenience in the coffee-room, that Dai was 'creating something terrible' on the beach.

"What's the matter with him?" asked Anabel, as she buttered toast and helped herself to marmalade.

"Dai's boat is missing, and he says it's been stolen."

"But who would want to steal an old boat like that?"

"She's old but strong."

"They'd soon be found out."

"Oh, the thief won't get far in this gale; and the boat is well known along t'coast. But I wonder the chaps in the lighthouse didn't spot him," commented Mabel. "But we'll hear something when the reliefs go up and the chaps come back to dinner. They won't half get teased, because the folks here think they were asleep."

"*If* the boat was really stolen," said Anabel. "It will probably be found that Dai's boat was swept away at high tide. And she's kept so snugly under the cliffs I don't see how the men in the lighthouse could be expected to keep an eye on her."

Anabel spoke indifferently. Her head ached badly this morning, and she felt tired out, as though instead of sleeping someone had beaten her. She hurried over breakfast so that she could go for a walk, to some quiet spot where the full force of the wind could play on her hot head.

But Mabel was inclined to gossip. With the door shut, no one could see what she was doing in the coffee-room. Mrs. Groom would not feel inclined to disturb Miss Robinson during breakfast, and Mabel, counting on this, lingered to talk, hoping that by the time she left the room the beds would have been made.

Now she said, "It might be that, too, only we don't get t'high tides until September, and Dai's boat is always drawn up above high-water mark."

Anabel sighed and wished Mabel would leave her in peace. Dai's boat and what had happened to it, whether stolen or lost, were Dai's concern, and had nothing to do with her. She grinned suddenly, remembering Tim's serious face last night when he spoke about fairies. "Perhaps the ghosts have been at work," she said lightly.

Mabel stared. "Say, miss, you — *you* don't believe in them, do you?" she asked curiously.

Anabel shook her head. "I don't think I did even when I was small. I seem fated to have been surrounded by realists who preferred to call a spade a spade."

She was about to pour herself out a second cup of tea when Mabel seized the pot. "I'll do it; I know how to pour out a decent cup of tay," she said. "Now, there's no need to be frightened, even if you do see things in t'churchyard."

"Then you've seen these fairies?"

"Oh yes — most every night in summer. Our cottage looks out over t'churchyard."

Anabel did not reply.

After breakfast, the weather having cleared somewhat, she went down to the beach, with the intention of sitting on the rocks and watching the heavy seas break and foam over and between the rough crags.

The rain had stopped, though the wind remained high, and the waste of water around the island was wild and restless. The sky was grey, but with swiftly moving lowering clouds of a darker grey travelling in an ever-changing pattern to the north-east. The force of the gale was broken. As the day wore on so the weather might be expected to improve.

Tim was a good weather prophet.

Old Dai, instead of sitting in his favourite spot, on the gunwale of his boat, was squatting on a rock near which was a mound of empty mussel shells, relics of his self-appointed job of finding bait for the fishermen on the island.

His clay pipe hung, unlit, from the corner of his mouth. He was in fighting mood, and appeared anything but woebegone over the loss of his boat, and Anabel's plan of sitting on the rocks and watching the seas was ruined. Dai was tired of repeating himself to one old crony and a handful of children — probably because he knew their answers to his diatribe by heart, and wished for a larger and more unfamiliar audience. Seeing his face light up at sight of her, Anabel thought, 'Now I'm in for it!' And aloud, "What is this story about your boat being lost in the night, Dai?"

"It wasn't lost, miss. She were stolen," Dai replied.

"What makes you so sure?" Anabel asked and sat down on a rock beside the old salt, with a resignation of spirit which, of course, he did not see.

"That there boat of mine couldn't move without hands," Dai asserted. "She were above high-water mark — and there's a rift where her keel has been dragged down over the shingle. Someone powerful strong took my boat out in those seas during darkness last night." And Dai showed in pantomime exactly how this had been done. "At first, I thought it was one of them there naval chaps who 'scrounge' anythink they fancies, and don't call it stealing, an' neither. But now I knows better, look you."

Anabel listened politely, her eyes fixed on the turmoil out at sea. Here, under the cliffs, there was practically no wind, but seawards the wind and tides were rough. "Then you know the thief?"

And Dai said, shaking her out of her calmness, "I know for sure, because I been talking to old Rube, from up t'Bella Luce, and he says his master bean't turned out to milk t'cows this morning. There be something wrong up t'farm, and I knows what — and it's all because of what I've seen coming for a long while — Robert Smith ain't turned out to work because he aren't there. He's broke loose from the old wiman, and has gone over to Luvelly or Doonehoe. He's joined up."

Having relieved his mind of all this, Dai set about lighting his pipe, and waited for Anabel to digest his words and answer him. It pleased him to think he had roused this stranger from her cool indifference to his great loss, and from time to time Dai glanced sideways at her from under his bushy eyebrows.

Anabel's eyes searched Dai's face wonderingly. It was easy to picture Robert breaking away one day from the confines of Bella Luce and the limited scope on the island, but it was difficult to understand why he should wish to do so at this particular moment — and so suddenly. She thought, 'I think he might have waited until I'd gone. He seemed so pleased to have me here.' She said to Dai, "But why should Mr. Smith do that? I saw him yesterday, and he didn't say a word about leaving Luniette to join the Forces."

"Well, for why should he take my boat and go over to Bankshire, if not to join somethink?"

"But if it had been in his mind, he would have told me," Anabel persisted.

"Then why did he go?"

"I don't know," Anabel replied slowly.

"You went to Bella Luce yesterday; what happened up there to make him leave on the sly? That's what I'd like to know." And Dai's tone said, 'You know what happened. Why don't you tell me?' And aloud, his sense of grievance deepening, "But I'll have the law after him. It won't be so easy for Master Robert. He won't get away with it. Why didn't he take a naval cutter if he must take a boat? The Admiralty is so rich it can afford to lose a boat or two, but I'm a poor working man. I can't."

Dai had been watching Anabel's face as he spoke, and saw the deep flush that appeared suddenly in her cheeks and spread to her neck, so that her whole face was suffused.

For it had dawned upon Anabel's mind that Robert had taken swift advantage of the first sign of a break in the weather to go to Bettycombe and get her clothes, and he had taken Dai's boat because it was in readiness to put to sea, and possibly also because he knew the old sailor.

Anabel was pleased at the thought of getting her clothes, but she felt vexed, too. Everybody on the island knew by now that Robert Smith had taken Dai's boat to sail to the mainland, and assuredly everybody would know when he returned of the circumstances of his errand. It would set the gossips' tongues wagging. Tim would tease her about Robert's interest in herself. The affair would be given an importance which Robert might misunderstand, giving a false value to their friendship — one which he might presume upon in the near future. It was most annoying.

So Anabel said in an odd voice, "I am sure that if Mr. Smith has borrowed —"

"Borrowed!" echoed Dai.

"If he has taken your boat," Anabel amended quietly, "he will be back again in a few hours."

"He'd better be," said Dai darkly. "But it's dirty weather, and my boat aren't so young as she was." He pointed a gnarled forefinger out to sea. "What would you say to going over to Bettycombe in my boat today?"

"I probably wouldn't be saying anything — I'd be seasick."

"So would anybody else like you — only Smith aren't normal. He's batty — but he's stronger than I thought. What I'd like to know, though —"

Dai began to talk, giving the history of his life ever since he was a small boy, in detail, and Anabel's attention wandered.

Now her vexation was tempered with worry in case Robert had risked his life for her sake, and lost it. If this happened — or had happened — what on earth could she say to Mrs. Smith? And Tim would never believe that her friendship with Robert was of the slightest. He might think she had gone out of her way to encourage the farmer, and lay the blame for his death at her door.

Anabel pictured Tim's face, as she had seen it last night, when the polite mask was momentarily removed, and for some reason or other it hurt even to imagine that he might think ill of her.

She turned impatiently to Dai, who was rambling on. "What time do you expect your boat back — if she comes?" she added hastily, seeing that Dai was about to disclaim the boat's safe return.

"About dinner-time. For why?"

Anabel opened her bag, took out a half-crown and offered it to Dai. "As soon as you can, buy yourself a drink and some tobacco."

Dai was delighted with the money. He bit the coin and spat on it before slipping it into his trouser pocket. "Thank ye, miss." His tone was more respectful than it had yet been. "I hears you are staying on the island for a while —"

Anabel turned sharply to ask, "Who told you?", thought better of asking, and closed her lips. Not one but many had probably told Dai her plans. It had probably been common knowledge in the bar last night. As Dai had said, "We are all one big family on Luniette." Everything was known to the islanders, who heard things, or knew them instinctively.

So she half-smiled, saying, "I shall be staying here for a few weeks."

"I'll do my best to make your stay a happy one, miss. All being well with my boat, and if the weather keeps fine for a spell, I'll be willing to take you out for a sail or a bit of fishing any day you like — just say the word, miss."

"I will remember."

"You see, miss, we don't often get people like you on Luniette. Usually the young ones pass on; it's only the old who stay. But we're in luck just now because there's the Navy here, and now you —"

Anabel went slowly up the beach, and mounted the cliff path, wondering what on earth she should say to Tim about Robert's mad escapade, and how she would face the inquiring looks of the islanders, all of whom would make conjectures as to why Robert went off in the middle of the night to fetch a strange girl's clothes. Then, too, there was the little nagging worry which could not be put aside: supposing Robert were not safe? Supposing —

Though Anabel had no intention of going into the hotel, she was obliged to follow the one roadway to the village green, and that ran past the hotel.

And here she was caught by Mrs. Groom, who, despite being busy, seemed to have been lying in wait for her visitor.

The landlady was mixing pastry at the open window of the kitchen, and as Anabel walked past, leant out and called softly, "The mystery has been solved, Miss Robinson."

"Oh! Has it?" And Anabel tried to look innocent, but failed because she could not dissemble easily.

Mrs. Groom was ready for a chat, for she wiped her floury arms with a cloth, and seemed bursting with news which she wanted her guest to share. "You haven't heard?"

"Well — not really, though Dai has a shrewd idea as to who took his boat, but —"

"Mr. Smith has taken the boat. One of the chaps at the lighthouse phoned down to me just now. They *saw* Robert Smith run the boat out, and were fair 'mazed at his strength, pulling the boat down over the shingle as easily as if she was a dinghy, and with that rough tide coming in. They said he was—"

But Anabel could guess what the lighthouse crew said about Robert, and she did not want to hear, so cut in, saying, "I expect Mr. Smith will return about midday — but what a day to choose for a trip."

The forced light note fell flat, because Mrs. Groom was too full of her subject to drop it easily. "Mr. Smith didn't choose the time, miss." And now Sarah Ann came to the crux of the matter. "He was anxious to do you a good turn, miss, in case others did it before him."

"Oh!" Anabel was nonplussed. 'In case others did it before him'! That meant Tim, of course. Mabel must have been listening outside the door when Tim made the suggestion last night. But how did Robert guess that Tim would send for her clothes?

"Mr. Smith's gone for your baggage, miss."

The impressive tones pulled Anabel together, and she said calmly, "There was no hurry for my clothes. They are certainly not of sufficient importance to permit anyone risking his life to get them. It was a kind thought of Mr. Smith's, but he should not have done it."

Some of Anabel's calmness fled when she said the last words, and Mrs. Groom, who had her own opinion of young people's friendships, and who also had a soft spot in her heart for this rich girl, and a longing to see the kind of baggage she possessed, said, "Oh, I shouldn't worry. That's the kind of thing Robert Smith would love to do. He's a young feller, a bit like my Alf, who courts danger — anything to break the monotony of life on Luniette."

"I don't know why he stays to exist here if he feels like that."

"Well, his home is here — and there's Mrs. Smith. She's like a shackle, never easy to shake off."

Then Anabel confided, and was herself surprised at speaking so, "She'll blame me for this, I suppose?"

"Oh, sure, but need you ever see her again, miss? The old lady only comes down here on Sunday mornings for church. You could avoid meeting her."

"Could I?" Anabel replied grimly. "Not if Mrs. Smith were determined to see me." And then suddenly she felt ashamed of herself for discussing Mrs. Smith with her landlady; and she was disgusted, too, with Mrs. Groom's manner, her understanding nods and sly winks which implied that more was known about Anabel's friendship with Robert than they themselves were aware of.

Anabel's cheeks burned with anger against Robert for exposing her to this kind of gossip. He should have known the natives better than to have shown such open friendship for a girl. He must have guessed how they would talk.

Anabel's cheeks were still red as she crossed the rough grass of the village green, and felt rather than saw the peeping eyes behind card-lace curtains. Such curiosity as this about the little happenings in other people's lives could spoil any holiday.

But it was lovely on the top of the Downs, where Anabel quickly forgot the natives and their ways, and a queer happiness seemed to surge through her veins because of the beauty about her — the purplish-grey blooms of cloud, the tossing sea beyond the island, the silver-white gulls, and the emerald-green grass at her feet.

Southwards on another height stood the white pillar of the lighthouse, with a path, picked out in white stones, leading to a black door at its base. Westwards, between the spot where she was standing and the tumbling grey-green sea, was a field of golden brown wheat stooks; and beyond the wheat, like a miniature native village on some tropical isle, were the brown tents which housed the camp-builders; while nestling in a hollow, away from the wet west winds, were the huts of the naval unit.

To the north stood the Copper Mount, like a policeman guarding the island; and close by, was it Anabel's fancy, or was it really the weathered old façade of Bella Luce, turned towards the west?

But seeing the farmhouse reminded Anabel of the Smiths, and she had come for a walk to forget people, so she turned away her head, and presently moved on, following a worn path which led to the tents where one old man pottered about a fire-devil which was full of blazing coals. Before Anabel was in speaking range, the path forked to a little-used track, and she took this one, scattering a flock of thick fat sheep, and continued towards the sea. Remembering her experience of two days ago, Anabel walked warily and alertly, making for a point on the high cliffs beyond the wheat belt, where fertility seemed to cease. For though the rough grass was still a vivid green, it was patchy, and there were numerous cracks in the soil which presently became arid. And there was a thunderous sound from below the cliffs as though water seethed and boiled furiously within a narrow space, a phenomenon on these wide free cliffs which made Anabel long to investigate. She proceeded cautiously, for at her approach the terrifying sound deepened into an ear-splitting roar. The air was fresh and clear, and had the tonic quality of wine. Gulls screamed eerily above the cliff edge, the sound rising thinly in the deep thunderous roar of imprisoned water hurling itself against granite rock.

Anabel's head was raised to the wind, which streamlined her soft hair and whipped the blood to her cheeks, while her skirt was wrapped tightly against her slim legs. She had never felt so free or so gloriously alive. Then she peered down over the cliff.

As she did so, a voice which boomed like a fog-horn shouted at her elbow, "It seems you like getting yourself into dangerous predicaments. Obviously you are not a safe person to be allowed to run loose on this island."

As he spoke, Tim slipped his hand familiarly in the crook of Anabel's arm and held it in a grip of steel — Tim in heavy oilskins and sea boots who had stolen up behind her.

Anabel started to find someone speaking so near to her, and turned quickly in response to the warning to smile and say she was all right.

Then she paused and stiffened, turning her face from his in perplexity, for there was a quality in that easy voice which ordinarily was so attractive, a familiarity in Tim's touch, which were new and wanting in respect for her, and instinctively aroused her resentment, so that despite her precarious position, Anabel moved her arm swiftly to free it from Tim's grasp.

"Don't," she said sharply, failing to loosen the steely grip on her arm.

"Don't what? I'm not hurting you. Am I not to save you? Shall I let you fall into the Devil's Cauldron, and so lose your delightful company at dinner tonight?"

Anabel's mouth set primly. "I'm not going to fall in." But she had to scream the words at Tim twice before he could hear what she said.

"I shouldn't try, because if you do it will be all up with you. I'm not the same cavalier who was on the spot to help you up at Bella Luce. He isn't here now." And there was no mistaking the sneer in Tim's voice. It showed him to be in a nasty mood.

Anabel looked at Tim's profile, but it was like the face of a stranger, and her eyes narrowed in astonishment and annoyance. It was new to her to have to worry about other people's moods, and she had no idea how to meet Tim's. What had happened to upset him? Or was Tim's nature changeable, and subject to chancy whims? It might be wise to take no notice of this vagary. Perhaps Tim had regretted confiding in her last night; or the confidence had brought back the past afresh to him? Evidently Tim's was a more constant nature than hers, for Anabel recalled with a guilty feeling that she herself had been able to forget Paul for a few hours this morning.

But conjecture like this led nowhere, and Anabel said laughingly, as with a quick twist she released her arm from his hold, "No, but you are here, and I'm sure you'd do your best to help if I were in difficulty."

"Oh—" disagreeably — "so that's it. *Any* man's help will do."

Again Anabel frowned. She told herself impatiently, 'Why do I bother about you?' But there was something wrong with Tim, and she longed to know what it was. She felt stung to say, "What on earth is the matter with you this morning?" And she thought quickly, 'What a bear he is! Do I seem like this to other people, at times? If so, then the quicker I snap out of making myself a public enemy the better.'

There was a pause, during which the two eyed each other moodily, then Tim seemed to decide to speak his mind, for he cried, "It makes me hoarse to shout. Come here," and turning, led the way to a dell where there was a fallen tree. It was quieter here, for all sounds were dulled.

Anabel sat down on the tree-trunk, but Tim stood before her, his hands plunged deep into his oilskins' pockets, and said in a hard tone, "Why didn't you tell me last night you had arranged with Smith that he should go to Bettycombe for your gear? You knew I was going to send my men over to collect it when the tide turned and the weather moderated. You went so far as to give me a chit last night to take with them. A nice fool I looked when I had to countermand my order — having heard during the morning that Smith had arrived at Bettycombe in Dai's craft."

Anabel looked up quickly, with an expression of relief upon her face which was not lost on Tim. "Robert got there safely, then?"

Tim nodded dourly.

Then Anabel said earnestly, "But I didn't arrange anything with Robert about fetching my clothes. I was as surprised as you must have been when I heard he had gone."

"But you were glad he went?" Tim insisted.

"As a matter of fact, taking Dai's boat with the intention of getting my luggage across — something everyone here seems to know — has made a lot of unpleasant gossip for me amongst the cottagers. They seem to delight in coupling men and women's names together — even where visitors staying here are concerned. I'm rather livid about their silly talk. That kind of thing is new to me, and I don't like it. And as for making you look a fool, Tim, surely you aren't going to blame me for your looks —"

There was a little silence after this last pointed remark.

Then, suddenly, Tim was sitting down beside Anabel, looking at her and grinning boyishly, his whole manner changed.

"I'm sorry. I boiled over when I heard that Robert had gone for your gear. It was an impulsive conclusion that you had arranged for him to go, and of course, quite wrong. I thought —" Here Tim broke off, then added ruefully, "The truth is I was annoyed to think Smith had stolen a march on me."

"Well, he has — on both of us."

"But you'll get your gear,and it will be through his efforts—"

"I'm not so sure I want my clothes now—"

"Of course you want them." Tim took out a packet of cigarettes and presently the two were smoking. "D'you know, Anabel, what I like about you is that you don't hold out on a chap; you're so ready to forgive and forget —"

"Oh, shut up!" But for some reason or other Anabel blushed. After a while she asked, "Aren't you supposed to be working?"

"I am; but when I saw you crossing the wheat field, I decided I wanted a break — some 'elevenses', if you like — and so ran after you. Besides, I was afraid you'd fall into the Devil's Cauldron."

"Is that it?" asked Anabel with interest.

"Doesn't it sound like a boiling cauldron? Let's go and look at it."

So the two climbed up into the wind, to the top of the hill again, and Tim pointed downwards, to a curious rock formation like a shutter, which barred the entrance to the chasm in the cliffside, so that the sea, rushing in on either side of the shutter, met with terrific impact in the hollow beyond, and seethed, moaned and foamed like an imprisoned spirit seeking outlet.

"That's the famous Shutter Rock," Tim shouted close to Anabel's ear. "It's a natural barrier to that deep pool, the devil's cauldron, which is below this sheer cliff. You see, no one could save you if you fell over here."

Anabel stayed for some moments watching the water, which was in constant boiling movement, and her breath came fast, while her eyes were smarting in emotional appreciation; and a curious thought came to her — that she was glad it should be Tim to show her this mysterious pool, and not Robert. There was something comforting in Tim's presence, just as there was danger, excitement and something terrifyingly sinister about Robert's. Instinctively she moved closer to Tim.

Anabel was silent for so long that Tim inquired in a loud tone, "What are you thinking about?"

But Anabel shook her head. "Only that I shouldn't care to fall in," she screamed back.

It was windy and cold on the top of the cliff, the clouds still lowering and threatening rain, and Anabel was not dressed for bad weather. She wore a woollen cardigan, but no coat, and had not cared to borrow Naomi's mackintosh which had kept her dry the day before.

Tim suggested they should walk back to the beach, which was sheltered, to see if Robert had returned. "He's about due, and it is warmer under the lee," he said.

Anabel agreed readily, saying, "If you are seen with me crossing the village green, the cottagers will gossip more than ever."

"Oh, you needn't mind them," he said indifferently, as they turned inland, keeping below the bluff and out of the wind and noise. "A stranger here is an event, and the poor things must have something to talk about, tales to store up for the cosy bar in the hotel, or by the warmth of the hearth on a winter's evening. And you, being especially —" But here Tim broke off, thinking he was saying too much, or as he might have put it, giving too much away, for he knew he was liking Anabel, the girl, and Anabel's company very much, a liking which could easily increase if he knew her long enough — only, he told himself, he was never going to make a fool of himself over a girl — ever.

So they walked in silence downhill, along the track, and then on the more familiar footpath, and so to the wretched-looking village green flanked by the stone cottages, standing like a row of dour sentinels on one side of the rough grass.

Faces appeared behind the pots of geraniums and maidenhair ferns filling the sills of low latticed windows, but were hastily withdrawn as curious eyes were abashed by Tim's full bland look of inquiry.

And so past the open kitchen window of the hotel where Mrs. Groom's alert sixth sense made her 'chance' to look out of the window at the moment Tim and Anabel passed by, just 'to see if it had begun to rain again'.

Tim still looked bland and inquiring, and made no answer to the obvious; and Anabel's eyes went swiftly from Mrs. Groom to Mabel, when she saw the latter's eyelid flicker gently but unmistakably.

Again Anabel felt annoyed and said crossly, "There's one thing I know I shall never get used to, even if I stay here for years —" when Tim cut in.

"Oh, heaven forbid that! You'd become a troglodyte!"

Whereat Anabel laughed, "Well — ever."

"That can be any time, too. But what's biting you now?"

The hotel was behind them and they were descending the path to the beach in single file, with Tim leading.

"These people's curiosity; the way they poke and pry into one's affairs."

"They're harmless, and you've got nothing to hide; or have you?" And Tim stopped in his tracks, and turning round looked straight down into Anabel's eyes.

"Of course not."

"Then why are you worried?"

"I'm not used to that kind of thing — at least," said Anabel truthfully, "I suppose it does go on, only the people around me take more care to hide their feelings."

"Because they are not so simple as these natives. From what you tell me, Anabel Robinson, you've been utterly spoilt."

Anabel stamped her foot at him. It was meant to show her power and dignity over all men. But as the path was muddy with rain and slippery, something she had not troubled to look down to realize, the foot carrying her weight skidded, and she fell ignominiously at Tim's feet, and all but brought him down too.

Tim yanked her to her feet, and in doing so held her against him for a few moments. Then he released her suddenly and stood away from her, and looking up at his face Anabel saw that it was a brick-red shade.

"I was just going to enlarge on how they have spoilt you by saying you were too independent and untouchable —" Then he stopped and laughed in a queer, low, thrilling way. "But you're not, Anabel. This island won't let you be. Before you've finished with it — and us — you are going to learn quite a lot."

Anabel looked anywhere but at Tim's eyes, and at first she did not see his hand stretched out towards her.

Then Tim said, "Won't you let me help you, Anabel?"

And suddenly she saw his hand with the long lean fingers that could grip like steel. "Oh — yes," she said nervously. "Of course." And put her hand into his. They went down to the beach in what seemed to be a harmonious silence; but when they reached the pebbles and the going was slower, but safer, Anabel withdrew her hand from Tim's fingers, which were suddenly nerveless and loose, saying ungraciously, "Your 'elevenses' are lasting a long while, aren't they? I heard the church clock strike twelve just now, and soon it will be lunchtime." Anabel spoke hurriedly, even garrulously, as though to hide some emotion, and congratulated herself that Tim had not seen her nervousness.

He laughed easily, waiting every now and then for her to catch up with him. "I've never had 'elevenses' before, so we can count today as working off an accumulate of short leaves which are due to me. But it's part of my job to know who comes and goes on this island. How do I know that Smith is not bringing over contraband to store in a cache for an agent who'll come across from the North Channel coast?"

"Oh, poor Robert!"

They both laughed heartily at the idea, and Tim said, "Between you and me, he looks a suspicious character."

But oddly, though they were amused at Robert's expense, Anabel had the feeling that Tim had really come to the beach to watch her meeting with Robert. It was as though Tim were jealous, and yet — he couldn't be.

CHAPTER 9

Though it was past his dinner-hour, old Dai had not gone home. He was sitting on rock beside the pile of empty mussel-shells, a dogged look on his face, which was turned towards the sea.

But as he heard people approach on the shingle he withdrew his gaze to the sea and looking at Anabel, smiled. The smile was bestowed upon her of all people because of the tip she had given him, and instinct had told Dai that where that tip came from others would be forthcoming.

"You're looking better a'ready, miss," he exclaimed, struck by the new soft look on her face which he naturally put down to the tonic air of the island.

"Oh, I'm feeling fine."

Dai grunted, Anabel's health reminding him of his grievance. "That's more'n I am," he replied.

Tim laughed unfeelingly, took out his tobacco-pouch and passed it over to Dai, with a laconic, "Help yourself to a bit of comfort, Dai," an offer which was eagerly accepted by the old rascal.

"When do you expect her in, Dai?" inquired Tim, looking out at the lively grey seas, hoping to spot Dai's craft returning to her beach.

"Allowing for the wind, and the mad hand at the tiller — any moment."

"Wind's dropped, and shifted a couple of points. The sun should be out presently," said Tim, looking at the sky, at the breaks in the scurrying clouds.

Dai nodded. "It'll turn warm, too." He was acting so furtively with the pouch in his predatory fingers that Tim smiled at Anabel, and with one mind they both turned their backs to Dai.

Tim said quietly, "It won't be much fun taking a stroll at midnight — too dank, and all the mosquitoes will be out, which you won't like. But the weather will be settled tomorrow night. There'll be a moon and a clear sky, but perhaps a gentle sea. Keep tomorrow evening free for me. Or had you forgotten our bet?"

She smiled back at him, and shook her head. "I hadn't forgotten."

Then at a sound from Dai, Tim turned to face the old man, and received his pouch back — but considerably depleted. "Thank ye, sir." But Dai did not light his clay pipe. Empty, it hung like a short grey stick from the corner of his mouth.

Tim pocketed the pouch absently. He had been gazing out to sea, and now pointed excitedly into the distance. "There she is! By Jove, Smith's made it, and I didn't think he would. Well done, Robert!"

Anabel noticed that Tim's praise was unstinted. She realized, too, that he must have felt some anxiety about Robert's safety, for he heaved more than one sigh of relief. She followed the pointing finger, straining her eyes seawards, but drew a blank.

But at Tim's words Dai had jumped to his feet with an agility that would have done credit to a far younger man, and taken his place beside Tim and followed his direction.

"Oh, ah! I see her," he said in a curiously flat tone, at last. Then his manner seemed to change, for he scowled heavily and spat on the pebbles near him. "And now to welcome that young madcap, for of course he'll have t'pay for this escapade." But Dai could not keep his eyes from the tossing seas. He would have liked to find fault with the way 'she' was being handled, but he could not. If it had been another man's boat instead of his own cherished possession, he would have given unstinted praise. But praise was left for Tim to make.

"You know, Dai," said Tim placatingly, but bluntly, "there's really nothing due to you but the hire of your craft. No one, not even you, could have handled her better than Mr. Smith; and taking the storm into consideration his seamanship is superb — there's no other word for it."

Dai did not answer for a while, then he said, "There's t'stealing, sir. You aren't going t'tell me it's *right* to steal. And there's t'anxiety that young feller give me — the wear and tear to my nerves."

"Rubbish, man! You ought to be proud your craft was chosen for the journey. It proves that though she's old, she is thoroughly seaworthy. You've preserved her well to stand up to such a gale."

Dai nodded. He accepted the praise for his boat as a matter of course. "It shows all that, no one's got any right —"

"Mr. Smith had no choice. Indeed, he showed judgment in choosing her from among all the other craft beached here —"

"Oh, those!" Dai's tone was eloquent. He did not trouble to glance at the 'other craft'. "But the risk —"

"To your craft? Remember it was his life, too."

Dai pursed his lips, and the pipe stuck up at an angle. "That young feller, that landlubber — took my boat," he reiterated with exasperating monotony, and the sneer which he managed to convey into the word 'landlubber' was indescribable.

Tim could now catch glimpses of the black hull of Dai's craft as she bobbed about in the trough of one wave, then was heaved to an eminence among the spindrift on the top of another — the glimpses becoming more frequent as she approached the beach. Tim said, "You know Mr. Smith borrowed your craft for a good purpose — to get Miss Robinson's luggage from Bettycombe?"

"I did hear that — sometime," admitted Dai reluctantly.

"It's true, and you won't have to wait long to prove it. But if you make a fuss, Dai, you'll be making a mistake."

"How?"

"It will be unfair to our visitor, Miss Robinson. She'll feel unwelcome and want to leave Luniette. As it is, and if the weather holds, she'll want to do some sailing and fishing —"

Dai nodded his head reflectively. "I don't know what you're making all this fuss about, sir," he said innocently, at length. "Seems to me there's too much interest taken in that young Smith — he's cock-a-hoop with his own importance. I believe he'd like me to take it up with the law. He's too fond of showing off, and this would give him a chance."

Tim withdrew his eyes from the sea and fixed them on Dai's face. "You're quite right, Dai," said Tim solemnly — and listening, Anabel could not make out quite what Tim meant — if he really agreed with Dai over some profound truth, or whether he was pretending to agree to please Dai.

By this time all three were watching the dark wet sail which was clearly visible, as the little craft made the last tack before reaching the safe harbourage of the island.

"There's a heavy ground swell," commented Tim, as the mast seemed to be rolling uncomfortably from side to side.

Gulls seemed to appear from nowhere, soaring about in circles above their heads, as though they knew that this was to be a landing-ground, and hoped for some tit-bits from the boat.

"She's a stout little craft, Dai," said Tim.

"I knows it."

The craft was coming swiftly in at an angle. Suddenly the sail came down, but the progress of the boat was unchecked, for the engine was working to help the sail, and its beat could be clearly heard throbbing through the roar of the sea.

Robert was standing at the tiller, his attitude tense, as though aiming the boat at a given spot on the beach, and determined to make it. He looked rather a lonely figure in dark wet oilskins and a big sou'wester tied under his chin, in that small black boat tossing among that waste of water. Someone hailed Robert from the beach. It might have been Tim or Dai. But Robert made no answering sign, only leant forward and then straightened up again, when the throb of the engine ceased.

Anabel saw that the sail was roughly reefed — just folded until there was time to tie it up properly. She looked again at Robert, and noted that his face was pale and his eyes staring, and pity for him arose in her heart.

There was a grating noise on the shingle, and as though he had come suddenly to life, Robert moved, jumped forward and clear of the boat, and turning gripped the gunwale and began pushing her up the beach — all in one long movement.

Meanwhile, both Tim and Dai had rushed out into the shallow sea to meet the boat and help her in so that the curling waves, as they broke along the shore, should not swamp her. Everyone timed his efforts neatly to coincide with the last upward lift of a wave which, rolling beneath the keel, carried the boat forward to land.

Then Anabel lent a hand — or she liked afterwards to think she did — with her small fingers gripping the gunwale of the heavy boat, and pulled her up over the shingle.

Everyone stood back for a space to regain breath, and to smile triumphantly at Robert, who swayed like a drunken man. But Robert had eyes only for Anabel, and he scarcely heard

Tim, who was loud in praise of his seamanship. Even Dai managed a twisted kind of smile which bore little resemblance to any kindly expression of emotion, appearing like a gargoyle's grimace rather than anything human.

As they seemed to be waiting for him to say something in reply, Robert pulled himself together.

"Here she is, Dai. Let me know the damage," he said nonchalantly and unexpectedly, not bothering to glance in Dai's direction. But his manner was understandable, for he was obviously dog-tired. Then Robert went on, speaking to Anabel in a lower tone which was, however, marked with weariness, "I've got your baggage. It's safe in the cabin, covered with oilskins. At first the hotel people wouldn't let me have it. They didn't believe me when I said I'd crossed over from Luniette, and laughed until I took them down to the quay, and showed them Dai's boat — and then they knew. Even so, I had to threaten and cajole before they'd hand over your stuff. Since you went away they have discovered you are a personage, and didn't want to let you go."

Robert tugged off his sou'wester, and with fumbling fingers unfastened the many buttons of his oilskin which fixed the flaps so securely that no wet could get in.

A little crease of worry deepened between Anabel's brows. A personage. She was afraid to ask Robert what he knew about her. Obviously he was too tired to care much about that now — and glancing sideways at Tim she saw that his attention was momentarily diverted to Dai's boat.

Then suddenly Anabel ceased to worry about herself. She forgot her anger against Robert. To think of holding it against him because she was gossiped about by the cottagers would seem petty in the face of such bravery — even if it were a foolhardy thing for him to do, and the risk was unnecessary.

She recalled Tim's unstinted praise, and Dai's grudging appreciation, and she had seen for herself how marvellously Robert had handled the boat in tempestuous seas. And it had all been done for her, to satisfy a wish to have a change of clothing...

There was a real maggot of worry in her mind now, too, because she could not help asking herself why Robert had done this for her. The answer was pretty obvious. That was the problem, for surely Robert would expect some return for all his trouble and risk? And what return could she hope to offer when, in her heart, there was a growing fear of him, but fear of what she could not say.

"Thank you for getting my things here," Anabel cried rather theatrically, looking up into Robert's eyes with gratitude in her own. "But you shouldn't have risked your life for me." And she held out her hands to Robert.

It was an intuitive movement, and whether in gratitude for her clothes, or for Robert's safe return, no one ever knew.

But immediately, as Robert's hands grasped hers, Anabel knew she had made a mistake and flushed painfully. And to make matters worse, Tim had turned and was watching her with a curious expression on his face, so that her confidence seemed to vanish.

Weary as Robert appeared, there was an unusual hard quality about his clasp which revealed a cruel hidden strength which filled Anabel with fresh dismay.

Then Tim spoke. "I congratulate you, Smith," he said quietly, holding out his hand. His big form seemed to come between Anabel and Robert, driving them apart, while his outstretched hand could not be long ignored.

Suddenly Robert loosened his hold of Anabel's hands, and looked at Tim almost inimically. "What for?" he demanded roughly. "I did nothing. Anyone could have got Anabel's baggage — if they'd thought of it."

"Oh, I wasn't referring to Anabel's gear, but your seamanship. On the tail of a gale, with that off-shore wind, too, you drove her in, right at Dai's feet. I've never seen anything like it. Who taught you to sail?"

Robert stared, not knowing what to make of this. He was unused to praise. Indeed, ever since he could remember he had never done anything right. Then he laughed shortly. "I picked it up. No one taught me. And I've been out in worse gales than this — and survived. The sea's a bit choppy, but a child could handle Dai's sloop, she's so easy. That's why I took her. I wanted to have time to think."

Tim laughed. "That's a good one."

Thus Robert dismissed Tim's praise, not because he felt it undeserved, or wished anyone, himself least of all, to belittle his feat before Anabel, but nothing that Tim could do or say would be right. Yet, once, Robert had liked Tim Northorn — but that was before Anabel came to Luniette, and he had seen her laughing and talking in a carefree manner to Tim. Everything was changed now.

Tim felt himself dismissed. He looked at Dai, who had boarded his craft, which lay at an angle, like something tired and spent, on the pebbly beach, and was examining her inch by inch and with much grunting, seeking for damage — half hoping to find some — trying the pulleys and testing ropes and tackle. It had once been a sloop with racy lines, but fashions in little ships had changed since she left the stocks, and though she still had a trim, seaworthy air, there was nothing streamlined about her to make her appear smart.

But staring at her, it crossed Tim's mind that only a madman would have ventured out in her on such a night when visibility was nil and the seas were mountains high. Whichever way one looked at it — whether the craft were stout, or the seamanship superb — it was a foolhardy adventure to undertake.

Tim's eyes went reflectively to Anabel's face. He liked watching the play of expression on it. She was talking animatedly to Robert, who seemed to have forgotten his surroundings, his mind intent only on this slip of a girl.

Her words of praise and thanks sounded sweet, and her gay laugh clear as crystal — even to Tim's ears, though what he heard was not intended for him.

And it came to Tim, slightly chagrined now, that the prize was certainly worth the risk.

Anabel was saying to Robert, "And now come back to the hotel to rest a short while, and then lunch with me."

It was a charming invitation, and Tim, hearing it, wished that it might have been offered to him — but he was not the hero of the moment. And, to be fair, Tim knew he did not deserve any of the plums of success.

No one was surprised when Robert replied, "That's exactly what I want — a little rest, and a lot of drink — and later, something to eat. And afterwards, unless you are in a tearing hurry to unpack, I'll come down here and get your luggage."

Only pausing to get out of the heavy oilskin and throw it carelessly over the gunwale of Dai's boat, Robert turned with Anabel to leave the beach.

Suddenly the girl stopped and called back to Tim, "Are you lunching at the hotel, Tim?"

"No, I must return to the camp. You two carry on. Go ahead!"

"We mean to," answered Robert.

Tim watched them go with mixed feelings.

Dai's voice cut across his thoughts. The old man was down in the cabin. Now he poked out his head, and leant his arms on the sliding roof of the cabin. "Pretty cool customer, ain't he?" said Dai eloquently.

Tim swung around. "I don't know what you mean," he said haughtily.

"No? Well —" Dai reared his body slightly, like a porpoise moving in the sea, and spat well and truly into the white foam of a broken wave. "You'd think this was that landlubber's boat, and *she* was *his* girl. But it's *my* boat, and *your* girl."

Tim looked startled. "My girl! Who said so?" he demanded roughly.

"I did — no offence meant, sir."

"Well, you keep that opinion to yourself. D'you hear? I have no girl. I don't want one — and any woman who is attracted to a chap like that, the opposite from anything I am or would wish to be, couldn't possibly belong to me — see?"

"Oh yes, I see, sir; but bless you, he's just risked his neck to get her clothes — and you know what store gals set by clothes. It's natural she's taken up with him — for a coupla hours, anyways."

Meanwhile, as Anabel, followed by Robert, struggled up the slippery slope from the beach to the cliff top, she had time for reflection. Thankful though she was to get her clothes, it would be wise not to overdo her thanks to Robert, who might quickly take advantage of any warmth on her part.

When they reached the hotel, Mrs. Groom, Mabel, Olly and Joe came out to greet them.

"I am that glad you're safe back, Mr. Smith," said Mrs. Groom, as spokeswoman for her staff, who, Anabel suspected, had downed tools and come to the door more through curiosity than with a desire to extend a welcome home to

Robert. And to lend colour to this idea, Mrs. Groom's appearance belied her words, for she did not look particularly glad to see the adventurer — her eyes were goggling too much.

"Thanks, so am I," was the surly answer.

"I've brought Mr. Smith to lunch, Mrs. Groom," said Anabel, her eyes a little anxious. "Have you enough for an extra?"

Mrs. Groom looked annoyed. "When have I ever been short of food?" she inquired tartly of each one of her servants in turn, and preened herself in a satisfied way when the answer came promptly in chorus, "Never."

"But I want a long strong drink first," said Robert. "I'm just about all in." He leaned against the jamb of the oaken door for support.

"I'm sure you are," Mrs. Groom agreed — and to Joe, "Go get a double whisky for Mr. Smith — and bring along a syphon from the icebox."

"No syphon," corrected Robert. "I want my drink neat." He pushed his way into the hotel, and so to the bar, where he sat down at a small table by the distempered wall. His slender frame sagged forward, and Anabel saw that he was far more tired than he had admitted to being on the beach. Her eyes followed his long arms to the hands tightly clasped between his knees.

And in that moment Anabel had some insight into what Robert had endured in the darkness when he had battled some twelve miles across the raging seas in that cockleshell of a boat, just to get her clothes.

Mrs. Groom, Mabel and Olly stood around silently, and Anabel moved over to the window, feeling distressed, while Joe got the drink and brought it over to Robert, who took the glass and drained it.

Then he sat up and ran his fingers like a comb through his black hair several times. "Where am I?" he asked in a dazed voice — and began to laugh when Mabel told him he was in the bar of the hotel. "Oh yes — I thought —" Then he paused before telling them wonderingly, "I was in Davy Jones's locker." He glanced swiftly at Anabel, and said to her profile, "D'you know where that is, Anabel?"

She turned and nodded gravely, her eyes full of pity. She came over to the table and sat down opposite Robert, and studied his face earnestly, wishing she could comfort him as he so badly needed comfort.

Mrs. Groom burst in, "That's where we thought you'd gone," and she pointed downwards expressively with her thumbs. "I can tell you, Mr. Robert, you gave us all a fright." Then as a new thought struck her, and with a commiserating look as befitted the subject: "Your poor ma! Shall I phone her and say you are safe?"

"No. She knows I am the bad penny that always returns."

But Robert knew his mother would be angry at his absence, and there was bound to be a row when he returned to the farm.

The answer struck a jarring note, and soon afterwards, having watched the young farmer toss off a second double whisky, neat, Mrs. Groom glanced significantly at Anabel, and said firmly she could allow no more drinks on an empty stomach. Then with a sign to her staff to follow, Mrs. Groom went majestically from the bar.

While waiting for the landlady to dish up the lunch, Robert beguiled the time by singing energetically, if drunkenly:

"As Jack was walking through the square,

He met a lady and a squire;

Now Jack he heard the squire say,

'Tonight with you I mean to stay.'
Doo-me a-ma, din-ghy a-ma,
Doo-me a-ma day."

"What is that?" Anabel asked.

"That song? I dunno. It's an old sea-shanty I used to hear Dai sing when I played on the beach as a kid. Dai served his time before the mast, and has been round the Horn umpteen times. Or hasn't he spun the yarn as yet?"

"No — remember, I've only been here a short while, and most of the time a terrific gale has been blowing."

"Don't I know it?" But he looked better, and the colour had come back to his cheeks.

Over the roast beef and Yorkshire pudding, Anabel asked him, "What made you do it, Robert?"

"You think me mad, don't you?"

"Well, it was a crazy thing to do."

"That's how I'm made and I'll never change. I thought it would be fun."

"And you took Dai's boat."

"It was the best of the bunch huddled under the cliffs — and only the best could survive the storm. I had sense enough to know that."

"You should have waited until it was calmer."

"Listen, Anabel; if I'd waited until the gale had spent itself, I'd have had to ask Dai for the loan of his boat, and knowing him I'm sure he'd have refused me."

"But why?"

"Partly because he doesn't trust me, though in his heart he must know I'm a finer seaman than he's ever likely to be; and again because he doesn't like me. And, too —" Here Robert paused and looked sly.

171

"Go on," coaxed Anabel, her gentian eyes fixed on the dark face with its overnight stubble of black hairs on the chin.

"If I hadn't gone then, the Navy might have got in first; and I wanted to be the one to get your clothes. Then, too —" and here Robert ceased to look sly, but spoke hurriedly, even shyly — "it was true what I told Tim on the beach. I needed space and time to myself to think, and darkness to get things clear in my mind. I've been confused the last two days, with my thoughts in a maze, and moving around as though I were in a dream. And it couldn't go on. Something had to be done about it."

Anabel looked down at her plate, and did not reply. She knew quite well what Robert expected her to say, to ask a question that would lead to the answer he wished to make. Aided by the whisky, which seemed to give him a false courage, he was ready to unburden himself; to load his heart-searchings onto her.

Anabel did not want to hear. Indeed, she told herself half-angrily that Robert, as a close friend, would be actually repulsive to her.

"Well, aren't you going to say something?" Robert asked at length, finding her unresponsive to his mood.

"I'm sorry: I wasn't listening. What *did* you say?" Anabel apologized and inquired smilingly.

Robert's lips set in a straight line. "Oh, if that's all you're interested, I can't be bothered to say it all again. But what *are* you thinking about with that soulful look in your eyes?"

"Food. Isn't this beef delicious?"

"Is it? I hadn't noticed."

After lunch, when Robert would have tarried, Anabel persuaded him to go home.

"Your mother will be worrying about you?"

"No, she won't; but I bet she's all set for a row. I left the farm to Rube today, and he's long ago forgotten how to work."

"I'm afraid Mrs. Smith will blame me for this?"

"How can she? It's not your fault. You didn't ask me to go."

"No, but you fetched my clothes."

Struck by the same thought, they both laughed.

"My clothes!" exclaimed Anabel. "I had forgotten them."

"I will get Joe and Olly to help me with them. I'll have to hurry or Dai will turn them out of the cabin, and be auctioning your entire wardrobe on the beach," said Robert.

But even as he spoke, and to his chagrin, four sailors appeared in the passage of the hotel. They had been ordered to collect Miss Robinson's gear and take it to the hotel.

This, of course, was Tim's doing, and Anabel laughed again, but Robert's face looked dark. "A piece of unwarrantable, high-handed impertinence," he said angrily.

It needed all Anabel's diplomacy to win back Robert's good temper.

But later, when she had soothed Robert, tactfully glossing over the fact that Tim had stolen his thunder, Anabel felt tired, and was impatient to be rid of her guest whose friendship made such demands on her nerves. 'He's a stormy petrel. There is trouble wherever he is,' and, 'I've paid in kind for getting my clothes,' were among the thoughts that passed through her mind.

Before he finally left for Bella Luce, Robert said, "When am I going to see you wearing some of these precious clothes?"

"I haven't unpacked them yet," was the obvious reply, and not for the first time that day did Anabel wish that her wardrobe had not been made to seem so important through Robert's adventure; or alternatively she hoped that people would find her clothes were worth Robert's risk.

"Tonight?"

"Oh! Are you coming down tonight?" Anabel inquired, with a sick feeling in her heart. "Aren't you worn out after your trip? You really should rest."

Robert looked at her quickly. "That sounds as though you don't want to see me." And as Anabel made a swift gesture of dissent, and wondered whether she would have to begin all over again the weary business of coaxing this temperamental man into a good mood, Robert continued, "But even if I don't come down, Naomi will."

Anabel heard the name with a kind of shock. She had entirely forgotten the girl. "Naomi!" she echoed, with an edge to her voice.

"*She'll* want to see your clothes."

Anabel suppressed an exclamation, and said flatly, "Yes, of course; and there's the mackintosh which Naomi lent me yesterday. She will want it."

"That's to be her excuse for calling here," Robert commented briefly. "And Naomi must come tonight or wait two days. Tim is on duty tomorrow evening, and there'll be no attraction for Naomi at the hotel."

"I see," Anabel replied slowly.

If that were the case, then Tim could not keep his appointment with the fairies in the churchyard. Well, probably he never had meant to keep it, for the whole thing was just a piece of nonsense.

"Why are you smiling so secretively?" Robert asked jealously.

"Not at you — only my thoughts…" And before he could speak again, Anabel urged desperately, "Now please go home, and for goodness' sake don't quarrel with your mother, or I shall feel even worse than I do coming between you over this adventure."

"Don't talk rot. You knew nothing of my intentions. No one can blame you for anything."

"But I put the idea into your head — unwittingly and foolishly; and there's no doubt that if something had happened to you, Mrs. Smith would have been right to lay some of the blame on me."

"Don't you worry, Anabel. I'll square things with Mother. She shall meet you at church on Sunday, with an angelic smile on her face, a friendly word for you, and — who knows, perhaps another invitation to Bella Luce — only let's hope the weather will be kinder then."

Anabel hoped she hid her dismay at these words. She managed to smile, however. "But you must promise not to drive her in any way —"

"Drive my mother!" echoed Robert, and laughed harshly. Suddenly he came close to Anabel, and looked down into her eyes, and said in a different voice, "Look at me, Anabel —"

Unwillingly, and with some effort, she did so, and their gaze held for some moments, until Robert sighed and turned away, saying inconsequently, "I can't decide upon the exact blue of your eyes. Last night — out at sea — they were the colour of some pansies I once saw growing in a garden on the cliffs about Luvelly; and today they've got the glassy brazenness of a cloudless sky in torrid, midsummer heat."

CHAPTER 10

When Naomi arrived at the hotel in the early evening, it was obvious that she had been at some pains to compete with Anabel's wonderful clothes which had caused so much stir to bring over to Luniette.

It was all to no purpose, for Anabel, afraid of hurting Naomi's tender feelings, had deliberately not changed into one of the many dresses now hanging in her wardrobe upstairs, and wore the same jumper suit which everyone knew.

Naomi's face fell for a moment when she saw that Anabel was wearing her old clothes, then brightened miraculously as it occurred to her that there was no competition to her finery. Naomi Smith was beautiful as a peacock in her best yellow muslin dress with the wide scarlet sash, and Anabel was drab as a dove.

Brother and sister joined Anabel in the lamp-lit dining-room where dinner had been cleared, and she was sitting with a book alone before the fire.

"Where's Tim?" inquired Naomi, her large limpid eyes looking about her as though she suspected Tim to be hiding somewhere.

"He hasn't come back yet," said Anabel, putting down her book, not sure whether the Smiths were her guests, or Tim's, or visitors to the hotel.

"Then he wasn't in to dinner?" And there was satisfaction in Naomi's voice.

"No, and he phoned Mrs. Groom not to keep anything hot for him, that he would dine at the camp — at least, that is what Mabel told —"

"Oh!" Naomi looked dashed. Presently she brightened up and asked, "Haven't you unpacked yet?"

Anabel smiled. "Oh yes, and Mrs. Groom and Mabel had a glorious time helping me. In fact, I think they know more about my belongings now than I do."

"Then why didn't you change? I thought that was the idea in getting your luggage over."

Anabel shrugged. "Too tired," she lied.

"Aren't you glad to have your things?" asked Robert, who was disappointed not to see Anabel so gaily dressed as his sister.

"I'm delighted, of course," was the ready reply.

"Don't forget Robert risked his life for you," Naomi reminded.

Anabel faced her eager little tormentor. "I shall never forget it," she said quietly. "Did you think I had?"

"I wasn't sure," Naomi answered pertly.

"Oh, shut up, Naomi!" cried Robert, as he saw Anabel look sharply at his sister. "If you're trying to pick a quarrel, you'd better clear out before I box your ears."

"I'd like to see you try," said Naomi.

They were an undisciplined couple, and if not squabbling with others, were sparring between themselves, and Anabel felt sure from their touchy manner that they had been quarrelling before they reached the hotel.

There was a commotion outside, and a deep joking voice and a hearty laugh were heard, and Tim came into the room.

Anabel looked at him with relief in her heart, and Naomi, forgetting everything but that Tim had come, ran forward to meet him and claim his attention.

Watching her youthful advances, Anabel admitted that only a hard heart could withstand such a joyous, gorgeous creature.

"Hallo," Tim laughed, "why the finery? I say!" And he walked admiringly around the pretty figure. "This is a pleasant sight for tired eyes. Is it a fiesta, a birthday or a ball?"

"Silly, I dressed up because I thought Anabel was changing and she might look grander than me and put me in the shade. But she hasn't, the cheat —"

"I say!" Tim's eyes widened. "You mustn't talk like that about Anabel. She mightn't like it. She doesn't know you don't mean half you say."

He paused as though waiting for Naomi to apologize, and when she didn't, but merely looked charmingly mutinous, he moved over to the window and stared out in silence, his back expressive of the disapproval he felt.

Naomi followed him, and pushed her hand into the crook of his unresponsive arm. "Now you're angry. Oh, please, don't be cross. I'll tell Anabel I'm sorry if you like, but —"

"What's the use if you say you're sorry with your tongue in your cheek?" Tim said, looking down at the rebellious face, with a more kindly expression on his own.

Mabel brought the coffee in. "Weather's not settled enough to have t'coffee in the garden," she announced, placing the tray in front of Anabel. "But it's getting finer every minute now."

As soon as Mabel had left the room, Naomi came over to the table, turned the tray so that it was in front of her and began to pour out.

Quick as she was, Tim was quicker. "That's Anabel's job," he said firmly, and twisted the tray back to Anabel. "She's older than you, Naomi, and she's staying at the hotel."

"Oh, I don't mind," said Anabel hastily, sick of being the centre of a storm. "I'm not too keen on pouring out."

"That isn't the point. It's your place to do it." And Tim looked stern and old and more determined than the Smiths had ever seen him.

Naomi drew in her lips. "I've always done it," she said sulkily.

"That isn't the truth," Tim reminded her imperturbably.

Naomi glared angrily at Anabel, who thought, 'For two pins she'd throw the whole tray over me,' and aloud, "I shall pour out my own, and you can all do as you like." Anabel deliberately poured out a cup of coffee, helped herself to sugar, and taking the cup rose from the table and walked to the other side of the room.

"Now *you're* being unsociable," Tim cried in an exasperated tone.

Anabel laughed. "I'm trying to keep the peace," she smiled.

That was going to be a difficult thing to do. And presently, in a spirit of renunciation, Anabel decided to leave Naomi alone with Tim, and try to work out her own salvation and happiness with him.

Anabel would have preferred staying in the room with Tim, who was a good companion and easy to get on with. Instead she must go somewhere — out of the room — with Robert. 'I'm a fool, and I don't suppose Naomi will have the decency to thank me,' she thought.

"Robert and I are going out on the cliff for a breath of air," Anabel said.

This was news to Robert, but his face lit up at once, and he rose with alacrity. "That suits me."

"I should have thought you'd have had all the fresh air you want for a bit," said Tim. Then, "We'll go with you, though."

Anabel shook her head smilingly. "We don't want you and Naomi. I want to talk to Robert," she said pointedly.

Tim agreed at once. "Of course. Sorry, I didn't mean to butt in."

"Oh, but you're not," Anabel replied hastily.

Tim did not answer.

It was Robert who appeared jubilant as he and Anabel walked in silence to the edge of the low cliff which overlooked the bay. Not that his manner was annoying — but joy was in his light springy step and the lift of his shoulders, which were squared confidently.

They paused at the cliff-edge and looked out to sea. The tide had turned, and a string of rocks, like a graduated necklace of beads, which were submerged at high tide now stood out sharply amid the foamy wash of green seas. The largest rock, Mouse Island, was farthest out to sea, and already gulls were standing on it hoping to find titbits in the pools as the tide receded.

Lights shone palely on vessels coming down-channel, each one laden heavily. Already the bright lamps from numberless lighthouses dotted at dangerous points along the north and south coastlines of the Channel shone intermittently, like beacons in the grey haze of evening. The wind having died down, there were no creamy crests to waves, and no spindrift was flying riotously as it had done less than twelve hours ago; and though it still heaved, moved by a heavy swell, the sea had lost its restlessness. The sky was a calm, pale blue and had a clean, washed look, and there were no grey blooms of low-lying cloud, and early evening stars shone steadily...

"And later," Robert said, as though following his thought to its logical conclusion, "there will be a moon; and tomorrow it will be a fine, warm day."

"One wouldn't believe a scene could change so quickly," replied Anabel.

They lit cigarettes and sat down on stones on the cliff top, when Robert asked, "Did you really want to talk to me, Anabel?" And his tone said, 'If you do, why don't you begin?'

Anabel shook her head. "Not especially; that was an excuse to leave the others alone."

Robert was silent for a while, digesting this; then he said, continuing the conversation where it had left off, "I don't think Tim liked being left with Naomi."

Anabel shrugged. Though sorry for Naomi, try as she would, it was difficult to like the girl whose dislike for anyone who crossed her path and seemed to spoil her good time was so active. "She is rather young for him. But there aren't many young people on Luniette, and we must all make the best of the material that is here."

That sounded pedantic, but Robert only remarked, "Naomi can be so blind."

"She's got to learn lots of things some time," said Anabel enigmatically. But what she really meant was that Naomi would have to learn sooner or later that men and girls could be good companions without falling desperately in love with each other.

"I'm glad you left them to it, though I believe Tim likes you best."

"Tim! Well, so he should. I'm new and I think he needs change. Besides, I get on with most people; I've never done him any harm."

That sounded so philosophical and disarming that Robert said fervently, "I wish I did!"

"What?"

"Get on with people like you seem to do."

"It's easy, once you get the habit."

"Which means that in your heart you are indifferent to people."

Anabel laughed. "It's an attitude which saves one a lot of worry in the long run."

"Where did you learn all that?" Robert asked curiously.

There was a long pause, then Anabel replied in a queer, strangled voice, "Through bitter experience."

"Tell me," Robert pressed.

"I can't." She thought how silly she would be even trying to make Robert understand.

Robert was labouring under some deep emotion which made thought confused. He was conscious of a longing to help her. "Do," he urged tactlessly. "It means so much to me if you are happy."

Anabel heaved a deep sigh. She had brought this on herself. She said in a hard voice, "It would make me unhappy to tell you because it would remind me of something I am trying hard to forget — the reason I was so ready to stay on Luniette."

At that moment she turned from contemplating the sea and looked at Robert, and he thought he had never seen such a sad face before — so lovely, and yet with such poignant grief in her blue eyes.

It occurred to him he had been tactless in reminding her of what was best forgotten, and with unusual consideration, for the Smiths were a selfish, thick-skinned family not given to thinking of other people's feelings, Robert turned his face resolutely seawards, albeit he was puzzled at Anabel's hint of tragedy. He cogitated for a long time; then, unable to resist asking, he inquired suddenly, "You aren't married, Anabel?"

It relieved him to hear her emphatic, "Oh, heavens, no! Do I look matronly or haggish? What made you think I am?"

"I didn't, but — there is some fellow in your life?"

Anabel answered shortly, "Yes, there is — or was, because that's all finished with now."

"Someone in London?"

"Yes."

"I was afraid of that somehow. But you're so sensible you'll forget…"

Anabel shrugged. Her eyes took on a martyred look. She was deeply wounded, but if only Robert would stop probing this wound. She said, "Oh, of course, I shall — I have to —"

"Yes, and I mean — in time — when it's all forgotten in the past — perhaps you could —"

But that was too much to bear just then.

"Never!" Anabel cried out, and then laughed shortly to prevent herself bursting into tears. "Never is a strong word," she said in a smothered kind of voice. "I may change. One can never be sure. But just now — oh, please, Robert, don't let's talk about me anymore. Tell me about yourself — what you do in your off-time — anything —"

Robert replied doggedly, "There is no free time. If I want a holiday I take it — by force, as it were. I just walk out on the farm and leave Rube and the women to carry on as best they can."

"As you did last night?"

Robert nodded gracelessly.

"I hope Mrs. Smith wasn't too angry about last night?" Anabel asked, feeling better now that she had got Robert to talk about himself.

Robert looked indifferent. It was easier for his long, saturnine face to appear cold than it was for him to seem happy, young and gay. "Mother hasn't said much — as yet. There hasn't been time. She's probably storing it up for tomorrow. But I don't care, because I've made up my mind to take lots more holidays now you are here. I want to take you places."

"On Luniette?" And Anabel glanced about her. "Where is there to go?"

"Well, after taking you *over* the island, I can take you for a sail around it, and show you the Knoll, Pins, Gannets, Seals and Gall Rocks — the Hen and Chicken Reefs, the Skerries, and the Lamatry Isles. Strange wild birds nest on some of those rocks, and the fledglings make rather a pretty sight just now. And at high water I'll take you right up to the cliff face on the west coast, and give you a close-up of the granite formation…" Here his voice changed to a lower and more confidential tone, "And we'll collect a keg of spa water —"

Anabel looked at Robert with quick interest. "Spa water!"

"Well, it isn't fresh, and it's not salt. I've tasted it, so I know. I call it spa water, and it rises like a spout in the floor of a cave which is only get-at-able at high water, and then, of course, by boat."

Anabel visualized the jet of water. "And what becomes of your spa water?"

Robert smiled crookedly. "It flows out over the cliff face to the sea below."

"What a waste! If my father were here —" It occurred to Anabel that if her practical father had found a natural spring in this little island, he would have sent a sample of the water away to be analysed. But she stopped talking suddenly, for Robert had no idea that her father was a money-spinner, and she was not minded to tell anyone on Luniette. It was a new and gratifying experience to be liked for herself and not for what she could give — or what it would be expected she should give as the daughter of a great financier. Anabel asked in a business-like tone, "Is this 'spa' on your land?"

"If you can call that stretch of barren cliff-top land, I suppose it is."

"But the owner of the island may claim any minerals found on your land, and that would go for a mineral water. You hold the farm on lease?"

Robert said, "When I was very young I was interested enough to look up our lease, which is a long one. Perhaps whoever drew up the lease thought it a waste of time putting in a clause about minerals. It is such a small island, and naturally they knew nothing about the spring."

"How did you discover it?" Anabel had all the zest of a pioneer in her veins.

"An old pilot found it, and told me where it was."

"Does anyone know about it?"

"Only you. And I've told you because —"

Anabel cut across his softly worded confession, "And you've done nothing about it?"

Her practical mind left him with a sense of frustration, and he replied shortly, "There isn't anything in it."

"You don't know until you try. Just think, Robert; if this spring were properly exploited, you might grow so rich that — if you wanted to — you could leave Luniette. The whole world could be an open book to you. You could —" Anabel had jumped to her feet in her excitement, which fired Robert's imagination so that he, too, rose agitatedly to his feet.

"I could," he cried in a ringing voice, his face lighting up. "And what's more, I'd have a shot at marketing the spa if I thought —" Here, with difficulty, Robert hesitated, looked sideways at his companion, closed his mouth with a snap, and relapsed into his habitual melancholic mood.

But Anabel was still being carried forward by enthusiasm. "Take a pot-shot at success," she advised largely. "Fancy, with this way of escape at your feet all this time, you've wasted months moaning against Fate, when you had only to look down, and there were the riches to buy you freedom and anything else you could want."

Robert smiled at her eagerness, but he was taken more by the beauty of her animated face than worrying overmuch about what she was saying. "And don't forget you were the one to point the way to me," he reminded. Then suddenly, in a flashing vision, Robert saw other things that riches might win for him, and with rising emotion he turned to Anabel and caught her hands in his, pressing them so tightly in his excitement that he hurt. Leaning towards her, his face came close to hers. For a few seconds they talked eagerly one over the other, laughing, with rising excitement, at the future prospect each took a delight in showing the other.

It was at this moment that Tim and Naomi, coming to look for them, saw the two standing close to each other, in animated conversation. Robert's face was altered out of all recognition; and Anabel, young and eager, her expression ever changing, was chattering like a monkey.

Tim would have retreated decently but hastily, aware that this was one of the great moments in two people's lives, more than half guessing what sort of a moment it must be — certainly one which would tolerate no outside gate-crashing.

But as he turned to go back, Naomi's shrill voice halted him. She called out half-vexedly, "What are you two up to?"

There was a short pause of consternation, and Anabel and Robert started, facing the newcomers guiltily. What had they been saying? How much had Tim and Naomi heard?

"Shall we tell them?" Anabel asked softly.

"Heavens, no! If we do the whole island would know, and that would never do. We'll keep the secret for the present," said Robert, but he seemed oddly youthful, having caught some of Anabel's eagerness, and for once he seemed entirely unselfconscious.

A feeling of envy — that some other fellow had found happiness with Anabel — rose in Tim's heart. And on top of that feeling came a curious wave of emotion which Tim freely translated, 'Anabel's managed to console herself quickly — are all girls alike?' He remarked with a dryness foreign to his nature, "Hold it tight, then, because in your present moods you are in danger of letting it fall, when it might be so brittle it would break."

Robert heard the enmity, and said, with a hostile stare, "Did you want anything?"

"I? No, nothing; but your sister thinks it time you went home."

It was barely dark. The Smiths never went home until night had fallen.

"Naomi does?" exclaimed Robert, looking at his sister in some wonderment. "That's odd; she's usually the last to leave a party."

Everyone waited for Naomi to speak, but she remained silent, standing a little apart from the group, gazing intently out to sea.

So Tim answered for her in a cheerful voice, saying, "Naomi doesn't like the company in the bar tonight. In her words, they are louts. I took her there thinking to please her, but apparently Naomi is not in the mood to be social. She won't even play darts with me in the skittle alley, which *is* a little less crowded than the bar."

And having said his piece, Tim took out his pipe and set about lighting it, his manner tantalizingly urbane.

Meanwhile, Anabel glanced at Naomi in the greying evening light, and saw that though the girl still looked like a gorgeous bird of paradise in her gay dress, she was sulky as no bird of paradise could possibly be. Her dark eyes were hooded and lowering, and the look she gave Robert when he exclaimed impatiently at her depressing mood was venomous.

Anabel saw, too, that Naomi's small fingers were plucking nervously at her skirt, and the sight touched her deeply. It needed little to realize that Naomi was desperately unhappy to the point of tears, and Anabel felt that Tim was behaving badly in speaking so unpleasantly about her in public.

When brother and sister had gone home, Anabel turned hotly to Tim.

"I think you're perfectly beastly. If you had spoken to me like you did to Naomi, I'd —"

"Ah," cut in Tim easily, "but you would not have misbehaved as Naomi did, so there would be no need to make a public example of you — that is, if you count you and Robert as the public."

They were standing on the hearthrug in the dining-room, where for want of attention the fire had gone out. Anabel had picked up her book and was going to bed. She was only lingering to tell Tim what she thought of him.

"You were very cruel to Naomi," she told Tim sharply.

Tim stared, "Well! If you aren't the most difficult person to please. I like that." His voice rose with righteous indignation. "First you tell me I have no business — in my old age, of course — to amuse myself with Naomi; then, when I turn a cold shoulder to the girl, you upbraid me for cruelty. I don't know where I stand, or what I should do for the best to please either or both of you."

So that was it! Apparently Tim had made some effort to treat Naomi rationally. Having taken to heart her, Anabel's, homily about the girl, he had attempted to keep Naomi at a distance — not an easy thing to do with Naomi. It would be like trying to dam a fast-running stream, for Naomi's emotions were warm, and until tonight Tim had rather encouraged her obvious liking for himself.

No wonder Naomi had reacted — well, as Naomi would...

While Anabel was thinking along these lines, Tim, annoyed by her silence, continued crossly, "You told me it wasn't fair to play with the child — and though I wasn't aware I had been playing with her, I did see your point and tried to reform; but I like the way you walked out on me tonight and left me alone with her."

Anabel thought ruefully, 'He's right. One can't please Naomi in that special way anymore. It is too dangerous.' Then, light-heartedly she dismissed Naomi from her thoughts with, 'It's only calf love. She'll get over it in time.' Aloud, she said, "Apparently *you* didn't enjoy yourself either this evening?"

"I could have — in the bar — where I took Naomi. But that wasn't Naomi's plan for tonight."

"I expect she didn't want to share you with the natives."

"Listen, Anabel, we'll cut Naomi out. What she does or likes doesn't forgive your parking her on to me while *you* and *Robert* flirted outside."

As Tim rightly guessed, Anabel forgot Naomi in the attack on herself.

"We weren't flirting!" she cried indignantly.

"No? I always understood that playing at being in love was flirting."

Anabel straightened her lips, then she asked, "Can you imagine Robert playing at anything — even pat-ball?"

"Well, no; but when Naomi and I came upon you out on the cliffs you were behaving —"

"Yes?" Anabel said icily, as Tim paused for a word.

"As though you were in love," he said bluntly.

"Thanks, then I'm afraid you didn't see very far."

"Can't you explain it?"

"Why should I?"

"No reason at all, except — are you in love with him, Anabel?"

"You know I'm not," Anabel retorted witheringly.

"I'm so glad. You're too nice for Robert Smith. But it would be understandable if you were fond of him after what he went through on your account last night."

Anabel interrupted quickly, "If you mention the word 'clothes' I'll go crazy."

"All right, I won't — and whether you're in love with him or not — it's plain that Robert is with you."

"Pooh! So are lots of men."

So far, the talk had been fairly amicable, with neither side very deeply moved, though there had been a fine show of mock indignation, and a pretence of icy aloofness on Anabel's part.

She had just spoken in ridicule, and without much thought, and was unprepared for Tim's reaction to her lightly spoken words.

This was real temper. It was in Tim's eyes, making them look like blue fire in the lamplight; it was in his voice, which was harsh and peremptory; and it was in the grasp of his fingers, which caught her arm in a clasp of steel.

"What men? Which ones?" He had acted and spoken instinctively, and seemed hardly aware of his manner and action.

"Please, let go. You are hurting my arm." And when Tim did so, and Anabel rubbed her arm to relieve the pain, she went on, "Oh, no men here. I don't know any on Luniette — only you and Robert — and I suppose Dai, but you couldn't count *him.*"

There was a slight pause. Then Tim moved away. "Sorry. But you haven't answered my question. What men, Anabel?" And even now, when Tim had had time to think and marvel why he was so upset at Anabel's random words, there was more vehemence in his tone than he was aware of.

Anabel smiled slowly. "It was perhaps a thoughtless figure of speech, but since I've been grown up I have learnt that I'm not exactly unattractive to men — and a girl like me is bound to have men friends, you know."

"Yes." The word was clipped. "I see. You're the sort of girl that nine men out of ten would go crazy about." Tim drew a deep, steadying breath, and smiled into Anabel's eyes, and though his eyes still sparkled it was not with the brilliance born of anger. "I say, don't go to bed yet. You're not tired — or if you are, you can stay in bed to breakfast in the morning. Come and have a drink with me in the bar. I want to talk to you — and look at you…"

Anabel could have pointed out that Mabel would willingly have served them any drinks they required in the dining-room, where Tim could have talked and looked to his heart's content.

Apparently Tim did not want that kind of privacy tonight. It occurred to Anabel that possibly Tim thought no more seriously of her than he did about Naomi, which was perhaps as well — for Anabel told herself firmly that she had definitely finished with love and all that kind of thing. But Tim *had* behaved queerly just now — especially for a man whose pride still smarted under another girl's scorn.

Both Anabel and Tim were warmly welcomed in the bar, and once they had settled down in the homely, if heady, atmosphere — a swift process in the small, intimate room — they were left pretty much to themselves. The hum of friendly voices and cheery, robust laughter formed an unobtrusive background, while the air was redolent with the smell of wine, spirits, tobacco and sawdust — the last having been liberally sprinkled over the floor by Olly before the evening rush began.

It was a busy night in the bar, and Anabel and Tim were squashed close together in the middle of the counter, and neither could move much without endangering someone else's drink.

Mabel was too busy at the beer-engine to give them much attention, though Mrs. Groom, in her usual black bodice, and wearing her Welsh flannel check apron, smiled benignly at Anabel — the smile was called forth by the quantity and quality of Anabel's wardrobe, which Sarah Ann Groom had appraised, and could not easily forget.

"Well — here's to a fine tomorrow — one filled with sunlight," toasted Tim softly and significantly, lifting his glass to touch Anabel's.

"But —" she began.

"No buts — drink it down — and no heel-taps."

Anabel drank obediently. Then she asked, "But what if it is fine and warm and filled with sunlight?"

"You don't mean to say you've forgotten our date already?"

"No, but you are on duty, and won't be free to keep it."

"Wise bird! Now who could have told you that?" inquired Tim.

"Robert."

A curious expression flitted across Tim's face, but was gone almost immediately. "Ah, Smith knows a lot — but not quite everything," he remarked.

"But you *are* on duty?"

Tim nodded. "During the evening — at a time when the Smiths might be sticking around. But our date is for midnight."

"Then we are going?"

"I haven't changed my mind, and I hope you won't?"

"Oh, I'm dying to go — so curious I can hardly wait."

"That's what I thought, and why I shall strain every nerve to keep my date with you — unless you want to tell the world, in which case count me out."

"I won't tell," said Anabel.

"Because if you break faith over that, I'll be the laugh of the island."

Anabel smiled wistfully. "I wonder what all this is about really?" she ventured.

"You'll see," oracularly.

After a second drink, Anabel asked Tim speculatively, "I thought you liked the Smiths."

Tim stared. "What a funny question! So I do — in small doses." Then hastily, because Tim's was a kindly and fair nature and he did not want to convey the wrong impression, "Naomi's a nice child — a charming girl — and amusing. It's Smith who is so difficult — or perhaps it's me. Anyhow, we don't hit it off."

Someone challenged Tim to a game of darts, and he readily assented, saying the room was growing too close for comfort, but he must be allowed to finish his drink first.

Anabel's drink was lukewarm and wishy-washy, so she left Tim in the bar, which was buzzing with sound, and went up to bed.

It was pleasant to go into the cool bedroom, light the candles, and see all her own pet possessions around her — the miniature of her mother on the dressing-table, and a large photograph of her father opposite it. But there were poignant memories wrapped up in other articles, and Anabel wished she had not put them out — the gilt cigarette box with the small oval painting of a Gainsborough lady's head in the lid — the carved ivory stamp box — even the paper summer fan, were all gifts of little intrinsic value, which Paul had given her from time to time — given them with his love, and treasured for that reason. These Paul had not wanted back; he had probably forgotten them. But he had snatched away instead the thing she had valued most of all — his love.

For the first time, looking at these things with hard, bright eyes, Anabel asked herself whether she had perhaps put a fictitious, even false, value on Paul's love. Her thoughts still whirled confusedly whenever she remembered that fatal day of discovery, when Paul had actually walked out on her, and the bottom had dropped suddenly out of her world. But tonight, as through a kind of mist, she fancied that Paul's stature was smaller than she had thought — or was it only in her imagination that he had been high, wide and handsome? Surely it would be sensible to suppose that a man who for no apparent reason could treat a girl so cavalierly was not worth troubling about — certainly not worth Anabel Robinson. These last words were said aloud, to the likeness of Anabel Robinson in the dressing-table mirror — and were continued: 'If the said Anabel hasn't the strength of will to realize this then she'll be lonely forever, for who cares about lost loves? It must be *finis*.'

With the springy step of new resolve Anabel walked away from the dressing-table, where she had been talking to her image in the glass, and went over to the open window, and perching herself sideways on the sill, gazed out to sea with interest.

To Anabel, a townswoman from London, it seemed extraordinary the part the sea played in the islanders' lives; and yet, of course, not so extraordinary considering that each time one raised one's eyes, there was the sea — in varying mood — filling one's vision.

Anabel now looked up at the tranquil star-bespattered sky, and then at the less tranquil but beautiful sea, shimmering like some live silver thing under the caressing light of the moon. And there were the passing ships, with lights twinkling from masthead and cabins, moving slowly towards the ports, or outward bound, in the Channel; and farther away were the intermittent flashes from the lighthouses along the coast — known to sailors by the length of their beams. And just below Anabel, in the bay below the cliffs, was the restless tide breaking rhythmically on the stony shore — and she could just see the lines of 'Praying Nuns' which seemed like a reverent congregation kneeling in the moonlight, and lent an air of the supernatural to the scene — 'for why should people kneel in shallow water and pray silently? There must be something strange about Luniette.'

Odd thoughts drifted across Anabel's mind, some of them too nebulous to be called thoughts, coming out of the blue and ending abruptly, having no bearing on a pattern, but just scraps of the visit's happenings. She wondered about Robert and his spa water, and if there were anything in the rock spring; why Tim had blazed with sudden anger when she spoke of other men in her life; if Olly would remain on Luniette, or cut loose;

and why someone didn't pull Dai up over his nasty habit of chewing tobacco and spitting on the beach.

Stray pictures flitted before Anabel's vision, like a film reel — the mellow facade of Bella Luce, as she remembered it best, with the western sun making diamonds of the window-glass, and the first evening star shining in the pale sky above the house; the Rockingham china tea-service; Naomi's crimson trousers; Keziah's deaf and dumb language; Robert's strange eyes; the storm at sea; Tim's merry quizzing glance; spindrift; Tim smoking a pipe; Tim... And here, smilingly, Anabel drew a blind over these mental pictures.

The bar clock struck eleven raucous notes, which meant that it was five minutes to the hour. There was a distinct pause in the buzzing sound of voices and laughter, and Mrs. Groom's voice could clearly be heard saying in pleasant, regretful but firm tones, "Time, gentlemen, please!"

Someone joked, but it was only a half-hearted attempt to break a custom, and was not taken up by the other customers.

There was a scuffling on the gravel outside the hotel, and many 'goodnights' fell cheeringly, in high and low tones, on the night air. And soon the sounds of departing guests diminished, and the music of the sea, which had dwindled to a monotonous, somnolent accompaniment of Anabel's thoughts, came into its own again. A feeling of happiness surged in Anabel's heart.

Then she heard something else, and withdrawing her eyes from the sea looked towards her closed door.

Nearby was a familiar and pleasant presence.

It was Tim coming up to bed, pausing to put out the lamp on the landing, stumbling at the first step at the turn in the staircase, then resuming with firm tread to his room, and shutting the door. That night Anabel slept more peacefully than she had done for weeks, and awoke in the morning rested.

She put this down to the fact that the elements had chosen to behave. The sea was calm, the sky a ceiling of blue — it was indeed a day filled with sunlight.

CHAPTER 11

That evening, Anabel chose to wear one of the best of her dresses hanging in fragile loveliness from a hanger in the wardrobe. It was of tulle of a lovely midnight blue colour, cut on simple but flowing lines, and held trimly at the waist by a narrow velvet ribbon of a darker blue, while threads of matching velvet ribbon caught the full sleeves at the wrist. It was, perhaps, too smart a dress to wear in a little island inn, but Anabel remembered her date with Tim, and felt that she must wear her best to meet fairies.

Anabel was wearing the dress when she sat down in lonely state to dinner, and was waited on by Mabel, who could not help exclaiming at the beauty of line and colour.

After dinner, when Anabel had settled down by the wood fire to a quiet evening with her book, ready for Tim when he should finish work and come to take her out, Robert Smith walked down from Bella Luce.

Anabel heard him say to Mabel, outside the dining-room door, "Don't bring in any coffee for me. I don't want it."

And Mabel's answer, given in a tart tone because Robert was no favourite of hers, "I wasn't bringing any, sir. Miss Robinson's alone tonight, and she's had hers."

Then Robert burst into the room, and stopped short at sight of this strange Anabel in a lovely new dress. "I say!" he stammered in an awed kind of voice, his sombre eyes lighting up, "How nice you look!"

That was a great deal coming from one who seldom paid any girl a compliment. The words had dropped from his lips almost before he was aware of saying them, and as soon as

Robert realized he had spoken, a dull red crept beneath his brown skin, and he looked embarrassed.

Anabel was smiling at him in her usual friendly manner, so Robert recovered his poise, shut the door carefully, and came slowly into the room, feasting his eyes on the small figure in the chair. Now that Anabel had shed her tailored, workmanlike clothes and wore this soft, clinging stuff which he longed to touch, but dared not, Robert thought she seemed more feminine and fragile than he had previously imagined, and this sense of apparent weakness made him long suddenly to protect her, but how or from what he did not know.

He spoke, and his voice was gentle. "I knew you might change your dress, and was prepared to find a stranger sitting in your chair, but I never expected anything so — wonderful."

Anabel smiled broadly, delighting in this wholehearted praise. "I'm so glad you like it," she replied, and put her book aside, guessing that Robert's demands on her would prevent any more reading until he went home.

"'Like' doesn't half express what I think. A princess might envy you such a dress."

"You really are saying pretty things tonight," approved Anabel.

At that moment, the evening, which had promised to be dull, spread like a pleasant prospect before Anabel, so it was shattering to watch Robert's expression change as his suspicious mind created an evil thought.

"Did you expect me down?" he asked, standing on the hearthrug, and looking down at Anabel with avid eyes.

"Not really; you see —"

"Then you didn't wear this dress to please me; or did you?"

'Here we go again,' thought Anabel with a curious sinking of her heart. And aloud, with carefully suppressed impatience showing in her clear modulated voice, "I put on this dress because I was sick of wearing the clothes in which I have been scrambling about the rocks on Luniette."

"Not to please Tim?" asked Robert stiffly, taking no notice of her warning voice.

Anabel replied abruptly, "Tim is on duty this evening. You know that. It was you who said Naomi wouldn't be down because there was no chance of seeing Tim." Anabel inferred that Tim would not be seeing her — or the dress — tonight, and her face flushed because she was not telling Robert the truth. But she hoped that the fitful firelight would screen the blush, and went on speaking rapidly. "Don't spoil everything by dragging in Tim's name. It seems to upset you so much, and there's really no need for it."

And now there was a cool note in her voice, a shade in her happy feelings — a withdrawal, that was not lost on Robert.

He pushed his hands deep into his trouser pockets and paced to and fro in the narrow confines of the hearthrug, and Anabel had a picture of a beast of prey, wild and untamed, padding restlessly in a barred narrow cage.

Robert said, "No, I suppose there isn't after what passed between us last night." And at once Anabel racked her brains to remember what they had talked about, and what special confidences had been exchanged — and drew a blank. "I must try to fight my black moods which drive me to want first place in everything and with everyone — or fade completely out of the picture."

Then Robert looked at Anabel's dress, which made so impressive a difference to her personality, and he added shyly, "You're so grand and remote, Anabel. I'm almost afraid of you. I believe you could do what you liked with me tonight."

Anabel thought, 'You sound almost tame.' And to Robert, her mild eyes looking up into his fiery brown ones, "In my heart I'm plain Anabel. I seem different because this room is nearly dark and you can hardly distinguish me, and so imagine spooky things."

"You're never plain to me — or indeed to anyone," Robert said, taking her literally.

Anabel could not answer this. She rose from her chair, and in sheer admiration Robert caught his breath.

He stood still, watching her every movement, not offering to help Anabel as she went over to the lamp which was standing in the centre of the largest table, and raising the globe, and lifting off the glass chimney, put a match to the wicks. He was feasting his eyes on her slender waist, following the gracious folds of the full skirt that swept to the floor, revealing the toes of her midnight-blue satin slippers. Then Robert spoke abruptly, his voice spurred by an unwelcome thought, and the sound broke the soft silence in the room like a pistol-shot. "Are you a rich girl, Anabel?"

Anabel paused to look over her shoulder at him, and catching sight of his luminous brown eyes which glistened in the lamplight, turned her back on him quickly, and busied herself carefully replacing the lamp chimney and adjusting the screw of the wicks. "I'm just Anabel," she replied lightly. "Why do you ask?"

"Because that dress cost money — even I can see that. You must have lots of money to buy clothes like that."

"So what?" she replied crisply, the modern slang entirely out of keeping with the soft dress.

"I don't know — exactly, only Naomi couldn't afford such a dress."

"This particular style of dress wouldn't suit your sister."

"But she could never buy one if it did — and yet the Smiths are supposed to be successful yeomen-farmers."

Anabel had finished with the lamp, which now filled the low-ceilinged room with a pale, mellow light, and she turned to go back to her chair. But Robert barred her way, and Anabel looked up into his face in cold, startled surprise.

"You can't put me off with a cold look, Anabel," he said roughly.

Anabel stood still — waiting. "I'm not trying to put you off anything, but I should like to return to my chair."

"You can't — anyway, not until I've finished talking."

Anabel pulled out a dining-room chair from the table and sat down. "It seems to me you've been doing most of the talking this evening. But if there is anything more you want to say that you've forgotten, I'm willing to listen." She spoke quietly, her look resigned, but there was a growing irritation in her heart against Robert, who seemed to enjoy creating difficult situations.

"Oh, if you're going to make a business of our talk..." he began violently.

Anabel interrupted with a frown, "Give me a cigarette. Thanks." She tapped the cigarette on the back of her hand before putting it between her lips and bending towards the light he held out. "Now let's sit down quietly and get to the bottom of what's worrying you." And she spoke soothingly, as to a child. Then, as Robert hesitated, "If you don't, I shall leave you and go to my room, and then the evening will be spoilt for both of us." Secretly Anabel wished that this might happen, for only that way would she find peace.

The threat seemed to calm Robert, for he moved aside from her path, and returned to his former position on the hearthrug.

"What I'm getting at is this: you're too good for us on Luniette."

"Have I said so?"

"No, but money talks..." He glanced at Anabel's figure. "That dress."

"Yes?" Anabel stared in bewilderment.

"I wish I had a packet of money."

Anabel could understand that. "I suggested how you could make some," she told him easily.

"How? Oh, the spa water." Robert shrugged. "There's probably nothing in it. Everything's too much in the air, and I couldn't count on it."

"Why do you suddenly want money?" asked Anabel curiously.

"Because nothing can happen between a man and woman unless money comes into it too."

There was a long pause. Robert continued to stare sombrely at Anabel, and her eyes were fixed on the glowing heart of the fire.

Then Anabel spoke, and Robert could not guess how her heart quivered, for money had counted in her relations with Paul. It had been the stumbling-block to their happiness. "Are you trying to tell me that money is a barrier or a help between a man and a girl?" she asked quietly.

"A fellow must have cash; but it could be a bar to happiness if only the girl had money."

"It's luck if a girl has a 'packet of money', but why shouldn't a man share her luck and be happy with her?"

Robert shook his head. "I don't know, but it would seem wrong. A man likes to give. Take us. What could I offer you that you haven't already got?" Impatiently he threw his half-smoked cigarette among the ashes, and during the long silence which followed, Anabel did the same.

Then she said firmly, "I shouldn't worry myself over a situation that can't arise between us, if I were you, Robert. Supposing I don't want you to offer me anything — ever?"

"You mustn't talk so hopelessly," Robert told her. "That is a continuation of last night's talk. But this is a new day, and you are young and must live. That being so, I feel free to tell you that whatever you may say, or wish, or hope, doesn't stop my feelings for you growing hourly stronger and deeper." To Anabel's discomfiture, Robert dropped on his knees beside her. "I never thought it would come like this to me — suddenly and without warning — and I feel confused and lost with everyday things. Anabel — I love you."

"Oh no! Robert, please! We must not talk about love. I don't want to. I can't." Her voice trembled with distress.

But Anabel might as well have spoken to the wall for all the notice Robert took of her words. Only he caught her hands, which were lying clasped loosely in her lap, in his own hot ones. "I must speak. You can't stop me. I'm only human. Since you came to Luniette —" Robert's tone was low and thrilling, but Anabel, forced to listen because she could not get away from him, felt her heart sink.

"Only three days ago."

"It's been long enough to change the course of my life. See, Anabel, you admit you're not happy, and neither am I when I'm away from you. Why not forget the past, cut yourself adrift from every mainland tie, and settle down on Luniette at Bella Luce with what I can give you? Let me try to make you happy?"

The prospect to Anabel was anything but alluring. Indeed, the thought of being cooped up on Luniette, in the atmosphere of Bella Luce farm, with Robert alternately playing lover or jailer, was not only unattractive but even repulsive.

Anabel said sharply, and with more ill-feeling than she had ever shown towards Robert, "I'm happy enough — or I could be if only you'd leave me alone. This following me about and talking so intimately is nothing short of persecution, and if it goes on I shall be forced to leave the island."

"Persecution!" Robert repeated, dumbfounded. "But surely it isn't persecution when I talk about love!"

Anabel pulled away her hands from his clasp. She said firmly, "This has gone far enough, Robert. You are being absurd, and when you think it over quietly you will be the first to agree with me. Three days may count as eternity to you when speaking of your emotions — but to me they are just three days. I'm sorry I can't look at the matter through rose-coloured spectacles. You must forgive me for being so prosaic; it is as I'm made."

This was not the truth. Anabel was known among her friends as a 'romantic, sentimental little fool', and they were probably right. But Robert's personality was rapidly outgrowing Anabel's comprehension, and she guessed that if a halt was not called soon there would be no knowing what measures he might take to gain his ends.

Robert sat back on his heels, then rose to his feet. "Are you turning me down?" he asked forlornly, and with such a stricken look on his face that Anabel spoke more gently.

"I can't be doing that because I'm not taking you seriously. You must know that a girl brought up as I have been, in the middle of a city, could hardly be happy on Luniette."

"But you said you liked it here?"

"It is ideal for a rest and change, but to live here — I think I'd go crazy."

"You don't mince matters," said Robert bitterly.

"You make me speak plainly, Robert."

Robert continued to stare down at her in silence, wondering what he could do to soften this girl's heart, having no previous experience of love to guide him. But there was nothing he could do about it at the moment — nothing at all. After a while, he asked, "Are you terribly annoyed with me?"

"Oh no." But Anabel knew that she was in a far worse state than mere annoyance from Robert's point of view. She was completely indifferent. Robert's impassioned words, and the red streaks in his brown eyes, left her unmoved. There was no answering thrill in her.

Then he said, "I've startled you. I should have held my horses for three weeks, and then approached you. That is what I could have done, only you might have left Luniette hurriedly, or others might have cut in ahead of me in your affection." And then he laughed mirthlessly. "As you've probably found out, I was born under an impatient star."

Anabel stifled a yawn. Robert's was a wearing kind of personality, and after a couple of hours in his company Anabel felt as limp as a rag. Happily Robert left the inn early, and gave clumsy advice to Anabel that she should go to bed at once.

And Anabel thought, 'Robert's leaving early in the hope that I shall be in bed before Tim comes in. If Tim were not here, Robert would have remained until midnight.' Perversely, Anabel said, "I shall go very soon."

"Go now."

And though Anabel nodded, she had no intention of following Robert's advice. When he had gone, not feeling inclined to read any more tonight, Anabel looked about for recreation to recover from Robert's prolonged visit. She was conscious of a growing excitement at the thought of her coming absurd adventure with Tim.

It was after eleven, and the bar was empty and the hotel quiet for the night. Mabel had flitted out from the kitchen like a ghost while Anabel was seeing Robert off at the door — and now the passage and kitchens were in darkness, the back door closed, and Mabel gone home.

Anabel went over to the cottage piano which Mrs. Groom had begged her to use whenever she liked, saying that it was tuned regularly, but that the notes were stiff because no one ever played the instrument. It had a fretwork front which revealed a lining of pleated rose-coloured silk and ornate oxidised candle-arms with pink candles. In a spirit of extravagance Anabel lit the candles, then sat down on the revolving stool, and raising the lid, sat for a few moments with her hands folded in her lap, wondering what she should play — then ran pliable fingers gently over the notes.

Anabel was not a great musician, and the piece she chose was simple and more in keeping with a harpsichord than a piano — a little old-world French melody, a morceau that had once been played at the court of Louis XIV.

And as she played, someone came softly into the room.

Anabel thought it was Mrs. Groom, to see if all was well before retiring for the night, and she called out absently, "It will be quite all right, Mrs. Groom, I'll lock up."

There was no answer — only silence, and a protesting squeak from a weak floorboard near the door as some heavy weight passed over it.

Then suddenly — unexpectedly — a pair of hands, with long fingers of a steely quality, were placed lightly over Anabel's eyes.

"It's not Mrs. G. Guess who?" cried a gay voice.

Anabel stopped playing with a crash, instinctively raising her hands to remove the pressure on her eyes — but the alien hands were removed. "That's too easy," she flashed, and twirled around on the stool to face Tim.

"You knew my voice."

Anabel grinned. "Oh, you — Tim!"

"Right first go. And now what shall I give you for forfeit —" Tim broke off. It was as though he saw Anabel, the woman, for the first time. He cried out, "By Jove, how beautiful you are in that thing! I had no idea you paid for dressing like this."

"Thanks," said Anabel tartly.

There was a strange note in Tim's deep tones, and clearly he meant so much more than the perfunctory words he used. Anabel was familiar with that note in Paul's tenor voice, and hearing it again coming from a new friend disturbed her profoundly. She was not afraid of herself, only disturbed, and not a little puzzled at her reactions.

She thought, 'When Robert praised my dress, I didn't feel a thing. Why should I do so now?'

Tim put his head on one side and studied Anabel through narrowed eyelids. "You're like — moonlight." He stooped and fingered the soft stuff of the skirt, his touch lingering. "Is it French? How lovely it feels — so soft, like the downy feathers of a fledgling." And then he let go and stood upright, smiling down into Anabel's eyes. "And as smooth and soft as a girl's skin."

So they remained looking at each other for a few moments.

Then suddenly Tim walked over to the fireplace. "You're a disturbing creature, Anabel. Do go on playing. I felt so soothed when I came in and heard you playing that little French minuet."

"Shan't I disturb Mrs. Groom?"

"I don't think that need worry you. Mrs. G. sleeps at the back of the house, looking on to the yard. I doubt if she could hear any music being played outside her room for the noise within it — because she snores like a pig." Tim laughed gracelessly from his vantage point on the hearthrug.

So, reassured, Anabel played several haunting airs and presently was aware that all was silent behind her.

Having come to the end of her repertoire, Anabel turned to look at Tim again, and saw him seated in her favourite armchair with his legs crossed, one hand, holding his unlit pipe, hanging over the arm of the chair, the other covering his eyes and shading the upper part of his face.

Tim broke the silence, saying quietly, "Thank you, Anabel, that was charming."

She closed the piano and rose, and crossing to the hearth stood in front of him, and Tim removed his hand to look at her.

There was a faraway look in his eyes, which Anabel guessed had been called forth by the sentimental music — thoughts in which she had no part.

But Tim exerted himself to be sociable, and asked, "Any visitors tonight?"

"Yes."

"The Smiths?"

"Only one — Robert."

"Ah! And did you play to him?" And Tim slipped his pipe into his jacket pocket.

"No." How school-girlish Anabel felt she sounded: yes — no — when there were so many words she might use.

"I'm glad. I couldn't bear to think Robert had sat here — perhaps in this very chair — and watched you play so charmingly."

Tim's tone was purposely light, and Anabel had the feeling that he was concealing irritability with an effort. But she might have been over-sensitive or even wrong, for Tim's next words were ordinary enough.

"I've been meaning to ask you, Anabel," he said, "but Smith remarked yesterday that the people at your former hotel at Bettycombe talked about you as an important personage. Should I know you? You aren't by any chance an actress?"

Tim's words were so wide of the truth, and her own feelings so correspondingly relieved, that Anabel laughed heartily. "Do I look as though I could act?"

Tim studied her from the crown of her soft, mouse-coloured hair to her blue, satin-covered toes, then said briefly, "I think you could act to deceive — if you were so minded. Who are you, Anabel?"

"Nobody much," was the reply. Robert had translated her dress in terms of money; but Tim was not so much concerned with money as to how she had acquired the dress.

"That's not giving anything away. I suppose you think me cheeky. Aren't you even a rich little good girl?" he said ironically, but she knew from Tim's tone that he did not think her actually rich — only used to spending money, which was an entirely different thing.

Anabel turned away from him and looked into the fire, and Tim only glimpsed her in quarter-profile. "Not your idea of riches, I am afraid," she said, and knew that she was purposely deceiving Tim — for Anabel knew full well that her idea of riches was far bigger than his.

"You won't tell, eh?"

"There's nothing to tell — really."

Tim addressed the white wood-ash on the hearth. "Righto! I understand. I'm an inquisitive brute, and I deserved that snub — but I honestly wanted to know. Sorry."

He was unprepared for Anabel's passionate outburst, especially as she had seemed so quiet and pliable. She turned to face him and cried out in a tortured kind of way, "What does it matter to you whether I'm poor or rich — or what I am? Are you going to like me more or less if I say I am an actress? Must I conform to some standard in womanhood which you have set up as your ideal? Because I won't. I'll be myself, and if you don't like me as I am, and for what I say, then you can lump it."

Tim stared in amazement. He leaned forward in his chair. "My dear girl! Don't be so upset about a simple question. I don't give a damn who you are. I like you just as you are, even without the trimmings of this dress, though I must repeat they're jolly attractive trimmings. But when you know me, if we ever get that far while you're on the island, you'll find out I'm the kind of chap who sets value on what people are, not what they have."

Anabel looked a little ashamed of herself, but she faced Tim bravely, though she was still breathing hard with emotion. "You sounded as if you were just being curious about me, belittling me in some way — poking fun at my manner."

"Belittling! I belittle you! Why, Anabel, what can I have said or done to give you such a false impression of what I do think about you? I'm a tactless chap, a bit blunt perhaps, but I admire you immensely. And in that dress I think you're a perfectly gorgeous person. In fact, I'm so impressed with your loveliness I'm speechless and clumsy. Nothing is further from my mind than poking fun at you."

He had risen as he spoke, and now stood facing her, looking earnestly down at her distressed face.

While Tim looked, it seemed as though light came to him, for he said in an ordinary voice, tinged with kindly feeling, "I know what's the matter with you. Smith has been harrying your nerves. I don't know what there is about that chap, but he's only got to enter a room and the peaceful atmosphere becomes stormy and electric. One of these days —" his voice grew dark — "I'll take it upon myself to tell him not to come here again if this is the effect it has on you."

Anabel felt distinctly better now. She said, with little trace of her quick anger, "You won't be able to stop him."

"He's a surprisingly strong chap, but I could try." Tim glanced at her keenly and approved of what he saw. Then, raising his sleeve, he looked at his wristwatch. "Time to go," he said. "Will you get a wrap? It isn't cold, but you must cover up that lovely dress. And please change your shoes because the long, coarse grass bordering the churchyard is still damp after the heavy rain."

Anabel went upstairs to carry out Tim's orders, and presently came down again wearing a short hooded cloak of black satin, whose sombreness was relieved by an oyster satin lining.

Tim was waiting for her in the hall, which was warm and shadowy, lit by the small wall lamp from above, and watched her approach down the stairs in silence.

"Does Mrs. Groom know we shall be out?" Anabel inquired.

"No, and she won't be any the wiser unless you tell her."

They turned to the inn door, which was closed for the night, and for some reason — the lateness of the hour; the sense of adventure before them; or Anabel's outburst, which had somehow increased Tim's interest in her — there was a new intimacy between them. It was as though they had turned a difficult corner in friendship's lane, and now at this late hour of night the two crept forward like conspirators.

Tim opened the door carefully, letting in the cool night air. "Feeling creepy?" he inquired softly, standing aside for Anabel to go out.

"Not with you — only terribly excited," was the whispered reply, as Anabel passed him, leaving behind her on the still air a whiff of the subtle-smelling perfume she used.

"What's the name of your scent?" Tim asked, closing the door quietly and catching up with her, as she moved slowly along the lane.

"There isn't a name, only a number."

"It's French."

"I bought it in Paris."

"Oh, so you've been to Paris."

Anabel could have pinched herself for giving so much away. "Yes, when I was very young."

"Well, you're not much more than a child now. And I know you can be gay."

It was not a dark night, for the moon was shining, and the lamp in the lighthouse made light and shadow on land and sea as it revolved. But picking up her skirts, Anabel stumbled, and it seemed natural after that for Tim to take her arm and guide her over strange places.

Everything was very still around them. The sea was a rhythmic murmur, breaking on the pebbly shore with the rustle of tissue-paper. Crickets chirruped in warm corners, and a bat hurled itself silently about their heads, swooping with terrifying swiftness.

The cottages were in darkness, hidden in the thick shadows of elm trees; a black cat, disturbed in its prowling among the grass at the side of the lane, rushed across their path, and Anabel made an involuntary movement closer to Tim.

He laughed lightly at her timidity, and she said, with some reproach in her tone, "I believe you are staging an atmosphere."

"On my honour, no."

They had reached the first yew tree which grew in the corner of the churchyard.

"Here we are. There's no necessity to go into the churchyard. We can sit on this low wall and watch."

Subconsciously Anabel lowered her voice. "Shall we have to wait long?"

"I dunno. I've never tried it before."

"But you said you had seen them?"

"Only because I happened to be passing when they were about. I came tonight to prove what a sceptic you are — and perhaps to renew your faith in fairies."

Now they parted, and sat sideways, facing each other on the old stone wall of the churchyard, their heads turned towards the grim dark shadows among the old gravestones.

"This is eerie," Anabel shivered, feeling the need of talking.

"And you don't like it!"

"Not especially."

"Well, don't talk. It will soon be over. Ssh! Keep your eyes fixed on that row of long grass mounds."

"Oh, Tim — they're graves!" Anabel's voice was shocked.

"Yes?"

"One doesn't associate fairies with graves."

Tim's eyes went to Anabel's face. It was white and warm in the grey light. "These aren't real fairies," he explained tenderly, "only something we see which may take the forms of little people."

They did not speak for a while, only watched from the shadows, and more than once Anabel shivered apprehensively.

Then suddenly, as she was staring obediently and unblinkingly at the row of dark mounds lying within a few yards of the wall on which they sat, Anabel saw what appeared to be an opalescent wisp of smoke curling upwards above a grave. It was perhaps a foot long, and parts of it seemed to disintegrate from the main wisp, which writhed like a luminous snake, and took on fantastic and ever-changing forms, and disappeared into the atmosphere. Anabel held her breath. She was frightened and excited, her heart thumping noisily in her breast, and there was a drumming sound in her ears. It was hard to believe her eyes.

Still staring, spellbound, fascinated, and feeling sick, Anabel saw other fragments of luminous mist rising from the graves, wreathing into strange shapes, some of which seemed human, and others monstrous and grotesque — and then flicker into nothingness.

And now Anabel was genuinely frightened. Her one need was for human companionship, to touch something warm and real.

Hardly realizing what she was doing, with one convulsive movement she left her perch on the wall and flung herself at Tim, into the circle of his arms held out to meet her.

From this safe vantage point, with round, popping eyes, Anabel turned once more to look at the strange fantastic spectacle in the churchyard which was glowing with a greeny, spectral light. Night dew settled on the grass, and the moon sailed high in the heavens, so that it shone through the yew trees, dappling the graves with a shadow pattern, as of long clawing dark fingers stretching over them — all of which lent colour to Anabel's vivid imagination that living people were about her.

Suddenly the silent churchyard seemed alive with flickering pale, yellowy-green quivering mist which dissolved into shapes, wriggling tirelessly and disappearing. Then new luminosities appeared, twisting tortuously, merging into one another — separating — disintegrating — pale ghosts of light in a damp old churchyard by the sea.

"It's like a madhouse," Anabel whispered in Tim's ear, and he held her closer to him as though silently telling her not to be afraid, while she stared fascinated at the weird, uncanny sight.

One grave in the centre remained in darkness, and passing her tongue over dry lips Anabel asked in a shaking whisper why this was.

"Because the dust in that grave has been there so much longer than in the others," was the quiet reply, "or perhaps there's a slab of concrete below the grass."

Anabel realized then what was happening, and wondered why she had not thought of it before — and some of her fear went. "It's phosphorus from bones, isn't it?"

"Yes, I thought you would have tumbled to it. But I must say this is a fine example of phosphorescence. One could almost see to read here."

"Somehow I never thought of phosphorescence, though I've seen it before on the water at sea during a voyage. But this does look like little people dancing."

"Aha! I remember seeing this phenomena in a churchyard in the Isle of Wight, where my father held a living, when I was a boy. I was frightened until I got used to seeing this sort of thing…"

So they talked for a while in whispers until Anabel grew suddenly alert, and looked about her.

"What's the matter?" asked Tim.

"I heard a noise."

"I didn't. It's your nerves."

"No, I distinctly heard a rustling sound."

"Then it's that black cat again. We're in for a spell of good luck."

But Anabel shuddered. "Let's go back," she suggested, and then realized with a queer thrill that Tim's arms were about her, and why she felt so safe, warm and comfortable.

Still holding her, Tim slid from the wall — and stood looking down into her white face and big eyes, and the dark outline of her lips. And suddenly, he did not want to let her go. "You're adorable, Anabel," said Tim huskily, and held her closer. "Such a little thing, and so frightened!" And swiftly, without further warning, Tim bent his head and kissed her cheek lightly.

"Don't, Tim."

"Don't?" he repeated in a shaky voice. Then, before Anabel could stop him, he had seized her tightly, and bending her back kissed her again, not on her cheek, but with swift, fierce passion on her mouth.

At first, Anabel tried to pull away from Tim, and then as instinctively to push him away from her, but his arms were about her like steel bands, and she was powerless against their strength.

Directly Tim's seeking lips had found her mouth, his hard, possessive kisses roused an answering passion within Anabel, and instead of struggling, she allowed herself to be carried away by emotion.

Her last clear thought was what did anything matter? Surely this was what love with Paul would have been like — only Paul had seemed more gentle than this man.

Last night — when had she thought it? — that the lovely things of life were not now for her? And yet here she was enjoying them.

And Tim was whispering in her ear — disjointed murmurs — the loveliest names — Anabel felt limp with emotion...

It was the moon that disturbed them. It shone in limpid golden shafts through the branches of the trees and beamed on their faces.

With a little cry, Anabel woke from her trance, and Tim stirred, loosening his arms so that they stood apart, looking at each other in a dazed kind of way.

Anabel saw not Paul's face which had been with her in this lovely dream, but Tim's. She remembered everything then, and in her disappointment spoke harshly. "Is this why you brought me out, to play upon my nerves with those silly spooks, so that you might kiss me?" she asked.

Tim had let her go, and was now leaning against the churchyard wall. He panted a little as though he had been running and was out of breath, but he did not speak, only watched Anabel rearrange the hood of her cloak which had gone awry when he held her in his arms. His blue eyes were like glass, and his manner dazed.

"Good sport, wasn't it?" cried Anabel, so hurt herself that she wanted to sting Tim too. "You'll have some fine yarns to spin to your messmates on a winter evening up at the camp — or in the bar — when I'm gone —"

A puzzled look crept into Tim's eyes, and he moved suddenly like a man awakening from a dream, then paused as Anabel continued:

"Well, that goes for me too. I shall boast about you to my friends when I go back to London." She, too, was panting as though running a race, but Anabel's emotion was chiefly anger — and she was forced to stop for breath to continue her tirade against this silent man.

Then Tim spoke, and his voice was languid and tired, but still rich and throaty with passion. "That's always assuming, my darling Anabel, that you will be in London and I shall be on Luniette."

"I'm not your darling," she snapped.

"You were just now."

"Well, anyway, I don't know what you mean."

"I don't quite know myself, yet, but surely there is a possibility we might take compassion on each other's loneliness and be together — in the winter."

"Is that a proposal?"

"Oh, lord, no! — I haven't got that far."

Anabel sighed audibly with relief. "How silly you are! As if I could remain a winter on Luniette."

"In my saner moments I know I shall call myself silly, too. As you say, it is unthinkable."

Anabel frowned. Was Tim poking fun at her? She could never be quite sure whether he were laughing or serious.

Tim straightened. "This is a queer spot to make love," he said laughingly.

"You chose it," Anabel replied stiffly.

"One doesn't 'choose' in love. I couldn't help myself," he pointed out. "Anyway, let's get back." He glanced at his wristwatch. "By Jove! We've been out here an hour."

They walked swiftly and in silence down to the hotel.

"Don't forget to lock up," Anabel advised shortly as they crossed the threshold of the inn.

"Oh, nobody locks a door on Luniette," was the light reply.

Anabel swept past him, brushing so close that a fold of her cloak caught on his hand, and was pulled from her shoulders. She turned to seize it, but Tim, swift to catch any opportunity, seized her hand in his.

"Not really angry, Anabel?" he asked softly.

But Anabel was deaf to this new wistfulness in Tim. She regarded him as Paul's usurper. Tim had taken something that belonged to Paul. Anabel quite forgot that Paul had long ago willingly forfeited any rights to her love.

So she replied tersely, not looking at Tim, "Terribly angry," and drew away her hand, and threw her cloak over her arm — and somehow, suddenly, she felt quite cold.

"I see." Tim let her go then, and she went upstairs, flinging a quick "goodnight" over her shoulder.

"But you did promise me a handsome apology, Anabel. You owed me something," said Tim, coming to the bottom of the stairs.

"I don't," Anabel said sharply.

"Oh, not now. You've paid the debt. We're quits — and — it was very nice." With a hand on the newel post, Tim watched her go.

At the turn of the staircase, Anabel turned and saw him staring upwards. She had a queer impulse to chase down the stairs again, throw herself into his arms and let him kiss her again. But the impulse went.

Tim might laugh at her. And obviously he couldn't be serious even about love.

So Anabel paused long enough for him to realize that she was not smiling 'goodnight', then to emphasize her feelings towards him she tossed her head with what she hoped looked like haughty disdain, and ran the remaining few stairs to the landing, and so to her room.

By the candlelight, Anabel saw with dismay that the bottom of her dress was wet and bedraggled, and the lovely blue was marred with ugly grass stains.

'I've ruined my dress,' Anabel thought furiously. 'And how on earth can I explain it to Mrs. Groom? Either she or Mabel will spot what has happened the next time they visit my wardrobe.'

Anabel sat on the bed and gave herself up to gloomy thoughts. Ten to one somebody had been awake in one of the cottages, and spotted her and Tim at the churchyard. There would be a fine island scandal.

'It was a crazy thing to do. I wish I hadn't gone,' she thought.

Yet if Anabel had not gone out into the moonlit night, she would not have known what it was to lie within the shelter of Tim's strong arms and feel his passionate kisses on her mouth.

If — if — if one small thing leading inevitably to another, all following Fate's immutable finger in one direction, towards fulfilment — to love. Only a few weeks ago, in terrible mental trouble, feeling that her heart was irrevocably broken, Anabel had renounced all thought of ever being happy again. Yet, now — tonight — at Tim's first kiss, a sweet unreasoning happiness had stolen over her, making Paul's memory dim, and her love for him a pretence. Anabel pursued her thoughts. 'I know exactly how narrow-minded these people can be. Just because I was out with Tim at midnight and he kissed me, they'll expect us to marry. As if I care what they think. Why, I shouldn't dream of marrying Tim.'

Anabel's eyes then widened suddenly.

A girl mightn't want Tim for a dream-husband because he was hardly of the stuff that dreams are made of, but she might do worse than have him for a real one.

It certainly was an idea.

Anabel felt more cheerful as she kicked off her shoes and began to undress.

'I'll make it all up to Tim tomorrow,' she thought, not quite clear as to what was to be made up.

CHAPTER 12

Something happened the next day which made Anabel decide to forget the episode in the churchyard and that she must never see Tim alone again.

The following morning, feeling washed out after a sleepless night, Anabel, like a criminal, visited the scene of last night's crime.

The churchyard looked a calm and peaceful resting-place in the golden warmth of the morning sun, while the graves, which had seemed so alive in the moonlight, were just ordinary long, slender, low grass-covered mounds, such as are seen in any churchyard. The centre mound of grass, which Tim had said was dead, seemed as innocuous as the rest, only perhaps a little more sunken into the ground.

The parson, opening up his church for the day, saw the slim figure in the pink cotton dress contemplating the graves, and came along the gravel path to speak to her.

Having introduced himself, and hiding his natural curiosity at the somewhat incongruous sight of a lovely smiling girl looking at his tombstones, he said, "We heard you were at the inn, and my sister means to call on you today."

He did not add that gossip was rife around Anabel's attractive personality, and that some of it had penetrated to the Vicarage.

His was a kind, intelligent face, and Anabel was drawn to tell him what she had seen in his churchyard last night, and they had an interesting chat.

While talking to the parson, Anabel caught sight of Naomi watching her from the other side of the wall.

With an apologetic, "There is Naomi Smith," to the parson, she broke off to call, "Hallo, Naomi."

There was no reply, only at the sound of Anabel's voice Naomi ran away towards the hotel.

'What an odd girl!' Anabel thought indulgently.

The parson's eyes followed Naomi, and there was a contemplative look in their serene blue depths, but, of course, he said nothing.

With a faint shrug of her shoulders at Naomi's queer behaviour, Anabel continued to chat to the parson, who offered to show this visitor to Luniette over the church, and extended a future invitation to take her over to the 'big' house of the owner of the island, which was shut up because the family was not in residence at the moment.

Later, Anabel walked up the lane towards Bella Luce, not with the intention of going anywhere near the farm, but having no choice for a walk without following in Naomi's footsteps and meeting the girl, something Anabel felt queerly reluctant to do this morning.

With the sun shining warmly upon her, Anabel struck off the stony, beaten track, across the gorse-patched ground, to a high bluff eastwards, again disturbing the flock of fat sheep she suspected belonged to the Bella Luce farm. They, as with one mind, at Anabel's approach, broke into a headlong gallop down towards the churchyard, kicking the stones with a clattering sound as they went. Then for no apparent reason they swept at an angle to the sea.

'They'll destroy themselves, like the Gadarene swine,' thought Anabel anxiously, surprised how nervous she was at the thought of conflict with the Smith family. 'And Mrs. Smith will take a delight in sending me the bill, which will probably be so big I shall have to pass it on to Father to pay.'

But the sheep had no mind for self-destruction. Indeed, they were sure-footed beasts, and having galloped madly around they came to a standstill near some gorse bushes, and quietly began to graze.

Beneath the bluff, which proved to be a large rock overhanging a slate platform, which in spring was a nesting-place for certain sea-birds, Anabel found a clean, shady spot, and sat down with her back resting against a granite and slate rock, with legs outstretched before her, to contemplate the boundless blue sea, which, with the lavender-coloured horizon of mainland coastline, filled the picture about her — and think.

It was a golden-blue morning, and there were many ships of all kinds — tramps, coasters, colliers, banana and oil boats — passing up and down the Channel, and coming towards Luniette, looking like a duck swimming hurriedly on placid water, Anabel espied the pleasure paddle-steamer on a trip from Bettycombe, with a wide white wake in her rear. From this height and distance she did not look like a real ship, but a child's pretty toy on a greeny-blue lagoon.

Gradually the scene lost its consciousness for Anabel, but she still continued to stare at the sea, though with her mind on other things. She tried to analyse the thrill of happiness that had been surging, with ever-increasing power, in her heart since Tim had kissed her in the night. And there was no need to wonder why the sky was such a heavenly blue, or the sea green, or that the sun seemed to shine with more golden warmth than ever before. Anabel was so happy suddenly in her heart that everything in life appeared roseate and lovely, and nothing ugly. There was a lightness and gaiety of spirit which she found disturbing, and which she had never known before — and all because of this new rich emotion in her heart which confused thought and made her long for Tim with a strength that surprised herself.

Anabel was not sure whether this was love. She only knew that this was the first time in her life a man's kisses had found an echoing answer in her soul — not even Paul had moved her so — Paul to whom she had once been engaged, and who had meant so much to her. She realized now there had always been a certain part of her heart which Paul had never touched, a corner that was shut off, kept in reserve, as it were.

Now everything in her heart had gone out to Tim.

It was not her doing. Anabel was the pawn of Fate, and had been powerless to control the feelings which had rushed over her, swamping all other considerations, like a mighty tide in flood.

Anabel did not at this stage consider how deep were Tim's feelings for her. He was attracted to her, and that was sufficient to satisfy for the moment. For herself, all she wanted in life was to be near Tim, to talk to him and hear his merry laugh.

And when with Tim, Anabel forgot about Paul.

It was lovely sitting in the warmth, half-listening to the dash, break and splash of water against the rocks below the steep cliff, and letting her mind drift idly on Tim.

Anabel was annoyed when Naomi rudely disturbed her solitude.

"It's no use your trying to avoid me," began Naomi stormily, breathing hard from rushing uphill. "I watched you coming here and followed you."

Anabel withdrew her gaze from the sea, and contemplated Naomi's clouded face instead, and her manner was one of icy immobility for a while. Then she said with some spirit, "I wasn't trying to avoid you, and I don't like being followed. I came up here to get some peace, but it seems I was mistaken."

"Why do *you* want quiet?" said Naomi roughly.

Anabel paused, before she advised coldly, "It would do you good, my child, if *you* sought a little peace. For a girl who lives in a back-woods island like this, and who should have sound nerves, yours are in a shocking state."

"We'll leave my nerves out of this." Naomi glanced down at Anabel, glad that she had shaken the latter's pleasant outlook on life.

Anabel shrugged. "They're yours, of course."

Naomi's face was angrier-looking than ever. She had not rushed at breakneck pace up the hillside to talk about nerves. She came to the point at once, in a bald way, without any finesse, which gave away her extreme youth, making her seem childish. "I suppose you think it a fine thing to settle yourself on Luniette, where you are not wanted, and try to upset everybody on the island? That would be so like a town lady — to make fun of the natives, enjoy herself at our expense, take anything good that's going, greedily and with both hands, and spoil everything for *me*."

Anabel wanted to advise this ill-mannered, scornful girl to shut up and go away — and leave people to their dreams. But she guessed why Naomi was so rude. The girl was jealous. And Anabel well knew what evil thoughts jealousy aroused in the mind because she had been through such a mill herself, and the remembrance made her tolerant.

Anabel knew, too, that this thing which was worrying Naomi and spoiling her nature, and which had come between them like a black cloud, would have to be faced, so she said quietly, "I don't think I'm unwanted, and I certainly don't wish to upset you or anyone — and no one has ever before accused me of greediness. By spoiling everything, I suppose you are referring to your friendship with Tim?"

Naomi was surprised at Anabel's pointed words. She had not expected them, but it did not alter what she meant to say. "Yes," she replied sharply, nor realized how sharp was her voice, or how ugly she was with her face so expressive of storm. "You've been talking to Tim about me — gossiping, backbiting —"

Naomi gasped when Anabel cut in coolly, "I only said you were rather young to be played with, that you couldn't possibly understand —"

"There, you *are* trying to spoil things. You admit it. And I know why. You don't particularly want Tim for yourself, but he's someone to amuse you, while, of course, it is a fine thing to take him away from me."

"Don't be silly, Naomi. I'm not out for amusement on Luniette. And when I told Tim you were young and inexperienced with men, I wasn't thinking of myself, honestly I wasn't. I was thinking of you."

"Then don't. I can do my own thinking. I'm not so young I don't know my way about. You may not know it, but there are far more men than girls on Luniette. And —" triumphantly — "if you weren't amusing yourself with Tim in the churchyard last night, what were you doing? Answer me that." Naomi screamed in temper, and some gulls skimming about screamed too.

A strange silence followed Naomi's words.

Anabel had not been able to suppress a start of astonishment, which she tried to cover up by leaning forward and pretending to take a closer interest in the steamer nearing the island to give herself a chance to think. A clear thought streaked through the sudden confusion in her mind that both the Smiths had a singular aptitude for intruding on one's private life, and discussing intimate subjects as though they were public commodities and not something sacred.

Of course, Anabel could have refused to say another word and leave Naomi to think what she liked about the position, an attitude that would not have surprised Naomi in the least, for she was well aware that because of her youth and stormy personality most people were afraid of her, and so she got away with things which no other girl would have cared to voice. But now Anabel was curious to find out exactly what Naomi did know, and asked as calmly as possible, "Did you see us in the churchyard?"

"I was watching you," Naomi said angrily.

Anabel sat bolt upright. "Why?" she demanded crisply.

Naomi studied her rival with hard eyes. "Goodness knows why I trouble to tell you. But when Robert came home yesterday, he was full of how wonderful you looked in a blue dress. He knew you weren't wearing it for his benefit. So I guessed you had put it on to impress Tim, and I went down to see."

"You were out at midnight?"

"After midnight. But I meant to surprise you. You wouldn't expect to see me then."

"Did your mother know?"

Naomi glared down at Anabel. "I told her this morning," she replied curtly.

"Oh! Well, if she doesn't mind your being out so late, I mustn't." Anabel sighed wearily. "Well, go on," she said in a resigned voice. "Let's hear it all, and perhaps when it is off your chest you'll feel better."

"I got as far as the churchyard, and —" Naomi struggled for breath, then cried in a strangled kind of voice — "I saw you in Tim's arms."

Anabel stifled an exclamation. 'Tim's arms.' The very words made her thrill. Then she said with scorn, "And you took a ringside seat and stayed to watch the performance. How nice for you! And I wonder how many other people on Luniette couldn't sleep, and, hearing voices in the night, peeped from behind their curtains to get a glimpse of what you saw."

"I don't know about the others — and you can believe me or not, but once I'd seen you standing close to him, with Tim's arms about you, I was so utterly miserable I went home. I wished I could die."

Anabel *did* believe Naomi. She was indeed thankful that Naomi had not seen Tim kiss her; and if Naomi were not so blind with anger, surely she must tumble to the fact that kisses would be the natural sequence to a girl being in Tim's arms — or any man's arms.

Presently Anabel said, "It was unlike you to leave Tim to me."

"I know that now. I should have stayed. But you shan't take Tim away from me."

"My dear child, have you ever had Tim?" And Anabel held her breath.

Naomi talked wildly for five minutes, then she said to Anabel, "You like him, don't you?"

"Of course I do — who doesn't? Tim's a likable man."

"But I love him!" Naomi cried dramatically. "That's all the difference. I love Tim."

Anabel said nothing, because she could not think of anything to say. She contemplated her brown antelope shoes, which, stretched out before her, were in her line of vision, and there was an unaccustomed mist before her eyes.

But Naomi noticed nothing unusual in the silence, and she went on passionately, "How long are you going to stay here?"

"I don't know."

"A month?"

"How can I say?" Anabel was purposely vague.

"Why don't you go away?"

"Why should I?"

After a little while, Naomi said cuttingly, "Of course, Anabel Robinson is not bound to time because life is one long holiday for her. The things that rule ordinary people's lives don't count with her. I bet you're relying on your father's wealth to win Tim over to your side."

It was the one thing Anabel, after her experience with Paul, was afraid of: that Tim would learn she was richer than most girls, and turn from her on the threshold of love. She looked searchingly up at Naomi's face, hoping that this angry girl would never realize what a loaded weapon she held.

Naomi, smart enough at most times, was too angry to be clear-minded, and had twisted her knowledge to suit her furious mood.

"You don't seem to have nice ideas about Tim," Anabel said presently.

"Oh, shut up, you make me sick!"

"Sorry; who told you about me?" Anabel's voice quavered.

"I don't know," Naomi replied impatiently. Then, "I saw your picture in some rag of a paper —"

"Oh! Did Robert see it too?"

"No, he's not interested in social things, though he would have been if I'd shown him *your* picture." Then, as though hating herself for explaining that much, Naomi continued fiercely, "But if you think I'm going to be a press agent for you and broadcast to Luniette who you are, you've got another guess coming. I'm not out to paint a pretty picture of *you*."

"No, I suppose not."

An imperceptible silence ensued.

Then Anabel made a swift pact with Naomi. She said, "I don't want you to tell a soul — in fact, if you give me your word to keep this to yourself, I'll promise to give you a clear field to improve your friendship with Tim."

It was sheer sacrifice for Anabel to leave Tim in Naomi's hands, even for a few days. Yet, if Naomi talked, it would mean losing Tim forever. It was the best idea that occurred to Anabel just then.

Naomi sat down beside Anabel. "D'you mean that?" she demanded.

Anabel nodded.

"For how long?"

"Shall we say three days? It should be long enough for you to find out how Tim feels about you. Remember, you'd known him for months before I came." Three long days without Tim! Anabel felt like crying out against Fate. If only Naomi didn't exist; how simple everything would be.

"Why are you doing this for me?" Naomi asked suspiciously. "What's the snag?"

Anabel could not say, 'I already know what Tim thinks about you, Naomi Smith.' Instead she shrugged, "Oh, so that you can't say I haven't played fair."

Yet there was something more behind all this which Anabel could not tell Naomi. Everything in life was changed suddenly since last night, and Anabel realized she must have time not only to prove her own feelings for Tim, to see if this time it were real love or only a strong passing affection for an attractive man. If she were not to be hurt again after her experience with Paul, she must proceed cautiously. Then, too, Anabel had not forgotten that Tim had spoken of a previous time, and obviously it would be madness to fall in love with a man who had remarked less than two days ago that he was so disappointed in love he would never trust another woman again. And after those problems were settled to their satisfaction, there would still be the hurdle of the Robinson money, which confronted Anabel like an evil thing ever since her trouble with Paul. Sometime Tim would have to be told — and how would he take it? Would his love be strong enough to bear out his creed of liking people for what they were instead of for what they had? Would Tim throw her over as Paul had done so easily, and perhaps turn to Naomi, who made no secret of wanting him?

Would all this thinking take three long days, during which Naomi would be doing her best to win over Tim? Either one loved or one didn't love. If the former, then shouldn't everything arrange itself without hours of wretched thinking? For after all, what does anything matter so long as a girl is with the man she loves? All the thinking in the world couldn't alter things, because all thought was just the trimming to the fact of being in love — a state that happened.

In sudden fear that a three-day wait would be so much waste of precious time, Anabel turned suddenly from staring unseeingly at the sea to recall the promise she had made to Naomi — but never spoke.

For Naomi was sitting back on her heels, picking pieces out of the face of the rock, and looking so childish in her mischief that Anabel began to laugh.

"What's so funny?" Naomi asked stiffly, pausing nervously.

"You — us. What on earth is all our squabbling about?" For surely there could be no choice for Tim between Anabel the woman and Naomi, who was such a child?

Naomi regarded Anabel's hilarity sourly. "You're hysterical," she said.

"Even that might be excused," laughed Anabel.

But in spite of her amusement, Anabel was tired of being with Naomi, in whose presence there could be no real relaxation, and who made her feel so weary, and scrambled to her feet.

"I'm going down to watch the trippers being carried in," she said, and was delighted when there was no answering enthusiasm to see the trippers in Naomi's face.

Having gained her point, Naomi found she had nothing further to say to Anabel, except to repeat, "Don't forget your promise?"

The two girls came out from the shelter of the rock and began to walk in opposite directions.

Anabel called out over her shoulder, not stopping in her downward stride, "If you come down this evening, you can see Tim alone." Her voice was thin in the morning air, and sounded unlike herself, and Anabel felt a queer tug at her heartstrings for being ready to hand over Tim so easily.

"Hey, what'll you do?"

"I've no idea, but enjoy yourself while you've got the chance," was the laconic reply.

"You bet I will." Naomi's voice was almost amicable.

Anabel turned then to look at Naomi, who had paused on the hillside, a brilliant figure with the morning breeze blowing through her black curls and whipping her short skirt against her legs.

Anabel waved and turned around again, and walking fast reached the beach.

The trippers had landed, and in small groups, gazing about them curiously, scattered slowly inland. Some people were already seated on the rocks above Mouse Point, eating sandwiches from packets of food they had brought with them.

'Did I look like that?' thought Anabel, feeling like a true islander when she looked at these 'landlubber-bumpkins'.

Dai, with his peaked cap between his knees, the top of his head bare and shining as a billiard ball, with a fringe of ragged grey wisps of hair outlining the crown, was busy counting out the money he had made carrying trippers pick-a-back to shore. The old man looked up as Anabel approached him across the shingle, a toothless smile broadening his rugged face, an ingenuous look in his blue eyes.

"I was just thinkin' about you, miss. The barometer's rising proper, and the weather's right for a nice sail. If you'd care to come out along o' me this afternoon — well, I'd be glad to take 'ee." He spoke tentatively, his eyes, dreamy and innocent, bent on the girl.

Anabel rose to the bait, just as Dai hoped and expected she would do. "I am longing for a sail. I'll be down at two," she said.

That did not suit Dai, who was loth to lose money over the trippers returning to the steamer, and he objected, with the freedom of old age, and perhaps a little of the cupidity of a 'Taffy Welshman', "I won't be starting until the visitors have gone home. That'll be half past two. We'll have time for a couple of hours' sail afore dusk."

Anabel agreed. Time didn't count much on Luniette. "And tea?" she asked.

"Better bring lots of 'tay', because the sea'll make you hungry; and sun glasses, or the glare on the water will give you a headache, and you won't enjoy your trip and want to go again," ordered Dai wisely.

So in the afternoon, when the trippers had gone, and the peace of a siesta in the tropics had descended on sun-baked Luniette, Anabel went for a sail with Dai in a sea which was a

235

mirrored blue expanse, with no more movement in the bay than in a pond.

"It'll be fresh enough for you when we get round t'Point," said Dai, busying himself with the sail ropes while Anabel took the tiller. "If you'll set a south-west course, miss," he said; he pointed his finger like a compass, and watched Anabel's wrist work carefully, observing how she twisted the boat's course to catch every scrap of wind in the sail.

And presently, satisfied that she was no novice at the helm, he sat in the cockpit beside her, alert as a man like Dai must ever be in a boat, yet relaxed, too, because he could give an order and know that Anabel would understand and obey.

They rounded the headland in fine style, tacking to south, then sailing back in their tracks. It was fresher, as Dai had predicted, with an oily swell sweeping in from the Atlantic. Waves dashing against the west coast of Luniette, which acted as a barrier to the Channel, were wild, strong and loud as they stormed the granite barren cliffs.

Anabel felt refreshed. She forgot Paul, Naomi and Tim — looking long at the high, inaccessible coastline.

She had a good view of the scene of her mishap that first day on Luniette, and saw, by the sheer fall below the ledge, where she had landed after her fall, how nearly she had escaped death. For there was no hold or platform under the ledge in the hard face of granite from which Robert had so coolly rescued her, and cruel jagged rocks like sharp teeth stuck out of the foaming seas forever beating the cliffs.

Struck by the way Anabel handled his boat, Dai became friendlily disposed towards his passenger. He was a gregarious soul, though naturally suspicious of strangers, and dearly loved a gossip with his cronies. For old age is as grey as the hairs on its head, and can be a lonely time. But this afternoon he opened up.

"Is your father a sailor?"

"Oh no."

"He's a landlubber?"

"Yes." And because she knew it meant little to Dai, Anabel added, "He's by way of being a financier."

"Oh, I know a chap who was a pigeon fancier once, and a tidy bit of money he made out of it. Well, tell your dad to come to Luniette. I'll teach him to sail." Dai took some lugworms from an old tin can, and tearing bits of them apart with his unfeeling, gnarled fingers, he fixed a line which floated behind the boat. "Perhaps we'll catch a few mackerel for breakfast. You'll like that."

Mrs. Groom had provided Anabel with enough tea for four people, and Dai and Anabel ate heartily before returning home from N.W. Point, sailing skilfully among the islets and submerged unnamed rocks littering the sea, shrieked at as interlopers by the birds resting on the rocks.

Now Anabel knew where the Hen and Chicken Reefs were — the Gannets and the Seals.

Smoke came from a spot behind the high cliffs.

"That be the kitchen fire up at Bella Luce," said Dai. "Keziah, her be lighting up for t'night."

It was Dai who spotted someone looking at them through glasses.

"That's the Navy look-out," he grinned, and did not say if he knew which particular unit in the Navy was looking out, but Anabel felt uncomfortable under his merry look and flushed.

"Is there anything that escapes notice on this island, Dai?" she asked, half impatiently.

"I guess not. This be a small world on Luniette of its own when the smallest thing calls for remark. And living on an island is something like being in a ship, and a chap is trained to watch for signs."

Then Dai laughed again, making a hideous cackle of sound so that Anabel did not pursue the question further, but said there was something on the end of the fishing line.

They caught a dozen mackerel.

"It's getting towards the end of the season now," said Dai, taking out his jack-knife and slitting and cleaning the fish expertly, then carefully putting them into the shade, out of the sun. "But there's some nice flat fish swimmin' about near t'bottom of the sea."

Then Dai opened up still more, and told Anabel yarns of long ago, of the smugglers that once infested the Channel coast and Luniette, and the ghost of the Moriscos that was said to haunt the island.

By the time he was on the flood tide of his reminiscences it was early evening, when the heat was going out of the sun, and the sky in the west was a glory of pink and lemon — and the boat entered the bay, and they were home again.

Anabel helped to pull the boat up the beach, conscious now that her head, if clear, was aching badly. Having paid Dai generously, and given him the whole of their catch, she returned slowly to the hotel.

Here she saw Mabel loitering with Joe, and sent a message to Mrs. Groom that she had a bad headache and was going to bed and must not be disturbed.

'This headache is timely,' Annabel thought, as she hurried past the open door of the bar which seemed packed with people all talking and laughing at once, with a resultant ear-splitting din. 'It'll give me an excuse not to see Tim tonight.'

Her heart felt heavy at the blank evening which stretched like an eternity before her.

'I have got it badly,' she admitted ruefully, as she shut her bedroom door.

Try as she would, she could not stop thinking about Tim for long.

'It has been a perfect afternoon,' she decided as she undressed, 'or it would have been, if Tim were there too.'

There was an emptiness about everything, a queer ache in her heart which vied with the throbbing pain in her head, which nothing seemed to alleviate — not even the aspirins she took before creeping thankfully between the cool sheets.

For a while she lay, alternately shivering and burning with fever, in a world of pain, when her mind thought of every rich kind of food which made her feel more squeamish inside than ever.

But later, when the room was filled with grey light, Anabel woke from a deep stupor feeling much better. Through the open windows came the sound of voices — Naomi's light childish accents, then Robert's voice with its soft, west-country burr — and then Tim's deep tones. It gave Anabel a queer sense of peace to hear Tim's voice. It was as though he were closer to her than in the garden of the hotel, as if he were holding her hand.

Presently the bedroom door opened, and Mrs. Groom came into the room, carrying a tea-tray and some thin slices of toast in a rack. She put the tray down on the bedside table, and looked commiseratingly down into Anabel's pain-darkened eyes. "How are you feeling, miss?"

"Oh, much better, thanks."

"Then drink this tay while it's hot, and try to eat a bit of toast." And Mrs. Groom continued sepulchrally, "I blame Dai for this, taking you out on such a hot day, too. He's a camel, that old man, thinking only of his pocket —"

"Don't blame Dai," said Anabel weakly, unable to repress a smile at Dai being miscalled a camel. "I loved my day, and I shall go again soon… Besides, I like Dai, he amuses me with his yarns —"

"I know — and aren't they endless, starting from the time of Noah, then to the storm on Galilee with the Sankey and Moody hymn, 'Pull for the shore, sailor', and *then* Dai tells you all about the 'Wreck of the Hesperus', as if everybody didn't know that — and after all that comes the windjammer stories of how Dai rounded the Horn seven times — and oh, Lor', how sick I am of those tales!"

Anabel opened her eyes in astonishment, expecting to see the glum Mrs. Groom laughing at Dai's yarns, but the landlady's face was as set and melancholy as ever. "Now, my Alf," she was beginning, when Naomi's laughter rose rudely above Mrs. Groom's voice, and she stopped talking with an exclamation of annoyance. "What a noise! There's that Smith girl carrying on something disgraceful downstairs, in the bar and in the garden. What is her up to, I can't think."

Mrs. Groom, with that lightness of movement which often goes with a buxom figure, crossed over to the window and closed it with a bang.

"Now perhaps you'll be able to enjoy a cup of tay," she decided, moving about the room, picking up Anabel's garments which she had shed and left lying about, and folding them neatly on a chair.

"I was to give you messages from the two gentlemen," she went on as she worked. "'You're to hurry up and get well', and, 'Poor little thing! Tell her, Mrs. G., to stay put and rest.' I'm to see you take some aspirin, and make the room dark."

Mrs. Groom left it to Anabel to decide which man had sent each message, though it was easy to detect from her tone where her sympathies lay.

Anabel quickly forgot Robert's message, but she thought, 'Dear Tim, how thoughtful he is.'

Mrs. Groom had finished her tasks and came to stand beside the bed, saying confidentially, "Miss Naomi's looking as black as thunder down in the bar, and nearly turning my beer sour, snapping and snarling at the boys like a little toy dog. She's getting herself disliked with those heavy frowns, and that nasty laughter which sends shivers down your spine to hear it. Scowls and discontent sit ill on a girl's face. If she were mine I'd spank a bit of that nonsense out of her, but Mrs. Smith can be hard enough on everyone, but she's too soft over Naomi. There —" as Anabel closed her eyes wearily — "I'm talking too much. I won't say 'goodnight', miss. I won't be free to say that until we close down for the night."

Much later, when it was quite dark, and the Smiths had gone home, the hotel was quiet and the loquacious Mrs. Groom had gone for the night, Anabel got out of bed. Wrapping herself in a warm dressing-gown she went over to the window, and opening it wide again, sat down to enjoy the air, which was heavy with the smell of salt and seaweed, and the wrack that lies damp upon a beach when the tide is running out.

Anabel looked out at the moonlit beauty of the sea, a serene study of light and dark shadows in velvet and silver. Over beyond Mouse Point was a pale, glowing reflection of light cast over the waters by the stationary lower lamp of the lighthouse; while its revolving upper light threw a periodic beam of gold athwart sea and island.

It was a clear night and the visibility was perfect.

Big ships and little ships were going up or down the Channel. Some of the lighthouse lamps on the south coast could be seen flashing gold dots on the grey horizon — flashing and then disappearing. The glorious beauty of the sea beneath twinkling stars and a large quiet moon was not without its effect on Anabel's spirit.

Anabel had given her word to Naomi to keep out of Tim's way for three days, and possibly for that very reason he was always more or less in her thoughts — while, of course, tonight, with the big romantic moon sailing high up in the heavens, Tim's picture filled Anabel's mind.

CHAPTER 13

Mrs. Groom insisted that Anabel should breakfast in bed next morning, and being a woman who liked to cosset young people, she enjoyed bringing in the tray herself, though as a sop to her pride as mistress of the hotel, Mabel had to carry the tray to the door of Anabel's bedroom, when Mrs. Groom, with a high-priestess look, took it in.

"What with you being so ill and all last night, I forgot to mention, miss, that the Rev. Mr. Henable's sister called to see you yesterday afternoon, and left this note for you which I was to be sure to deliver," she said, taking a letter from her apron pocket and handing it to Anabel.

To Mrs. Groom's secret joy, Anabel opened the letter at once. It ran:

Dear Miss Robinson,

As your stay on Luniette is so short, I shall be so glad if you will waive ceremony, and come to supper with the Vicar and myself tomorrow, Friday, about six o'clock. Do come, as it is such a pleasure for us to meet someone from the mainland who can tell us what is happening in the big world outside this small island — happenings which, I fear, do not bode well for our country.

Sincerely yours,
Matilda Henable.

Anabel looked up to see Mrs. Groom's blue eyes fixed avidly on the letter in her hand. Obviously the landlady wished to know what was in the note, and as clearly, by hook or crook, Mrs. Groom meant to read its contents — sooner or later. So

Anabel put her out of mental torment by saying carelessly, "Miss Henable has invited me to supper this evening."

Mrs. Groom nodded her approval. "Supper!" she exclaimed. "That's a polite name for high tea. There's no such thing as supper at the Vicarage. They have a high tea, and Olive washes up and goes home, leaving a bowl of bread and milk for the Vicar to heat up later on. Miss Henable has a glass of hot milk. Well, I'm glad they've asked you to a meal. It shows they want to be friendly. Now you'll feel proper when you go to church on Sunday." Having said so much of the inevitable duty expected of those who lived on Luniette, Mrs. Groom turned her attention to food. "Let me see what you'll have to eat," she said in the absentminded tone of a housewife viewing her larder and arranging the day's menu. "There'll be blackberries and apples for sure, because I saw Miss Henable up on the Downs yesterday with a stick and basket, and Olive mentioned to Olly that there were some fine berries on the hedges; and there'll be soused mackerel, because I saw Dai bargaining with Parson over your catch last night. Friday is the day when Mrs. Smith sends down a bowl of clotted cream for Parson, while I myself told Mabel to take over some cheese I made out of sour milk. So though the fare will be plain it is good, and you won't starve."

Anabel began to eat her breakfast. She said tentatively, "I was going out with Dai again this afternoon —"

"Impossible!" cried Mrs. Groom, aghast at the idea of refusing such an invitation.

"There would be time to do both things. Dai could arrange—"

"No, he might say he'd try just to please you, but he wouldn't keep his word. You'd be sure to pick up another headache — or, worse still, the sun might blister you, and you couldn't go to supper at the Vicarage with a red nose. It would look unseemly, and Parson mightn't think it was the sun. He might blame me." Mrs. Groom changed her tone and beseeched Anabel, "And I want you to go, miss."

Anabel smiled. Apparently this invitation gratified Mrs. Groom in some way. "Very well, but only to please you. I don't want to seem ungracious or ungrateful, and I suppose there'll be lots more good sailing days before I go home."

As Mrs. Groom said afterwards when speaking to her bosom friend, one Winnie, whose husband was postmaster, verger and gravedigger, "Would you believe it, Miss Robinson wasn't going to the Vicarage, and I don't know for why, I'm sure, unless her wanted to be here when Mr. Tim came home. So I made up her mind for her. I don't often put my foot down, as you know, even with my Alf..." Then having digressed somewhat, Mrs. Groom returned to the main theme, "But I says to myself, 'You're going to the Vicarage even if I have to drag you there.' I nearly says, 'You can't treat nobs like that!' Then I remembered Miss Robinson was a nob herself. But being so friendly-like, you forget her's a fine lady, judging by her clothes and what-nots, perhaps finer than we know. And that reminds me: Keziah was telling me the dog, Con, up at Bella Luce was howling his head off last night. Her couldn't hear him, of course, but Mrs. Smith did, and came to Keziah's room and woke her up to go down and give him something t'eat to stop his row. Fancy Mrs. Smith being nervous and all! What is the world coming to? But even she must know it means a death."

After another warm day, which Anabel spent on the rocks, reading and writing letters which could go off by Monday's mailboat, came a cool evening.

When Tim arrived home from work at the camp, his first thought before having a drink was to seek out Mrs. Groom, who for once was not in the bar, but in the kitchen, and ask after Anabel.

"I've been worrying about her all day," he said simply. "I did think of phoning you, but I was afraid Miss Robinson might not like an inquiry going through you." Tim knew that sounded a lame explanation for his real worry about Anabel. He had tried to put the girl out of his mind, but the effort of doing so only made him remember her more.

Mrs. Groom accepted his explanation naturally. She had commented to others that 'Mr. Tim was gone on Miss Robinson'. But she had said the same about Robert.

The question which puzzled everybody was which man Miss Robinson favoured. On Tim's side of the scales was a handsome man in attractive uniform — one who had a way with him. On Robert's side was an equally handsome man with a forceful manner — one who usually managed to get his own way. Bets in the bar were evens.

"Miss Robinson is much better," replied Mrs. Groom emphatically.

"Oh, good! She's up then — downstairs?" Tim glanced towards the closed door of the dining-room.

"Miss Robinson is out — and if you please, sir, she wanted to go sailing again with Dai — as if yesterday afternoon wasn't enough for anybody to stand."

"It would have been foolish," agreed Tim. "Better lay off sitting for hours in a glare until Miss Robinson's got her sea-legs and is acclimatized to Luniette. Where is she, though?" It occurred to Tim that he might stroll out to meet Anabel. "I haven't seen her on the Downs today." And he did not realize he was giving away the fact that he had been looking for Anabel.

"Miss Robinson didn't go to the Downs."

"To Bella Luce?" sharply.

Mrs. Groom made a note of Tim's jealous interest, and later enlarged upon it to Winnie. "No — but Mr. Smith had tea here with Miss Robinson."

"Oh! Here?"

"In the coffee-room."

"And afterwards they went for a walk?" And Tim felt decidedly ill-used. Robert was his own master and could work or not as he pleased, but *he*, Tim, was a servant of the State, and had to obey orders, and follow a routine faithfully.

"Not exactly." Mrs. Groom was enjoying herself keeping Tim in suspense. Then seeing his impatience explained, "But he took Miss Robinson to the Vicarage."

"What on earth for?" demanded Tim.

"Miss Henable invited Miss Robinson to supper tonight — not what I'd call supper but high tea, and I don't honestly believe Parson would call it that either, but Miss Henable, her knows that the word supper looks better on paper than high tea."

Tim was not listening. He was annoyed to think that Anabel had made this engagement without consulting him. She might have known he would be alone. "What time will she be back?" Tim asked, and wondered how on earth he should kill time this evening until he saw Anabel again.

"Miss Robinson didn't say, sir; but I know Parson goes to bed at ten, reg'lar as clockwork, and naturally he'll want to bring Miss Robinson home."

"I see — well, it's all rather annoying, a bit of a washout for the plans I'd made for Miss Robinson's amusement. I'd arranged to take Miss Robinson up the Policeman tonight, on a kind of moonlight picnic, but that's off now."

"Just you two, sir, on that lonely mountain?" asked Mrs. Groom in a shocked tone.

"It's hardly a mountain," corrected Tim. "But I suppose the Smiths would join us. I've already asked a couple of young fellows from my unit to join us, but now I'll have to phone to put them off. I thought of taking up some drinks and celebrating on the Policeman's head —"

"And rolling down into the sea at dawn," added Mrs. Groom acidly.

"Nothing of the sort," said Tim shortly.

What Tim had not planned, but earnestly hoped for, was a lonely walk home with Anabel, and a repetition of what had happened in the churchyard a few nights ago; and this news that Anabel was spending the evening at the Vicarage gave him a feeling of frustration.

Tim had not seen Anabel for two days now, though she had been a good deal in his mind. Yesterday he had determined for the sake of his own peace of mind — because nothing, of course, could come of any flirtation with a girl — to avoid her. But when evening came, and Anabel had not been around to join him in a drink at the bar, Tim changed his mind, and found himself longing to see her.

Last night, when everyone was in bed, he had been tempted to go to her room and talk out this worry that had been in his mind all day, but remembering that she was not well, he had resisted the temptation.

Today, after a wakeful night spent in thinking about Anabel, with her lovely picture always before his mind, he was filled with a bittersweet yearning to see her in the flesh, and perhaps touch her. He had looked forward impatiently to the evening when they would meet at the evening meal. There was an intimacy about sitting at the same table to eat, alone together in the dining-room, which made them seem very close to each other.

Now this unexpected invitation had come for her and Anabel had accepted it, forgetting that he, Tim, would have to eat alone. He would not see Anabel now for three whole days, and that was asking too much of a man who liked girls' society, and Tim felt irritated with his surroundings as he had never done before.

At a loose end now, Tim thought of Naomi, with whom he had quarrelled last night. Both sides had indulged in plain speaking: indeed, while Tim was drinking in the bar it occurred to him to be thankful for not having to be pleasant this evening.

Later, having finished dinner, and smoking a solitary pipe in his favourite chair by the hearth, Tim felt sorry for himself, and welcomed Naomi warmly, though expressing surprise that she should have come.

"Hallo, Naomi!" he called out cheerily. "I didn't expect to see you down after last night, when you told me I was the rudest man you had ever met, and that you would never forgive me. Still hot and thundery? Or have you decided that it doesn't pay?"

Now Naomi had also done some thinking in the meantime. Last night she had made the mistake of thinking that because the Smiths had been yeomen-farmers on Luniette for two generations, they were in a position to rule anyone on the island body and soul. She had been proud, disdainful and overbearing, moods that seemed naturally to suit her best, and which had the effect of subduing any adverse criticism or show of independence.

Naomi was forced to admit that she hadn't cut much ice with Tim, who had poked fun at her. He had been ebullient and overflowing with high spirits which had not somehow rung true; and he had laughed at her and joked about her until Naomi could have screamed with rage. Tonight she was different, having planned to be soft and gentle.

Tim was alone, and that was a piece of good luck, and a portent of good fortune. And she was alone, too, for Robert had returned home soon after tea, in a difficult mood. Naomi guessed either he had not seen Anabel, or if he had their meeting had not gone according to his liking. Though before Naomi reached the hotel, Winnie, who was on her way home after cleaning the church, told her where Anabel was, and with such a malicious smile on her face that Naomi cheerfully wished Winnie's husband would dig a grave and push Winnie in.

So now Naomi knew where Anabel was, why Robert did not come down to the hotel tonight, saying surlily that he had something better to do than stick around the hotel, and most important of all, that Tim would be alone.

In pursuance of her scheme, Naomi answered Tim's banter softly and smilingly. "I've been such a fool, Tim," she sighed.

Tim glanced keenly at her. "I'll say you have, Naomi."

"You know I don't mean to be hot with you—"

"I only know it if you tell me so. It's as well, though, because if I thought you meant it, I'd apply for a ship straight away — anything to leave Luniette at the double."

"Oh, Tim," said Naomi anxiously, "you won't do that?"

"It depends upon your behaviour."

"D'you mean that?"

Tim looked closely at Naomi. "What's the matter? Are you ill?"

"Nothing's the matter; and I'm quite fit, thank you."

"Then what's wrong?"

"What should be?"

"Quit that, Naomi! You know what I mean quite well. You're not yourself."

"But I am. This is the real me."

"Is it?" Tim asked disbelievingly. "I'm delighted to welcome the change. I foresee that we shall get along like a house on fire from now on."

Naomi sidled close up to Tim. "Do I mean even a little to you, Tim?"

Tim's mouth tightened, and he took a step backwards, away from Naomi. Then he put his pipe on the mantelshelf and spoke firmly. "Now, listen, kid. We had all that out last night, and the upshot of it was that you were never going to speak to me again, even if I were the last man in the world. And I told you that sounded good to me — if it held. Apparently it hasn't. I believe as a parting shot, you picked up a stone in the lane outside and threw it at me. Remember?"

Naomi nodded laughingly. "Yes, of course I do, but I didn't hit you."

"Because you are a bad shot, m'dear, and Providence saved not only my eye, but one of Mrs. Groom's windows. One of these days, Naomi, if you are not careful, and you happen to have a gun in your hand when quarrelling with your best-beloved, poor shot as you are, you'll find a bullseye in him — and then what'll happen to you?"

Naomi looked properly forlorn and said demurely, "I've said I'm sorry, Tim."

"I seem to have heard those exact words before, but they are not words that bear repeating too often. But I think you mean them, and so I will accept your apology," Tim said grandly, disquieted at Naomi's changed attitude, and stalling for time, hoping that someone — Tim did not know who — would come into the room and 'break it up'.

Only Mabel answered his 'bachelor prayer', and she was not in uniform, but dressed ready to go home and in a hurry.

Tim sighed as Mabel bustled about the room, then went out banging the door after her. He waved his hand towards the coffee-table, which Mabel had placed on the far side of the hearth from his own favourite chair. "Will you pour out, Naomi?"

She was delighted to do so, left Tim's side, and sat down in Anabel's chair. "It is like old times," Naomi smiled. "Before — " Then she stopped, biting her lip, and opening the lid of the coffee-pot peered into its steaming darkness.

"Yes?" said Tim helpfully, as he sat down opposite Naomi.

"Before Anabel came," Naomi was forced to say, hating herself for so stupidly dragging in Anabel's name.

"'Old times'!" echoed Tim. "D'you know it's only a few days since Anabel joined us, and in a way it seems like eternity." He sighed for no apparent reason — and then, seeing Naomi's dark eyes fixed on his face, laughed, as though afraid of seeming sentimental. "Now there's a chance for you, young Naomi."

Naomi clasped her hands tightly together in her lap. Tim was going to say something to her which she knew would be unpalatable, and she prayed for strength to keep calm. "What do you mean?" she said quietly.

"It just struck me you might do worse than learn something from Anabel while she is here, and take a leaf out of her book."

"How?" Naomi's voice was ominously quiet.

"I don't know — but it seems to me —" Tim was about to enlarge on his phrase when Naomi cut in, and could not keep the tremor of indignation out of her voice.

"What for?"

That Tim should dream Naomi Smith could learn something from Anabel Robinson! The cheek of it! Naomi's heart sank. Had Tim compared her with Anabel already, and found her wanting?

"To improve you, of course."

Naomi shook her head with a suggestion of helplessness which sat ill on her glowing face. "You think Anabel could teach me something?"

"Well, Anabel has poise, and knows how to dress, her manners are easy, and she's invariably kind to people. She's thoughtful, too, and doesn't try to rub people up the wrong way. Anabel —"

But Naomi could bear no more, and forgetting her carefully considered pose, she cried out angrily, "In other words, Anabel's perfect. Go on, say it."

"No, I wouldn't go so far as to say that. Anabel would hate the idea, which wouldn't be true. But —"

Naomi tossed her head. "Well, we can all have this envied poise and look pretty if we have the money to buy nice clothes; and if I lived in London, as I've always wanted, perhaps I'd have the rough corners rubbed off me. I could be thoughtful if I lived with the right people —"

Tim hardly heard her, though the last words made him say impersonally but authoritatively, "Hold hard! Surely one can be thoughtful for others in any state of life? At least, that's what my father used to preach."

Naomi didn't care a rap about Tim's father, or what he preached. Her anger was rising in spite of her efforts to keep it under. Either Tim was teasing her, or — horrible thought — he was in love with Anabel. She said hoarsely, "D'you realize what you're saying?"

"What?"

"You are praising Anabel to me," Naomi reminded angrily.

Tim stared, then he laughed easily, and for a few moments Naomi's worst fears slept. "So I was," said Tim. "It just happened that Anabel came to my mind as the one person who could be of some use to you these days. You meet so few girls of your own age on Luniette."

Naomi exclaimed with annoyance, "But I keep telling you I don't want help. I don't need to be changed, because I am quite satisfied as I am. You see, Tim, the last thing I want is to be a cheap copy of Anabel. You'd be the first person to pick holes if I were. We're entirely different. I can do things your precious Anabel can't — dairy work, ploughing fields and running a farm. These practical things appeal to some people who prefer them to uselessness in girls. Anabel can only sit pretty, say smart things and wear nice clothes, and take holidays without earning them." It was extraordinary the scorn Naomi managed to put into her voice while belittling the absent Anabel in Tim's eyes.

"Shut up, Naomi," Tim advised now. "There's more to Anabel than that, and you jolly well know it. I made a perfectly innocent remark, with the best intentions in the world for you, and this is how you take it."

"I won't shut up, and you can't make me."

"You have a down on Anabel."

"And if I have, it's your fault. I was willing to be friendly with her; I tried hard — but she —"

Tim knew the two girls could have little in common. "Well, don't upset yourself about it. I thought you meant to be nice to me this evening?"

There was a pause. Naomi softened at once, and remembered her good resolutions. She calmed down, and Tim was surprised to find how swiftly her mood changed.

"Why, so I did. I am. It's only that Anabel's name makes me see red."

"Oh, the poor girl!"

After a little while Naomi began, "Tim?"

"Yes?"

"Promise you won't be angry if I ask you something?"

"Go ahead."

"Are you — in love with Anabel?" whispered Naomi.

She was astonished at Tim's vehement reply. "Oh, good lord, no!"

There was a deep silence in the room.

Tim kicked the logs in the hearth, which were already burning brightly, into fiercer flames. Then he turned to Naomi, saying mildly, "And now, if it isn't too lukewarm to drink, perhaps you'll give me a cup of coffee," and he went towards her to fetch his cup.

No sooner had that storm blown over than another came up. This time Naomi, like an evil sprite, called it forth.

Peace must have been proclaimed, for they were chatting easily, drinking second cups of coffee.

Tim was relaxed, and feeling fairly content — or as satisfied as he could be without Anabel. For he was beginning to realize that unless Anabel was before his eyes, and if he did not hear her crystal clear voice, or hear her merry laughter, there was something definitely missing in his day. It was an odd feeling, and he did not like it, but there seemed nothing to be done about it — nothing at all.

And Naomi's curious question, "Are you in love with Anabel?" was disquieting. For, of course, he wasn't in love with Anabel — or any girl. He never could be — now. But it was strange how his mind kept returning to that question. However, just before Naomi broke a long comfortable silence, and spoke in a most confidential tone which made him feel that there was something around the corner he was going to hear, Tim was as nearly at ease as it was possible to be in these worrying times in the world about him.

Naomi said, "I met Winnie tonight." Her voice recalled Tim to the present, to the rather dingy, warm room and to the glowing little face, a study in the lamplight, looking at him across the room from Anabel's chair.

"Winnie!" Tim exclaimed blankly. "Should I know her?" And for the life of him Tim could not place Winnie.

"Winnie is the church cleaner. She sits in the pew by the font on Sundays; and she also lays out the dead. Everyone knows Winnie."

Tim nodded vigorously. He remembered Winnie, a thin woman with a sharp nose, untidy grey hair and a scrawny neck.

He thought, 'No wonder Naomi has such a queer outlook on life. She mixes with such odd people — Keziah, Rube, Carrie — and now this Winnie who apparently knows more about dead people than live ones; who sees their dead as no member of the family does.' And aloud, "They would. Winnie's calling gives her a unique position on Luniette. Goodness knows I'm not a ghoulish man, and I have no liking for Winnie. If she lived in the Middle Ages, they might consider shortening her tongue. If she were a Spaniard in those robust days, I've no doubt the Inquisition would have chopped out the whole of her tongue. You should know better, Naomi, than to listen to Winnie's tales."

"But you hear what's going on through her. She knows what people are talking about."

Tim laughed, wondering where all this was leading, sure that in a few moments he would hear. "And I'm supposed to show curiosity to ask you what they are talking about?"

"Can't you guess?"

"No — unless it's the European situation. Now that should be occupying people's thoughts just now. But this being little insular Luniette, with a nice clean green sea all around it, I suppose the people here are wondering if the storm cone is up at the lighthouse, when the mails may be late; when Mabelle and Joe are going to the altar; how many glasses of beer old Rube put away last night; or how much Dai made over the mackerel he sold to Parson — oh, there are many trifles which might be worrying the heads of the worthy natives, keeping them awake at night. Well, what is the latest gossip, Naomi?"

Afterwards, it came to Tim that subconsciously he must have guessed what the latest gossip was before Naomi repeated it. And his voice must have sharpened quickly, for Naomi looked at him across the hearth with startled round eyes, and Tim was vividly reminded of a stag which he had surprised rooting turnips on Exmoor once.

"Can you take it?" Naomi asked softly.

Tim paused before he said grimly, "Yes, providing it's not about you and me, when I'll go off the deep end."

Naomi sighed, but her eyes were hard and bright, and belied any feeling of softness or self-pity. "It's about Robert —"

"Yes?" said Tim breathlessly, as though he anticipated what was coming.

"And Anabel."

There was a pin-point silence. Tim heard the gentle tick-tock of the clock on the mantelpiece, and it was a quiet timepiece.

"Of course!" Was that his voice? It was like the croaking of a frog. Tim fixed his eyes on Naomi, and drew himself up in his chair, his hands gripping the arms. "Just what are they saying, Naomi?" His very quietness made the words sound dramatic.

"Why, don't you know? That they're in love."

Slowly Tim removed the pipe from his mouth and put it in his jacket pocket. Then he said, "That Robert is in love with Anabel is as plain as my hand. But that Anabel has fallen for Robert! I'll not believe it. Winnie's gossip! Winnie, whose tongue would have been cut out if she'd lived in Spain in the Middle Ages." Tim laughed shortly and bitterly. It was an unhappy sound. Then he said loudly, "And what do *you* think, Naomi?"

And though his expression was much as usual, Tim could not keep the anxiety out of his eyes — something which Naomi saw and caused her heart to turn over in her breast.

"I haven't thought much about it at all," she confessed, feeling more cowardly than she cared to own; and she wished she had not spoken at all. For now Naomi knew that Tim cared for Anabel — not deeply perhaps, as yet, but he was beginning to realize that he was growing fond of the girl.

Tim said, "But you admit you've thought a little."

"Yes."

"And would you mind?"

Naomi hesitated, then replied readily, "Not a bit. It would be a fine thing for Robert to marry. Perhaps then he'd settle down quietly at Bella Luce, and not want to roam abroad as he often says he will now. Besides, the farm needs a younger mistress than Mummy."

But Tim only said, "I can't see Anabel living there. It would seem like being in prison to her."

"What a nasty thing to say! It's a lovely house; Anabel adored it. And Robert's so crazy about Anabel he'd do anything in the shape of redecorating and refurnishing to please her."

It took a little while for Tim to think this out. Then he rose and went over to the window overlooking the sea, and stared out at the grey waste of water, and the pale moon rising to turn the colourless Channel into silver, and found inspiration there.

For presently he whirled around to confront Naomi, who seemed to have shrunk into a forlorn heap in a corner of the big chair, and he laughed gently — and even happily, like a man relieved of a load of care.

"Naomi," he began, "if you don't mind Anabel and Robert marrying, why do you show so much dislike towards Anabel?"

Naomi did not meet Tim's eyes. "Because — well, though I think marrying would be good for Robert, I don't think Anabel would fit in with our family, that's all. It might make Robert unhappy."

"A fat lot you'd care."

"He's my brother," Naomi said with dignity.

Tim raised his eyebrows, but made no further comment on that score. "Yet you say it would be a fine thing for Robert to marry?"

"He's got to marry someone, sometime," Naomi cried out with unnecessary emphasis, "and there aren't many girls on Luniette — none that Robert likes. He's always been so difficult to please until now. He loves Anabel."

"So you've said before." Tim stretched himself, then glanced at his wristwatch to see the time, a movement not lost upon Naomi. "D'you know what I think, Naomi?" And without waiting for a reply Tim continued, "That you're a little liar. I'm not saying that Robert isn't crazy about Anabel, for that seems fairly obvious to anyone who isn't blind. But Anabel couldn't be in love with Robert. You wish she were. You are terrified she'll fall for me — perhaps that I will for her. That's right, isn't it?"

But Naomi had quickly uncurled herself, and was on her feet. Tim's remarks, said in a cutting voice — careless or cruel — perhaps both — were meant to hurt. And they were as a whiplash to Naomi, who rushed over to him, and caught his arm, holding it fast. "Oh, Tim, you won't do that! Promise me you won't ever do that!"

But Tim unloosened Naomi's arms roughly. "What a child you are! Surely you know that this love business can't be directed into channels of your choosing? One can't say to one's heart, 'Do this, do that.'" Then more quietly, "Why should I promise you anything, Naomi, you who have only a nuisance value for me tonight?"

Naomi moaned. And she had thought herself so charming, and had meant to behave so well! She looked up at Tim, who was staring at her with hard eyes, and to his horror Tim saw that tears were not far off. "Because —" her voice quavered, as she grimaced in her effort to keep back the tears — "we've been such friends."

Tim said harshly, "You have a strange way of showing your friendship, Naomi. That is the worst of you Smiths. You are your own worst enemies — nothing ordinary is good enough for you. Whether it is friendship or love, you must have sole possession of a man's soul. Are you human, Naomi? Sometimes I feel that you and your brother are a couple of vampires. If so, how could I be expected to have any use for you?"

Naomi did not answer, but hung her head, and Tim had a good view of the crown of her dark head.

Then slowly she raised her face, and he saw that her eyes were swimming with tears, which were running down her cheeks.

Tim was not cruel at heart. He was frustrated by Anabel, and hurt by Naomi, and feeling defenceless before these emotions, which were new to him, had retaliated swiftly — if blindly. But when he saw how his words had hurt Naomi, Tim was stricken afresh with remorse, and quickly relented towards her.

Placing gentle hands on her bowed slender shoulders, Tim said quietly, "As you were! I shouldn't have spoken so roughly. D'you know, I don't think living on Luniette agrees with me. I'm catching Winnie's complaint and growing malicious. There," and now Tim moved his hand and put it gently, if clumsily, on Naomi's dark curls, rumpling her hair affectionately before dropping his hand. "I didn't mean to hurt you to the extent of tears. Do stop crying and smile."

And presently, when Naomi's tears were dried, and they had exchanged friendly, shy smiles, Tim went on, taking himself generously to task. "The trouble with me, Naomi, is that I forget you are growing up. You always seem such a kid to me that I expect you to behave like one, and must be ready to spank you when naughty. Now in a few months' time, when you've really grown up, I shall have to remember to mind my p's and q's, or the mids. from the camp, who will be your friends then, will be out for my blood."

But with almost disquieting passionate intensity, Naomi replied, "It's all my fault. I can be such a beast, letting my temper get the better of me. And don't ever want to be on your best behaviour with me, Tim. Never change, I like you best as you are."

"But that's all wrong," protested Tim. "You must insist upon every man treating you like a princess."

Naomi smiled wanly at his extravagant advice. "And I don't want boys of my own age for friends. They're all so silly, with ideas that seem to jump about in their minds like fleas; and they're so intense about everything because they think it's the grand thing to be to make people notice them. But a girl never knows where she is with them."

Tim looked down at Naomi, and his eyes were very kind, so much so that Naomi had to look away again quickly to save herself bursting into tears.

"You're wonderful, Tim," she said in a low voice.

Tim stood still for a while looking at her, searching for something deeply felt to say. But, "I'm hanged if I see why you say that, Naomi," was all he said.

When he had taken Naomi up to the head of the valley leading to Bella Luce farm, and watched her run home, a dark pencil of a figure in the moonlight, Tim returned to the hotel feeling inexpressibly sad — not only for himself, but for Naomi, whose life at best was a wretched travesty, with no one to turn to, at least no one who could explain how unwise it was for a girl to allow her heart to be gnawed out by an idea; and Anabel, so beautiful, bright and brave, about whom his thoughts were so confused.

The Vicarage was in darkness, the inmates of the house apparently asleep in bed, and Tim knew that Anabel must be back at the hotel, and hurried home to meet her. He was aware of an odd tugging at his heartstrings which gave him a queer thrill of happiness. It was as though he had been asleep and had suddenly come to life again. Soon he would see Anabel again, when the fret of the evening with Naomi, which had racked his nerves, would be a thing of the past, and he could feel light of heart once more.

Tim's step quickened almost to a run, and he smiled broadly to himself at his own impatience.

At the hotel, too, the place was in darkness, with no friendly yellow glow from the wall-lamp on the stairs. Tim shut the oak door and proceeded slowly and disappointedly to his room, pausing as he saw a thin line of light under Anabel's door and knew that she was awake.

The happy expectation faded from his heart.

'Anabel must have guessed I should have to see Naomi safely home,' he thought. 'She might have waited for me.'

CHAPTER 14

When Dai and Anabel launched the former's yawl the following afternoon, to go for a sail, other hands — brown, lean and with amazing strength in their grip, came unexpectedly to help them, and their task was made much easier. And as this happened, Robert's voice said, "May I go with you? I promise to work my passage."

Anabel turned her head quickly, and her first feeling was one of dismay, for surely Robert's disturbing presence would spoil the afternoon's enjoyment? It was in her mind to say Robert could not go with them, but directly she saw how he was dressed, in a pair of old grey flannel trousers tucked into half-sea boots, and a navy sweater with a fisherman's collar, she knew that Robert's question was perfunctory, and by way of appeasement to Dai, who hated idle landlubbers in his boat. Robert meant to go sailing with them in Dai's boat.

So Anabel made the best of things by saying, "Come, if you're good."

"I'm always good when with you."

Anabel made no reply.

Dai grumbled. "Two's company," he said. "I haven't enough bait for three to fish, and there's no tay for you."

"Ungracious pig!" said Robert in a low tone to Anabel. "Dai's afraid he'll have to take me out for nothing, that he'll not get more than his share of a 'dish of tay', and he'll have to share the catch with me — because I'm not unselfish like you, and shall demand my fish."

Softly as Robert spoke, Dai heard him. "I'm a-goin' to be paid passage money for you, though I expect you to lend a hand," he paused to say dourly, and it was evident that Dai had no liking for Robert.

"And so you shall be — overpaid," agreed the young man in an agreeable tone. "Now let's get a move on, or if we start arguing we'll miss the tide."

So the three sailed out into the bay, which was from five to twelve fathoms deep, where big ships could anchor, and rounding Mouse Point went down-channel towards the western horizon lying in a pearly-lavender haze.

Robert's skill in handling a boat was quickly evident; he seemed to know by instinct what should be done.

Dai had moved for'ard, so that the yawl would sail easier, and to bring her up to the wind — and, too, he had to shift the foresail.

This arrangement was to Dai's liking, for he could not bear Robert. The old man took out his jack-knife and a plug of tobacco, and cutting off a wedge put the juicy morsel into his mouth, and settled himself with his back to the young people. They sat close together in the cockpit. Anabel, as helmswoman, sat, of course, on the weather side of the helm, and talked to Robert. It was a perfect afternoon for a sail, with the sun hot and strong in the blue heavens and a freshening breeze to temper its heat, while the yawl skimmed lightly through the green water. At first they spoke of Dai's boat and discussed sailing, but when they had settled down, Robert, tiring of this, talked of personal things.

"You're twice the girl you were when you landed on Luniette," he said admiringly.

"D'you mean I've doubled my weight?" asked Anabel in mock alarm.

"I was thinking of your looks," Robert smiled, and stared at Anabel so boldly that she felt the colour deepening in her cheeks.

"Don't," she said at last, turning her head away from his ardent gaze.

"A cat can look at a queen!"

"You embarrass me."

"Don't let it. Try to think of my enjoyment in wondering how long those lashes shading your glorious blue eyes are, and the pleasure it gives me to count the freckles on your nose, and —"

"Oh, stop, Robert! I'm not used to compliments."

"Aren't you? But you love admiration — all girls do."

Robert was in such good form that Anabel inquired, "Is this a birthday treat for you?"

"Mine or yours?"

"It isn't mine, but — you sound so gay. I've never known you in such a frivolous mood. I thought it *must* be a feast day."

"Every day is a fiesta for me when with you," Robert cried extravagantly, but with an underlying fervour that gave a note of grimness to his gaiety, which was more like the Robert Smith Anabel knew. "I'm gay because I am happy."

Anabel remarked, "It has taken little enough to make you happy."

"Well, here's a boat, which I love to sail, and a nice girl like you. We're good friends now, with perhaps the promise of a deeper friendship —" And Robert's voice was soft with intimacy, and he put his head close to hers, as though determined not to let Dai hear what he was saying.

Anabel stared, fascinated by the fiery, untamed look in Robert's brown eyes, but she was repelled too, and pushed her back hard against the edge of the cockpit to get away from

Robert — but it was of no avail, for he seemed to follow her until his brown face was within a few inches of hers.

Then Dai's voice rose in a protesting roar. "Up helm, miss," he shouted. "Look what's bearing down on us."

As he spoke, a ship's hooter rent the peace of the afternoon.

Anabel obeyed Dai immediately. Robert instinctively put a hand over hers on the tiller, and leant forward to attend to the mainsail with his other hand.

Anabel saw a deeply-laden tramp pass close to them, and caught sight of laughing faces of some of the crew who had lined the rails to look down at the yawl.

"What the plague are you two talking about?" Dai asked angrily, as the tramp passed up-channel. "Do you expect me to have eyes at the back of my head to see if you're doing your duty? Remember, the Lord only gave me one pair of hands." And he spat into the swell of the sea. Nobody answered him, but presently, when Anabel and Robert relaxed, the latter began to laugh, and because she had never seen Robert laugh so heartily before, Anabel joined in too.

It seemed as though Robert, too, had come to the conclusion that violent tactics led him nowhere; and like his sister he had changed his technique, and seemingly with more success, for Anabel apparently liked his company. Robert knew, although Naomi had not told him why, that Anabel and Tim had not met for days, and that was a big contributing factor to his lightness of heart today.

Robert also gained by Anabel's change of heart. When her heart was empty, and soured after her experience with Paul, Anabel had been critical of all men, but there was a warm feeling within her these days, and she saw goodness in everyone — even Robert.

The yawl passed close to a tanker from Panama, coming into port, and all three waved to the officers standing on the bridge aft.

Then they sailed past a buoy, and at once seemed to be amongst sailing craft which looked like a fleet of swallows, skimming about on the surface of the water, putting about round the buoy, jockeying for position in the race for home.

Dai said they were competing in the Luvelly Regatta which was taking place that afternoon. Robert and Dai had a heated argument about the handicaps of the craft engaged in the race, while Anabel spread the tea. After tea, Dai put out the lines, and after an hour's fishing drew in the lines and counted the catch — fourteen mackerel and seven other kinds of fish, including a dog fish which Robert caught over the side, and which put up a great fight before it was killed.

Dai divided the fish into three lots. He accepted Anabel's offer that he should have her share, but refused vehemently Robert's easy, "You can have mine, too."

"I don't want your fish." And listening to the old man's decided tones, Anabel felt uncomfortable.

Foolishly, Robert persisted in trying to force the fish upon Dai. "Why won't you take them, Dai? The fish are all out of the Channel, and there's nothing to choose between any of them."

"They belong to you," was the stubborn reply.

"That doesn't make them poisonous."

"Perhaps — and perhaps not —"

"Well, if you don't want them, chuck them back into the sea," was Robert's careless retort.

He would have liked to look well in Anabel's eyes, and this stupid old man would not allow it.

To Robert's and Anabel's amazement, Dai scooped the dead fish back into the sea, where the gulls swooped down upon them.

Then Dai got out his mop and swabbed the deck viciously, and without looking at either of his passengers took out his jack-knife and began to chop off the heads of the fish that were left, talking to himself, saying he was going to "cut out their guts".

"That's what Dai thinks of me, and Heaven knows what I've done to deserve it," said Robert, grinning at Anabel, and whistling gaily, to show he did not care. But Robert did care. And as he smiled Anabel saw his pointed, strong white teeth, with the gums bared, and Robert's face was like the mask of a wolf, and she shuddered. "Cold?" asked Robert at once.

"If anything I'm too warm."

"Then someone is walking over your grave."

"Oh, I hope not. I don't want to die just yet."

"Who said anything about dying?"

"But I haven't decided where my grave shall be."

"It might be on Luniette."

"Silly, of course not. I shall be leaving Luniette soon and —"

Robert said more earnestly than the occasion warranted, "Supposing you settled on the island? You might do worse than be married in the church there, and life —"

"Oh, no —" Then Anabel paused abruptly, for it had occurred to her that Robert was growing serious again, and she edged further away from him.

Dai had finished cleaning the fish. The deck was swabbed again, and Dai had gone for'ard.

Anabel wished that Dai did not dislike Robert so much, and would talk to them occasionally, and not leave her so much alone with this strange, ardent man. Alternatively she wished that the men would change places for a while.

But Dai stubbornly refused to be friendly. His manner had been strained all the afternoon, and he had shown plainly that it made him unhappy to have Robert aboard.

Apparently Robert wanted to be friendly, for he asked Dai once, "You didn't find your boat any the worse for her adventure with me the other night?"

"No, nothing was wrong," replied Dai slowly, and Anabel saw that the old man's eyes, though fierce, were troubled. "Only the atmosphere wasn't right, as if an evil spirit had been aboard."

Anabel turned away sharply, and looked over her side at the green sea, and tried hard not to listen to what was being said.

Seeing her distress, Robert said lightly, "Oh, Dai's an old sailor and chock full of superstition. If a boat shows signs of strain, then it's an evil spirit in man's shape that is aboard."

Anabel was thankful when Dai decided to turn for home.

And so, with the setting sun behind them, they steered for Luniette, a grey-green hump of land lying athwart the Channel.

But the afternoon, though from a weather point of view, glorious, was not the success Anabel's first outing had been. It seemed to Anabel that Dai's manner with her was short, as though he blamed her for Robert being with them. As if anyone had the power to stop Robert doing anything once he had made up his mind.

The hours at sea had one beautiful moment, however, which remained in Anabel's memory for a long while afterwards.

It was when they had turned to go home, with the evening west wind behind them, and the pace was quickened. There was the tang of salt in the air and on the lips. Robert had broken into song, the chorus of "Rolling Home":

"Rolling home, rolling home, rolling home across the sea: Rolling home to dear old England, rolling home, dear land, to thee."

And it seemed as though Dai, his mind returning to the palmy days of sail when he served before the mast, could not stop himself joining in. His voice was old and cracked, and he sang out of tune, but the timing was good — and for a few precious moments there was the fellowship of the sea in the little yawl that marked the pleasantest time of the day.

Ahead of them stretched Luniette, acting as a breakwater to the Channel, with its high, inaccessible cliffs, with Mount Policeman rising like a pyramidal cone from its heart. Astern came a couple of sea-going ships, with the pilots aboard, and overhauling them fast. To starboard, towards Luvelly, were the white sails of yachts — white wings on a green sea. The sound of the sea dashing against the rocks of Luniette could be heard like the distant rumble of thunder.

The yawl rounded Mouse Point and entered the bay, where there was the peace of early evening.

Dai and Robert were busy with the sails, the former giving Anabel orders from time to time. Then Robert went below to switch on the engine, and Anabel looked ahead, saw Tim on the beach, and her heart gave a great leap of joy.

Tim was evidently waiting for them to come in, for as they approached the shore he came to the frothing edge of the sea to meet them, and cupping his hands to his mouth called out in a cheery voice, "Had a nice afternoon?"

"Grand," replied Anabel, because no one else answered. A queer excitement swept over her as she watched Tim's tall figure, so that unconsciously she jumped to her feet and waved her hand, and never had Tim's presence seemed more welcome than at that moment on the beach on Luniette.

Dai spoke, but Anabel never knew what he said, only she heard the note of relief in his voice and guessed that Dai, too, was glad to be back.

And presently, as the yawl struck the shingle, Anabel, pleasantly tired, and assisted by Dai and Robert, who held the bows secure, made a flying jump to the beach, where Tim caught her neatly. Anabel quickly regained her equilibrium, and talked animatedly to Tim about the trip, but Robert, at sight of his rival, had drawn his accustomed saturnine reserve around him like a cloak. He did not speak much, only helped Dai drag the boat well clear of the tide; then, drawing a handful of money from his pocket, Robert asked the old man what was owing.

Dai had a queer maxim in his dealings with his fellowmen. He only rooked the people he liked. Men like Robert, who Dai disliked, could always be assured of a square deal.

Meanwhile Tim was saying to Anabel, "I had no idea Smith was going out with you today."

"Did you know I was sailing at all?"

"Yes, because Dai told me."

"Oh, and since when has Dai to report to you about my movements?"

"Always, where your safety is concerned," was the reply, the laugh that went with the words robbing them of any deep meaning.

But the quick coolness in Anabel's voice served to remind Tim and her that they had parted on an unfriendly note three days ago. It occurred to Anabel, too, that in keeping with her word given to Naomi, it was not fair to see Tim alone, for Naomi must have a clear field. How to manage this was going to be a puzzle. It was disappointing for her, but this was the third and last day.

It would be difficult for Anabel to pretend she had a headache and retire to her bedroom for the night.

'I've never felt so fit and alive,' she thought.

The Vicarage people had not thought to ask her to supper two nights running, though no doubt such friendly people, given the hint, would have invited Anabel to their house again.

"Glad to see me, Anabel?" Tim was asking. It was only later, when going over those confused moments of their meeting on the beach, that Anabel recalled Tim had spoken seriously, without a trace of laughter in his voice.

"Glad!" she echoed. "Rather! I mean…" And then Anabel frowned, and turning sharply to Robert, who was standing awkwardly behind her shoulder, said, "You will have supper with me tonight, Robert?"

Then, as though aware of the silence that followed her invitation, Anabel glanced sideways at Tim, who had stiffened, and said, "I suppose I should ask you if *you* mind, considering we eat together."

"I don't mind," said Tim quickly, even offhandedly, as though Robert's joining them at supper was a matter of no consequence to him. "In fact, I like visitors — the more the merrier. Only let's get a move on if we want a drink first, because Mrs. G. gives us hot supper on Saturday night."

Robert smiled at Anabel. That was how he liked things done. It pleased him to see Tim's face — a man trying to make the best of a setback.

And so to the hotel, where Anabel went to her room to change for supper.

Dressed in a pink cotton dress, Anabel came out of her bedroom and closed the door, to be confronted by Tim, who had evidently lain in wait for her, and seemed literally to pounce upon her.

Anabel smiled disarmingly, as though she guessed instinctively that their meeting was not to be an agreeable one, but no answering smile lit up Tim's face, which was stern and angry.

He crossed the landing towards Anabel, caught her wrist in a steely grip, as though afraid she might elude his grasp and run downstairs, and asked grimly, "Now just why did you do that to me, Anabel?"

"Do what?"

"Oh, don't pretend to look innocent, I'm in no mood for it. You know quite well what I mean. Why did you ask Smith to supper?"

"Several reasons; don't you want him?"

"You know I don't."

"Then why didn't you say so?"

Tim looked helplessly at Anabel. "I couldn't without being rude."

A glow had filled Anabel's heart at sight of Tim's anger, and she glowed again at his words, which implied that Robert was *de trop*, and Tim wanted her to himself.

But nothing of this secret exultation showed on her face as she said coldly, warming to her subject as she proceeded, "Would it matter if you were rude? It seems to me that no one on this island cares what they say to the Smiths, or how they behave towards them. There is such a thing as being fair, even to the meanest criminal, and surely the Smiths must know how they are treated and resent it."

A little silence followed this championship of the Smiths' cause.

At first Tim had an inclination to laugh at Anabel's defence as at something comic, but swift thought made him seek for a reason behind this sudden change of front. And Tim thought he knew why.

He said angrily, "Oh, so you're on their side! Now just tell me what that man has been saying to you to win you over to his point of view; spinning a long yarn, I'll be bound. As I've warned you —"

Anabel twisted her hand out of Tim's grip. "Robert hasn't spun a yarn. I wouldn't listen if he did. I don't need to be warned against people; I should rely on my intuition."

"Then all I can say is that your instinct has gone to sleep on Luniette," cried Tim angrily, aware that matters were fast getting beyond his control, yet somehow, in this special circumstance, he was powerless to stop them.

Anabel gazed at him steadily. Her voice was even steadier as she told him, "Perhaps; one imagines this island is the kind of place where one could run to seed quickly."

So they faced each other in the twilight and silence of the landing, though from below, through the open door of the bar, came the usual cacophony of sound.

Tim thought Anabel was looking lovely in the simple dress, but he could not appreciate her loveliness tonight, for obviously the dress was worn to impress Robert Smith, who was her guest.

He was not, however, insensible to her appeal. Confused as he was about his own special feelings for Anabel, Tim yet wanted to stand well in her sight. And this quarrelling, which was of his own making just now, and even if he felt justified in every word that was said, got them nowhere. It came to Tim that if he wished to make Anabel hate him, then this might be the right way to make her. So his voice was several degrees softer as he asked, "What's the matter between us, Anabel?"

"Nothing."

Tim refused to let her airy manner upset him farther, and he pursued, "But there is something. I know it. You're so different from the Anabel I knew — or thought I did — less than a week ago." Then, as though he remembered something that had happened between them a long while ago, "I say, you're not holding out on me because of the other night?"

Anabel's fixed stare was almost insolent. "I had forgotten it," she said distinctly and hardly.

Tim winced, but he replied with his usual swiftness, "Then I needn't apologise again, and say I'm sorry for hurting your feelings." He ran impatient fingers through his hair. "But what have I done that you're so changed?"

"I've told you: nothing," Anabel replied woodenly.

"But that isn't true. I must have done something to upset you, however unwillingly. If you'll only be frank and tell me so that I shall know where we stand, and never make the same mistake again. It's so unfair on your part to leave me groping about in the dark."

Anabel shook her head.

Tim did not see that her hands were clenched tightly behind her back. He only saw her looking infinitely young and pathetic, desirable, standing before him like a schoolgirl on the carpet before her headmistress, with her hands clasped behind her, and that fixed look in her big eyes.

He asked, "Then why have you been avoiding me lately?"

"Does it seem like that to you?"

"It certainly does. I'm beginning to think: I say, did you really have a headache the other night?"

"Yes."

"But you fished for that invitation to the Vicarage last night?"

"Oh, no; that came out of the blue."

"Don't tell me Fate arranged it to fit in with some plan of yours?"

Anabel half smiled — a ghastly kind of smile, gone almost before her lips widened to the humour of Tim's question. "Well — yes."

"Thanks," said Tim sarcastically. "And now we come to this evening. You know I have no liking for Smith. Yet you ask him to join us at supper?"

"It is only chance there are no other visitors on Luniette, when we should have separate tables, and could ask whom we liked to eat without inconveniencing anyone."

Tim scarcely heard Anabel. He was pursuing a track of his own. He said, "You've been seeing quite a lot of Smith these last few days. You arranged for him to go sailing with you today."

That was a shot in the dark, and it drew a swift reply.

"That was not my doing. You and Dai can blame me as much as you like, but it won't be true. I was as surprised as Dai when Robert said he was going with us."

The faint pleading note in her voice placated Tim, who said, "When I went down to the shore to meet you coming in, I thought you were pleased to see me, but now — I don't know what to think." Tim did not explain that he had hurried through his work to leave as early as possible so that he could be on the beach to meet Anabel.

"I *was* glad, Tim."

He smiled then, but said seriously, "Then it all points to one thing. You like me, but not well enough to endure my company for a whole evening, so for want of someone else you must needs inflict Smith upon us. Have I got that right?"

Anabel could see no end to this questioning, or rather, she could see the end which by deft questioning and eliminations Tim might reach. So she said with some spirit, "I don't see how I could do less. Please be reasonable. It is true Robert invited himself for a sail, but he did his full share of the work. Dai knows that Robert can handle the boat as well as himself, and so leaves the heavy work to Robert. And even if Robert went up to Bella Luce now supper would probably be over, and it seems so silly sending a man supperless to bed when there is so much food down here."

Tim stared down at Anabel approvingly. "Very prettily said," he commented drily. "But surely all that supposition is Smith's look-out? No doubt, as master of the farm, he can get food from his own larder at any hour. But to ask him here to spoil our evening —"

"That's entirely up to you," Anabel replied laconically, showing little apparent interest in what Tim said. She dared not utter the words that came to her mind, for fear of upsetting Tim further. They were 'Naomi will be down to console you after supper.'

That wouldn't be giving Naomi the promised square deal, for Tim, angry as he was, might well have said, "Oh, hang Naomi!" And he would certainly have cut short any overtures on Naomi's part.

And though Anabel longed to plead with Tim, and smile lovingly at him, and win him over to being on his best behaviour for a couple of hours, for her sake — something she felt sure of being able to do — it was impossible to let Tim see how it was with her.

Then Tim said, "And to crown everything, you've dressed up for Smith."

"What! In this old thing? Why, it's only fit for the rag bag!"

"The colour suits you," admitted Tim morosely, "and it will give Smith a wrong impression of how he stands with you. Is that fair or wise?"

"Anything's fair," flashed Anabel. "As for being wise — I don't want to be too wise."

Tim laughed, but a sigh quickly followed. "I wish I understood you, Anabel."

"Do you? And talking about dressing up: I wore my best dress for your benefit the other night, and ruined it. Now Mrs. Groom's mind is thickly patterned with question marks whenever she opens my wardrobe door and looks at the dress."

Anabel's grin was so friendly that, looking at her, Tim's cross expression softened. He was about to say something more, to make a supreme effort to bridge the gulf that was between them, and establish friendly relations again, but Anabel spoke:

"I really must go down to my guest, or he'll be wondering what has happened to me."

She walked away from Tim, downstairs to Robert, who was waiting for her in the hall.

But there was a dragging feeling in her feet, making them seem tired and heavy, and Anabel thought, 'Does Tim honestly think I want another couple of hours of Robert after having him for a whole afternoon? Does Tim really imagine this is going to be fun for me?'

Robert had washed himself and brushed his hair. "Mabel has been along to see if you are ready to eat," he said when he saw Anabel. "You are to ring the bell when you come down."

Anabel nodded to show that she had heard. It wasn't easy to switch over from talking to Tim, however acrimonious their talk, and be natural with Robert, whom her instinct distrusted. She led the way in silence into the dining-room, and rang the bell as she had been asked to do.

By that time Anabel felt calmer, and able to face Robert, and meet the curious high light that flickered like a smouldering fire in his brown eyes as they rested upon her.

"Will you put some logs on the fire?" she asked. "Mabel sometimes forgets to make it up, and by the time we have finished supper it will be nearly out, and so unwelcome-looking."

Robert bent to do as she asked. "Are we going to sit here after dinner?"

"I wasn't thinking of doing so, but Naomi and Tim will be here."

"Tim's a horse and Naomi isn't used to a fire. Why leave the cosy spots to them?"

"I hope to go out on the cliffs."

Robert grumbled, "I should have thought you'd have had sufficient sea air for one day."

"I have, but I tell myself it would be wise to store for the winter. Remember, I'm a town bird."

"You needn't be," Robert straightened himself to say, looking squarely at her.

Anabel did not reply, only looked out of the window at the sea which was losing its colour in the twilight. Robert turned again to making up the fire, a job he was still doing when Tim entered the room, and at once jumped to the conclusion that Robert was making up the fire for Anabel and himself.

"It's stifling in here," remarked Tim, blowing out his lips in exaggeration at the over-heated room. "I was thinking of opening another window."

"Why not?" Anabel replied brightly. "There is nothing more beautifully extravagant than a huge fire necessitating wide open windows."

"A fire in August is a luxury," said Robert, dusting his hands with his handkerchief.

"It's Mrs. G.'s idea of comfort for her guests," Tim told him.

"Don't you ever have fires in summer at Bella Luce?" asked Anabel, but remembered the dank smell in the farmhouse, and knew that few fires ever warmed the rooms.

"Good gracious, no! And very seldom in winter. Of course, the kitchen fire is always going; but we're usually too busy to sit by fires," Robert said.

"What do you do in the evenings?"

"When work is done, there's supper, and that finished we go to bed," the farmer said simply.

"So that coming down here is the wildest excitement for you," suggested Tim.

Robert paused as though not sure how to take this, and regarded Tim suspiciously; but the latter met his gaze calmly. "I have only indulged in the pastime this summer, and I find it most exciting."

CHAPTER 15

For several reasons Anabel remembered that evening, chiefly because it was tiring keeping a friendly balance between two men so suspicious of each other as Tim and Robert. After the first questionable skirmish before supper, Tim appeared to accept Robert as his guest, too, and played the part of host with such graciousness and tact that Robert's suspicions were increased. As the meal progressed the latter grew more silent and morose than he usually was when Tim was present. And when Robert did speak it was in a dictatorial, hectoring manner well calculated to upset the peace. Anabel pretended that everything was normal and found it a strain to her nerves. It would have been a very insensitive person not to realize Robert's boorish manner, and to know that he was doing his best to pick a quarrel.

Anabel could imagine Tim saying to himself, 'This is indeed an unpleasant fellow. What on earth you see in him, Anabel, beats me.'

Tim allowed nothing to disturb his calm demeanour, and Anabel awarded him full marks for his efforts to make the supper a hospitable and pleasant meal.

Things were a little easier when Naomi, looking like a flamingo in a short white dress with pink stockings and shoes, joined the party. And seeing her vivid young beauty and lovely legs, Anabel realized that this was Naomi's 'test' night with Tim, and he would be a hardened man who could withstand the girl with her fresh, flower-like appeal.

And suddenly Anabel found the room even stuffier than Tim had suggested it was.

It was odd what new feelings Naomi's presence tonight awoke in Anabel's heart. Just to hear the relief in Tim's voice when Naomi came to break up the dull party hurt Anabel. She hated seeing Tim and Naomi together, and called herself every kind of fool for making such a silly pact with this girl who had known Tim for so long, and who had surely enjoyed every advantage for furthering her friendship with him long before a rival's appearance on the scene.

'It's been a hateful meal,' she told herself. 'Robert was heavy weather, and somehow I let him get me down.'

Excusing herself from having coffee, feeling it would choke her, Anabel left the room, and walked out of the hotel onto the cliff where there was fresh air. She sat on some granite stones in full view of the hotel and contemplated the incoming tide. At first she fretted, wondering what Naomi was saying to Tim, and if Tim were enjoying himself.

'I hope he isn't,' Anabel thought uncharitably. 'If I imagined he was…' But here Anabel stopped, and made herself listen to the wash and rustle of water on pebbles, and gradually her nerves became calmer.

Robert joined her, as Anabel expected he might, and sat down beside her. "Are you going to sit here for the rest of the evening?" he asked, and his voice was normal and quiet, as though pressure from his nerves, in the shape of Tim, were removed and he felt free again.

Anabel wanted to tell him to go away, but she had asked him to supper, and it was her duty to be pleasant to him; and then there was Tim's example of good breeding which she tried to copy. She replied, "It's comfortable enough, and I see little enough of such lovely green water in London."

"There's a better spot on the beach, more sheltered from the night air, and not so public as this. We could talk there without being interrupted."

Anabel made no answer, and remained where she was. Robert could never be made to understand that she preferred the sea to being in his company.

"Unless, of course," he said presently, "you don't feel like talking."

"There's nothing much to talk about," Anabel said tiredly. "It soothes me to watch the sea."

A mist had arisen, dimming the moving light of a steamer going slowly into port, and the melancholy sound of warning hooters came regularly across the quiet waters. Clouds had obscured the moon and the night was dark and, except for the wash of tide on the beach, silent.

Robert looked around him at the thickening grey mist. "There'll be a change in the weather tomorrow. We're in for some squalls," he said. And after a long pause he ventured, "I wish you would talk to me, Anabel. Tell me all about yourself — your home, and what you do with yourself."

At first, Anabel was reluctant to talk, then realizing that Robert had shifted his position slightly, and was closer to her, and that his head was turned so that he stared at her, within a few inches of her face, she thought talk might be wiser than keeping silence, and stop him behaving sentimentally, something which would be repugnant to her. So Anabel talked until her mouth was dry and her tongue ached, and at last she fell into silence, too tired even to think clearly, while she hadn't the faintest recollection of what had been said between them.

Robert, who had been listening quietly, threw away the end of his cigarette, and it lay among the scrub like a glow-worm in the darkness. "I wonder if you know how you really appear to others, Anabel?" he said in a low tone, catching her cool fingers in the hard warmth of his hand.

"What do you mean?" Anabel croaked. She shivered and tried to withdraw her imprisoned fingers from the iron clamp of his hold, and without success.

"Shall I tell you what I think?"

"It might be interesting to hear."

Robert half-smiled to himself in the darkness, but he said seriously, "You've painted such a lovely, delicate and attractive picture of your life that I feel rather like a beggar boy looking from the street into a warm, lamplit room; but you seem so terribly lonely and unhappy. I know your father is on the other side of the world, newly married, and with a fresh interest in life in which you cannot share — a young wife, and perhaps children to come … and I do not forget your recent personal affair — but there's something more behind all that."

"Yes?" Anabel was on the defensive. She braced herself for what was coming.

"You are nearly as lonely and unhappy as I am — or was until you came to Luniette." Robert waited, expecting Anabel to give him a lead to go on.

But she was thinking, 'So that is what all this means, telling me how lonely and unhappy I am to emphasize his own wretched state. As if I care.' Anabel felt she could not bear much more of this kind of talk. "Now, Robert," she warned, but spoke too late.

"This is as good a time as any to say what is in my mind, and a fellow couldn't spend an afternoon with you and not feel something in his heart for you."

Anabel thought wearily, 'Oh, dear, now I'm for it!'

Robert continued, "I know I said I wouldn't talk about love; I realize it's an emotion we each approach from opposite angles because our manner of life is different; but I do think my feeling for you is strong enough to make you happy, even if, for a time, you don't lòve me as I do you. If you'd only agree to give me a chance, I'd be content for a bit."

What faith Robert had in himself! What a queer notion he had of his power to attract anything to himself! What a wrong perspective he laboured under of his attraction for women!

Anabel dismissed Robert from her mind with one word. Cheek! Where was Tim, and what was he saying to Naomi? Take herself to task as she would, Anabel could not forget how pretty Naomi was looking tonight, and that Tim liked pretty girls around him.

Robert squeezed her fingers, and Anabel started in fear, and this time managed to wrench her hand from his hold.

"Don't. I hate people pawing me." Then more moderately, "I came to Luniette for the sake of its peace, so that I could forget one man, and need not think of any man — and even here, I cannot find peace or escape men."

"Because you're too good-looking. That attitude is all very well for a short while, whatever its cause, but life — real life for a woman — demands a man in it — and vice versa. Living without the love and companionship of one's opposite number is mere existence; that's why you and I are so unhappy — and why together we could live."

Anabel was tired, and weary of fighting Robert, but she shook her head, saying, "I don't want to think about it."

"Then, later?"

"Later! That could be any time in the future, and I have tried not to look too far ahead —"

But Robert was persistent. He heard the weariness in Anabel's cracked voice, and he was relentless in his pursuit of her, driven by a mad longing to have this lovely girl for himself forever. Robert could see no unsuitability in his proposed plan.

Then out of the fog they heard Tim's voice, with a note in it which sent a wild thrill through Anabel's veins. "Hi, you two! There's a mist rising."

"What of it?" Robert shouted back, resentful of the interruption.

"Anabel's wearing a cotton dress."

"And it's pink. So what?"

"And thin. Savvy? Snap out of it, Anabel, and send the fellow in for a woolly or you'll be in bed tomorrow with pneumonia."

Tim's deep and robust tones gave Anabel fresh heart, and now she did not feel so tired, and the weariness fell from her like a cloak.

She rose, realizing that it was indeed damp, and her dress was clinging to her figure.

Seeing this, Robert was full of remorse. "I could kick myself," he said. "I should have thought —"

"So should I, and as I shall probably be the sufferer, there is no excuse," was Anabel's retort. Her mind was full of questioning. There was no sign of Naomi. Tim was alone, and his manner unruffled; if his nerves had been fretted by Naomi, they were well under control.

Anabel longed to ask questions, but dared not, and she heard with joy the answer to Robert's, "Where is my sister?"

Tim said casually, "Naomi left me ages ago. I believe she went to the Vicarage. At any rate, she said you were to call there for her on your way home."

The three stood for a few minutes in the light of the porch. The bar was in darkness, with a smell of beer, tobacco and sawdust heavy on the atmosphere through the open door.

Tim dismissed Naomi from his mind. He was looking closely at Anabel, and seemed to find some comfort in her neatly-arranged hair and generally calm appearance, for he smiled suddenly down into her eyes, while the look of anxiety in his own faded.

There was a period of squally weather which lasted with heavy hissing showers and bright intervals for several days. Anabel, after a good night's rest, went to church for morning service. Her pact with Naomi was at an end, and Tim had done nothing rash with Naomi, and Anabel felt free again and even happy. Perhaps Fate was at last on her side. Possibly everything she had gone through were as stepping-stones to bringing her and Tim together. The feeling of uncertainty that had been with her for days had disappeared and her mind was at rest, and able to look forward to making her peace with Tim and enjoying his companionship, when everything would have a chance to turn out well for them both.

So she went to church confident in the future and thankful for all her mercies, and joined in the singing, her clear, flute-like voice, which had been well trained by a competent master, rising above the usual chorus of adult and children's voices which made up the choir.

At the close of the service, with the peace of the Sabbath in her heart, Anabel went out into the rain with the congregation.

Waiting under the dripping yew trees, a gaunt, mackintoshed figure, was Mary Smith. With her hair tucked under a close-fitting cap, she looked very like her son.

Anabel, with head bent to the rain, smiled as she passed, and would have hurried on, only the mistress of Bella Luce put a detaining hand on her arm.

"One moment, Miss Robinson." It was not a request but an order, and with resentment in her heart, Anabel stopped.

There followed a spate of words in a low tone which none of the few passers-by could hear. Mrs. Smith told Anabel what she thought of her behaviour, and the way she had wilfully interrupted the routine of farm work at an important time of the year by keeping Robert from his duties.

It was useless for Anabel to protest. Mrs. Smith was implacable.

"I know it means nothing that you have caused me annoyance and unhappiness, but I should wish nothing more than that you leave Luniette at once, so that I can try to remedy the misery your being here has caused."

Anabel would have liked to gain time by saying she did not know what Mrs. Smith meant, but stalling would get her nowhere. Both knew the position well. Naomi wanted Tim, and obviously she could not make him do as she wished and was unhappy, probably venting her mood on her mother. Robert wished to keep her, Anabel, in Luniette as his wife, which was too preposterous an idea to be worthy of serious consideration; but naturally, feeling for her as he did, Robert neglected his work to spend all his time at the hotel.

Anabel resented Mrs. Smith's tone more than her words, and replied frigidly, "This is a free country, Mrs. Smith, and I intend on staying here as long as I please."

"I have no doubt about that. You will remain here just long enough to ruin my children's lives, to undo what I have striven to strengthen in them; and now I do not know what will become of either of them."

Anabel shrugged, as though indifferent to the Smiths' fate.

"But — I shall hold you responsible."

The word 'responsibility' in connection with Naomi and Robert frightened Anabel, and she repudiated it swiftly, in unmistakable terms. "They are grown up, and certainly know their own minds — or they should do so. They're not children to be guided by you and me. Robert and Naomi have got to face life someday, and learn to take what it gives — or does not yield — as we all have."

The spirited reply made Mary Smith realize that this stranger to the island had a will equal to her own, and for once she could neither browbeat nor drive her into submission.

"It's all very easy for you to talk, Miss Robinson. When you go, it will no doubt be with a light heart and a careless smile, such as you wore when you discovered you were marooned on Luniette. You may wish to wipe the dust of Luniette quickly off your shoes, and in the midst of your gay London life forget the people you have left behind, who are suffering because of and through you — but the results of all you have done here will remain long after you have gone, and it is for these things you will have to answer, no matter what you say — that is, of course, if you have any sort of conscience."

"I have done nothing to be afraid of the consequences, Mrs. Smith," Anabel repeated.

"And I say you have. I know. Naomi is at home crying her eyes out. Robert hasn't spoken to me since he came back after seeing you yesterday. How can you stand there and tell me you've done nothing to my children?"

When Mrs. Smith had gone, Anabel was left standing alone near the lich-gate, angry, dumbfounded and not a little bewildered at the attack, with the rain dripping from the trees on to her best hat.

What was this savage attack about? What was she, Anabel, supposed to have done?

'Robert and Naomi must always have their own way, it seems,' Anabel thought wrathfully. 'I've made enough sacrifices for them. I stood aside with Tim to give Naomi a chance; I've been bored by Robert. Surely Naomi must see that Tim doesn't care two hoots about her; as for Robert, I've made it plain I don't like him. Anyway, Mrs. Smith's attack has settled everything nicely for those two as far as I am concerned. Even if Robert were the angel Gabriel himself, and I adored him, I wouldn't take him on with Mrs. Smith as a mother-in-law.'

Through Mrs. Groom, Anabel received an invitation to visit the lighthouse, and as the weather cleared in the afternoon she walked across there.

The head keeper allowed her to look through his powerful glasses, and Anabel was astonished at all she was able to see on sea and land.

She stood for a long while with the glasses trained on Tim's camp, with the faint hope of seeing him when he was not looking at her. And then, with the acrid taste of the morning meeting with Mrs. Smith still in her mouth, Anabel saw Bella Luce at close quarters, and wondered afresh how such a beautiful facade could hide so much wretchedness and misery. And all at once Anabel was sorry for Naomi and Robert as she had never been for anyone in her life, for in both these people was the zest of life, twisted out of recognition for them by a repressive mother and the ugly confines of the house, thwarted as the motif for living has no right to be.

After her visit, and she had waited until a passing squall was over, Anabel walked up to the Devil's Cauldron, anxious to hear again the hollow thunderous roar of imprisoned water behind the Shutter Rock, fascinated by the seething mass of snowy froth that preceded a split second's silence while the water found the level of the clamouring sea outside, and before the next violent surge sent a fresh mass of water into the narrow cove.

Remembering Tim's warning, Anabel approached cautiously, and stood for a long while, unaware of the passing of time, her mind blurred to a kind of dreamy self-consciousness, marvelling at the strength of the rock formation that could hold such a mass of riotous water without being burst asunder.

As she stood, Anabel had a half-hope that, as had happened once before, Tim might see her from his office in one of the huts, and join her. But, except for the crying gulls, whirling suspiciously about her, and other wild cliff birds' cries, and the movement of that imprisoned energy below the cliff top, there was no sign of life about her. Yet there were men in the lighthouse, men in the camps under the hill behind her — life at Bella Luce.

The atmosphere was clean and windy, but redolent of Sunday, for there was a peace which was of the Sabbath about Anabel, when possibly all men were finding repose.

Followed by three white ponies who were grazing in a field, Anabel walked slowly back to the hotel, and had tea in the coffee-room, afterwards finding idle amusement in flicking over the pages of old *Graphic*s, with yellowed pages, depicting 'The Boxer War in China', and 'The Carlist War in Spain', and a double-page lugubrious picture of five shipwrecked mariners at sea in a ship's lifeboat, two of them lying athwart the gunwales having died of madness after drinking seawater.

Turning back to look at the date on the cover, she saw that it had all happened before she was born. And now there was another war in China and a Revolution in Spain. How history was repeating itself! To Anabel's keen disappointment, there was no place laid for Tim at the supper-table, and upon inquiry Mabel informed her that Tim was on duty up at the camp, and wouldn't be down until late.

"They're that busy up at the camp just now, a chap hasn't no time hardly to think," Mabel told her, but made little impression on Anabel, who had formed the opinion that everybody in the camp must have spent the afternoon in sleep.

"Why are they so especially busy?" inquired Anabel impatiently.

"There's this war they're expecting at any minute, when this lot of navy chaps'll be posted to ships immediately."

"And leave Luniette?" asked Anabel, in dismay at the thought of losing Tim to a ship.

"We'll get a new lot," replied Mabel cheerfully. "I like new faces, they're so jolly. It's only after they've settled down on Luniette, and feel they can't get away whenever they like, it becomes monotonous and gets them down."

Anabel thought resentfully, 'Tim could find time to tell Mabel what he expects to happen to them in the event of war, but he's never said a word to me.'

The same thing occurred the following night. Tim did not come in to supper, and, nonplussed, Anabel put on her thinking-cap, and decided that Tim had taken a leaf out of her own book and was purposely avoiding her.

'I won't be treated like this,' she thought, when Mabel told her during the evening that Tim had gone to supper up at Bella Luce for the first time since he had known the Smiths. 'I think I shall leave Luniette tomorrow. It will save so much trouble all round.'

Brave words.

On the morrow the pleasure steamer *Lady Elizabeth* called at Luniette, and Anabel had not the moral fortitude to drag herself away from Tim if there was the faintest chance that he might love her.

She tried to tell herself, 'There is some easy explanation to all this. Tim is incapable of playing a mean trick on me. If he preferred Naomi, I am sure he would have told me so. And I'll never believe he has changed and is attracted to her unless he says so — only I should know. But why is he keeping away from me? He seemed so keen.'

And Anabel put her hand over her heart to still its agonizing pain. She felt ill with suspense and longing, and scarcely touched any supper, which caused Mrs. Groom great concern in case her guest was going to be ill.

"Are you sure you haven't been near some kind of infection? D'you know anyone who had developed measles, chicken-pox or fever before you left London?" she questioned earnestly.

A gleam of humour came into Anabel's eyes. "Or smallpox," she added. Then impatiently, because since yesterday her patience had been so short, Anabel went on, "How should I know? People don't go around with placards or yellow shirts saying what they've got. Usually you only know people have had these diseases when they are getting better."

Anabel's unusual irritation made Mrs. Groom certain that her guest was 'sickening for something'. "I should go to bed early," the landlady advised soothingly. "I'll put a fire in your room, and bring you a basin of gruel. If you're not better in the morning, I'll consult with Miss Henable."

"Don't be silly, Mrs. Groom, I'll be as right as rain in the morning. And if you dare talk to Miss Henable about me, I'll leave by the next boat."

This 'leaving by the next boat' was to be Anabel's slogan for a few days. She was sick at heart, and nothing anyone could do

— except Tim, and he seemed loth to put in an appearance — could help her.

Anabel went to bed and cried; waited in the darkness for Tim's familiar step on the stairs, and cried again, because she saw the long void of years stretching into the future, alone and without Tim.

She tried to sleep, but that was impossible for her brain seemed alive with thoughts which kept going round in circles, leading nowhere unless it was to more confusion, and a fever of misery.

She had been a fool throwing Tim at Naomi's head. This would never have happened if she had not felt so safe about Naomi. And now through silly championship of a lost cause, Tim was lost to her forever.

After a sleepless night, Anabel rose feeling heavy, and in her own words to her image in the glass, "looked like a piece of chewed string."

She told herself it would never do to let this new setback to her romantic hopes get her down. Having learnt a severe lesson from Paul, no one must be given the chance to hurt her again.

Of course, the only cure to the situation, to cut all losses, as it were, lay in flight.

Anabel definitely decided to return to Bettycombe. There seemed no point in staying any longer on Luniette. Tim was lost. Robert was a pest. And the everlasting noise of waves breaking on the shore, and washing over shingle, whether the tide was going out or coming in, and there was a gale or the weather was calm, got on her nerves, so that she felt she must scream to find relief.

Anabel added to this summary, "And the clothes I've ruined on this island — my blue model gown, and the hat which was ruined in the rain outside the church, talking to that old gargoyle, Mrs. Smith, and which I had to throw over the cliffs into the sea."

To give point to her decision, Anabel drew out her cases and packed a few clothes. And having done this she felt better, and put on a white dress with a blue belt, and went down to the dining-room to wait for her supper. That night, as though he knew of this decision, and the preparations for Anabel to leave Luniette, Tim turned up again for supper.

There was no place laid for him because he had left word he would not be in; and he came in late, when Anabel was seated in solitary state, pretending to read a depressing book called *Beulah of the Salt Lakes*, which she had fished out of the bookcase on the landing upstairs, thinking to find a little comic relief among the well-thumbed pages.

In contrast with his usual mode of entry, which was blithe and boisterous, Tim opened the door quietly and came into the room, shutting the door again before Anabel was aware who had entered.

She turned around sharply, rose from her chair, and with heightened colour cried in a glad tone, "Tim!"

He did not answer at once, though there was an odd light in his blue eyes, as though he were suffering from a fever, but looked at her face, and then at her dress, in silence for what seemed a long while.

"Oh, hallo, Anabel! Fancy finding you alone. This is unusual: or is it? Have you quarrelled with Smith?" said Tim.

Anabel's gaiety died away. "I don't know why you should say that," she said in a flat tone.

"Because he's been sitting in your pocket lately, and you seemed to like it. Are you expecting him this evening?" The bland tone, coming from Tim, tore at her heartstrings.

"What if I am?"

Tim shrugged. "In that case, I should make myself scarce."

But Anabel had recovered from her joyous surprise at seeing Tim, and though the colour remained in her cheeks she was able to say easily and quietly, "I am not expecting Robert. Why?" But she continued to stand facing Tim, though her legs were wobbling under her, and she had to put her hand on the back of the chair for support.

"Just the party dress!" Tim sounded only half convinced.

Anabel took a deep breath to steady her voice. "It's a gala occasion! If a boat comes tomorrow, and I am hoping the weather will hold so that it will, I'm going back in her," Anabel said loudly, hoping she looked as courageous as she sounded, and at once felt grand now that she had shot her bolt.

Anabel was unprepared for the swift change in Tim, and if she had not been so confounded by his unexpected presence, and still more unwelcome attack, his anger at her decision would have been most gratifying, and made up for all those bad, lonely days she had been through.

For in a bound Tim was across the room, standing angrily in front of her, demanding, "Since when have you decided to go?"

Anabel's voice quavered as she replied, "I made up my mind this evening. I have found it lonelier here than I thought — and I'm not used to being alone; it makes me miserable."

"Rot! You must unmake your mind again. D'you hear me?"

A half-smile played for a moment about Anabel's soft lips, and then was gone. "I am not deaf." Her voice was steadier.

"You can't go."

"Why not?"

"I forbid it. Imagine me left alone on Luniette — without you. It's unthinkable. I'd go off my head."

"You've managed to do without my company for several days."

"No, I haven't. But I've given myself a helluva time. You haven't been out of my thoughts for a moment. I've been a fool keeping away from you. I know that now."

"Oh!" The feeling of not knowing where she stood with Tim, which had been in Anabel's mind for days, went in a flash. Suddenly she was riotously happy again, confident in herself.

"I should have sought you out, had a surfeit of your society, found out all your faults, got sick of you, been bored, as I often am with girls, and then —" Tim spoke hardly and looked fierce.

"Yes?" said Anabel breathlessly, and she sat down again.

"Then you could have gone tomorrow for all I cared." Something in the large blue eyes looking half-smilingly up at him made Tim catch his breath, and say in a very different tone, "You nearly did go. I am only just in time to stop you."

"I should have to go *someday*, in any case," Anabel replied softly.

"Someday isn't tomorrow. The plain truth is, Anabel, I can't lose you so soon. I haven't shown you half the secrets of Luniette I simply must show you one day, and I haven't said a quarter of what I mean to say. And we haven't had a sail together. We've wasted time — I have, I know —" Here Tim broke off suddenly, as confused as Anabel.

He turned away from her and rang the bell, and when Mabel came running to answer it with a, "I didn't know you were in, sir," Tim found relief in saying:

"Ha! I've caught you up on one thing at last. So there's one thing that's happened on this island which you didn't know.

298

See here, Mabelle, tell Mrs. Groom I'm hungry as a pirate, and—"

"There's plenty in the larder, sir. Miss Robinson's only been pecking at her food, so we haven't served her a full portion, only dainty titbits to tempt her appetite —"

Tim swept around to Anabel. "What's this? Off your food! What's the matter?"

"Nothing's the matter," Anabel replied laughingly, for suddenly she felt light and happy — silly and gay, irresponsible and hysterical... For whatever was wrong between them was in the past, and now all was well again.

"Sure?"

"Quite sure."

"This calls for a celebration. Shall we have a bottle of Graves Superior, very dry?"

"That will be nice."

Tim turned to Mabel, who was staring from one to the other slightly mystified, not sure what occasion was to be celebrated. "Tell Mrs. Groom I want a sound bottle of wine — and if she hasn't a Graves, I'll try some Barsac." And he went into detail as to what he wanted.

When Mabel had gone, Tim said to Anabel, "I sometimes think I'm the questioner and you the person who answers in 'A Child's Guide to Knowledge'. 'What's the matter?' 'Nothing's the matter.' 'Why don't you eat?' 'Because I am not hungry.' We get nowhere: or do we, Anabel?" Tim sat down at the table, and leaning towards Anabel, looked tenderly into her eyes. "I was so afraid you'd be cold to me — like a stranger. I richly deserved punishment though I should have hated it. But you're so sweet to me: so warm and kind. Your features are just as I've been picturing them in my waking moments as well as in my dreams. And this dress: I haven't seen it before, but it seems familiar — white, as you were in my dreams last night… I've tried to forget you and I can't."

After they had drunk several toasts, Tim broke off in the middle of some shop talk to say, "I've learnt so many new things about life lately, I realize now that none of us is master of his Fate. We are all her children, progressing through a series of 'ifs' towards fulfilment."

They looked into each other's eyes, and Anabel said, "It's been so lonely, Tim."

He nodded. "I should have thought about that." Then, "What about a sail tomorrow afternoon, Anabel? I think I can make it."

"I'd love it. I don't suppose Dai will mind you. It's Robert he seems to dislike so much."

"We won't use Dai's boat. A friend of mine, over at Luvelly, is going to lend me his craft. It is only half the size of Dai's, with a sprit sail, and is more manageable, because it's not only that I want to sail with you, but to be alone with you, out of sight of prying eyes from all odd corners."

CHAPTER 16

But Tim could not make it the following afternoon — or the next.

Robert spent many hours hanging about the hotel, in the hope of talking to Anabel, who tried her best to make him return to the farm and work. But Robert refused point blank to work regularly, though he made herculean efforts to catch up the lost hours during the time when Anabel was not available.

Anabel did not speak to Naomi. Several times she caught sight of the gay little figure in the coloured trousers and vivid jumper — or both, talking gaily to a couple of 'mids.' who had recently arrived at the camp; but whenever Anabel waved, Naomi pretended not to see and turned her back.

But there was something missing about Naomi, the carnival spirit that had gone well with her colouring which being with Tim always seemed to call forth. And when Anabel could watch her unseen, something which happened occasionally, she saw that Naomi was tired and listless.

Tim did not seem to miss Naomi in the evenings, though he must have noticed that her habit of coming down from Bella Luce for coffee was discontinued. Perhaps Naomi had warned him she would not visit the hotel again. For Anabel heard from Mabel that the two often met. There might be nothing in these chance meetings, there probably wasn't, but the way Mabel spoke about them was in undertones fraught with meaning. Anabel was uneasy about Naomi, knowing well how impossible it would be for any girl to forget Tim easily, but she said nothing of this worry to Tim, who seemed particularly gay and friendly on these evenings, when work was over for the day, and the two met for supper and had long chats afterwards by the fireside.

Tim did not repeat his visit to Bella Luce, and Anabel concluded either he had gone to the farm on some business connected with the camp, and made a pleasure of such business, or he had not enjoyed Mrs. Smith's hospitality.

And then, one afternoon, Tim phoned Anabel to be ready to start for a sea voyage in ten minutes.

Just long enough for Tim to get down to the hotel from the camp! The sudden order, which was so like Tim's impulsive decisions, knowing that the recipient would obey blithely and blindly, made Anabel laugh.

"How young and gay Miss Robinson is," said Mabel wistfully, in the middle of washing up after dinner, as the happy sound wafted down from above came into the scullery window and made dishwashing seem the world's worst drudgery. "And how lovely she is these days." Mabel's soapsud-covered fingers slid slowly and precariously over a meat-dish.

Mrs. Groom uttered a warning cry, and when the meat-dish was rinsed and put up in the rack to dry, said proudly, "Luniette's done Miss Robinson no end of good; her cheeks are quite rosy."

"Oh, it's not Luniette that's making Miss Robinson bloom like a beautiful flower. Don't you know, Mrs. Groom, it's love. Now I wonder —"

But Mrs. Groom wasn't going to be told anything by Mabel, even about love, which emotion was so long out of her system as to be classed among the 'delicate and unnatural' list of things a lady didn't talk about — anyway, only to her best friend, and then in seclusion and in whispers.

"There you go with your highfalutin romantic notions, Mabel. Since you've taken up with Joe you think about love all the time, and that's bad for any young couple. I should never be surprised if one of these days, with your cheek, you don't join Keziah with old Rube."

Mabel looked serious. "And so I might," she said solemnly and wisely, at length, "but it won't be love that drives Mr. Rube to her. He told me, one Saturday night, when he'd had a drop too much, that now he's a widower he'll have to be looking out for the second Mrs. Rube, not because he wants another wife to nag him on a Saturday night, but because it's cheaper to keep a wife than a housekeeper."

Mrs. Groom was indignant. "Well, I never, the horrid old man! I pity the woman who takes him on."

"Not, look you," continued Mabel, delighted that her news had stirred Mrs. Groom, "that you'd put a wedding between Keziah and Mr. Rube in the same lane as Miss Robinson —"

But Mrs. Groom thought it wiser to put a stop to the nonsense Mabel talked, and she interrupted sharply, "Stop that, Mabel. Don't run away with those ideas, now, or repeat them to Carrie, who, though she's my best friend, has the busiest tongue on Luniette. All your talk now is about love — and when you're married it'll be about money — that is, if I've summed up Master Joe rightly."

There was a tea-basket on the table, and Tim was waiting in the hall, when Anabel, dressed for the weather in trousers and sea-boots, and carrying her oilskin, came downstairs.

"I hope I haven't kept you waiting," she said.

Tim glanced at his wristwatch. "You're here on the dot. Good girl! I like punctual people — especially when the tide's on the turn, and running out fast."

With that Tim picked up the basket, and taking the oilskin from Anabel's arm and throwing it across his shoulder, they went down to the beach, chatting lightly and casually as they went.

What made the prospect of an afternoon together so wonderful was the fact that Tim was taking a legitimate holiday. There would be no black looks or harsh words waiting for either of them if they were late.

A few yards out on the restless sea, just out of reach of the breaking waves, a fourteen-foot white-painted boat was lying at anchor. Tim looked up at the sky and sniffed appreciatively at the keen air. Out at sea, beyond the shelter of the bay, it was a windy day, with the clouds flying from the south-west.

"It's a gorgeous day for a sail," said Tim. "But we're going to get wet, I'm afraid." His voice softened as he turned his head to look at Anabel. "Trust me, Anabel?" he asked.

She met his look squarely, but glanced away again almost at once, unable to stand the warm glow in his eyes unmoved. "Of course, Tim."

"Supposing I capsize our craft?"

Anabel laughed. "Then I'll drown in good company."

"Nice person to say that! But I don't think you'll be drowned. I'm a strong swimmer. You'll be safe with me."

Dai was waiting at the water's edge to see them off, and appeared to take Anabel's defection in employing his services calmly enough. "You'll be in for a rough time, miss," he warned. "Better avoid this cockleshell like the plague and come along o' me. My *Polly* will stand up to anything."

But Tim advised good-naturedly, "Oh, shut up, Dai: what an old pessimist you are! Here, take this —" and he passed over the tea-basket and oilskin to Dai, and turning swiftly picked

Anabel up in his arms and carried her out to sea, waiting his chance to avoid the oncoming waves.

As Tim neared the boat which was tossing about on the water, as though eager to be off, he paused and looked down at Anabel in his arms, her cheek near to his heart, staring up at him, a soft smile in her eyes.

"A penny?" he invited.

Anabel shook her head.

"Two — a shilling?"

"I was only thinking I've never before seen your face at this angle."

"I should think not indeed." And then laughingly, "D'you like what you see?"

"That would be telling," was the teasing reply.

"Suppose I say I'll drop you into the water if you don't tell me?" And he loosened his hold a fraction so that instinctively Anabel flung her arm around his neck and clung tightly to him.

She released her hold almost at once, blushing at her boldness, just in case Tim misunderstood.

But he only laughed gently, and put her into the boat, saying, "You're far too precious to drown like a cat."

Anabel moved swiftly over to trim the boat while Tim heaved himself in. Dai handed them the tea-basket regretfully.

"It feels heavy, and I know it's good," he remarked.

Anabel whispered to Tim, who stood between her and Dai, "Shall we take him?"

"D'you really want him — he'll make a third?"

There was such disappointment in Tim's tone that Anabel said, "No."

"Neither do I." Then: "Better put on your sou'wester and oilskin, we shall probably run into dirty weather." And Tim helped her on with the cumbersome oilskin and did up the buttons for her, then tied the tapes of her sou'wester.

When everything was ready to his satisfaction for getting off quickly, Tim hauled up the anchor and waved to Dai, who stood watching the start, looking like a faithful dog whose master has decided he shall be left behind. Tim hoisted the sail and Anabel took the tiller, and away they went out of the lee of the island, rounding Mouse Point and making for the ocean; and presently, when everything was ship-shape, the sail well filled with wind, Tim, the rope in his hand, came and sat beside Anabel and put steadying fingers over hers which rested on the tiller handle.

They began to talk of many things, though Tim was always on the alert. Anabel saw that Tim had no use for 'pretty sailing', that he had the keenness of the professional in the sport, and handled the boat as though it were some live thing. There were long silences between them, while Tim smoked his pipe contentedly.

Once, meeting her eyes, he smiled and asked, "Nice time, Anabel?"

"Perfectly gorgeous."

"Sort of thing I'd like to last forever — sailing westwards with you! When I was a 'mid.', I used to think there were only three things in the world that counted for happiness — a boat, a motorbike, and a pretty girl. Well, I've had all three. I've outgrown the motorbike, and my tastes in boats and girls have changed with the years. But this afternoon I've still got two of my old loves — and am I lucky!"

Soon after that a squall blew up and there was a heavy shower, when the rain came hissing down.

The cloud passed, the rain stopped and the sun came out, and Tim drew Anabel's attention to a school of porpoises rolling in line.

"They're after the fish,"he told her."If we had a line now —"

"There's no bait."

"No, and my pal doesn't like his boat smelling of fish. But does it matter?" And it was as though Tim continued '— So long as we're together.'

All at once, as though she read his mind, Anabel heard herself saying recklessly, "No, nothing seems to matter much this afternoon." She added as a face-saver, "I suppose it's the space and colour all about us — the changing sky and the green sea." And she could have said, "And the fact that we're alone."

Tim looked vaguely around him, and his eyes came to rest on her face. "It is all very beautiful," he said, so earnestly that she coloured under the emphasis of his words and the intensity of his gaze.

It seemed natural for Tim to transfer his hand from hers on the tiller-handle and put it around her. "Keep her up to it, Anabel," he said, glancing up at the sails which shivered as Anabel's hand on the tiller trembled, changing the boat's course ever so slightly.

Tim spared a moment to turn towards her smilingly — then swiftly, as though moved by some uncontrollable impulse, he bent his head to hers and kissed her lightly on the mouth.

"Your lips taste of salt," he grinned, but his voice shook. "And your face is all wet with spray."

"Oh, dear! And I suppose I look a sight," she said softly.

"You look beautiful as you are, Anabel — a dream creature in sun or moonlight — such an old story to you, I am afraid, but it's from the bottom of my heart."

It was so unusual for Tim to speak so deeply, and in that tone of voice — deep and slurry — that Anabel could think of nothing to say, only a wild happiness that made her feel dizzy took possession of her. This was what she longed to hear Tim say, what she had prayed for lately.

'If only I can make him love me,' she had wished, 'as I am beginning to love him! How happy I could be.'

In the early evening, when the clouds had rolled away, and the sky looked clean and washed, Tim and Anabel reached the bay. Here, on that side of the island away from the light sunset sky, it looked dark, grim and forbidding. There was little sign of life, though the hotel was lit up and appeared like yellow eyes in a white face against the sombre hillside, and a cow mooing in pain and loneliness seemed to add its note of melancholy to the scene.

Dai was waiting to give them a hand in — and with Dai, so Anabel noted with a queer sinking of the heart which presaged misfortune, waited Robert Smith.

For three hours Anabel had forgotten him.

Tim asked her, "What does *he* want?"

"I don't know." But the edge to Tim's voice, no less than Robert's presence on the lonely, darkening beach, troubled her.

"Like his cheek coming down to wait for you. It's as though the fellow doesn't trust me."

Anabel laughed a little, finding comfort in Tim's slang which lightened the shadows she felt to be gathering about her. But she was puzzled too, for Robert looked more gaunt and gloomier than ever. She said, "But you did exactly the same when I went sailing with him, and it was his turn to feel annoyed."

"That was different," said Tim shortly.

"Was it?" asked Anabel, trying to sound impartial. She was busy removing her oilskin, aware that it was hot and heavy, and was engrossed in pushing the buttons back through the stiff buttonholes.

Hardly had Tim put Anabel down at the edge of the sea, greeted Robert, and returned with Dai to get the boat in, than Robert plucked at Anabel's sleeve and said urgently in a low voice, "Naomi's gone!"

At first the words did not register, partly, no doubt, because they were spoken quietly and not dramatically, as one might have expected them to be.

Anabel had taken out her powder compact, and was busy repairing the ravages of wind and weather to her face. Then she paused suddenly with her hand in mid-air, and turned sharply to face Robert. "What did you say?"

"My sister, Naomi, has gone!" he repeated quietly.

"Gone! But where?" Anabel exclaimed blankly.

Robert shrugged faintly. "Over to the mainland."

"When?"

"This afternoon."

"But there's been no boat today."

"No, she went with a couple of 'mids.' in a naval pinnace."

Anabel glanced at Tim. Sounds fell clearly on the thin quiet air, and she heard every word he was saying to Dai: "I shall be going out in her again tomorrow —"

In view of this news, would that be possible?

Anabel recalled Mrs. Groom saying once, "Although we're not related, we are like one big family living on Luniette. You'll see what I mean when you've been here a few weeks; but whatever happens, whether it's being born or married — or dying — seems to affect us all. We learn to share the good and the bad."

After a short while, during which Anabel finished powdering her face, she looked at Robert's moody face, and said, "You don't know where Naomi has gone, what she means to do on the mainland, and whether she has money to keep her going?"

"No."

"Well, I shouldn't worry if I were you. Naomi's probably gone to relatives or friends."

"I don't think so. There are some relatives my mother hasn't seen for years and whom neither Naomi nor I have ever met, but she won't go there."

"Naomi won't go far if she has no money."

"We don't know what she has. My mother paid her for work in the dairy, and there's nothing to spend money on here, so she has some savings to draw upon."

"I see. But I wonder what made Naomi do such a silly thing." Anabel spoke lightly purposely, not because this news was to be treated in a light manner, but in an effort to help Robert a little, to mitigate his worry. She was not surprised when Robert replied shortly, and with a penetrating look which brought the blood to her face:

"You know."

Anabel did know, and hadn't the faintest idea what to think or do. After the enjoyment of the lovely afternoon with its sense of spaciousness, uplift, and a kind of healing peace, which gave Anabel a tranquillity and happiness she had never known, meeting Robert and hearing his news was like shutting the door on bliss and being plunged into chaos — into a world of tumult and torment, where gladness was out of place.

How would Tim react to this news? Would he blame himself or her for Naomi's flight?

He was in earnest conversation with Dai, and Anabel had no idea how to tell him. A picture of the perfection of the

afternoon was spread suddenly before Anabel's mind's eye —
the long satisfying silences between Tim and herself. Each had
gazed seawards, studying, with an artist's eye, the exquisite
detail of light and dark greens in the curving shadows of
dancing waves, each wavelet crested with a snowy white drift
of spume flying in the wind, crashing in crystal drops in the
green shadows.

The picture went almost immediately, and Anabel sighed
regretfully for the memory.

Then, characteristically shouldering an unpleasant burden,
Anabel went over to Tim, who stopped talking to Dai at her
approach, facing her with a worried line deeply drawn between
his brows.

"Robert has come down to tell us that Naomi has left
home," Anabel said in a flat voice, carefully devoid of the
irritation she felt at having to mention Naomi's name, and
avoiding looking into Tim's eyes.

To her relief, Tim did not exclaim with surprise, and
Anabel's nerves, which had been strung up in anticipation of
Tim's reactions, relaxed a little.

"I know. Dai was just telling me that Naomi went off with a
suitcase, in one of our pinnaces, two hours ago," said Tim,
adding darkly, "Somebody'll get into trouble for that. To take a
boat without permission is bad enough, but to take a girl for a
joy-ride is absolutely forbidden." Tim looked beyond Anabel,
and called to Robert, "What are you going to do about it?" He
wondered uneasily whether the zealous but inexperienced
seamen had reached land, and where his own responsibility for
all three ended. And when he saw Robert standing idly at the
water's edge, with his hands in his pockets, one foot stubbing
at the pebbles, it was difficult to keep the irritation out of his
voice.

"What can I do?" replied Robert, not bothering to look up. "I haven't a plane that I can fly over to the mainland to search for them. If I borrowed a boat, I shouldn't know what port to make for. I came down to find out if you'd seen them at sea."

"We went down-channel, probably in the opposite direction to Naomi. Of course, if I had seen them I'd have ordered the 'mids.' back pronto. They, at any rate, must be back before nightfall, when we shall know where they landed Naomi, and you can get in touch with the police at the port."

"That's about all I can do — wait."

Tim went up to Robert. "I'm sorry about this, Smith. It must be a terrible worry for you and Mrs. Smith. But there, Naomi's a wilful girl, and these wild doings are not unexpected. If she were my sister, I'd shake a bit of sense into her. Why did she go? Was there a rumpus at home and Naomi flew off the handle? Don't take any notice of it, no one's to blame, and these things happen — and then settle themselves — somehow."

Robert eyed the sailor coldly. "There was no row. Naomi hasn't spoken to a soul in the house for days."

"How unpleasant! And how did Naomi, the chatterbox, manage it? And why?"

"She was too miserable —"

"Miserable!"

"Through you!"

"Oh!" The talk was depressing Tim, perhaps because he suspected that no matter how strenuously he might deny it, there was some truth in what Robert said.

"Yes, you were great friends once, and then suddenly you turned on Naomi, and that cut her up. My sister's a sensitive girl, and would feel any rough treatment from certain people."

Dai had drawn nearer to the two men, and was listening attentively to the conversation, and seeing this, Anabel hastily suggested, "Don't you think we'd better go back to the hotel and talk this over quietly?"

She felt dazed, and a little tired now that all the afternoon's enjoyment had been squeezed out of her by Robert's news. Anabel was unhappy, too, because — unknowingly, of course — both she and Tim were implicated in Naomi's flight. She was relieved when Tim replied quietly, showing that he had the matter well in hand, and knew how to treat Robert, "There's nothing to talk over."

Robert sneered, "Nothing? Well, so long as your conscience is clear —" and his tone implied that he thought Tim's conscience anything but clear.

"I promise you —" began Tim, but Robert cut him short.

"I said okay — or I implied it, didn't I?" And he glanced sideways at Anabel. "I thought you might like to know that my mother blames Anabel," Robert went on slyly.

"Blames Anabel?" Tim repeated stupidly. "What for?"

Robert raised his heavy eyebrows. "Rightly or wrongly, my mother thinks that Anabel has driven Naomi from home," he repeated.

"Well, of all the nonsense —" began Tim violently, roused in someone else's defence when nothing would induce him to defend himself.

But Anabel said quietly and with dignity which could not fail to impress her three listeners, "Of course it's nonsense, Tim, though I can well understand that Mrs. Smith had a distorted view about everything. I shall probably go to see her soon, when I can explain matters to her satisfaction."

That sounded prim and silly, because Anabel knew as well as the others that not only was Mrs. Smith inaccessible to callers at any time, but that if anyone tried to explain it would certainly not work out satisfactorily.

It was something to hear that even though Robert took pleasure in blaming Tim for Naomi's prank, Mrs. Smith did not. And Tim would not understand the lights and shades of Mrs. Smith's dislike of the stranger on Luniette.

Naomi's Smith's disappearance was the chief subject of gossip in the bar at the hotel. It was probably the only topic of conversation in all the little cob cottages around the church. It broke up Anabel's contemplated evening with Tim. And Anabel could not help noticing that the latter seemed more worried about the result of his 'mids." misdeeds than over Naomi's flight.

Tim did not linger at the hotel, whither he accompanied Anabel and Robert, but went straight up to the camp. This proceeding disgruntled Mrs. Groom, who said she had cooked a lovely supper to a turn for Tim, and it was now spoilt.

"He'll get something to eat up at the camp," said the aggrieved Mrs. Groom. "And as I happen to know the man who's looking after them up there, I know it'll be good food ruined."

Anabel was alone after supper, trying to read, when Mrs. Smith, a gaunt figure in deep black with the big cameo brooch pinning her bodice at the neck, came into the dining-room.

Anabel smiled tentatively at her visitor, and, with a pretence of brightness, jumped up and went forward with outstretched hand to meet Mrs. Smith.

"Have you come to see me?" Anabel hazarded, aware of a hot, dry feeling in her mouth, gathering her wits hastily about her to meet what she felt was going to be a stormy interview. For Mrs. Smith's facial muscles had not relaxed when she saw the girl. Indeed, at sight of Anabel, Mrs. Smith looked grimmer than ever.

"You've guessed right," was the hard answer, as Mrs. Smith shut the door with a click, then opened it again swiftly, looked outside, and closed it more quietly. "That there Mabel —" she said, and left the rest of the sentence to her listener's imagination.

"Mabel has gone off for a couple of hours," explained Anabel, wishing she dared smile at the thought of what Mabel was missing. Then, "Will you have some coffee, Mrs. Smith?"

The visitor made it plain at once that she had not called in a friendly spirit. "I couldn't touch anything of yours."

Anabel paled with indignation, but she replied easily, "It wouldn't be mine, but Mrs. Groom's."

"But you'd be paying. I'll not touch a thing you pay for."

Anabel watched Mrs. Smith come forward into the room and sit down heavily, with all the spring gone out of her step, and compassion for this suffering woman filled Anabel's heart, and she said softly, "I'm so sorry to hear this news about Naomi."

"So you should be, though it's rather late in the day to talk about pity, considering you are the cause of it all."

Anabel did not pretend to misunderstand. Unwittingly or not, she had been the cause of disrupting the friendship between Tim and Naomi, and it would be of no avail telling Mrs. Smith this. The mischief was done. So Anabel said, "Those are hard words."

"But the truth. Interlopers usually make trouble. Because my Naomi liked the commander, you must needs want him. And being on the spot, in this hotel, I suppose you worked until you won him over. It isn't a new story, and has been done before. When I first saw you I sensed trouble, and I was right."

Anabel did not answer at once. The hard bitter words had shaken her. When she spoke, it was quietly and gently as before. "That is rather a crude way of putting it. I helped Naomi all I could, but Tim only liked her as a friend."

"Yet she is winsome."

"She is charming. If I were a man —"

"But you're not, Miss Robinson. And the point is that Commander Northorn would have grown to like my girl much better if you hadn't come upon the scene. That is why I begged you to leave Luniette, to go away and leave us to our island. We could not pick up Bella Luce and take it over, lock, stock and barrel, to the mainland, when perhaps Naomi would have been cured of her attraction before much harm was done, but you could go. That, however, did not suit you. This naval man was a fresh type to you, and you set yourself out to attract him. You wormed your way into his good graces until you weaned him away from Naomi. You made her so unhappy she could not bear to live on Luniette any longer. I was robbed of my beautiful daughter, and now I am left to work the farm alone."

Until Mrs. Smith spoke about the loss of a farm hand, Anabel's sympathies had been with her entirely. There was a grain of truth in what Mrs. Smith said. Anabel was sufficiently honest to admit that. Much of it was not true, but a figment of Mrs. Smith's imaginative brain.

Now Anabel said in a business-like tone, "You have Keziah."

"Oh, Keziah, who is deaf and dumb! Keziah, who understands just as much of an order as it suits her! This is the busiest time of the year. The Welsh labourers, who usually help this month, haven't come over this year. With all this talk of war, they've joined the forces. I shall miss Naomi's help sorely."

Anabel thought, 'If I am kind to this woman, perhaps she will keep to herself all that has passed between us. For if she should go to Tim and say one half of what she has been telling me, then that lovely something that is growing between us, and which I do not want to die, must surely be spoilt.' And aloud, Anabel said, still with that same easy, quiet, conversational manner which was secretly surprising Mrs. Smith, "Perhaps I could help you out for a week or so?"

"You?" Mrs. Smith's thin lips curled. "What do you know about farming?"

"Not much, though I once had a two-week course in dairy work."

"Waste of time! Why, you'd be useless on a farm."

"Oh, I don't know. I'm practical and capable —" Anabel stopped suddenly. To be too practical and capable would only annoy Mrs. Smith further. "Try me," said Anabel. "I'm willing to prove my worth to you."

"I have no time to show you." But Anabel's idea was working in Mrs. Smith's mind.

"But I don't want you to spare valuable time on me. Just tell me what you want done, and leave me to tackle the job."

Mrs. Smith still looked incredulous. "What's behind all this?"

"What do you mean?"

"Some trickery on your part?"

Anabel shook her head. "I have no tricks," she said simply.

Mrs. Smith nodded. "I'll prove you," she said grimly. "Be at Bella Luce at five tomorrow morning — ready to begin work."

"But —" began Anabel, when Mrs. Smith broke in triumphantly and impatiently.

"I knew you couldn't get up so early. You're all talk. Put your kind to the test and they fail at the first fence."

Anabel told her, "I can get up, and I shall be at Bella Luce at five o'clock. Is that quite settled?"

Then Mrs. Smith seemed to remember her grief, and collapsed. Her face went white and was drawn with suffering, while her brilliant brown eyes were filled with anguish. "But there's still Naomi," she whispered tensely, and Anabel saw that her bony, work-worn fingers clasped the arms of the chair in which she was sitting, as though to draw some kind of comfort from the horsehair padding. "She's never been away from the farm, not even for a night. Your help up there won't bring Naomi back to me. Nothing can do that. And no one has any hold over her but Commander Northorn, and if he refuses —" Mrs. Smith paused expectantly, her eyes searching Anabel's face.

But the latter replied quickly and decisively, "I won't discuss such a position with him."

"Then Naomi's gone for good."

"Oh, I hope not. She'll soon come to her senses, Mrs. Smith. Naomi is still so young she can't be sure of her own mind."

The mother answered, "Naomi's stubborn; she will never give in and return unless —"

Anabel was not to be drawn. "It is impossible for me to help her like that."

"Then I've lost her."

The sallow face looked sinister with grief, and in spite of her express wish to help the grief-stricken mother, Anabel felt impatient and wished Mrs. Smith would go.

'I've had about as much as I can stand,' thought Anabel. 'Naomi is nothing to me. If she were not so spoilt, Naomi would never have dreamt of running away. If Mrs. Smith says much more, I shall scream.' After a while, Anabel said, "I am truly sorry for you about Naomi. It was a cruel thing for her to cause you so much distress."

"Don't you dare say a word against Naomi! She wouldn't have left me, only she was too upset to think about me. And who are you to call Naomi cruel? Speak for yourself. Try to remember the harm you've done to us on Luniette, and then see if you are able to speak so easily about cruelty. I know you've made all of us intensely miserable up at Bella Luce. Even Robert —"

Anabel listened in silence. She knew it would be useless trying to excuse herself to Mrs. Smith. 'Even Robert.'

Surely she, Anabel, wasn't to be blamed for not falling in love with Robert to order? Though that, of course, would have simplified matters for Naomi.

'Then I should have been the miserable one,' thought Anabel crossly.

When Mrs. Smith had gone, without a 'goodnight', her last words a reminder to Anabel that she would be expected to start work at five o'clock in the morning, Anabel went over to the window and flung it wide.

Standing before it, she gazed out at the dark sea, waiting a few seconds for the cheering beam from the lighthouse to sweep around and light up the turbulent waves and the patch of gorse over on the edge of the cliff. She raised her arms above her head and stretched and yawned tiredly. "If I'm ever going to wake at four o'clock, I'd better go to bed," she said aloud. "I wonder if Mrs. Groom has an alarum clock."

But Mrs. Groom was still busy in the bar, from whence came the usual hum of non-stop talk.

Meanwhile Anabel gazed out to sea, and watched the moving lights of a ship going up-channel into port.

CHAPTER 17

When Tim came in eventually, the bar was closed, and the house had quietened for the night. He looked tired and grim, but expressed no surprise at seeing Anabel standing dreamily at the open window, except to remark, "Are you trying to catch your death of cold? Why don't you come over here where it is cosy and warm, and where I can see you?"

Anabel took the hint, closed the window at once, and came back to the fireplace, where Tim had already kicked the dying fire into renewed life, and was staring down thoughtfully into a log in flames.

He said, "Having left Naomi at Combeford, where she took the London train, those two little blighters came back here. Apparently she told them she had a packet of money, and meant to join up in the women's branch of the Air Force which is now open for recruits. Naomi made no secret of her intention never to return to Luniette, and frightened, I suppose, they tried to make her reconsider this — and failed. I have already sent word to Bella Luce, but unfortunately Mrs. Smith was out, and heaven knows how much of my message will be passed on. I shall, of course, punish my 'mids.'; and I only wish I could spank Naomi, silly little fool, for causing so much bother."

Tim sat down in a big chair with a deep sigh, and took out his pipe and pouch, glancing across at Anabel, who was sitting silently in the opposite chair, looking at him.

"You look white, Anabel. Seen a ghost?" he asked, his voice softening unconsciously.

"No, but a vampire."

"You're over-tired. It's been some day! Better turn in soon."
But as Tim fished in his pocket for his cigarette-case, which he
handed to Anabel, she guessed he wanted her to remain
downstairs to talk.

They sat quite still for a long time, smoking in a kind of
dreamy silence, both looking into the heart of the fire, seeing
strange shapes among the flames. And after a while Tim spoke,
quietly and softly, as though telling her his thoughts.

"This afternoon, when we were sailing in the Channel,
everything seemed so beautifully simple — just you and me in
a boat, sailing around in a choppy green sea, with the fret of
the world so far away that it seemed no price could ever be
asked by Fate for those tranquil hours in paradise. And now, a
short while later, and we are back again in the world, nothing is
straightforward, and every darn thing complicated — and all
through a chit like Naomi. I've been asking myself back there
in the camp, why should I have to worry about her?"

Anabel could have told him in a very few words, but she held
her tongue.

For a long while they remained silent.

Then Anabel said, "Mrs. Smith was here this evening."

Tim replied somewhat unexpectedly and almost without
premeditation, "Ah! Is that why you opened the window so
wide?"

"What do you think?"

"I'm wondering what she wanted with you." Tim looked
directly at Anabel, as though he suspected she might not tell
him the whole truth.

But Anabel replied wearily, remembering her tortuous
interview with Mrs. Smith, "As Robert said on the beach, she
blames me for Naomi leaving Luniette."

"What rot!" said Tim vigorously, and after a little while, "You're nothing to Naomi." But his voice was not now so sure, and Anabel guessed that this least-conceited of men was troubled by conscience.

"Mrs. Smith seems to think I am — an evil genius to many people, in fact."

"They might as well blame me, because I know Naomi rather well."

"I already knew that," was Anabel's quiet reply.

Tim leant forward to knock out the ashes from his pipe against the corner of the hearth, and when he spoke it was bitter. "And Mrs. Smith called here to tell you so, and obviously with the intention of putting you off me. What a charming creature!"

Anabel smiled faintly, knowing that no one lived who could turn her against this man. She said quietly, "Mrs. Smith is distraught."

"I'm worried, too: we all are. But Mrs. Smith is not so much grieved at losing her daughter as she is about having no one to help her up at the farm. But perhaps even she wouldn't be so tactless as to mention that point —"

Anabel grinned suddenly, and at once the atmosphere in the room, which had been so fraught with emotion, changed, and the tension slackened, so that everything seemed more normal. "I don't think Mrs. Smith left anything out. You see, she has no intention of repeating her visit to me, and so everything had to be got off her chest in a short space of time. And what she said was to the point —"

Tim frowned. He was sitting back in his chair again and had crossed his leg over his knee, nursing his ankle with one hand, while with his free hand he held the unlit pipe in his mouth.

He released the pipe, holding it in mid-air, and looked at Anabel. "You should have refused to listen to Mrs. Smith's nonsense, and turned her out — or gone yourself. Even she would have seen the futility of wasting her breath in an empty room. The fact that you stopped to listen to her must have seemed a sign of weakness in her eyes. You must learn to stand up to a bully, Anabel."

But Anabel shook her head at these barbarous suggestions. "I was sorry for her," she said.

Tim laughed hardly. He was feeling sore with the Smiths. Such gentleness as Anabel had in her make-up should not be squandered on the unappreciative Smiths — and he included Robert especially. "That's rich, coming from you. But I hope, for your own sake, you didn't lay on your sorrow with a trowel?"

"No-o, but I felt I wanted to help her."

"How?"

"I hope you won't think it funny, and laugh at me, but I offered to take Naomi's place on the farm until either Mrs. Smith finds someone else or Naomi comes home again." Tim grunted and Anabel knew he was angry, and said quickly, "It's none of your business."

"No?" He stared angrily at her, and then changed his mind and smiled affectionately. "You funny little fish!" he cried softly. "You don't know what you are letting yourself in for. If I know Naomi, and I like to fancy I do, now that she's broken adrift at last, she won't ever return home to the narrow confines of Luniette. While if you are useful, Mrs. Smith won't trouble to look for outside help. There'll be precious little coming over from Combeford, and the girls here don't like Bella Luce farm. There's known to be something wrong with the atmosphere of the homestead." Tim slipped his favourite pipe into his pocket, and unwinding his limbs from their comfortable, if inelegant, position, rose and went over to Anabel, and putting his hands on either arm of her chair bent to look down into her wide eyes. "You have let yourself in for a fine time, Anabel," he said half-smilingly.

"Have I?" But her voice was tremulous at Tim's nearness, while her eyes wavered and fell away from his glance.

Anabel looked up again in surprise, as with a quick change of tone Tim asked abruptly, "Does Robert know of this crazy plan? Is it perhaps his idea, behind Mrs. Smith's visit, to get you up to Bella Luce?" And Tim frowned menacingly, in a manner which boded ill for Robert if he harboured designs on Anabel.

"So far as I know, Robert doesn't dream that I shall turn up at the farm at five tomorrow morning," Anabel replied with composure, knowing well the effect her last words would have on Tim.

"At five! You're crazy, Anabel! Apart from the fact that this plan is quite the wildest I've ever heard, there's absolutely no reason on earth why you should put yourself out like this for a stranger like Mrs. Smith. Don't you understand that hers is a vengeful nature, and once she's got you working up there, preying on your good nature to help her out of a hole, she'll move heaven and earth not only to keep you there, but to make your life a hell for you? She'll think up some revenge —" Tim paused for breath. He knew he was letting his tongue run free, and probably talking wildly, but he was frightened for Anabel, who was already so much in his mind and heart — more deeply enshrined than he was then aware of.

Anabel smiled broadly as she reminded Tim, "What could Mrs. Smith do to me? What can anyone do? This lonely island is still England, and it is a free country. If I don't like it at Bella

Luce, if the work is too hard, or Mrs. Smith tries to make life the hell you suggest she will, then I need not stay."

"Words, Anabel — and you say them so easily that I know you have no fear. But — oh, I can't explain — the mischief may be done before you can get away —"

Anabel frowned. "I don't follow you."

"And it's beyond me to figure out what is in my mind. It's so nebulous — but there all the same. My intuition tells me you should beware of a woman like Mrs. Smith who is suddenly bereft of her young, and blames you for coming between them."

"You are speaking of a human being, not a mad dog."

"I liken Mrs. Smith to a mad dog — and one without a chain, because though people realize she is queer, no one knows just how abnormal."

"I thought you didn't believe in intuitions."

"I don't usually, but where you're concerned it is pretty lively —" Suddenly Tim raised his hand, and putting his fingers under her chin, lifted it firmly but gently.

Slowly, as though her eyelids were heavily weighted, Anabel opened her eyes to meet his compelling gaze.

"Anabel!"

She thrilled to the core, and for a moment felt dizzy and confused.

"Don't go to Bella Luce... I haven't asked you ever to do anything to please me, but I do now... To please me, Anabel —" Tim's voice dropped to a whisper.

There was a long silence. Then Anabel's eyelids dropped so that her eyes were concealed, and she sighed like someone awaking from a trance. "I wish I could, Tim. I'd love to —" She frowned fiercely because unbidden and rare tears were burning under her eyelids. "But I told Mrs. Smith I would go. I hate having to break my word to anyone, especially to someone I dislike —"

Tim's fingers relaxed their hold, and he walked abruptly away from her, so that she felt cold and shivered.

"Tim —"

"Well?"

"Don't be angry with me."

"Haven't you asked for it?" Tim's voice was strained.

"Have I? For doing something I think right?"

"Apparently you get some sort of kick out of it, or you wouldn't do it," Tim replied drily, "though heaven alone knows what."

"D'you imagine I shall enjoy working up there — and for her?" Anabel demanded, now very close to tears.

"You are being quixotic, of course. But I don't know what to think, Anabel. I've tried to see your point of view. I've made every effort to clear my brain of trimmings and get down to the truth about you, but I'm still terribly confused. It's as though the hurt I had when I first came to Luniette has soured my outlook on life, and time alone can cure me completely, and make me whole enough to — well, to fall in love again, I suppose." Then Tim laughed, an unhappy sound, as though amused with self-mockery. "I couldn't have admitted that much a week or two ago, so perhaps time is already at work, and shaping me as Fate wishes to some end — but what end, Anabel?"

Anabel did not speak. Tim's words had made her feel happier, and the tears which were so close, threatening to fall, seemed far away again.

Tim said more briskly, "And now go to bed, Anabel. You look all in. Have you an alarum clock?" And when Anabel shook her head, "Then take mine. What time shall I set it for?"

"Four o'clock, please."

Tim glanced at her small white face quickly. "It'll still be dark then."

"I know, but I must have a bath, and I've got to climb the hill. I must be on time."

He frowned. "And your hours of work and pay?"

"They haven't been discussed."

"And won't be." Tim sighed. "Well, I can see it is no good talking — but I don't like it at all."

Before going to bed, Anabel had written a note to Mrs. Groom, telling her what she was doing, and saying that she did not expect to be back at the hotel before six o'clock. Anabel had decided it would be wiser to be frank with the landlady, who would anyway learn very quickly what was taking place, and might, unless warned beforehand, put her own — and perhaps wrong — interpretation on things.

It was dark when Anabel left the hotel the following morning. She soon grew accustomed to the blackness, but when passing the churchyard kept her eyes on the grass at her feet, not wanting to experience again the eerie feeling of seeing phosphorescence rising from those dark mounds on either side of the churchyard path.

It was easy to keep her mind off such things by concentrating on Tim.

'Here he held me in his arms! Here Tim whispered all those lovely, inconsequent endearing things!' Anabel thought. 'I shall never forget, even when I am an aristocratic old lady in a lace mobcap, with a sleek footman standing behind my chair, and an overfed lapdog on a needlework footstool at my feet.'

The remembrance of Tim's passionate kisses stirred Anabel deeply, the emotions such memories aroused remaining with her until she lost breath running up the stony incline to the valley opening on to Bella Luce. The atmosphere was clean and the air keen. There was a sense of waiting about her. If the birds were awake, they stayed quietly in their nests. Here Anabel paused. Her quick breathing sounded loud in that stillness which presaged the dawn; for the sound of breaking surf, and water dashing against those immutable rocks at the bottom of the granite cliffs, and which could be heard continuously, loudly or softly, according to weather and tides, seemed distant.

There were moving lights in the Channel, most of the ships steaming into port, with their streaks of smoke from galley fires, bent like black threads against the pale morning sky in which the stars were swiftly waning.

The thin keen air freshened Anabel's senses like wine, and made her eyes water. She coughed, the sound cracking across the intense stillness about her. In the occasional sweep of the lighthouse lamp falling athwart sea and land like an ever-watchful eye, there was a peacefulness and steadfastness and sense of security which had a tranquillizing effect on Anabel's mind.

Black and forbidding, down in the shadowed hollows in the lee of the island, were the cottages and hotel — a spinney, and the squat tower of the church.

And, nearer, was old Rube's cot, with its washed walls and thatched roof, looking like a mushroom in the sheltered dene — dark, silent and cold.

Over in the east the first pink finger of dawn gleamed, and as though it had been waiting for this signal, a bird fluttered up from its nest in the ground, shrilling heavenwards.

Anabel smiled and faced Bella Luce, thrilling at the beauty of its faded facade, the windows looking like dark lustrous eyes in the early light. There were sounds in the outbuildings, and hearing a low moo, Anabel stepped aside and went towards the open door through which streamed a gentle golden glow from a hurricane-lamp fixed to a wooden stall.

A warm sweet smell greeted Anabel as she entered the byre, and there was a quiet restfulness which she liked.

Old Rube and Keziah were milking the cows.

The latter looked up as Anabel approached, mute inquiry in her expressive eyes, but after a startled pause went on with her work of milking a cow with the name 'Polly' written in chalk on a blackboard over her stall.

Old Rube, with short legs, long arms and a powerful body — with an old felt hat perched on a grizzle of hair, got up from his milking-stool and ambled like a great ape towards Anabel, coming to a halt so close to her that she stepped back involuntarily, a feeling of repulsion towards this man sweeping over her with such strength as to make her feel sick.

"What be you wanting here?" he asked, his voice surprisingly clear, considering the mat of hair around his face, over his lips, and on his cheekbones. "What be you doin' up here at this hour of the marning?"

"I've come to help in the dairy," Anabel said, trying to speak firmly, and wishing she had gone directly up to the house instead of side-stepping in here.

"It don't take more'n me and Keziah to milk the cows. Does her know?" Rube jerked his thumb and head backwards, expressively, towards the house.

"Yes, Mrs. Smith expects me. I am to do Miss Naomi's work," Anabel explained stiffly.

"That's what oi thought. Miss Naomi, she never had patience to milk cows. But can you make good butter?"

"I think so." At this moment, having lost all confidence, and being aware of her colossal ignorance, with only a fortnight's theoretical experience of farming to draw upon, Anabel could feel sure of nothing.

Rube seemed amused. He shook with silent laughter, and Anabel, gazing fascinated at this hairy monster, saw a yellow tooth gleaming among the fuzz around his mouth.

Rube turned with agility, twitching Keziah's blouse, and when she looked up, proceeded to go through a series of pantomimic contortions of someone making butter, pointing at Anabel, and nearly doubling himself to the ground with his horrible silent laughter.

Quickly understanding his meaning, possibly thinking that Rube looked more like an Italian organ-grinder than a butter-maker, Keziah made curious sounds and stopped milking Polly to roll about on her three-legged stool. Naturally she rolled off, which increased Rube's mirth so that he slapped his corduroy breeches at the knee in a helpless kind of gesture.

This whacking frightened Polly, who began to kick, and tipped over the pail of frothing milk — whereat the peace of the cow-byre was broken by loud wails from Keziah, who shook her fist at Anabel.

Rube sobered down too. "What be oi going to say to her about the waste?" he cried in a sing-song voice to Anabel, his laughter gone and his eyes baleful, as he eyed the spilt milk.

"It wasn't my fault," disclaimed Anabel, foreseeing what was coming.

"Then oi am not to blame. If so be her hadn't drove Miss Naomi away —" Rube was beginning to say to Keziah, when Anabel cried:

"Don't you dare speak to me like that! How dare you accuse me of driving anyone away! You must know it is the last thing any decent person would do."

Rube looked worried and sheepish, though the eyes that peered under his bushy eyebrows had no likeness to a sheep's; they were cunning, as those of an ape. "Then oi don't know why ye be here, miss," he burst out.

"Because I am sorry for Mrs. Smith, and want to help her."

"Sorry!" Rube repeated. "Ye be sorry for her! For why?"

Meanwhile, Keziah had stopped making uncanny noises, and was clearing up the milk which filled a gutter running along the bottom of the stall, doing the job so thoroughly that Anabel realized later Keziah would never tell Mrs. Smith about the spilt milk.

But Anabel only shook her head and looked blank, and presently Rube returned to his milking.

Then Anabel went round to the back door of the homestead, and with a perfunctory knock entered to find Mrs. Smith standing, a lonely figure, in the middle of the big kitchen — doing nothing.

She turned suddenly to see the girl, slightly nonplussed, waiting with her hand on the knob of the kitchen door. And in the lamplight Anabel saw that the yellow face was even yellower than she had thought, the eyes were swollen and red with recent tears, and there were deep brown shadows under them. Cheeks and chin were sagging dejectedly, and Anabel noticed that Mrs. Smith was not dressed so neatly as usual, and there was no cameo brooch binding the collar of her bodice together, which was left open, revealing the wrinkled scrawniness of a tired old neck.

"So you came after all!" was the uncompromising welcome.

"Good morning, Mrs. Smith. Did you think I wouldn't?"

"I wasn't sure. The likes of you make facile promises which they have no intention of keeping."

"Well, you see one has kept her word," replied Anabel, determined not to be upset.

"But you're late. It is ten past five." And Mrs. Smith glanced significantly at the kitchen clock hanging on the wall.

"I have been here for some while. I saw a light in the cow house, and went to see if I could help Rube."

Mrs. Smith stared at this over-willing worker. "I hope Rube had the good sense to refuse your help, though he's so bone lazy he'd let anyone do his work."

"He didn't want mine," was the candid answer. "Anyway, I came to take Naomi's place as far as I could."

"As far as you could!" Mrs. Smith mused, pursing her thin lips. "Well, the first thing to do is to clean out the outer dairy, ready for the new milk to set which Rube will bring in before breakfast. Then skim the milk which has been standing all night in the inner dairy. That cream will be slightly sour when the second butter-making day comes later in the week. The pans of cream you will use today are on the right-hand side."

Mrs. Smith asked Anabel what temperature she used for churning, and nodded when Anabel said she was taught it should be as near 60 degrees as possible.

"And when do you know your butter is ready to wash and press?"

She received Anabel's answer in silence.

"The buttermilk you draw off is for pig swill," Mrs. Smith said at length. She pointed towards the dairy, which Anabel remembered from her first visit to Bella Luce, with the parting instruction, "And don't make a mess of things. I can't afford to waste sixty gallons of milk."

Anabel closed the dairy door carefully, and tiptoed across the brick floor to the inner dairy, and contemplated with some dismay, and her courage in her shoes, the neat rows of huge shallow tin pans. "Heavens!" she exclaimed. "Supposing I do make a helluva mess of everything?"

But just using Tim's habitual expression made Anabel feel better. At seven o'clock Anabel was called to breakfast. She was tired and hungry by then, but so interested in her work that she went unwillingly into the kitchen.

Robert and his mother were already seated when Anabel entered, but as soon as he saw her Robert smiled and rose to pull back her chair and ask if he could cut her some bread.

"You needn't treat Miss Robinson as a visitor, Robert. She has come up here to work, and must take us as she finds us."

Robert took no notice of his mother's advice, and continued to wait on Anabel, asking her how she was shaping. "If you want any tips about butter-making, ask me," Robert said, and looked proudly at Anabel.

"I'm rather slow," confessed Anabel. "This is all so strange to me, but I quite like it. I shall soon get into my stride." And secretly she added, 'I hope.'

"And what is your stride?" demanded Mrs. Smith coldly.

Anabel half-smiled. "I have the reputation of setting a good pace, carrying on steadily, and always finishing the course," she replied demurely.

Mrs. Smith glanced at the girl sharply, as though she suspected Anabel was belittling her before Robert. "Let's hope you can face up to one week of hard work then, without having to go sick."

"I'll try to," said Anabel confidently.

Then Robert asked, "Bacon and egg, Anabel?"

"Please."

"Is that how you like your bacon fried?" he said.

Mrs. Smith interrupted sharply, "This isn't an hotel."

"Fancy it's one of those hospitable farms! Who would have thought it?" Robert answered imperturbably, but his eyes looked black in the morning light.

Mrs. Smith gave Anabel a withering glance as though to say, "This is your doing." But Anabel would not meet those dark accusing eyes, and looked out of the window to where Keziah and Rube were eating their breakfast of bacon and potatoes at a wooden table under a shelter roofed with corrugated tin — the dog, Con, straining at his chain, hopefully waiting for titbits.

Robert said, "Made any butter yet, Anabel?"

"Good gracious, no! I've only just finished scrubbing the slated shelves of the dairy."

Robert fixed his eyes on his mother. "Anabel is here to do Naomi's work, but Naomi never scrubbed a thing in her life. You took care of that. Why do you set Anabel to scrub?"

Mrs. Smith glanced at her plate. "The shelves were dirty — someone had to do them," she remarked sullenly.

"They can't be dirty. I saw Keziah preparing them, as usual, yesterday afternoon."

"Oh, Keziah! I couldn't be running down the hill and watching Keziah. She never works hard unless I am standing over her."

Anabel intervened to say cheerfully, "Well, it's done now."

After breakfast Robert suggested, "Now rest awhile, Anabel, before you start work again, or you'll crock up — take it easy, I say."

"I'd rather go ahead," Anabel replied, rising from the table with an, "Excuse me, Mrs. Smith."

Robert was before Anabel, opening the door, saying, "Don't forget if you want any help to ask me."

It was kind of him to make things easier for her, Anabel thought, but such an attitude only angered his mother.

And when Anabel was in the cool gloom of the dairy, with the door shut, she could hear mother and son quarrelling, their voices reaching her clearly through the slatted window. It required little imagination to know that they were squabbling about herself.

Before making the butter, Anabel carefully washed her hands in oatmeal water, then began to strain the cream through cloths.

Robert poked his head in to say, "Don't churn too quickly, Anabel, or you'll burst the butter; or too slowly, or the flavour will be bad. You don't mind my telling you?"

"Not a bit."

It cheered Anabel that Robert wanted her to be a success, and she was glad of his tips, which were a great help. Mrs. Smith's attitude confused Anabel so that she could not think clearly, and was nervous of doing something wrong.

But luck is ever on the beginner's side, and Anabel churned until the butter globules were the size of sago.

By that time, Robert looked in again. "I've got five minutes to spare," he said, and helped Anabel wash and knead the butter until all the buttermilk was expressed.

It was a hard day and a long one, and Anabel suspected that Mrs. Smith went out of her way to create petty chores, find endless trivial faults, and make the work trying. On the other hand, Robert left his work in the fields to visit the homestead on some pretext or other, and though his presence eased Anabel's work considerably, it also increased Mrs. Smith's spite towards her.

Once, when Robert had given her several tips, Anabel thanked him gratefully.

"The gratitude is on our side," Robert said generously, and Anabel liked him at that moment better than she had ever done. "I could do no less than try to help you. I think it is most sporting of you to give us a hand. If my mother were not so upset about Naomi, she'd be grateful, too. You're working much better than my sister ever did — and you're cheerful about it, which Naomi was not. This house was always in an uproar, with one and another quarrelling. Gossip says that my mother is only happy when she's quarrelling with someone."

Then Mrs. Smith caught Robert in the dairy, and sent him about his business, watching him as he disappeared through the yard door, when she said to Anabel, "You two like each other, don't you?"

"I think so, Mrs. Smith," was the wary reply.

"I only asked because people are talking about you and Robert."

Anabel's colour heightened, as she said lightly, "Well, people must talk about something — and there isn't a great deal to discuss on Luniette."

"When I was a girl and people coupled a boy's and girl's names together, those two were expected to marry."

Anabel's eyes were alert, but she only remarked coolly, "How funny! Well, people are more sensible now — happily for the boy and girl."

"Then you don't mind what people say about you?"

"Oh, gracious, no! If they want to talk, let them."

"I thought you would mind it if the islanders said you were after my Robert — especially as you're supposed to be helping me because of Naomi."

It hadn't occurred to Anabel to wonder or care what the islanders thought or said about her and Robert, but she did pause to think what Tim would say if he heard such gossip.

Then she said quietly, "Whatever they think wouldn't be true, Mrs. Smith."

"Perhaps you don't think my Robert good enough for you?" Mrs. Smith sneered.

Anabel met the older woman's gaze squarely, and confessed, "I haven't thought about it at all." But on and off Anabel pondered over this talk for the next hour.

Then came dinner, which Anabel was too tired to eat. Her arms ached with turning the handle of the butter-churn, and there were blisters on the palm of one hand. Robert did not come in, and Mrs. Smith seemed not to care whether Anabel ate or not — though there was plenty of food on the table.

Late in the afternoon, when the rolls of golden butter were wrapped in paper and packed in a wooden kit to be taken down to the store ready for the boat coming in from Combeford in the morning, Anabel made some dough for bread which was put to rise in an earthenware pan beside the kitchen stove and covered with a clean cloth.

Robert came in. He wore no coat, and his shirt was open at the neck, revealing the beautiful bronze column of his smooth neck. Anabel thought, as she had done once before, what a handsome man Robert was — perfect except for the perpetual sneer on his finely chiselled lips and the wild bitter look in his eyes. Not that his eyes were bitter at this moment. They looked across the kitchen at Anabel and their expression was soft and tender.

"Don't work so hard," Robert begged. "Surely you've finished for the day? Naomi never did half what you are doing. It's so easy to put upon a willing worker."

"Naomi knew her way about, and I don't. And I must finish all my chores."

"Must you? There's always tomorrow, Anabel."

"I know, but your mother hates the work to drag on. She tells me Naomi is worth three of me."

Robert frowned. "Mother's a slave-driver, always behind people, pushing them on to work harder. That kind never get the best out of people, because we're all only human and must tire some time."

"Don't speak like that about your mother."

"It's true, and I only say it to you because — well, anyway, while you're here you are one of us. But don't take any notice of what she says. Mother isn't always so crabbed."

Anabel nodded sympathetically. "She's worried about Naomi."

"And it's giving her relief to take it out on you."

Anabel thought this most unfair, but she replied sturdily, "I can take it."

"I wonder."

"And if I'm any real help —"

"I believe Mother wants you to be a failure. She'll be disappointed if you are a success. You'll never know from her how well you've done. But did you notice how her face fell when she saw those perfect golden rolls of butter?"

Anabel had noticed that, though she refused to admit it to Robert. So she shrugged, "Oh, I don't spy around looking for trouble," she replied.

After that, Anabel had a welcome cup of tea.

Twice during the day, when Anabel was in the kitchen, Keziah had opened the lid of the well in the corner of the kitchen, and with a horrible clanking of the long chain had drawn up buckets of water for household use. Fascinated, filled with a nameless fear of that dark depth which the removal of the cover exposed, Anabel had stopped work to stare at Keziah, a baleful influence in any house, not because of her misfortune, but for her bitterness of spirit, something which warped her mind and dwarfed her outlook.

Once Keziah, by signs, had invited Anabel to look down into the darkness, and when the girl had approached the well with dragging unwilling footsteps, Keziah had hastened her by taking hold of Anabel's sleeve and pulling her playfully towards the gaping hole.

Anabel had screamed and Keziah had let go immediately, when the girl retired hastily, covered with confusion, ashamed of letting herself go.

But after tea Robert uncovered the well with the unconcern of habitual use, and brought up sufficient water for a bath.

"I'll run you down in the van with the butter, which must catch the boat in time for the market tomorrow," he said to Anabel, who was mixing chicken food. "Will you wait for me? I shan't be long."

But the prospect of sitting close to Robert, cooped up in a van, did not appeal to Anabel, and she said the first words that came into her head. "I promised to be down early. I think I'll hurry off."

"Whom did you promise?" And a strange and terrifying note crept into Robert's voice, and he paid out the bucket and chain rapidly and with a deafening rattle.

"Mrs. Groom — why?" Anabel's tone was bland. She was learning to defend herself against mother and son.

"Oh! I thought you meant Northorn."

Anabel did not answer.

CHAPTER 18

Tim, laughing and blue-eyed, so gay in comparison with the dour people she had just left that Anabel found her spirits rising fast, was waiting for her as she entered the hotel.

"Hallo, had enough of playing dairymaid?" Tim asked, his blue eyes fixed anxiously on Anabel's tired face — a look she did not see, because meeting him so unexpectedly, and catching the kindliness in his voice after the hard unsympathetic day, brought the sting of tears to Anabel's eyes, blurring her sight.

"I don't know about playing," she cried dubiously. "Just look at my hand after churning forty pounds of butter." She showed Tim her blistered palm, with one of the blisters raw.

Tim looked down and caught her hand in his. "Oh, I say! You poor child! What have those people been doing to you? I've got a first-aid outfit upstairs. Come up to the bathroom and I'll bind up your hand."

And when this was done in workmanlike fashion to Tim's satisfaction, he exclaimed, "That's a neat job, isn't it? Good enough for a hospital sister. Well, I hope this will be a lesson to you, and you'll never want to go farming again — not the real thing, anyway. If you must play, do it in the Marie Antoinette way."

Anabel sat on the edge of the bath. "Silly, I'm going tomorrow."

"With that hand?"

"Of course. Mrs. Smith thinks I can't stay the course, and I've got to prove to her that I can."

"That's absurd! If you've crocked up like this — with a bleeding hand and a haggish face — after one day's work, what will you be like at the end of a week? You'll harden, but you'll look a sight."

As he appeared to wait for an answer, Anabel replied flippantly, "Perhaps I'll be dead."

"Not with me here to stop it," was the robust retort.

And presently, when Tim, too, sat on the edge of the bath and they were both smoking, he asked, "And that reminds me, Anabel; have you discussed pay and hours yet?"

"No."

"Well, do so. Mrs. Smith will underpay you, and deduct, so that you will find in a week's time that you've been working for nothing."

"Oddly enough, that would give me joy."

Tim studied her face in silence. She was tired, but game, and a great admiration for Anabel filled his heart. "You funny little thing!" he said softly. Then in a louder tone, "D'you mean to tell me you don't believe in the national creed of the labourer being worthy of his hire — with the labourer's worthiness a thing beyond price, and the hire a trifle?"

Anabel laughed, forgetting her fatigue. "I don't think of my work in terms of money. You've no idea how interesting it is and what a lot I'm learning."

Tim eyed her as a curiosity. "Obviously you don't have to think ever of money," he said. "Well, tell me all about your day. I'm curious to know more about the Smith *ménage*. Did Robert behave himself?"

"Oh yes."

"I'm glad to hear it," replied Tim succinctly. "Mrs. Groom doesn't approve of what you are doing — Mabelle is scandalized — Winnie, or should I say the whole island now that Winnie is talking? — is like one big question mark. So what, Anabel? It's your move now."

Anabel digested this in silence. Then, "I can't help it, Tim. They must just talk. Perhaps when they get it all off their chests they'll stop talking. You know what little communities are like, everywhere."

Tim nodded. He got to his feet and stood looking down at Anabel. "Now listen to me seriously, Anabel —"

But he got no further, for Anabel, driven by some sudden driving urge, seized Tim's hand, and held it closely to her hot cheek for a few moments, as though deriving some comfort from the contact. "Please don't say it, Tim. Just be kind and patient and understanding with me — and perhaps it'll all come right."

Just what Anabel meant Tim did not know, but that Anabel felt she was in some manner in the Smiths' debt was clear.

Tim did not like the position at all. Anabel was young, pretty and defenceless, and, as he put it, had crept under his skin, so that he thought about her during the day, when her face got between him and his work; and he dreamt about her at night.

Tim was beginning to feel that life would be a dull existence without Anabel. Indeed, it would be impossible.

She was precious, and he had to care for her. He distrusted the Smiths, and Anabel spent, and intended on spending, all her days there. It was unthinkable. And who were the Smiths?

But he resolutely put these worrying thoughts behind him, and responded to Anabel's appeal. "Of course it will," Tim said, patting her shoulder awkwardly. "At least, I hope so. But this is a foolhardy undertaking, Anabel, and it would be wrong of me not to tell you what I think." He bent and touched her bandaged hand playfully. "A tenderfoot among the Spartans! Well, what about a drink? I think we both need one."

The atmosphere of the bar was not so friendly as formerly. When Tim and Anabel entered, there was a noticeable break in the smooth flow of talk. The *habitués* were uneasy, not so hail-fellow-well-met, and there were sly looks at the couple, though everyone tried to pretend that everything was as usual.

Anabel appeared not to notice it, and it was easier for her because she was a woman and quick to adapt herself to her surroundings, and she had mixed more in society than most of these people.

Tim said nothing, though he could not pretend a *bonhomie* with his fellow men which he did not feel, and it galled him that they cold-shouldered Anabel. So after a quick drink, he yawned to show that he was bored, then said he was hungry and drew Anabel into the dining-room. Here, he rang the bell, and spoke sharply to Mabel when she answered it, asking how long supper would be.

Anabel cried out that she hadn't had her bath, and ran upstairs to take it.

After the bath, when she felt less tired, while dressing, Mrs. Groom came hastily to the door, and Anabel let her in.

"I've run away for a moment," Mrs. Groom said breathlessly. "I can't stop or they'll miss me and wonder where I am. Then their tongues will get busy again." Mrs. Groom, her hand fidgeting nervously under her dark flannel apron, took a deep breath and burst out, "Oh, Miss Robinson, whateffer made you do such a silly thing?"

Anabel stuck out her chin stubbornly. It was a family characteristic, and when business associates saw Anabel's father thrust out his chin they were wont to say, "Sam's gone to war again, and by the look of him he'll stick to his guns even if the enemy overruns him — somehow."

So now Anabel exclaimed haughtily, "Silly!" And Mrs. Groom wilted visibly.

But the landlady pressed on. Now that Alf was gone, a woman required a bit of willpower to stand up to Mabel, Olly and Joe — and sometimes the rabble in the bar, which got a bit above itself on a Saturday night.

Mrs. Groom said, "It's like putting your head deliberately into the lion's mouth — look you."

"What do you mean?"

Mrs. Groom opened the door a fraction to make sure nobody was listening, then she shut it again, and spoke in a sepulchral whisper. "The Smiths aren't ordinary people. Everyone round here knows that. And there's Winnie's mother, who's bedridden in her cottage this ten years, and no one hardly ever sees because she's got so thin she looks like a witch, and people are afraid of her; she used to work up at Bella Luce when old Mr. Smith was alive, and she says there were nice goings-on. That family —"

Mrs. Groom heard a sound outside the door and quickly put her hand over her mouth, while Anabel, though curious and mystified, suppressed a wild desire to laugh.

There was a timid knock, Mabel coughed suggestively, and then called out, "I've hurried up with the supper, miss. It's all in and waiting. And will you please to tell Mrs. Groom —"

"Now how did Mabel know I was here, considering I crept up while she was in the yard?" whispered Mrs. Groom. Then: "It'll have to keep." And in a louder voice, "They say on Luniette that if people want to talk secrets, they have either to go out to sea in a boat or go bathing."

When she was alone again, Anabel went over to the window. There was a pink reflection in the sky, the glow from a gorgeous sunset. But the heaving sea was more grey than green, and already the evening star was bright in the clear sky.

Anabel was mystified and full of misgivings, sensitive by the adverse criticism of what she had done and depressed by the lack of good comradeship in the bar. All her old fears of the Smiths rose in her mind like a crowd of ghosts. And once more she asked herself what the end of all this would be.

She did not waver in her purpose. She had given her word to Mrs. Smith, and in spite of everything it had to be kept.

Next day, a letter reached the farm from Naomi, and after reading it in secret Mrs. Smith hid it in the bodice of her dress, and later attacked Anabel again for driving Naomi from home.

And today, because she was still tired, Anabel worked without the zest which had been behind everything she did yesterday. There was no butter to make, but there was bread to be baked.

It turned out so leaden that even Robert, who thought everything Anabel did perfection, ate it reluctantly.

Anabel listened to Mrs. Smith's long saga of her failure in silence, but there was a faraway look in the girl's eyes which showed that only half her mind was listening to what Mrs. Smith said. With the other half Anabel was trying to recall what she had seen on her arrival in the kitchen in the morning.

Determined to give no cause for complaint in being late, Anabel had reached the farm a quarter before the kitchen clock struck five. The door leading to the yard was open. Con, barking at the cat which was its avowed enemy, drowned the sound of Anabel's light footsteps on the cobblestones as she entered the kitchen unobserved.

The cloth in her hand, Mrs. Smith was bending over the pan of bread that had been left to rise overnight. She jumped nervously when Anabel said, "Good morning, Mrs. Smith. Has the dough risen nicely?"

Mrs. Smith covered the pan quickly, and looked with stony eyes at Anabel. "I suppose so," she said sourly.

But later, when Anabel raised the cloth to take the dough from the pan, it occurred to her that the mixture had been touched. And a fleeting picture of Mrs. Smith's floury hand as she replaced the cloth flashed across Anabel's mind's eye.

However, the picture was nebulous, and though for a moment Anabel knitted her brows in perplexity, she quickly drove all unworthy thoughts out of her mind. Instinctively Anabel was aware that Mrs. Smith was her implacable enemy.

"I'll do better next time," she promised. "I've never done any cooking before."

"And in the meantime, my flour is wasted."

"I will replace it."

"You'll have to."

That evening, Anabel was too tired to keep awake and blamed the heat of the dining-room in the hotel for making her so sleepy. And Tim, disappointed in her companionship, advised her shortly to get to bed.

"I'm so sorry, Tim, but even if I stay down to talk as I should love to —"

"I thought I told you to turn in? Goodnight, Anabel."

And so the days went by for a week, and into the second week, with Anabel struggling through tasks of which she had little or no knowledge a couple of weeks ago, and registering more failures at her work than successes.

Yet she was true to her determination to let nothing Mrs. Smith said upset her. And, oddly, that was the easiest part of her day at Bella Luce.

As the week went by, Robert made more and more opportunities to be with Anabel, neglecting his work, flouting his mother's authority, doing anything to stay with this girl who fascinated him deeply.

And though occasionally Robert would have liked to burst into uproarious rage, and ease his overstrung nerves a little, he had evidently set himself to win Anabel's friendship, and perhaps something more, seizing the wonderful chance of having her in his house.

No one guessed that piously, every night, Robert knelt down by the side of his bed and prayed that such a storm would arise that Anabel would not be able to go back to the hotel where his rival, Tim, was awaiting her, but would have to sleep at the farm.

Anabel should have Naomi's little room, which was the most comfortable in the house, and was on the opposite side of the landing to his own, well away from his mother's bedroom.

And then…

Even Robert could go no further.

Tim struggled to keep cheerful, but he heard criticisms against Anabel which tried his patience sorely, some of them unjustified, and was glad that none reached her ears. She was busy and tired, and seemed to pass her time away from Bella Luce in a state of somnolence.

And one never-to-be-forgotten evening, when Anabel was hardening to the farm routine, and had taken a swift revivifying drink before Tim came in so that she should be fresh for him — it was Tim who was too tired to keep awake.

"I couldn't sleep last night," he apologized, when he had dozed off, and wakened with a start as a log fell apart with a shower of sparks in the grate.

"It's that night duty," commiserated Anabel.

Tim nodded, looked long and unblinkingly at Anabel with eyes bright with sleep, and agreed laconically, "Perhaps."

After a long silence, during which Tim nodded and slept, Anabel said briskly, "Let's turn in. We're both tired."

"No — I'll stop here — you go."

"But you are far sleepier than I am," Anabel protested.

"Oh, I can fall off anywhere so long as it's a comfortable spot. Unless —" ponderously — "you are expecting Smith down? But I should have thought you'd seen plenty of him during the day."

But there was that in Tim's tone which fell disagreeably on Anabel's ear — so she rose and went to bed and to sleep; and Tim, his heart more or less at rest, remained quietly dozing in the dining-room until Robert burst in, pausing when he saw that Tim was alone.

"Where's Anabel?" Robert asked quickly.

"Gone to bed. Is it important?"

"Yes." Robert's tone was impatient.

"Can I give a message? Cow sent her love? Pig's ill?"

"Don't be a fool."

"Whatever it is must wait," was the decisive reply. Then, as Robert was turning to leave the room, "Hold hard, Smith! Shut the door." And when Robert did so, "Now that we are at last alone, perhaps you'll tell me all about this new game your mother and yourself, for diverse reasons, are playing with Anabel."

"Game!" repeated Robert blankly. "Your mistake. Anabel's working for us."

There was such arrogance in the younger man's tone that Tim kept his temper with difficulty, and itched to knock some of the bumptiousness out of Robert. But he said calmly enough, "Can't Mrs. Smith find a more suitable person to work at Bella Luce than Anabel, who is a stranger to her and is new to the job?"

Robert's lips moved in a superior twisted kind of smile. "I dare say my mother could if she tried."

"Supposing you show your decency towards Anabel by asking Mrs. Smith to try?"

Robert shrugged. "Decency!" he repeated slowly, as though savouring the meaning of the word. Then stubbornly, and with a malicious light in his brown eyes, "That would be the last thing I should suggest. You see, having Anabel up at Bella Luce suits me. Down here, I never had the chance of speaking to her alone. There is always someone watching, or ready to interrupt. But up there, knowing exactly where Anabel is at any moment of the day, I can make many opportunities to talk to her. And who can blame me for seizing a chance I have never had in my life before?"

A dull flush crept under Tim's tanned skin, and his hands, which were partially hidden from Robert, were clenched so fiercely that the nails dug into his palms and drew blood — though Tim did not realize this until later. "I don't doubt but that you are making good use of your time — from your point of view," Tim was able to say coldly. "But the arrangement was for a week or so only."

"Yes — but the time isn't up yet," was the complacent reply.

The two men took each other's measure.

'I'd like to knock the fellow down!' thought Tim.

'He'd love to knock me out!' Robert thought. 'But I'd like to kill him.'

Tim said aloud, "It soon will be, thank heaven."

Robert laughed suddenly. For some reason he felt bold, confident and triumphant. "I don't know who put you up to question me. I'm sure Anabel doesn't know that you have appointed yourself her guardian. And being independent, she would be furious if she knew. You are nothing to her, and have no right to say what she shall or shall not do — yet to hear you, anyone might think you had some right."

"That goes for you, too."

"No — not yet — but I hope —" The short, clipped sentences were suggestive with meaning, and for the life of him Tim could not help asking in a dangerously quiet tone:

"What grounds have you for hoping anything?"

Again Robert laughed — easily, and with that new disquieting confidence that roused Tim's fears for Anabel to such a pitch it was difficult to hold back from kicking Robert out of the room. "Anabel likes me. D'you think she'd stay up at Bella Luce for a moment with my mother, even though she still sympathizes with her about Naomi, if I were not there? Even Anabel, conscientious worker though she is, must have relaxation, or go mad penned up each day in a gloomy dairy, or working in that great kitchen with Keziah. I keep Anabel amused at Bella Luce."

A vertical line appeared on Tim's forehead between his eyes. "D'you mean that, Smith?"

"Of course," Robert replied haughtily.

"You've got a darned big opinion of yourself."

"Not at all. I'm just being clever at turning a deal between my mother and Anabel to my own account."

"Anabel —"

"She likes talking to me. I help her in the dairy. We work together. I stand like a buffer between Anabel and my mother.

I do my best to make the work easier, and naturally Anabel appreciates it."

"Did Anabel say so?"

"Oh, rather, she is always thanking me. And believe me, she does it jolly well." Then Robert shut up suddenly, and looked suspiciously at Tim. And when he spoke it was in a flat voice, like a balloon that has lost its gas — and bounce. "And now, if Anabel is not downstairs to talk to either of us, I will go home. I shall see her before you do in the morning. I am a very busy man these days, because not only must I get through my own heavy work, but I like to help someone else, and also arrange it so that there is still a little time to be friendly — if you get me?"

When Robert was gone Tim relaxed, conscious that he felt sick at heart.

He was glad to be alone, to have time to cool down, and to try to forget the disgust and, yes, jealousy, which he felt for this odious young man.

Now Tim welcomed Mrs. Smith's presence at the farm, hard taskmistress though she seemed to be. It was easy to see that Mrs. Smith was working Anabel hard, meting out a kind of retribution against Fate for the loss of Naomi — hoping perhaps to break Anabel's spirit, certainly to impair her health. And, of course, it was not difficult to understand that Robert would naturally take full advantage of Anabel's being at Bella Luce. He was a man unused to delicate and sensitive girls... Tim was sure that Robert had never met anyone so beautiful as Anabel, with such poise and spirit, and that gracious manner which many women might well envy.

Robert was playing his mother's game for his own sake. Tim could even believe that Robert was glad Naomi had gone, for her going had given him Anabel — and in no other way could Robert have enjoyed Anabel's company.

But in Robert lay a danger which Tim could not name, and it worried him so much he could not sleep that night.

Next morning, when Anabel went up to Bella Luce, she walked in an atmosphere of red light, for the sky over in the east was a gorgeous and terrifying sight, a study in angry streaks of blood-red.

The atmosphere was heavy and still, as though presaging something awful.

Old Rube called out from the cow-byre as Anabel passed, "There be a big storm brewing. Them birds has kept oi awake all night," and he threw a stone at a gull perched on the shaft of a farm-wagon.

Anabel paused before the homestead, lost in admiration of its beauty. Like everything else, the house was bathed in the unearthly light of the sky's ruddy glow.

She had already, in this short time, seen the old house in many guises. Once the upper storey, with its towering copper beech as background, had seemed to rise above a white ground mist, looking like some beautiful desert mirage in the sky which cheers the weary traveller into believing he has found haven at last.

Anabel had seen Bella Luce in the pale light of a waning moon, a study in velvet, and again like an opal in the morning sunshine.

The weather-beaten frontage was like a picture when the western sun picked out its faded colouring, and beamed on the windows so that they shone like crystal eyes.

Robert's voice came softly over her shoulder. "What are you looking at?"

"Your house — and wishing I could see it in winter with the snow lying thickly upon it. I expect it looks like a Christmas card then. Have you ever seen it in the snow — or is it too warm on Luniette for snow to settle?" Anabel had spoken casually, growing careless, now that her time at Bella Luce was ending, of how she treated this man with the hot melancholy eyes.

Robert, his emotions rising, caught Anabel's hand suddenly in his. "You could see it then, Anabel," he said thickly.

"Oh no, I'm not staying on Luniette much longer," she replied swiftly, her voice impersonal, a tone she found most suitable in keeping Robert's amorous advances at bay — and there had been many lately, and were increasing in number and strength.

"You sound as though you'll be glad to go, and don't want ever to return," he said, thinking that Anabel showed far more enthusiasm for the house than she did for him.

"I'm not glad to go for many reasons, but my holiday must come to an end."

"Then you'll come back one day?"

"No." It was best to speak decisively. Lately Robert had been purposely dense, refusing to take a hint.

Robert squeezed Anabel's fingers until they hurt cruelly, but she bore it without flinching, and waited quietly until the pressure relaxed somewhat, then calmly withdrew her hand from his.

"What is the betting that Rube is watching us?" she asked half-smilingly.

"Let him," said Robert roughly. "Rube knows better than to interfere. Anabel —"

But Anabel chose to be deaf to the imploring note in Robert's voice. She said, "If there is a storm coming up, as

Rube prophesies, I must go in and do my work quickly, so that I can get down to the hotel before it breaks."

Robert did not answer, and looking at him, Anabel saw that he was staring up at the sky with a curiously rapt expression on his face, and a queer luminous light in his eyes.

"I believe you like storms," she told him teasingly as she left him standing there, and went round the house to the kitchen entrance.

Anabel thought the day would never end. She was in a fever of impatience to get ahead of the storm, for as the day lightened to a sickly grey pallor, and the crimson faded from the sky, the wind rose, soughing through the massive branches of the giant copper beech, and whistling eerily, like an imprisoned soul in pain, between the window slats in the dairy where Anabel worked.

As the day advanced, heavy blooms of greyish-purple clouds moved swiftly, and in a rolling formation across the darkening sky.

Mrs. Smith was in her most unpleasant mood. Nothing Anabel did was right. There was much work to be done, and some chores to be done again because Mrs. Smith was difficult to please. There were petty vexations which rasped Anabel's nerves, but through it all, on the surface anyway, she remained cheerful.

Then Robert for once did not help Anabel as she had fully expected him to do, a fact which Mrs. Smith commented upon with acerbity.

At dinner, Anabel said openly, ignoring Mrs. Smith's set face, "I haven't seen you all the morning, Robert," hoping he would take the hint and promise to help in the afternoon.

But to Anabel's dismay, Robert grunted something about Sue being lame, and that he'd have to poultice her leg during the afternoon to keep the swelling down, or she would not be fit to use for weeks. He had brought her round in front to the loose-box.

Mrs. Smith questioned him sharply, and with a malevolent glance at Anabel said the farm was going to ruin.

When Mrs. Smith and Anabel sat down alone to tea, Anabel took the opportunity to say quietly, "I shall not be coming here tomorrow, Mrs. Smith — or any other day."

There was a long silence, then Mrs. Smith asked with a sneer, "The work's got you down? I knew it would," and her tone said, 'I told you so.'

Anabel shook her head. "It has nothing to do with the work."

"Then Robert's been annoying you. Well, that was to be expected."

"It isn't Robert."

"No? He loves you."

Anabel shrugged. "I haven't encouraged him."

"Then what is it?"

"Why should I tell you?" Anabel queried.

"No reason at all. We hate each other. Put it down to curiosity on my part."

Then Anabel made a decision, and faced the sallow-skinned woman squarely. "It's this: I came here to help you not because Naomi went away, or I sympathized especially with you, or even because I liked Robert as you once suggested I did, and which I think you would not like — but to pay a debt."

Anabel paused to collect her thoughts, aware that her last words had astonished Mrs. Smith. Everything must be put plainly before this woman so that there should be no further misunderstandings, questions or recriminations, while it would be good for herself at last to unravel the confusion of motives in her own mind.

Quietly, and with dramatic effect, Anabel continued, "Naomi would never have won Tim Northorn. And eventually, perhaps for a totally different reason from disappointment over Tim, she might have left Luniette. It's a grand place for a holiday, but even you must admit there is little scope on Luniette for a spirited girl like Naomi. It just happened that my coming brought matters to a head, and it seems I have made a nice scapegoat for the failure of family schemes.

"Well, I did take Tim Northorn from Naomi — not wilfully, because I'm not the sort to poach on another girl's preserves. But Tim and I had a lot in common — we had suffered from the same experience of being jilted, an unpleasant thing to happen to anyone, and we were both sore.

"Anyhow, something drew us together in spite of ourselves, something more powerful than our wills to keep apart, stronger than your efforts — something nobody could control.

"But, and this is the funny part of the whole business, the mere fact that I was Tim's best friend, enjoying his society knowing he gave me his first thoughts, seemed to put me in Naomi's debt. It was my own idea, which I don't expect anyone really to understand — but there it was. And just because you had lost Naomi's help, I transferred the debt to you, and offering to do her work here seemed to be the best way to pay it off."

There was another long silence when Anabel had finished speaking, during which Mrs. Smith's eyes never left the girl's face.

At length the older woman spoke, asking harshly, "And you consider the debt paid?"

"Yes, amply — and my conscience is now clear."

Mrs. Smith rose quickly — her way of closing an unpleasant discussion. "I see," she said. "Well, there are a few odd jobs I should like you to do before you go, Miss Robinson —"

Anabel agreed pleasantly, then looked out of the window, and saw that the rain which had been threatening all day was coming down fast. "Oh, dear! Just look at the rain! And I had hoped to be back in the hotel before the storm broke," she cried in some dismay, rising to watch the storm.

Even as she spoke, Robert came into the kitchen. He was hatless and wet through, the rain streaming down his face and dripping from his saturated clothes. "You can't go home tonight," he shouted triumphantly to Anabel. "There's been a landslide, and the track is broken. Nothing can pass up or down."

Mrs. Smith ran to the window.

"There's nothing to see. It's just over the brow of the hill," Robert cried, rubbing his hands gleefully together. "What a bit of luck!" He laughed at Anabel.

But Anabel could say nothing, only stand there white and stricken, despair and fear in her heart. She felt crushed.

Meanwhile, when the wind was rising with phenomenal swiftness to hurricane speed, whipping the sea into a mass of churning white foam, and the rain was beating down like steel knives against a leaden sky, with a venomous hissing sound, Tim — in oilskins — went to see Winnie's mother.

She was a dreadful old crone lying bedridden in a small room under the eaves of a cob cottage. Here Tim heard a strange and terrifying story, which haunted him, so that he hurried back to the hotel to phone to Anabel that she must leave the farm at once, and he would meet her on the way down.

Tim was met on the doorstep by Mrs. Groom, who was on the lookout for him, and who told him in some agitation, "Miss Robinson isn't coming down tonight, sir. The bad weather has swept away a part of the track, and it would be dangerous for her to make the journey."

"Then —" Tim said twice, passing a dry tongue over his lips, making an effort to frame words, and failing. He took off his sou'wester and shook off the raindrops, and tried to appear natural.

"She's sleeping up at Bella Luce."

Then Tim asked hoarsely, "Did Anabel — Miss Robinson — speak to you?"

"Yes, sir."

"Was she upset at all?"

"No-o — very much as usual."

Tim was silent, staring at Mrs. Groom dumbfounded, rain falling from his oilskins, making pools of water on the hall floor. "But —" he began, frowning heavily. "Are you sure Miss Robinson said the track was gone?"

"Quite, sir."

Tim shook his head. "That's most odd. Somehow I can't understand it."

The unreasoning fear that had been with him all day, and which the revelations of Winnie's mother had put into concrete form, came to Tim with renewed force, so that he knew it was imperative for him to reach Anabel without delay and bring her away from the danger that lurked at Bella Luce, one which might break forth at any moment. This he must do if ever again he was to know peace.

And while he was making swift plans to be carried out immediately, Mrs. Groom remembered something else.

A message had been received from the camp: would the Lieutenant-Commander go up at once?

For a moment Tim stood looking at Mrs. Groom in bewilderment, then he nodded briefly. He had been expecting something from the Admiralty all day, and Fate had arranged that he must do his duty when every nerve in Tim's body yearned to go to Anabel's aid.

"Supper's ready, sir," said Mabel, coming out of the kitchen, her face woebegone because Anabel's bright presence was not in the house.

"Eh? I don't want any. I'm going out again — up to the camp."

"Shall I leave it on the table, sir?"

Tim stared with glazed eyes from one woman to the other — not really seeing either. "No. Yes — oh, do what you like —" And with that he put on his sou'wester and was gone.

Slowly, Mrs. Groom's eyes met Mabel's. "Look you, Mabel, he might be drunk."

"There's somethink on his mind. I believe he's gorn up to her — not to camp. There's romance for you."

Mrs. Groom let that pass. "He's nearly as upset as I am, and that's saying something. There are queer things going on up at Bella Luce tonight. I don't like it."

CHAPTER 19

Anabel's first reaction, after the numbing shock of Robert's news had passed, was one of terror, and she cried out, "What shall I do? I can't sleep here."

Mrs. Smith replied in such a matter-of-fact tone — calm and capable — that for the moment Anabel's wild fears were stayed. "Of course you can," said the older woman.

"Anabel can have Naomi's room," suggested Robert helpfully, and with a kind of suppressed eagerness in his voice which made his mother look at him sharply. And he said to Anabel, "There's no need to be so frightened about spending one night here. Naomi's room is opposite mine, and if you are afraid and can't sleep, just give me a call. I sleep lightly."

His suggestions only served to increase Anabel's fears, because she was instinctively on her guard against Robert.

Mrs. Smith, however, had other views. "Miss Robinson will sleep in the spare bedroom," she said.

Robert immediately raised objections. "In the four-poster? Why, that mattress hasn't been used since Father died —"

"I shall give Miss Robinson my own feather bed. That is aired," said his mother.

"It is very kind of you, Mrs. Smith —" began Anabel haltingly, when the older woman cut in sharply:

"I am not being kind, Miss Robinson. Don't mistake my motives. I am merely being practical."

"I think you're being stupid, Mother. What with the noise of the wind down the chimneys, the mice chasing around under the floorboards and in the wainscoting, and the dripping of rain through the window sashes, Anabel will think there are ghosts in the room and be terrified," objected Robert sullenly, for he hated being thwarted at any time, and to have Anabel in a room close to his own was something he wished for very much.

Mrs. Smith snapped, "Miss Robinson won't imagine there are ghosts if you don't put the idea into her head." And to Anabel, "If you will follow me, I will show you the room while there is still some daylight left."

They went upstairs to the spare bedroom.

It was nearly dark as Mrs. Smith flung open the door. A smell of must, though the room was chilly, greeted them.

Anabel hesitated on the threshold, the unnamed terrors seizing her again, so that she felt a strange unwillingness to enter the unused bedroom.

"It is a big room," Anabel remarked, "and a large bed."

"They say a king once slept in that bed," was the reply. "Presently I will find you some pyjamas of Naomi's — and a dressing-gown."

"Thank you."

Anabel remembered this room. About ten days ago, when a fierce thunderstorm had rolled up, Mrs. Smith, in fear of attracting lightning, had ordered all mirrors in the bedrooms to be covered with cloths. This was one of the rooms Anabel had visited then.

Now she shivered, and Mrs. Smith said, "An unused room always strikes cold. I will get some extra blankets from the airing cupboard. It is well to use them occasionally to disturb any moths. Now if you will help me carry in the feather bed?"

While she was helping Mrs. Smith make up the bed, Anabel asked suddenly, "Who sleeps in the room opposite this?"

"Keziah, why?"

"Oh! She wouldn't be of much use to me if —" Anabel tailed off, knowing that even if in danger she would hesitate to ask Keziah's help.

"Yes?" said Mrs. Smith coldly, as Anabel paused.

"If I needed to call Keziah in the night," Anabel finished boldly.

"But why should you want help?"

"I — don't — know."

"Don't be silly! If thoughts of ghosts are troubling you, put them out of your mind. There are no phantoms here — only those formed by uneasy consciences. Besides, Keziah won't be using her room tonight, and she isn't best pleased about it. She is a Christian woman and never goes to bed without *thinking* her prayers. And as she will be staying up all night making a dress for Naomi which must go off in the morning, she can't kneel down by her bed and *think* her prayers."

With that, Mrs. Smith left Anabel alone in the room, closing the door after her.

Anabel looked about her curiously — at the faded heavy curtains, at the rotting wall panelling in the corner of the room, where the damp had been coming in, and at the twelve candles in sconces on the walls, six on either side of the room.

"I shall light six when I go to bed, and keep them burning," she decided. "And when they are burnt out, I shall light the remaining six."

She inspected the door. There was no key in the lock, but there was a stout chair in the room which could be fixed under the handle and prevent or delay anyone coming in. Anabel did not specify even to herself who 'anyone' was. She went over to the window which looked directly down the short valley, and peered through the rain-blurred glass towards the grey-misted curtain of rain that hid the sea.

'It's going to be some night,' she thought drearily, and wished she had never set foot in Bella Luce.

When Anabel went to the kitchen for supper, the table was bare. Keziah was in possession. The shrewish little woman with the sly eyes was seated at an old-fashioned treadle sewing-machine, busy with some gaily coloured material which could only belong to Naomi. She looked up when Anabel entered, and made signs for the girl to go into the dining-room.

Here were Mrs. Smith and Robert; the former sitting in a horsehair armchair, darning socks, making vicious stabs with her needle, showing the nervy state she was in; the latter writing in a ledger at a modern roll-top writing-desk.

A cold supper was spread on the table, and there was a large bottle of cider to drink in place of the usual mugs of beer.

Robert turned round with a smile as Anabel entered. "Has my mother made you comfortable upstairs?" he asked. "And are you still frightened out of your wits?"

His voice was gentle and inquiring — friendly and hospitable — but the eyes that met Anabel's were bright as with a fever, and again Anabel felt sick with fear.

She rallied quickly, however, and said, "I shall be most comfortable — but the bed will be the biggest I have ever slept in." Then quickly, "But I must ring up Mrs. Groom and tell her I am staying here for the night, or she will be wondering where I am."

Robert started up. "Let me do that for you," he urged.

"I would rather do it myself." Anabel spoke nervously, for there was something about Robert's manner, a curious restraint expressive of inward excitement, which made her uneasy, especially as the Smiths were known for their lack of emotional restraint.

She wondered, 'What is he cooking up now?'

So Anabel went into the hall and telephoned to Mrs. Groom, and was at once comforted to hear the familiar sing-song voice. As the Smiths were probably listening, Anabel confined herself to facts and spoke in crisp tones. But underneath, Anabel was conscious of a longing to know if Tim were in yet, and a yearning to hear his voice — light and reassuring — which was almost a pain.

"You needn't have scared the good woman telling her about the landslide," Robert remarked crossly, when Anabel returned to the dining-room.

Anabel made no reply, but picked up Naomi's kitten, which was rubbing itself against her ankle and purring loudly. Sitting the animal on her lap, Anabel stroked its back from head to tail with firm rhythmic gestures.

Robert rose and came over to the table, drawing out a chair, and seated himself sideways facing Anabel, while his fingers closed over a glass which was on the table. He watched Anabel with dreamy, brilliant eyes for some time, then said, "How gentle you are with her, Anabel!"

"Am I? It is such a little thing!" Anabel tried to speak normally, but it was difficult to seem as usual with those sharp eyes watching her every movement, seeing everything and missing nothing.

Robert asked, "Are you cold, Anabel?"

"No — quite warm."

"Then why did you shiver?"

"Did I? The storm is rather terrifying," replied Anabel, glancing at the window against which the rain beat and the wind blew with an implacable fury, so that the curtains moved gently to and fro. The window-frames had warped with the years, and there was a gap between them and the windows, and the rain was dripping monotonously in dull thuds into a pan on the boards below.

Robert's answer was to get up from his seat and draw the curtains, remarking, "We are so used to these noises we forget civilized people may not understand them." He resumed his seat by the table and fiddled with the glass because he could not sit still.

Mrs. Smith said tartly, "Luniette seems determined to give Miss Robinson something to remember when she goes back to London. By the way, when are you leaving the island, Miss Robinson — or is it still a secret?"

Thus cornered, Anabel replied, "I don't know the exact date, but it won't be long now — a matter of days."

Robert took the news quietly. One might have thought he had not heard, so still he was. But presently a quick snap and crash brought the women's eyes to him, and they saw Robert loosen his fingers and let the broken glass fall to the tablecloth, and it was bespattered with blood.

"Oh, Robert, how careless of you! Couldn't you use your surplus strength on something other than my best glass?"

"Why do you put out your best glass if it's so precious?" Robert asked in a suppressed tone. He looked at Anabel's hand stroking the cat, then said, "Perhaps you would like it better if I had used my strength on that kitten's neck?" And was pleased when he saw how Anabel's hand paused, and tightened involuntarily on the kitten as though to shield it from him. He took out his handkerchief, a large light-blue silk square, and bound it roughly about his hand, and watching, fascinated, Anabel presently saw that the blue was covered with bright red flowers. Seeing it too, Robert drew the handkerchief tighter.

"Hadn't you better wash it and see if there is any glass in your hand before you bind it up?" Anabel said.

Mrs. Smith said, "I thought from your manner that Miss Robinson had told you."

"What?" Robert said quickly. "That she's leaving Luniette?"

"This is her last night with us. If it hadn't been for the storm, she would have gone by now. She's not coming up tomorrow. And that is why I put out the best glass, and we have cider and not beer to drink tonight. This is a farewell party." And Mrs. Smith laughed shortly — a queer, unusual sound.

Anabel took courage to glance at Robert, and saw that his burning eyes were fixed incredulously on her face.

He looked aghast. Then he said, and could not control his voice, so that his mother stared scornfully at him, "You were going to leave me high and dry — and without saying a word? Oh, Anabel!"

Anabel's eyes fell to the kitten. It was safer that way. "I don't know about high and dry, but I certainly meant to go tonight. I would have, too, in spite of the storm if the track were still intact."

There was a long silence. Then Robert said in a steadier voice, "But the track is broken, you are here, and it's up to us to make the most of it." He glanced gaily at his mother, tore the sock from her hand and threw it in a corner of the room.

"No more darning, Mother. Let's eat — or should I say feast?" He dragged her quickly out of her chair and brought her to the table.

But the feast was a failure. It was more like sitting down to a collation after a funeral, for after a few abortive attempts to be gay, Robert sank into a depressed silence.

Anabel tried to rouse him. "You never told me if you did anything about your spa water, Robert."

"Oh, I got a small keg the other day, and sent it off to London to an analytical chemist; but I'm not interested in it anymore — now."

"What a pity you feel like that! I thought perhaps you had found the foundation of a romantic fortune on Luniette."

"What's this?" asked Mrs. Smith, but neither heard her.

Robert replied morosely to Anabel, "I'm no longer interested. The whole thing is too much in the air — too much trouble to pursue."

Anabel had the impression then that Robert was even more unstable than she had thought, eager and interested in a thing one day and lacking enthusiasm the next — and yet he had seemed so keen such a short while ago.

She looked at him covertly, and thought how much Robert had changed lately, how quickly he flew into tempers, what trifles put him out; his eyes seemed more unfathomable and brilliant; and he was thinner, though his handclasp when greeting her seemed more terrifyingly strong than ever.

She saw a new watchfulness about him, too, a kind of furtive look about him which attracted Anabel in such a repulsive way that she felt sick.

There was only one crumb of comfort in the situation — that no night lasts forever, and that some time dawn must come — though long before dawn this household would be awake and at work — while as soon as it was light she, Anabel, would go.

Tim was right. She should never have come.

Soon after nine o'clock Mrs. Smith suggested bed, and Anabel rose with alacrity.

Mrs. Smith said, "If you will come with me, I will find some night clothes for you."

Robert seemed to accept the invitation, too, for he followed the two women into the kitchen, where Keziah was machining the long skirt seams.

"That is the dress for Naomi," said Mrs. Smith superfluously. "Keziah likes Naomi, and would do anything for her."

Anabel thought, 'That is why Keziah hates me, because she blames me for Naomi's going away,' and pretended to take an interest in Keziah's work.

Robert had been growing more morose as the evening advanced, and was now in a difficult mood. The tension in the atmosphere was such, Anabel felt, that a wrong word or move, and Robert would burst out like a volcano in eruption.

While Anabel was looking at the half-made dress, Robert went over to the well, threw off the lid with unnecessary violence, and began to draw up a bucket of water.

"What's that for?" queried Mrs. Smith in astonishment.

"I want a bath."

"What nonsense! You've already had one this evening."

Robert turned round on her with a snarl. "Can't I have another if I like? Or do you grudge me the cold water?"

Mrs. Smith's mouth tightened ominously. "You can have a dozen baths if it pleases you; but remember that too many baths dry up the natural oils of the body and lay you open to colds."

So Robert, with a kind of dogged obstinacy, drew up six buckets of water, throwing each one into a hip-bath that stood beside the stove, splashing the clean floor. When he had finished, he left the bucket in the middle of the kitchen, and the lid of the well off.

Anabel said laughingly, "If you're going to bath now, I'd better say goodnight."

Presently she went upstairs with Mrs. Smith, who had lit a hurricane lamp, and was carrying it high above her head like a votive priestess marching to the altar, making dark shadowy pools around her feet.

When nearly at the top of the staircase, which rose from a square inner hall, Mrs. Smith told Anabel to wait, and went on to disappear into a room on the other side of a passage, leaving Anabel in darkness.

From where she stood, nonplussed, Anabel had a good view of the kitchen, which was clean and neat, like a painting of a Dutch interior she had seen in an art gallery in Amsterdam.

As Anabel looked down she saw Robert go up to Keziah, seize the material she was working on with rough hands, bundle it in her arms, and point to the kitchen door.

'What a boor he is,' thought Anabel.

The kitchen door was slammed on Keziah, who moved towards the staircase in the dark. Suddenly Anabel had a fit of nerves. Keziah was fumbling her way upstairs. Soon she would pass Anabel, perhaps touch her — something Anabel felt she could not bear.

The noise of the storm beating against the house, the rattle of windows, and the soughing of great trees added to Anabel's unnamed terrors.

She stepped back swiftly, calling urgently, "Mrs. Smith," and ran blindly in the direction Mrs. Smith had taken.

Desperately Anabel opened the door of a room, through whose cracked panels came an irregular line of light — and paused wild-eyed on the threshold.

Mrs. Smith was fumbling in Naomi's drawers. She turned a ravaged face towards Anabel. "Why are you spying on me?"

Anabel thought swiftly, 'She's cracking! What the world sees is a mask! But why? What is underneath?'

"I'm no spy," gasped Anabel. "But you left me in the dark, this is a strange house, and I'm frightened."

Mrs. Smith had gathered her wits together by then. "Really, Miss Robinson, you surprise me! You are a grown young woman, and mustn't be childish. I've already told you there is nothing to be afraid of. Here are Naomi's pyjamas — and this dressing-gown is one of my daughter's favourites. She would be angry if she knew you were wearing it — but I can't look any more tonight."

Anabel took the dressing-gown, a crimson satin affair with broad gold tinsel stripes. It must have suited Naomi's flamboyant personality well, but it was not Anabel's style. However, she thanked Mrs. Smith graciously, and the latter brought the lamp to light Anabel to her room.

There was no one on the landing. From the kitchen came the sound of water splashing.

"You see how silly your fears are?" said Mrs. Smith, as she lit one candle over the mantelpiece in Anabel's room.

Directly Anabel was alone, she lit five more candles to keep the solitary one company. There were fewer shadows when the six candles burnt up, though their glow was not quiet and steady, but fitful because the room was full of draughts.

Anabel put a chair against the door, fixing the back under the knob.

She removed her short skirt and jumper, and put on the gaudy dressing-gown, looking with surprise at the strange image of herself in the glass — for the garment gave her a stagey effect. The girl in the mirror — because of the gown — had a look of confidence. But in Anabel's heart there was craven fear.

The bed was high, and Anabel removed her shoes before climbing up a three-step ladder to get on top of the feather mound. And though Anabel would have dearly loved to hide her head under the blankets, she did not dare, for surely this fear that was growing within her was a premonition, a warning that she must be on her guard against evil. Anabel had no special fear of Mrs. Smith or the house, though no doubt each made some contribution to her fears — but Keziah might do her an injury on Naomi's behalf, and certainly Robert, whose manner was erratic, dominant and excitable, was to be feared.

Despite the wind and the rain, the scuttling of mice, and the rattle of tissue paper in the grate, which caught the down-draught from the chimney, and the fact that she was only half undressed, Anabel was tired and dozed, though her legs kept twitching and waking her up.

It was a severe twitch which awoke her before midnight — and something else — a movement outside the door.

Anabel's blood ran cold.

It was Robert, of course!

Anabel got out of bed, sliding to the floor, and put on her shoes. If he succeeded in forcing an entrance, it would not do for Robert to find her in bed. Intuitively she went over to the window where the rain had seeped in, and was being driven about on the sill with a spitting sound.

'If the worst comes, I shall jump out of the window,' Anabel thought wildly.

To her surprise, she realized that the glass was clear. The rain had stopped. Swiftly Anabel wiped the mist from the window with her hand and peered out. As she did so, the beam from the lighthouse shone in a golden shaft along the valley and onto her face — and as it passed, Anabel drew a swift breath — not sure if in one illuminating split second she had seen something phantom or real. For close to the house, beneath a tree, stood a figure in oilskins.

Thought hammered chaotically in Anabel's brain. She glanced fearfully behind her at the door, and watched the handle being turned softly, and the door being pressed in.

In that second's distraction, Anabel had lost the next turn of the lighthouse beam. But the following beam picked out the figure standing as before. Who was it? Swiftly Anabel rejected Rube. He was short, and his oilskin was yellow, not black. It could not be Robert, for he was outside her door.

Anabel's heart beat fast. Could it be Tim? If it only was! Then remembering that the track had gone, Anabel could have cried with disappointment.

Her heart thumping wildly, nearly suffocating her, Anabel opened the window, drenching herself with water, and the cold night air swept into the room, the wind billowing the curtains to the ceiling.

Anabel saw the watcher clearly, and was comforted.

There was a stealthy movement behind her, and Anabel turned swiftly to see Robert, fully dressed, standing in the doorway.

"Why do you pester me like this, Robert?" cried Anabel angrily, but her heart seemed to be in her throat, choking her. She put one hand up to still the throbbing of her heart, and with the other she clutched the dressing-gown tightly across her breast.

"I'm not pestering you, Anabel. That's the last thing I'd dream of doing. I only want you to be kind to me — and surely that's not much for a lonely chap like me to want of a lovely thing like you?"

The words were normal enough, but there was such a queer light in his eyes that it frightened Anabel, and gave her the helpless feeling that Robert was beyond anyone's reasoning tonight.

She replied coldly, "That's a strange thing to ask any girl at this hour of night. I hope I am always kind to everybody — but there is a proper time for things."

"Ah, but I didn't mean that sort of kindness. I mean —" He raised his hands in supplication towards her. "Anabel!"

She held herself stiffly. "Don't move or I'll scream!"

They were the wrong words and gave Robert the impression that he held the whip hand.

"There's no one to hear you — only Keziah sleeps near you, and she's not in her room. She's gone down to the kitchen to finish Naomi's dress."

"All the same, I'll scream," said Anabel, knowing that the 'watcher' must hear any cry for help.

As though to test her nerve, Robert did move, but so obviously at an angle from Anabel, going to the window, and saying with some surprise, "It has stopped raining for a bit."

Anabel turned to face her enemy, and stared beyond him, out of the window.

Just then the lighthouse beam shone along the valley, on the dark muck outside the cowsheds, and filtered among the shadows beneath the tree.

There was no sign of the 'watcher'.

Anabel's pulses were drumming with fear, her brain alert to anticipate Robert's least move. He was standing by the wall between the two windows, and looked like a beast. Gradually in the silence that was between these two, Anabel became conscious of another kind of drumming — Sue's hooves against the door of the loose-box. There was power behind that frantic kicking, and Anabel realized it could not come from a sick mare.

Her eyes widening with knowledge, Anabel looked at Robert. "Sue isn't lame," she breathed. "You only said that because you didn't want to help me. You didn't wish me to finish my work. You wanted to keep me here." And as she spoke, other parts of this puzzling plot Robert was weaving against her for his own ends slipped into place, and Anabel accused, "The track isn't broken. That was a ruse to keep me here all night." Yet even as Anabel spoke, a wild relief clamoured in her heart. The way was open!

Robert began to laugh. "Sue is well, and the track isn't broken: how could it be when Luniette is made of granite and slate? But those things served their end. You are here, and what you think now does not seem to matter much. I've got you exactly where I want you, at last — see?"

Robert was not laughing now. He had moved swiftly while talking, and his hands had seized Anabel's arms as in a vice, and he was shaking her to and fro urgently, with increasing speed, so that her hair became tumbled — and soon they were both breathless.

"That's how I want to see you," he breathed, "not so tidy, bent to my will."

"Let go, Robert — you hurt!" Anabel gasped.

"It'll do you good to be hurt. Then perhaps you'll know what I've suffered — how I've been hurt through you."

Minutes passed — or were they hours?

Anabel could not free herself from Robert's hold, though she struggled grimly to do so.

Then, suddenly, before she could anticipate it, Anabel was in Robert's arms, with her face pressed so closely against his chest she could not breathe. It was unexpected — and cruel.

How long they remained thus Anabel never knew. One minute she was held so tightly in Robert's arms that she was in danger of suffocating, and the next she was free, reeling back against the bed, then sliding to the floor, holding her throat and whimpering.

Keziah was in the room, making strange noises at Robert. There was a pair of scissors in her hand, and on her shrewish face a look of outrage.

Anabel, watching her dully, knew that Keziah was a true Christian woman. Panting for breath, nursing his hip where Keziah had jabbed the point of the scissors, and crazy with frustration, Robert lunged out at Keziah savagely. It was an unequal fight, and Keziah must quickly have realized that there was little protection for her in the bedroom, for suddenly she turned and fled down the stairs to the kitchen, Robert, a rabid tormentor now, on her heels.

Anabel dragged herself to her feet, ran out onto the landing, and down two or three steps of the stairs. Looking into the kitchen, which was well lit by three oil-lamps, with Keziah's work still on the sewing-machine, Anabel watched Robert chase after Keziah, who showed the surprising agility of someone in the grip of fear.

They were like two evil things jumping about — Keziah with her voluminous thick skirts and Robert with his long thin legs.

Once he caught Keziah's hair, but she tore herself away; and the well-bucket was kicked over.

Anabel screamed a warning, but even as she did so the sound died in her throat. She raised her eyes.

Mrs. Smith was standing on the landing, holding the hurricane lamp above her head. "What's all this noise?" she demanded, in a harsh domineering voice.

As small details impress themselves upon the mind in moments of crises, Anabel saw that Mrs. Smith was dressed in a trained magenta stuff dressing-gown, with darker lozenges of the same colour dappling the surface — and there was ruching of the material round the hem and up the front, and edging the winged sleeves. Anabel pointed to the kitchen.

"Robert is chasing Keziah," she cried, her teeth chattering with cold and fright. "I think he means to hurt her. Come quickly." And again, as Mrs. Smith made no move but stared at her in a dazed kind of way, "I think Robert is mad!"

"Mad!" repeated Mrs. Smith, the word sounding like a knell.

Then something within her seemed to crack wide open, and she said quietly, and with the solemnity of a child, "Yes, it's true. He is quite mad!"

Anabel looked away from her and down again into the kitchen and, closing her eyes, let out a dreadful shriek.

For Keziah was jumping over the gaping mouth of the well — and the leap was short! And Robert, in blind rage, was rushing ahead too fast to stop.

And when Anabel opened her eyes, both Keziah and Robert were gone and the kitchen was empty — still and peaceful, with only the sound of the storm outside to break the uncanny silence of the house.

Then Anabel, as in a dream, heard Mrs. Smith saying, "I can't bear any more," and, dropping the lamp, which fell with a shattering crash at the bottom of the stairs, Mrs. Smith put both hands over her face and began to sob aloud.

"You shouldn't have done that," said Anabel, and ran downstairs, but stopped as with a burst a mass of flames seemed to shoot up the stairs. Anabel rushed upstairs, and catching Mrs. Smith's arm, hurried her into the spare bedroom and shut the door. "This way!" she cried, turning to the window.

And then it seemed as though Anabel's feet were on wings, for Tim was climbing in through the window. He was minus his oilskin, his manner cool and collected.

"Are you all right, Anabel?" he grinned.

"Oh, Tim!" There was sharp relief in Anabel's voice.

"Because the house is on fire. With this gale, there's not a moment to lose. Come." And Tim held out his arms to her.

He had a rope with him. "They told me the track had gone, and though I knew better I couldn't take a chance," he said. And touching his hip pocket, "I've got a revolver, too — just in case," he added grimly. "Don't be afraid. Just do as I tell you. And take off that awful dressing-gown — it doesn't suit you a bit."

It was a matter of moments until Anabel was safely on the ground, and already the air was full of acrid-smelling smoke, and an ominous crackle came from within the house.

"Now go and stand under that tree until I come for you. I'm going back to find the family." And as an afterthought, he said quietly in that deep voice she had grown to love, "Kiss me, Anabel. My brave girl!"

The hard warm kiss steadied Anabel as nothing else could have done. And when she reached the tree, she was able to look back at the house where a curious evil nightmare had just taken place, and thought that perhaps those lively yellow flames were cleansing fires.

They had the homestead in their grip, for there was much old wood within the house, and paraffin lamps in most of the rooms. There were minor explosions as they caught fire and spread the work of destruction. Several windows were lit up by the flames which streamed like red and yellow pennants in the wind.

Rube passed swiftly up to the house. He did not see Anabel — or if he did passed no remark, for there was much on the old man's mind.

Sue had kicked herself free, and had galloped off. The cattle were out at pasture. But there were flocks of sheep on the cliffs behind the house, and a herd of swine in the sties beyond the cobblestone yard, and terrified by the fire, they came sweeping madly round the house, rushing past Anabel, down the hillside — probably in their terror leaping over the cliffs into the sea.

Then the roof of the house fell in, and the building was a raging inferno, and Anabel stood rigid in an agony of suspense, in case something had happened to Tim. When he came at length, unscathed but tired, Anabel was hysterical. But Tim spoke sharply, and she was forced to pull herself together.

Tim asked in a curious tone, "How many were there in the house to save, Anabel?"

Anabel's voice was cracked and husky, as she said with emotion, "One."

"There were none," Tim replied quietly, and as he saw her shiver, "It is better so."

People from the village came up, and a party of sailors arrived from the camp with fire-fighting apparatus, but Tim told them, "You're too late! But nothing could have saved the house from the start of the fire. She went off with a bang — like a big firework."

Then, tired and grimy, Tim took Anabel down to the hotel. He held her hand tightly and encouraged her to talk. "Be open with me Anabel; get it all off your chest," he urged.

His questions sounded casual and gave her the confidence she so badly needed, steadying her shaken nerves. "The sea doesn't sound so fierce," she said. "I believe the gale is blowing itself out."

Mrs. Groom, faithful soul, was waiting for Anabel with hot coffee which she now laced well with brandy, and stood over the girl while she drank it, saying many times, "Thank God you're safe!" And to hide her emotion, Mrs. Groom indulged in a garrulous fit. "Not that I would have been surprised at anything happening. When I heard that the dog, Con, had howled all night, I knew exactly what to expect. The dog *knew* what was coming. There are always signs for those who can read them!" Mrs. Groom looked at Tim. "They're saying, sir, as there'll be an inquiry —"

Tim nodded. "Of course, but tell us all about that in the morning, Mrs. Groom. I'm too tired to listen tonight, and I'm sure Miss Robinson is. Get her to bed — *pronto!*"

Still dazed, not sure whether she had dreamt a particularly evil dream, or if what had happened were real, Anabel was taken to bed, where presently, helped by the brandy, and warmth of hot-water bottles, she fell asleep.

In the morning, Anabel awoke to find Tim bending over her, his blue eyes tender and kind as she had never seen any man's. He was smiling gently down at her, while Mrs. Groom, in a ringside seat, so to speak, at the end of the bed, was listening and approving of all that was being said.

It was Sunday, and the church bell was ringing to call people to early service, and there was a peace in the atmosphere which belongs peculiarly to a Sunday, and which was especially welcome after the turmoil of yesterday.

Anabel remained looking up into Tim's eyes for a while, then as remembrance came to her she started up, clutching his arm tightly, a look of horror in her eyes. "Tim!"

"It's all right," he soothed cheerily. "Look!" — and he pointed through the open window at the fresh sea dancing in the morning sunlight. "The gale has blown itself out, and the sun is shining brilliantly in a clear sky. It's one of those blue-and-gold September mornings which come to show us what a nice place the world is to live in — when the clouds have rolled away. There's nothing to worry about, Anabel. And Dai's down below waiting to know if he can book you for a sail this afternoon."

Tim pushed Anabel back gently among the pillows.

She lay back tiredly, looking at him, and presently noticed that he was wearing his best suit. With a queer sinking of her heart, Anabel said, "You're going away?"

Tim nodded. "But only for the day," he said. "This is going to be a fateful kind of day for many people —"

"You mean —"

"Yes. And I'm summoned to the Admiralty. I don't know exactly what for — but I don't think they'll post me to a ship yet. I'll be back tonight, Anabel."

"Promise?" Luniette without Tim would be unbearable.

Tim shook his head. He took one of Anabel's hands in his. "Darling, there need be no promises between you and me. But while I'm away, if I can do it on a Sunday, will it be all right with you for me to —" Here Tim paused, stuck because he suddenly realized how important for them both were the words he was saying. But he recovered himself almost immediately and went on, "to get a special licence, so that we can be married straight away?"

Anabel's heart felt like bursting with new sweet happiness, but her eyelids were weighted as with lead. She longed to look at Tim, but was too shy. It appeared that Tim was as much stricken as Anabel, and when he spoke again the words were halting and disjointed — so unlike Tim that Anabel stared at him in astonishment.

"Anabel!"

"Yes, Tim?"

Then Tim's eyes met hers squarely. "I — love you."

"Oh!"

"Is it all right?"

"I — think so."

"What do you mean?" said Tim in quick alarm. "Why did you say that?"

In the midst of this lovely happiness, Anabel had remembered the dreadful barrier that stood between them, the one which had once proved such a stumbling-block to her happiness with Paul — or what she thought *then* was happiness.

Anabel knew better now. But how would Tim react to the barrier?

She asked seriously, "How much do you love me, Tim?"

Tim paused — grinned at her — and then looked serious. "It's measureless, Anabel. I only know that without you to share everything with me, there's nothing left in life I care about. You *are* my life, Anabel." His voice was deep.

"And nothing could put you off me now?"

How anxiously Anabel waited for Tim's answer! "Nothing. You are Anabel. I should have known all along how it would be between us. I suppose in my heart I did, but was too blind to understand. But something powerful beyond our control must have been drawing us together ever since you were born — and nothing we could do — nobody — could hold us apart. It was ordained."

Anabel turned her face towards the window, and during the long silence that followed she counted seven ships rolling into port on the brilliant green Channel swell — all homeward bound.

Then slowly, her cheeks pink with life, excitement and happiness, she looked smilingly into Tim's eyes, saying softly, "I think so, too, Tim."

A NOTE TO THE READER

If you have enjoyed the novel enough to leave a review on **Amazon** and **Goodreads**, then we would be truly grateful.

Sapere Books is an exciting new publisher of brilliant fiction and popular history.

To find out more about our latest releases and our monthly bargain books visit our website:
saperebooks.com

Printed in Great Britain
by Amazon